Potent Pleasures

G·K
Hall
&Cº

This Large Print Book carries the
Seal of Approval of N.A.V.H.

Potent Pleasures

ELOISA JAMES

G.K. Hall & Co. • Thorndike, Maine

4/60

This novel is a work of fiction. Names, characters, places, and incidents either are the product of the author's imagination or are used fictitiously. Any resemblance to actual persons, living or dead, events, or locales is entirely coincidental.

Published in 2000 by arrangement with Delacorte Press, an imprint of the Bantam Dell Publishing Group, a division of Random House, Inc.

G.K. Hall Large Print Romance Series.

The text of this Large Print edition is unabridged.
Other aspects of the book may vary from the original edition.

Set in 16 pt. Plantin by Minnie B. Raven.

Printed in the United States on permanent paper.

ISBN 0-7838-8828-7

For Sharon Kosick,
of the wonderful bookstore
The Book Rack, Too,
who guided my reading
and encouraged my writing.
Thank you.

Chapter 1

Kent, England
April 1798

Charlotte was one week short of seventeen when her life changed, falling into two halves like a shiny child's ball: *before* and *after.* In the time before, Charlotte was staying with Julia Brentorton, her dearest friend from school. Julia and she survived boarding school together: the dreary grind of everyday Latin instruction, music instruction, dance instruction, art class, etiquette with the school mistress, Lady Sipperstein. Etiquette was really the only unpleasant class.

"Julia!" Lady Sipperstein would hiss, suddenly appearing behind her left shoulder. "Cross your legs at the ankle when you sit in a low sofa."

"Walk up the stairs again, Charlotte, and do *not* sway your hips this time! You are wiggling in an inappropriate fashion."

Lady Sipperstein was a terrifying woman with a bosom that extended forward like the prow of a ship. She knew to a hair how low one must bow to a duchess as opposed to a king, and she drilled her students as if they would do so every day.

She was full of maxims: "One dismisses a servant as if he were a young child: with firmness, brevity, and uninterest. . . . The appropriate gifts for the sick depend on where they live: If they live on your estate, instruct the cook to make bone-marrow jelly and bring it yourself, with fruit; if they live in the village, instruct the servants to deliver an uncooked chicken instead. And of course be sure to ascertain that any illness is not contagious before you enter a house: While it is important to show feeling, one must not be foolish."

Etiquette was an hour of unnerving questions. "Julia! If a footman enters the breakfast room with an obviously swollen jaw, what is the appropriate response?"

"Send him home?" Julia would suggest tentatively.

"No! Information first. Is the swelling the result of a distressed tooth or an improper brawl the night before? If he has been brawling, dismiss him. If not? Julia?"

"Ah, send him to a doctor?" Julia stammered.

"Incorrect. Inform the butler that he should be put on duties that will keep him out of public view. There is no point in mollycoddling servants."

For Charlotte, art class was the focus of the day. She was happiest in the white square room furnished only with twelve easels. They painted the same groupings over and over: two oranges, one lemon; two peaches, one pear. Charlotte didn't mind.

Julia did. "A pumpkin today!" she would chortle, mimicking Miss Frollip's excited tone when she introduced the latest still life.

For Julia, there was dance class — and that not because of dance, but because of Mr. Luskie. He was a rather hairy man, a family man: robust, friendly, not a bit of danger with the girls, the teachers all agreed. But Julia thought his whiskers were dashing, and she read messages in the gentle pressure of his hand as he directed her through the steps of a quadrille. "I *adore* him," she whispered to Charlotte at night.

Charlotte would wrinkle her nose: "I don't know, Julia, he's rather . . . well, he's not . . ." It was hard to put into words. He was common; but how not to insult Julia? She thought a bit uneasily of Julia's passionate vows of love: She wouldn't *do* anything, would she? Of course, Mr. Luskie wouldn't . . . but Julia was so beautiful. She was like a peach, Charlotte thought: golden and sweet-smelling and soft-looking. Would Mr. Luskie?

One of Charlotte's governesses had been stridently opinionated about men: "They want one thing, Lady Charlotte!" she would say. "One thing, and don't you forget it and get yourself ruined, now!" Charlotte would nod, wondering what the one thing was.

So she would whisper back, "I don't think he's *so* handsome, Julia: Did you see that he has red veins in his cheeks?"

"No!" said Julia. "He doesn't!"

9

"Yes, he does," said Charlotte.

"How do you notice so much?" Julia said crossly.

Finally school drew to a close, and one by one the girls were taken off by titled relatives, or simply by maids: taken off to be fitted and prinked and "tarted up," Julia said, for their debuts. It was time to start a process that would end in settlements and dowries, balls and weddings.

As the daughter of a duke, Charlotte was regarded enviously. Her debut would be magnificent. Her elder sister Violetta had made her bow to society in a ballroom draped from top to bottom with white lilies.

It was only Charlotte who didn't care much. She longed, if the truth be told, to stay in the white square room and paint another apple, or (if the market was particularly exciting that week) even a persimmon. She was *good,* really good, she knew she was, and Miss Frollip knew she was, but that was the end of it.

She had to debut; Julia had to debut; there would be little time for persimmons.

So when her mother picked her up at Lady Chatterton's School for Girls, Charlotte felt resigned, but not excited. Her mother arrived in full armor, in Charlotte's private opinion: in the ducal coach with *four* footmen behind, all in livery! The duchess was shy and quailed at the thought of an interview with the formidable Lady Sipperstein. Poor Mama, Charlotte thought.

She must have been in a terrible tizzy.

Finally Charlotte and her mother were regally dismissed by Lady Sipperstein and escaped in the coach. The duchess grinned in a most unduchesslike fashion, leaned back against the satin cushions, and said, "Thank goodness, you're finished, Charlotte! I *never* have to see Lady Sipperstein again! We can be comfortable. How did the last picture go, darling — oranges, wasn't it?" For Charlotte's mama was a devoted parent, who lovingly kept track of her children's latest exploits, even if in Charlotte's case that had simply turned into a long progression of watercolor fruits.

"All right, Mama," Charlotte said. "I'll show you when we get home." Charlotte frowned a bit. Her mama treated all her work the same: with reverence, delight, and a noncritical eye.

"Good," said Adelaide comfortably. "I shall send it off immediately to Saxony. We're doing quite well on that hallway, dearest. Why, two or three more and the walls will be full!"

Charlotte grimaced. Her parents seemed to view her painting as a decorating tool, a new kind of wallpaper. Each new painting was sent out to the best framer (Messrs. Saxony, Framers to the Crown), fitted into a gold frame with an appropriate matte chosen personally by Mr. Saxony, Sr., and solemnly delivered back to the ducal mansion. Then it was hung up in a long, long row of fruit (and the odd vegetable) that decorated a long, long hall in the east wing.

11

"Now, Charlotte," Adelaide said with resolution. "We must start planning for your debut immediately. Why, I happen to know that Lady Riddleford — Isabella's mother — has already taken the weekend of August nineteenth, which was precisely when I was planning your ball, dearest. So we must choose a time immediately and make it known. I was thinking of the weekend before. What do you think, darling?"

Charlotte didn't answer. She was thinking of her latest painting. But Adelaide was used to Charlotte's lapses into inattentiveness; she simply returned to her plans.

When Charlotte visited what her brother, Horace, called the orchard (the long row of pictures in the east wing) she could see change: hours of painting under Miss Frollip's tutelage had turned her oranges from misshapen to round; apples stopped being poisonously red and gained some reality.

What she was working on now was color. Color was so difficult: oranges, for example. When she closed her eyes, she saw groups of oranges, bright against her eyelids. She mixed and mixed for hours, a little yellow, blue, brown, but she couldn't find the orange she saw in her mind's eye. Oranges, colored the right way, had a slight brownish tinge at the top and streaks of blue: colors that smelled of the sun, of warm seas, of real orchards rather than of long halls or white rooms.

But Charlotte didn't have much time for

painting after they arrived at the Calverstill House in Albemarle Square. She endured hours and hours of poking and prodding from seamstresses, and days of her mother's planning.

"Dearest," announced her mother. "Delphiniums!"

Charlotte stared at her.

"Delphiniums what, Mama?" she finally asked.

"Delphiniums! They're *your* flower for the ball! I've been racking my mind . . . you know I did Violetta's ball in lilies. I had to avoid colors for her because of her name, but delphiniums are such a lovely blue. They will set off your hair perfectly."

Just now the rage was for blondes: blondes with curly locks and blue eyes, but Charlotte had jet-black hair, her mama thought despairingly. She did have green eyes, but her skin was so white — not a drop of color. True, with some coaxing her hair formed perfect ringlets, and her skin was creamy, but she was no sweetly pert debutante. Her eyebrows arched like question marks over eyes as green as the ocean on a cloudy day. In fact, her whole face was pointed like a question mark: Her chin formed a delicate triangle that simply lead back to her eyes and those flying eyebrows.

The duchess sighed a little. When Charlotte was happy, she was the most beautiful of her daughters: She would simply have to see that she had a happy debut, that's all.

Charlotte stood rock-still through all the fittings, closed her eyes, and analyzed the oranges that appeared in her mind. Perhaps more red. Perhaps starting very red, and working back to orange, in layers?

"Charlotte!" her mother said. "Miss Stuart is trying to do up your hem. Please, turn around when she asks you."

"Charlotte! I've asked you twice; please raise your arms."

"Charlotte!"

Finally the fittings were over and the last pearls were painstakingly sewn into Charlotte's presentation dress. Seventeen ball dresses fit for a duke's young daughter were swaddled in tissue and hung in a closet; the delphiniums were growing well, the duchess was relieved to hear; ten footmen were summoned from the country; the ballroom was polished and the chandeliers shined, and the London police notified of the extra traffic: the Calverstills were ready to launch their last child onto society. Invitations winged their way to the London *ton*. And the London *ton* accepted. The duchess may have been shy, but she was beloved, creative, and had money to spare. A Calverstill ball would never be slighted.

Perhaps most important, young men accepted, all of them — fops, courtiers, gallants, Corinthians — all the groups and cliques and sets of London. Charlotte was rumored to be beautiful (her two elder sisters were) and she was sure to have an excellent dowry as her father was plump in the pocket. And still two weeks remained before the ball.

So Charlotte was given permission to visit Julia in the country. Her mama didn't worry much.

"Charlotte, you mustn't be seen in public; this is a terribly delicate time," she said brightly, looking at her dutiful but somehow detached daughter.

Could it be that Charlotte wasn't really interested in her debut? No, no, the duchess thought: Why, she loved talking about her dresses, and we had such a good time looking at all the silks. She's so *good* with colors! And she had a positive surge of affection for her youngest daughter, who had never caused her any real trouble or anxiety. Charlotte was reasonable, calm, and unexcitable.

Charlotte was driven, in the ducal coach but with only one footman, a few hours out of London to Squire Brentorton's estate. Julia greeted her with glowing eyes. She too had ball gowns to show, with less embroidery and no pearls sewn in the hem, but beautiful all the same. And she had a passion — of course.

"He's adorable, Charlotte! I adore him! He's not at all like that old Mr. Luskie, Charlotte. He's beautiful, really beautiful; you'll love him; no red veins!"

Charlotte wrinkled her nose at her.

"What do you mean, beautiful? And who are we talking about?" She noticed with some dismay that Julia's violet eyes were dreamy with love.

"His name is Christopher," Julia said. "He has curls . . . he looks like Adonis, truly, Charlotte."

"But who *is* he?" Charlotte was getting suspicious: There was something evasive about the way her friend's dewy gaze kept drifting off into the corners of the room. Julia pouted, just a little.

"Julia!" Charlotte said threateningly, smothering a grin. Her friend was so *silly* about men. Just a few weeks ago she had cried heartbrokenly because she would never see Mr. Luskie again.

"He'll never hold me in his arms again," she'd wailed, "we'll never waltz together again," sobbing into her pillow. And even Charlotte was moved, and wondered if she'd been too harsh, constantly pointing out the plumpness of Mr. Luskie's backside and the growing bald spot on his head.

Julia cast her eyes on the ground. "He's a man of God," she finally said, softly.

"What?" said Charlotte, not understanding her.

"He's . . . well, he's a curate!" Julia said.

"A curate? Julia!"

"He has blond curls, Charlotte. He looks like, well, he looks like a painting!" Having confessed the worst, she ignored Charlotte's frown and listed the curate's many graces: He was young,

16

and more handsome than anyone including the seller of sweet lavender who sometimes came by the school and who, until now, had been consecrated as the most handsome, even if Mr. Luskie was the most cherished.

"Even *you* will like him, Charlotte. Because he's full of virtue, and quite thin — you know how you were always saying that poor Mr. Luskie was a bit plump. And he would be a wonderful person to paint." Julia sat up, suddenly, and looked speculatively at Charlotte.

"You don't suppose. . . . You can't keep painting fruit now we're out of school, Charlotte! Why don't you offer to paint Christopher?"

"You're demented," Charlotte said fondly. "I will not offer to paint a young man I've never even met! Why, my mother would collapse in shock."

"Well, Charlotte, you do have to start thinking about men instead of paintings now, you know," Julia said a bit sharply. "You just never seem to show any interest!"

The curate *is* more handsome than the lavender seller, Charlotte thought on Sunday, her heart sinking a bit. Julia stared at him so devotedly that Charlotte had to elbow her twice, so that she would bend her head to pray. Charlotte watched him too, out of the corner of her eyes. He was somberly dressed in a black cassock, blond curls smoothly shining. He didn't look like a painting; he looked like a statue — a statue of a mischievous fawn. There was something too smooth about his curls, and his face looked naughty, she decided. Like her brother Horace's when he'd been sent down from Oxford.

On the way out of church Charlotte watched the curate wink at Julia and give her a very small, very private smile while the cold spring sunlight shone on his hair. And when the squire and his wife turned to greet two friends, she saw him slip Julia a bit of paper, and her knees went weak.

All the way home, chatting pleasantly with the unknowing Brentortons, Charlotte's mind was racing. Julia was ruined! If anyone knew that a young man was writing to her, she'd never be able to go to Almack's. She'd never be approved by the patronesses. She would never find a husband.

When they got back to Brentorton Hall, Charlotte took Julia firmly under the elbow and swept her upstairs to her room. Then she pushed the door shut, leaned on it, and stuck out her hand, without saying a word.

Julia looked at her mutinously. Her eyes measured Charlotte's taller height against the oak door. Julia was slight and small. She would never be able to push Charlotte's willowy self from the door. She sighed and plumped down on her bed and pulled the small bit of paper from her bosom with a practiced air that chilled Charlotte to the bone.

"It's nothing," she said. "Nothing, Charlotte!" She looked up at her fiercely. "See?" She flashed the scrap of paper.

Charlotte snatched it. There were four words, written in peaky letters with blue ink: *Stuart Hall, Saturday, 9 o'clock.*

"Oh, Lord, Julia, you wouldn't — you aren't meeting him, are you? Secretly?" Charlotte slid slowly down, crushing her petticoats, until she was sitting against the door. "What is this place, Stuart Hall?"

"It's nothing bad." Julia leaned forward eagerly. "It's not a rendezvous — I would never do anything like that. It's a masquerade ball, you see: it's held every Saturday night, and I just happened to be talking to Christopher about it —"

"Christopher!"

"Well, Reverend Colby, then, but I don't like his last name. Anyway, it is nothing serious, Charlotte. It's a masquerade ball that lots of, well, merchants and servants attend, and Christopher — Mr. Colby — says that people of our class never get to see real life, and especially how everyone else lives. He says young girls, debutantes, are like houseplants. We never do anything, and then we're sold to the highest bidder, and he says that it is a perfectly amiable dance, and everyone wears masks the whole time, so no one could see our faces and —"

"*Our! Our* faces!" repeated Charlotte.

Julia leaned forward. "You must come with me, Charlotte. You see, don't you? If you're with me everything is quite proper, and Mama knows how correct you are, and even if she found out, she wouldn't be horrendously angry."

"Yes, she would," Charlotte said bluntly, picturing Julia's brisk and forthright mother.

"Don't you see, Charlotte? We're just like sheep, being sold to the highest bidder, and —"

"What are you talking about, Julia?" Charlotte asked with exasperation. "What does being a sheep have to do with sneaking off to go to a ball?"

Julia wasn't sure she remembered: It all made so much sense when Christopher explained it to her, his sweet face downcast as he talked of her sheeplike docility.

"You know," she said vaguely. "We just have to get married, and we never get to see anything. Oh, Charlotte," she said, abandoning the messy question of ethics, "it will be fun, don't you see? There's nothing improper about going to a party chaperoned by . . . by a theologian!"

A small thread of rebellion lit in Charlotte. After all, had anyone asked her whether she wanted to debut? Whether she wanted to get married? But of course she *did* want to get married, and the only way to do that was to debut, so that train of thought didn't lead anywhere.

"I won't go if you don't," said Julia in a small voice. "We'll just look."

The corner of Charlotte's mouth quirked up in a grin and Julia answered her unspoken consent with a squeal.

"You must promise me that you won't run off to dance with your curate and leave me alone,"

Charlotte said sternly.

"Oh, I wouldn't, Charlotte!" Julia's eyes were glowing. "We'll have to go up to the attic and find something to wear. Costumes. I think there are some old dominoes up there."

Charlotte tried to remain calm but it was no use. Her reasonable, unexcitable temperament had deserted her, leaving a racing pulse and a seductive taste of excitement.

Julia jumped up. "This is the perfect time to go to the attic, Charlotte. Mama and Papa always visit the tenants on Sundays until time for luncheon."

So the girls crept up the stairs, all the way past the servants' floor into the huge, echoing attics that lay under the timbers of Squire Brentorton's manor roof. Blocks of pale sunshine fell across old pine boards, the dusty shapes of covered furniture, trunks of outdated clothing. Charlotte paused for a moment and watched dust specks eddy and dance in the light as Julia briskly trotted across the floor towards the trunks. Within a minute she had found two voluminous black cloaks that would cover their whole bodies. At first it appeared that there were no masks, but then with a little shriek Julia pulled them from the corner of another trunk.

"Hush, Julia!" Charlotte's heart raced.

"It's quite all right," Julia replied, looking up from where she was bundling the dominoes into a clumsy parcel. "No one except one of the servants could possibly hear us."

21

"And what if one of the servants did hear a noise and came to investigate?" Charlotte demanded.

"Oh, Charlotte, you're such an innocent." Julia laughed. "We would bribe him, of course."

And, in fact, that very night Julia bribed her maid into airing out the dominoes and by the time she returned them, pressed and sweet-smelling, the excursion had come to seem inevitable. Giggling wildly, Julia powdered Charlotte's hair with her bathroom powder so that it looked vaguely like the old-fashioned hairstyles of twenty years ago.

Julia was delighted. "Look at me! I look just like that portrait of my mother upstairs on the landing! And no one would recognize you, Charlotte," she said encouragingly. "With your mask on, all I can see is powdered hair and a little bit of your face. Do you think we used too much powder?"

Charlotte looked at herself. Julia had certainly been liberal with the powder.

"Well, at least we don't have to worry about being asked to dance," Julia said, giggling. "A gentleman would probably start sneezing if he got too close!"

It should do, Charlotte thought dubiously. They could go see how the other half of the world danced, and then come home. Escaping the house was no problem. The east wing, where Julia's bedroom was, had stairs in the back for servants, but the servants were in bed in the west wing when the girls stole out at ten o'clock at night.

The curate was waiting around the curve of the drive as Charlotte and Julia rounded the bend. Seeing a dark figure leaning against the carriage door, Charlotte's footsteps faltered. She felt a wave of passionate conviction that this masquerade was a mistake. But Julia danced forward irresistibly, shouting "Christopher" and generally acting as if surreptitious meetings on dark roads were nothing new to her. Charlotte followed slowly, feeling that she really ought to tell the curate that they had made a mistake and drag Julia home.

Yet to Charlotte's relief, Mr. Colby was respectful when the two girls reached the carriage. He bowed solemnly when Julia introduced him to Charlotte, and mentioned that he had visited the chapel at Calverstill while at Oxford. Somehow that comment managed to give the whole excursion the air of a school outing. Charlotte felt immeasurably relieved and at any rate Julia bounded into the carriage before Charlotte had a chance to say anything about returning home. She found herself seated on the dusty seats of a hired hack, sitting forward gingerly so as not to crush the folds of her domino.

Then Mr. Colby pulled a bottle of champagne from a basket with such a flourish that it seemed they must join him. Did people really drink on the way to balls? Charlotte sipped at her wine uncertainly as the carriage gathered speed, lurching along the main road. Julia babbled of dances and balls and servants.

Finally Charlotte pulled herself together. Mr. Colby must think she was dreadfully ill-bred, sitting in total silence. She cleared her throat, a small uncertain noise, but Julia was deep in her normal flow of distracted chatter and there was no space for Charlotte to speak. In fact, Julia paused only to cast fascinated glances at the curate seated across from them, his head politely bent toward Julia.

Finally Charlotte seized an opening and began asking the kind of question she had heard her mother ask the curate: about his flock, so to speak, and how were the poorer people doing?

"This is a fortunate area," Mr. Colby replied courteously. "Miss Brentorton's father is more than generous in his support of the parish."

"My mother says —" Julia broke in and dashed away with the new subject, and so Charlotte relaxed even more and felt that while the excursion was daringly bold, it wasn't beyond reproach. Someday she might even be able to tell her mother, and laugh about it with her.

Charlotte was able to keep her feeling of calm equanimity when they arrived at Stuart Hall. It was an imposing brick building with long windows casting light across gardens: not so different from any gentleman's house, she thought. Inside, everyone was in costume, and most people had masks, just as Mr. Colby had said. There were many, many people there, pushing slowly through crowds in the hallway, and she could see, down the steps into the ballroom, couples lined up in close rows on the floor.

They wormed their way into the ballroom, and found a little space over to one side, between a statue of Narcissus and the open doors to the gardens. Mr. Colby pushed off and came back with some rather vile lemonade, and they stood about sipping the drink.

"Do you know," Julia said, "I think there's some liquor in this lemonade."

"I shouldn't think so," was all Mr. Colby said. "They simply can't afford the *best* lemons here, the way *you* can at home."

Charlotte and Julia both felt a flash of shame at all the best lemons they'd eaten in their lives, and they drank with renewed fervor.

Mr. Colby turned to Julia: "Shall we dance?" He looked respectfully at Charlotte. "You'll be perfectly safe here, and Julia and I shall return in a moment. They're playing a waltz, which was my dear mother's favorite dance, and I should love to honor her memory . . ."

He looked so apologetic and sad about his mother (she must be recently deceased), that Charlotte nodded, even though she had made Julia swear that she wouldn't dance, no matter what happened. And Julia, of course, turned quickly into Mr. Colby's arms and vanished into the press of people.

He's not wearing a cassock, Charlotte thought rather stupidly.

And then, vaguely, I wonder where his mother learned the waltz: I thought it was quite new. One doesn't think of the mother of a curate whisking about the dance floor.

It was rather embarrassing standing alone in the ballroom. Charlotte gazed out over the dancers as if she were looking for someone. Slowly she realized that the party wasn't, in fact, exactly what she might have expected. Quite a few of the ladies seemed to have taken their masks off, and their costumes were — well, revealing. For example, there was a lady dressed as Marie Antoinette. She was carrying a shepherd's crook and was wearing a towering wig. But her dress was so bright, and so low, Charlotte thought. Really, if it was any lower, her bosom would pop right out. And look what she was doing with that shepherd's crook! Charlotte felt pink creeping up her cheeks. The lady's escort was laughing and laughing, but every instinct told her that no one behaved like that at the balls her mother attended.

But after all, this was why she and Julia had come tonight, wasn't it? Of course the atmosphere wouldn't be exactly as it might be in London. Mr. Colby said young ladies were kept like houseplants, and not allowed to see anything, she reminded herself: Well, this must be how ladies and gentlemen actually behaved when they were not at debutante balls.

And so she lifted her eyes and tried to find Marie Antoinette again, but she just caught a glimpse of her going up the stairs; actually she must have been taken ill, because it looked as if her escort was carrying her up toward the ladies' room.

Then her gaze was caught by a man standing on the stairs. He leaned back against the railing as Marie Antoinette's thick skirts brushed past him. He was tall, taller than her father, wearing a dark green domino rather than a black one like most of the men. He looked . . . he looked arrogant, and lordly, and very handsome, even given his mask. He had broad shoulders and curly black hair shot through with silver.

Just then a very pretty girl, dressed as Cleopatra, stopped next to him. She seemed to know him; they were laughing and he rubbed a finger against her face. Charlotte instinctively touched her own cheek and kept staring. From here, his eyes looked black and his eyebrows arched just as her own did. People always said that she looked as if she had a perpetual question in mind; his eyebrows gave an entirely different impression. They made him look a little devilish: not childishly naughty, like Julia's curate, but altogether more dangerous. Something stirred warmly, deep in her belly: for the first time, she saw a man whom *she* would like to . . . to what? To kiss, she decided. Yes, she would even like to kiss him, she thought with a delicious shiver. Although kissing, Lady Sipperstein had said over and over, was something one only did with one's fiancé, and then only after all the papers were signed.

27

Suddenly the stranger's green domino swung elegantly out from his shoulder as he turned down the stairs and escorted the laughing Cleopatra to the dance floor. Charlotte tried to follow them with her eyes, even standing a bit on tiptoe, but there were too many people. He was taller than most men so she occasionally caught glimpses of his silver-black curls. Her heart thumped loudly.

"Oh, for goodness sake!" she said aloud. A tiny smile lit her face. She was behaving just like Julia, falling for the first handsome man she saw. He was probably a footman. But where *was* Julia? The orchestra had played at least two or three dances since she left; Charlotte had lost track. She felt a little anger stir inside her. How could Julia leave her alone, when the ballroom was full of people who were definitely behaving in a less than restrained manner? Even as she watched, a stout man dressed in a frayed domino grabbed his partner by her bare shoulders and kissed her, and they didn't even seem to notice the hissing annoyance of the other dancers who bumped into them.

Charlotte turned a bit and stared into the corner behind the statue. The room was papered in a perfectly unexceptional blue with gold flock. She drank up the rest of her lemonade.

Suddenly she felt a push and she toppled into the corner. She would have caught her balance, but her head was fuzzy and so she teetered and fell forward. And the person who had shoved her fell on top of her, heavily.

"Ow," Charlotte said. Her mask was twisted, she could feel that, and powder had fallen from her hair all over the polished floor.

But she was whisked to her feet in a second and large hands brushed the powder from her cloak.

She looked up. It was the man from the steps. Charlotte looked at him a bit owlishly. Just at that moment he looked up from brushing off her cloak, met her eyes, and froze.

"Thank you," she said, remembering to smile.

He didn't move. Charlotte looked away from his eyes. They were so intent: black and deep, like polished obsidian, she thought absurdly, and almost giggled. Would a footman wear a domino made of thick green silk? She crept another look at him. He was younger than she thought, and even handsomer. His eyebrows formed thick peaks over his eyes. He was still staring at her. At her mouth, actually. Nervously she bit her lip, unable to move, caught by the intensity of his gaze.

Then without saying a word he put his arms around her waist and pulled her against his body.

"What!" Charlotte managed to say, but he bent his head and a warm strong mouth descended on hers. She didn't say another word, not even when his lips opened hers and his tongue lunged into her mouth, not when he pulled back slightly and delicately traced the shape of her lips with his tongue, and certainly not when she — she! — leaned toward him in a silent request and his mouth took hers again.

He swung her about so that they were shadowed behind the Narcissus statue, safe from people's eyes. Then he swiftly pulled her mask over her head. Charlotte looked up at him. He wasn't wearing a mask anymore either. The light in the corner was rather dim, and it enhanced the strong planes of his face. He was staring down at her, his eyes glittering, as if she were a rhubarb tart ready for eating, she thought. She nervously wet her lips and his eyes darkened visibly.

Charlotte still didn't say a word. In fact, she had no thought of leaving, or of speaking. She was simply waiting. His large hands swept down her back and cupped her bottom through her cloak and dress, and even though she knew exactly what he was doing, she mutely raised her face for another kiss.

His mouth left hers and she felt warm breath on her ear, and shivered instinctively. A tongue swept around her ear, and a husky voice murmured, "Very nice, a lovely ear," and swept without a pause to reclaim her mouth again, his tongue stabbing into her mouth. Finally he stole her tongue altogether and sucked it into his mouth.

All the time his large hands kept up a disturbing rhythm on her back, and even on her bottom. He molded her to him, his fingers caressing her through the worn domino and her frock. He pulled her body up, against his hard muscled body; Charlotte's legs felt as if they were made of jelly.

Thinking back, she knew she couldn't have protested, even if she'd thought of it. Her body was hardly even hers anymore. Maybe she could have said something when he put an arm behind her shoulders and another under her knees and simply, smoothly, picked her up and backed out into the warm garden. Instead she just leaned against his chest and felt his fast beating heart against her cheek.

He was gazing at her, his eyes black as jet and thickly fringed with lashes. Charlotte blinked, her mind possessed by the idea of licking those lashes.

The insanity of this notion almost jerked her back to reality but then he was kissing her again and she heard herself moan faintly. He lowered her to the ground, and she smelled flowers and fresh grass, and felt the fierce warmth of the large male body hovering just above her. And so it was she who wound her hands in his curls and pulled his masculine pressure down onto her softness.

He pushed aside her cloak, but her eyes were shut tight and she was lost in the intense pleasure of the moment. When he ducked his head and his mouth closed on her breast, Charlotte — uncaring of the ballroom a few feet away, just on the other side of some trees — gave a moan that wasn't a moan but almost a scream.

His mouth sent trails of fire up and down her

31

body and especially down her legs, and she gasped and twisted in his arms, her body instinctively arching up, her hips lifting off the soft grass. And he was murmuring something, murmuring his strange, delicious kisses against her skin. Charlotte strained to listen and then forgot to understand. Lips moved down her body as if he were tracing messages, teaching her a language of which she had known nothing until now.

Charlotte was on fire and exploding at the same time, and so when his face appeared over hers, all she did was delicately put her tongue to *his* lips, and run her hands through his curls again. With a muffled groan, he did something, she didn't know what, and he was pushing about her clothing, but his hands were on her breasts and she couldn't think. And when he said, "Would you like . . ." in a deep, velvety hoarse voice that she still shivered to think about, she whispered, "Please," and strained toward him for another kiss.

A knee pushed between her legs, but he was bending down to kiss her and she swept into a swirling, breathless haze, her body ignited by the closeness of his. But then, in a split second, pain shot through her and she screamed.

"What the *hell!*" he said in a furious tone, rearing up on his arms. Charlotte shrunk back, suddenly coldly sober.

Alex McDonough Foakes, future Earl of Sheffield and Downes, looked down at the girl in stupefaction. She was a virgin, for God's sake. She was staring up at him, absolutely white in the face, her lips swollen with his kisses. Lovely lips, he thought wonderingly: such a dark, dark red, and she tasted like honey . . . And, not thinking at all, he lowered his body back down onto her softness and claimed her lips again.

She was devastatingly beautiful, this serving girl: so wild even if she was a virgin; he didn't remember ever feeling so frantic with need. He ran a slow hand down her lovely languorous thigh, and in spite of herself, Charlotte squirmed against his hand.

He cupped her delicate, triangular face in his large hands and pressed kisses on her eyelids. Still she didn't make a sound, just opened her mouth a bit and gasped when he drew his tongue over her eyelids. Which was such an entrancing sound that even though Alex knew he had to get out of there, stand up, deal with the unpleasant fact of having deflowered a wench, he bent back to her lips and brushed his across hers, tantalizing, asking, demanding.

His hand ran down her thigh again and then up the inside, sliding slowly over the gossamer silkiness of her stockings, over the slight bump of her garters, into the creamy smoothness of her inner thigh. His hand closed over her, and her body arched again, surprised by desire for something she had never felt before. Gasping, Charlotte's eyes stared blindly into the dark leaves overhead. Mindlessness descended and she moaned, small ragged sounds, parting her lips. The burning pain of a moment ago was forgotten.

Alex stared down at her, almost puzzled. She had a perfect, aristocratic nose, and such delicate, flyaway eyebrows. . . . She turned her head and looked squarely into his face. Her eyes were glazed, her mouth swollen. Alex was struck by such a bolt of lust that he shuddered all over. He reared over her again, easing his fingers from her, his knee thrusting between her legs.

But in that instant — before he could reclaim her, virgin or no — Charlotte struggled, a belated instinct for self-preservation replacing the unwelcome coolness when his fingers left her.

Alex let her go instantly, rolled himself off to the side. Charlotte ignored how unpleasant the loss of his heat and weight felt. She was shaking slightly all over, her heart pounding as if she'd run for miles. She tried not to look at him as she stood up, almost stumbling from the sudden pain between her legs, pulling her bodice together.

But she couldn't not look. He was much younger than she thought, probably only a few years older than her brother Horace, and Horace was only twenty-five. And he was so lovely: His skin looked golden as shadows of leaves played over his white shirt. Her eyes fell. He was politely looking away so she rearranged herself, straightened her cloak and put her mask back on.

The only thing she could think of, besides throwing herself back into his arms, was getting

34

home, so she gently laid her hand on his arm and said (with an inborn politeness which was natural to her), "Thank you. Good-bye."

She didn't think how odd it was to say thank you for being ravished — the worst thing that could happen to a young lady, after all.

His face jerked up when he heard her voice, but she slipped away without a backward glance and dashed through the tall windows into the crowded ballroom before he even moved. And when Alex cursed and sprinted after her, he couldn't distinguish her among all the cloaks and dominoes and masks moving about the floor. Burnt yellow silk brushed shoulders with rose cotton and the occasional greeny gold taffeta. Men dressed in shabby black coats peppered the floor. But there wasn't a black domino to be seen.

Alex sighed. The girl couldn't have just disappeared: She must have rejoined her party. And like a guilty thief, struck with remorse and eager to compensate for his crimes, he needed to find her. With a muttered curse he mentally divided the room into quarters and then patiently wove through each quarter, surveying all the young women who reached his shoulder. But he couldn't find her. Yet even when he knew rationally that she must have left the ball, he kept searching, doggedly, until the dance closed down.

She was gone. And whoever she was, she'd gone with her loss of virginity, and he'd paid nothing. But that wasn't it, and he knew it. He wanted to see her again. The thief was only hiding behind a wish to compensate for his crimes: In fact, he wanted her, with an urgency that made him feel slightly insane. He wanted to reclaim that lovely, untouched body, to kiss away her little pants, to repeat the crime again and again and again.

The odd thing was that she sounded like a lady. And she looked like a lady. But of course no ladies came to the Hookers' Ball on a Saturday night, and so she was just a very clever whore — but what was a whore thinking, to give away her most prized possession for free, in the gardens? Alex left the ball in a ferocious temper.

That night he woke from dreams of wild seduction completely confused, gazing around his room as if he'd never seen it before. His garden girl . . . her body had been just there, and he had been tracing the shape of her breast with his tongue, and she was moaning in his arms. For some reason she had stolen into his mind and wouldn't go away.

For a few weeks Alex treasured the hope that he'd receive some sort of a ransom note from her protectors or perhaps even from her parents, if she were a serving girl rather than a whore. He rather hoped she was; he would protect her, and find her a house in London, a quiet little house. But there never was a note.

And even though he went back to the Hookers' Ball the next Saturday night, to the distress of his

36

brother, Patrick, who had had no fun at all the week before, she wasn't there. He also went to a few society balls in the next two weeks, thinking if she *was* a lady he might see her, but he couldn't find any tall, slender girls with green eyes. The young girls in London were bouncy and curled and small, whereas he was looking for willowy and composed.

If only he knew the color of her hair it would be easier, but she had been wearing a ridiculous amount of powder. Alex's domino smelled faintly of lavender for weeks. He thought about it carefully and decided that she had red hair. With skin that white, her hair had to be red. So he looked for a red-haired girl who smelled of lavender; and Charlotte, whose hair was jet-black and who smelled of orange blossoms, never crossed his path.

When Alex wasn't dreaming about making love to her (and he didn't even think how odd it was to use that term about a probable whore), he dreamt she was weeping, and he was comforting her, and saying tender things. Probably, Alex told himself rationally, he kept thinking of her because he hadn't gone through with it and finished: but even thinking about how wet she had been, and how small, made him pale. She couldn't be a lady; there was proof positive. No lady enjoyed sex, let alone a virginal lady.

On her side, the truth came slowly to Charlotte. She ran into the ballroom and thankfully saw Julia and Mr. Colby standing by the statue of Narcissus, although she didn't notice the mutinous set of Julia's mouth. She didn't have to say anything; Julia simply shoved her across the ballroom and out into Mr. Colby's carriage. In fact, she didn't even think until later how odd it was that no one said a word on the way home; her mind was so tumbled that she barely felt as if she were in the carriage at all.

And when they got home and Julia babbled about Mr. Colby, that he had tried to kiss her — to kiss *her*, Julia! — and she had had to grind her foot into his in order to get him to let go, Charlotte just sat numbly on a chair and nodded occasionally. Finally Julia stopped.

"Are you all right, Charlotte?" she asked, seeing that Charlotte's eyes were shadowed and her face was waxen.

And Charlotte simply said, "I think I shall be ill." And she was, right on the Aubusson carpet in Julia's bedchamber. Which was problematic because it was the middle of the night and Julia did not want to sleep in a sour-smelling room, so finally they both went into Charlotte's bedchamber and prepared for sleep.

Except that Julia gasped when Charlotte was undressing, and when Charlotte looked down she saw blood on her thighs and nearly jumped out of her skin.

"Oh, aren't I silly," said Julia. "You've got your monthly: Do you have the right clothes?" And when Charlotte shook her head silently (it wasn't even due for weeks), Julia tripped off into her room and got the necessary items.

Charlotte washed at the basin in the corner, delicately touching that part of her which stung and ached and throbbed, and which she'd never really thought about before.

He'd ruined her, she suddenly realized. *This* is what is meant by ruined. She must be torn inside, changed.

And then, like a chill blowing down her back, she understood that she could never get married, because any man she married would find out, would know that she was ruined. Her mind went very, very quiet, and she even managed to smile at Julia when she rushed back in the room.

She put on her soft white nightgown and curled up in bed, facing away from Julia. But she couldn't go to sleep for a long time. And when she did, she sobbed aloud and woke up, imagining the faces of her mother and father. What would they say if they knew?

The next morning Charlotte lay in bed feeling miserable. Julia sat next to her, sipping hot chocolate and talking. Luckily, Julia never needed much of a response to engage in lively conversation.

"I simply cannot *believe* Mr. Colby's perfidy!" she repeated again and again. Charlotte noticed that "Christopher" was now definitively "Mr. Colby."

"I just can't *believe* that he tried to take liberties with me!" Julia elbowed Charlotte again, trying to get her attention. "Charlotte! This is important! He didn't just try to kiss me, you know. He put his hand — *on my breast,* Charlotte! *On my breast,*" Julia said again, emphasizing each word. "I could have been ruined," she said with relish.

Charlotte didn't respond. Julia peered at her. "Are you quite all right, Charlotte? You're awfully quiet. I could ask my mother . . . she has some good remedies for a bad monthly. Would you like that? Oh, no," she wailed, "I couldn't! Why, she would take one look at me and see that I was almost *ruined* last night!"

Charlotte thought dully that Julia certainly was enjoying herself.

"Why," Julia continued, "if I hadn't trampled on his foot, just at the right moment, well, who knows? He might have overcome my resistance!" Julia giggled. "But you know what, Charlotte?" she said. "His lips were rather wet, and it was revolting . . . I don't know what came over me! Kissing the curate!" She giggled again.

Charlotte listened silently. What was the matter with *her?* At least Julia knew Mr. Colby. She even adored him. But Julia hadn't lost her head. They both knew that if Julia had been able to tell her mother, which of course she couldn't, Lady Brentorton would have approved of her response to the curate's kiss.

But when a stranger, a total stranger, kissed Charlotte out of the blue, she collapsed into his arms as if she were begging for more. So Charlotte separated her guilt from her anger. How evil could the man be? He must have thought . . . she didn't want to think what he must have thought, and quickly covered her burning cheeks with her hands.

It was only when the huge house was quiet, around two in the afternoon, that Charlotte started to cry. Julia had gone riding with her parents; her maid was down in the kitchen. Charlotte soaked her pillow with tears: for the husband she would never have, for the babies she thought to have, for the unfairness of discovering that she — she, Charlotte — was an insatiable woman. She'd have to stay away from men, she thought finally, after crying hopelessly for a long time. She couldn't trust herself, that was clear. And she couldn't allow herself to be publicly ruined; her parents would be devastated.

Finally she got out of bed and rang for a bath. She sent the maid out of the room because she wasn't sure whether there might be other signs of her ruination. But she didn't seem to be bleeding anymore.

It was only when she leaned back into the steaming water that Charlotte remembered her paintings, and given the way the world had shifted in the last few hours, she allowed that to shift too. Since she couldn't have a husband, or a baby, she could learn how to paint properly. She would make a focus for her life in the easy sweep of new canvas and wet paint, far from the humiliation she felt at the moment. The thought — the plan — calmed the agonizing jumble of feelings inside Charlotte; she rose from the bath and allowed Julia's maid to button her into a chaste white gown.

Chapter 2

As Charlotte's world fell into *before* and *after,* so did the world of her mother. When Charlotte returned to Albemarle Square the next day, she didn't say much. She looked at her mother with a tearless, somber look that made her mother want simultaneously to shake her and to burst into tears. What on earth had happened to Charlotte? She wasn't herself anymore, as the duchess told her husband in bewilderment. Charlotte became moody and even harsh.

If the truth be told, Adelaide was exhausted, too exhausted to deal with a new, irritable Charlotte. Debuts were tiring: The planning had taken weeks, and just this week Gunther's had put up a fuss about the ices. She had ordered ices colored a delicate violet, and they appeared with a violently purple sample. The footman who was set to washing the center chandelier broke seventeen crystals before anyone noticed he was dead drunk. The new gown she had ordered (blue velvet, embroidered with silver fleur-de-lis) was ghastly. The sleeves were short and far too tight, and the overdress sagged, making her look old and matronly. So she had to pay four times the price to have Madame Flancot create a new gown of rose brocade, practically overnight.

And then, the very day before the ball, Charlotte announced that she wouldn't go to any balls, including her own debut. Adelaide stared at her in disbelief. She turned sharply to Charlotte's maid, Marie.

"Fetch Violetta please, Marie. And then you may go."

Marie slipped from the room. Her mistress must have gone crazy. That beautiful dress! How could she even think of not wearing it?

Charlotte's sister Violetta strolled into the bedroom with all the nonchalance of someone with two seasons behind her and an almost-for-certain marriage proposal from the Marquess of Blass.

Violetta tried persuasion. "You know, Lottie," she said, reverting to Charlotte's pet name from childhood, "I was terrified at my debut. Mama had the place absolutely covered in white lilies — which was very nice, Mama," she hastened to add, "but the perfume was so powerful. When I slipped downstairs to see the ballroom in the afternoon, I just kept sneezing and sneezing, and we all panicked. But then Campion suggested scotch, which he said was a perfect remedy for sneezing, and he was right. Of course," she said meditatively, "I don't remember much of what happened after the glass of scotch, but at least I didn't sneeze all evening."

Charlotte just looked at her sister miserably.

She hadn't cried since leaving Julia's house, but she felt like it, all the time. One minute she was desperate to see *that man* again; the next she was consumed with rage and self-pity.

Violetta sat down next to her on the bed, so close their shoulders were touching. "I wouldn't worry, Charlotte. You're the most beautiful of us three, you know. You always have been. And you're the reason for the whole ball: you don't have to worry about not having someone to dance with. . . ."

Charlotte just shook her head. Why go? She couldn't get married; she might as well start the way she meant to go on. She felt, in her old nurse's phrase, as stubborn as a pig about it.

"It's no use, Violetta," her mother broke in. "She's set against it! Why? Why, Charlotte!" Her voice rose perilously near a shriek. "At the least you owe me an explanation, after all the work I've done. If you'd said four months ago you didn't want this ball we could have discussed it rationally. But now you *must* tell me why you won't attend the ball or I shall summon your father!"

Adelaide was sitting on the stool of the dressing table, her eyes fixed on Charlotte's face. Violetta was staring at her equally intently from her other side. Charlotte felt as if she were being squeezed between two walls, as if she couldn't breathe. She looked down at her lap. Her hands were twisting, one over the other, around and around. She felt hot and nauseated. From outside her window came the rhythmic pounding of workmen building a huge marquee in the garden, for the supper at *her* ball.

"All right, Mama," she finally said.

"All right what!" snapped her mother.

"I'll tell you why," said Charlotte slowly. She couldn't look up, so she steadily regarded her linked fingers. "I went to a ball in Kent," she said, "secretly. It wasn't Julia's fault; I wanted to go too. It was a masked ball and I powdered my hair, so no one could recognize me."

Violetta had gone very still next to her. Her mother was staring at her in fascinated horror. She was too dumbfounded to ask why Charlotte had broken all the rules she spent years drilling into each of her three daughters' heads.

"And what happened?" Adelaide finally said, evenly, when the room had been silent for several minutes.

Charlotte raised her miserable eyes to her mother's. "I met a man," she said, her voice trembling. "I met a man and I went into the garden with him." Whatever was in Charlotte's eyes made all the anger in Adelaide's chest melt like snow. She whisked over to Charlotte's side, tucked herself against the bedboard, and pulled her daughter into her arms.

"It's all right, darling," she whispered, rubbing Charlotte's arm and kissing the top of her head, just as she had when Charlotte was a little girl and stubbed her toe. Charlotte didn't respond, but she didn't pull away. A silky curtain of hair

46

fell over her face as she leaned on her mother's chest.

"But — what happened then?" Violetta asked. "What do you mean, you went into the garden? Did you let him kiss you? What was it like? Did you enjoy it?" She reached over and gave Charlotte's hip a little poke.

Her mother gave her a look she had rarely seen before. "Be quiet, Violetta," she said. And Violetta didn't say another word. She had been about to admit to visiting the garden herself, with the Marquess just last week, and *she* had quite liked it. But Charlotte had never been very interested in men . . . unless, and Violetta's eyes grew round with horror, Charlotte allowed this man to take liberties with her, with her person. She drew in her breath and opened her mouth again, but her mother's eye caught hers and she relapsed into silence.

Adelaide gathered her thoughts. Unlike Violetta, she had an excellent idea what had happened. Her little Charlotte, her baby, she thought, with a pain like a knife twisting in her heart, had been violated. By a man whom she could kill with her own bare hands. She clutched Charlotte closer.

Finally she cleared her throat and eased Charlotte into a sitting position. She put both hands on Charlotte's shoulders and looked straight into Charlotte's tearless green eyes.

"Are you all right, darling? Do you need me to . . . should I summon Dr. Pargeter?" Charlotte turned even paler, and just shook her head violently.

Adelaide stared at her silently. She needed to find out exactly what happened, but not in front of Violetta.

"Violetta," she said. She couldn't even think of a good excuse. "Violetta," she repeated, looking at her elder daughter over Charlotte's bent shoulders, "I want you to go to your room now. No arguments," she said firmly, heading off Violetta's protest. "I will visit you in a few minutes and we will discuss all of this. Until then, *no one* is to know, Violetta, particularly not Alice." Alice was Violetta's maid.

So Violetta walked slowly out of the room, confident that she could pry all the details out of her mama later. Mama, she thought complacently, had always been putty in the hands of a good questioner. Why, she knew all about things she really oughtn't to, like what happened between a man and his wife, for example. She bet that Charlotte had never asked Mama anything, and so she had no idea. Or perhaps she had? Violetta trailed back to her room, bursting with questions.

When they were alone, Charlotte drew a shuddering breath and started sobbing and speaking incoherently. "Oh, Mama, I met a man . . . in the garden. I kissed him. I didn't think — he kissed me." Her voice broke on a sob and she bent her forehead against her mother's shoulder. How could she say it, what really happened? Her

48

mother would be . . .

"I went with him, Mama," she finally said, raising her head and meeting her mother's eyes painfully. "I went into the garden with him, behind the trees, and he . . . he took my clothing apart. I'm so, I'm so — I didn't stop him."

Adelaide listened silently, stroking her daughter's arm. It was both worse and better than she feared. At least Charlotte had not been raped. But she did seem to have abandoned all of the rules of society in an act of such recklessness that Adelaide's stomach twisted just to hear about it. Behind the trees! *Anyone* could have seen them!

"What was his name?" Adelaide asked.

"I don't know!"

"You don't know," Adelaide managed, and then, "Charlotte, he wasn't one of Squire Brentorton's footmen, was he?"

Charlotte gulped. "He could have been, Mama." She began to weep even harder. Details flowed out amid sobs: the ball, silver-black hair, a green domino, the curate, the statue of Narcissus, the lemonade made with poor lemons.

Adelaide's hand stopped its soothing motion. Who was this man? Charlotte's description was none too exact, and there were so many gentlemen in London — if he was a gentleman, Adelaide thought bleakly. He certainly hadn't acted like one. But Charlotte hadn't acted like a lady, either.

Something nudged the back of her memory, something she'd heard about a young man with silver-shot hair, but she couldn't quite remember what. They would just have to hope. She decided to send someone to Kent immediately to investigate the masked ball.

Finally Charlotte was cried out, and Adelaide came to a decision. She pushed Charlotte into a sitting position again.

"Now," she said firmly. "We simply have to forget that this whole incident happened." She looked into Charlotte's eyes with every bit of maternal authority she could summon. "You cannot allow your life to be ruined because you had a momentary indiscretion in a garden, Charlotte.

"We have *all* been indiscreet on occasion. Why —" she paused and looked at her daughter's innocent eyes. Not so innocent anymore, she reminded herself. This was going to be difficult. She had always thought of Charlotte as the daughter untouched by desire. In fact, she'd probably been much sterner with Violetta, given that Violetta was a girl one might picture enjoying a tryst in the garden! But Charlotte . . .

"Well, your father and I did exactly what you just did, before we got married. In fact, we weren't even engaged."

Charlotte looked at her with a gleam of interest. "You did?"

"We did," her mother replied. "Not, I am glad to say, in the garden. It was . . . well, I won't say where, but I will tell you that it was likely just as uncomfortable as your garden, and only slightly less imprudent. Believe me, child, people do odd things all the time. You were just terribly lucky." She gave her a brief hug.

"No one knows." Adelaide looked sternly into Charlotte's eyes. "If no one knows, then it didn't happen. Do you hear me, Charlotte?" She gave her a little shake. "It *didn't happen.*"

Charlotte looked back numbly. Her mother must be insane. What did she mean, it didn't happen? She could feel the imprint of the man's body on her own at this very moment. She gave a little shudder.

"But, Mama," she said uncomfortably. They had never discussed things like this before. "There was, at least, I, there was some blood, and . . ."

"Virginity," her mother said astoundingly, "is a state of the body *and* mind. And believe me, child, I stayed a virgin for a good two weeks. You'll see: When you find yourself in this situation again — *married* this time — it will hurt just as much the second time, and the third. There really isn't any magical formula. You may not bleed on your wedding night, but actually many women never do bleed at all.

"You are going to this ball. You are going to have a good time, because you are *my* daughter, and I didn't raise you to be a weepy child. You made a mistake, and luckily you got away with it. You must never think about it again, ever."

In the back of her mind, Adelaide reminded herself to send someone down to Kent to investi-

51

gate that ball (better talk to Campion; he was so discreet). And she must remember to check, casually, that her daughter's monthly flux appeared on time.

"You are beautiful and young, and a lovely person, Charlotte," Adelaide said seriously, stroking her daughter's hair. "I think you will fall in love and get married, and it will be just as if it were the first time. Because in reality it *will* be the first time. You must forget this."

You must forget this, Charlotte told herself dutifully that night in bed, on the morning of the ball, in the later afternoon as Marie delicately arranged the folds of her white ballgown, adorned with white-on-white embroidery and the faintest of pale green love knots.

The whole house hummed with noise. All the furniture in the reception rooms had been removed and stored: Every bit of space was needed for the five hundred gentlefolk expected. Cartloads of soft blue and deeper blue, velvety delphiniums had arrived that morning and been arranged in huge vases. Huge swags of delphiniums adorned the staircase leading up from the drawing rooms to the ballroom, and the temporary staircase from the marquee in the garden to the house was lined in them.

"It's quite blue," Charlotte said rather faintly to her mother as they stood surveying the ballroom in the late afternoon. The parquet floor had been polished so brightly that the blue flowers doubled themselves on the floor. The whole room looked like an aquamarine ocean.

"You'll see, darling," her mother said confidently. "When the rooms are full of ladies and all the candles are shining, this blue will make a splendid background. Now, off you go and see if Monsieur Pamplemousse is finished with Violetta's hair. He will take at least an hour, and you know we must eat by eight o'clock tonight, since the invitations are for nine thirty."

Charlotte wandered upstairs. How could she forget what had happened? Even now she could imagine the chiseled warmth of his lips descending on hers, the strength of his huge hands gripping her shoulders and sliding down her back. How does one forget something like that? Oh, why hadn't she said something! She was such a booby; she should have said — what? "Please, sir, what is your name? Reginald? And is it nice being a footman?" Charlotte stifled a giggle. She did see her mother's point. Forget this, she said firmly to herself.

Still, she couldn't stop hoping. Maybe he was a nobleman, or a gentleman. Maybe he would come to her ball, and she would meet his gaze across the room, just as she had at the other ball. And maybe he would shoulder his way through the crowd and bow before her. Charlotte's eyes glowed.

The Duchess of Calverstill's ball for her youngest daughter was a triumph. By eight thirty, spectators were thronging the streets outside

Calverstill House, hoping to see nobility, even royalty, going in. By eleven o'clock the ball was clearly the success of the season. Everyone who counted was there, and several scandals were circulating briskly, which made the party all the more delightful.

The formidable Lady Jersey herself had declared that Adelaide's delphinium scheme was "delicious"; she and her fellow patrons of Almack's had graciously extended permission for Charlotte to enter the sacred premises. The ball continued until dawn, long after supper was served in the marquee around midnight.

And as to whether Charlotte had a good time: well, she survived. She didn't enjoy it, her mother thought as she undressed in the wee hours. Anyone could tell that. Charlotte's eyes kept scanning the room anxiously, as if the guest of honor hadn't arrived, and finally she burst into tears in the ladies' lounge and had to be quietly whisked off to the upper reaches of the house.

But she looked lovely, Adelaide comforted herself. Many young ladies at their debuts were nauseated with pure nervousness, and if Charlotte was a bit, well, *damp,* who would blame her? Of course, no one in the ballroom was advised that the lady of honor had retired weeping to bed.

Around two in the morning Adelaide looked up from the middle of a rather slow quadrille and saw two young men standing at the top of the stairs, looking down into the ballroom.

She froze and stopped dead in her tracks, causing her partner, the Honorable Sylvester Bredbeck, to stumble slightly.

"Sylvester!" Adelaide said sharply. "Who are those young men?"

Sylvester looked around. "Well, they're not bounders, m'dear," he said comfortably. Sylvester had been her dear friend for years, and anyone he didn't know wasn't worth knowing. "I think the one on the left is Sheffie's heir (he's a trifle taller) and the other's his brother. Let me see, I think the heir is called Alexander and his brother is . . . Patrick. They are twins, as you can see, but Alexander got five minutes on Patrick and about two million pounds on account of it."

Sylvester guided Adelaide through a few more slow turns while she thought furiously. Of course! Sheffie was Sylvester's friend the Earl of Sheffield and Downes, and that was his heir . . . and his younger son . . . and they *both* had silver-shot hair. What on earth should she do?

Maybe she should excuse herself, dash upstairs, force Charlotte back into the dress and bring her back down? But then Adelaide despairingly remembered Charlotte's reddened eyes. Besides, these probably weren't the right men, or man, and Charlotte would be horribly disappointed.

The two men were still staring down into the ballroom. He's looking for her, Charlotte's mother thought suddenly. He's here because of *her.* Her heart warmed a little to him — well, to whom? Which *he* was the right man? They looked exactly the same to her. I certainly hope Charlotte would know the difference, she thought a little tartly.

Even as she watched, they wheeled and left the ballroom. Couldn't find her, so he left, Adelaide thought. Well, how very interesting. And I was quite right not to disturb Charlotte, because this is just the beginning of the season. Why, when she herself came out she attended fifty balls and sixty-three breakfasts, and if Charlotte didn't encounter the future Earl of Sheffield and Downes and his brother within the next week, she'd eat her hat!

"Sylvester, m'dear," said the duchess, leading her partner off the floor. "I should like a glass of lemonade, and a talk. Because we haven't talked all night, and you know I have to dance every single one of these dances, so I haven't had a moment of conversation."

Sylvester was charmed. "My dearest wish is to sit at your side, your grace," he said cheerfully, although he was a bit nonplussed to find that the subject of conversation was one and only one: the future Earl of Sheffield and Downes and his brother. But, like most men, Sylvester was a born gossip; he simply didn't bother to hide his inclinations. He bent his head near Adelaide's ear and agreeably related tales of Oxford mishaps and a reported fistfight at Vauxhall two years ago, when both brothers were accompanied by a lady of easy virtue and came to blows with another "friend" of hers. Then he burbled on with a few more tales expunged of too racy material.

But he said enough to convince Adelaide that Charlotte probably wasn't the first maiden this Alexander, or Patrick, had deflowered in a garden; and to explain why she herself didn't know them. Apparently the twins didn't spend much time in respectable surroundings. Another point that suggests that one of them came here looking for Charlotte, Adelaide thought.

Still, they were gentlemen, nay, they were noblemen. And their papa was friends with her husband, Marcel, and *if* one of them had a hand in this, Marcel would make perfectly sure that he offered marriage by tomorrow night.

"I hear," Sylvester rambled on, "that Sheffie is thinking of separating them; they're just too wild together. He was talking of sending them off to the Continent, or maybe it was one of them off to Europe, or some such thing, and I think the other one to the Orient . . . I don't remember what exactly he was planning, but that was it: yes, one to Europe and the other to the Orient. Probably get taken by pirates over in the East; he'd better not send his heir.

"Sheffie's not here, is he?" Sylvester peered around for Woodleigh Foakes, the actual Earl of Sheffield and Downes.

"No," Adelaide said absently. "I think he's poorly again; he suffers horribly from gout, you know."

Just then the music ended and the duchess's next partner, Sir Walter Mitford, appeared at her elbow as if by magic. Sylvester bowed, a little creakily (he'd taken to wearing corsets in the past few years), and her young partner led Adelaide onto the floor.

Sylvester stood for a moment, his lips pursed. I wonder why she's so interested in those boys, he thought, his gossip-loving soul sniffing a scandal. Probably no scandal, he thought with a sigh. One tended to forget that Adelaide was the mother of three girls, but she was. And the Foakes heir would be an excellent match.

The duchess herself puzzled over the situation throughout a country dance with Sir Walter. Finally she decided to let events take their course and say nothing to Charlotte about the future earl or his brother. She and Charlotte and Violetta were going to Almack's tomorrow night and those men almost certainly wouldn't show up there; they were too young to be hanging out for wives, and Almack's was nothing but a marriage mart, she thought dispassionately. But in four days the crown prince was giving a ball that all the *ton* would attend. The Foakes brothers might come late, she thought, given their appearance tonight, but she'd keep Charlotte there till dawn if she had to. And so, having worked the whole problem out to her satisfaction, she dismissed it from her mind and turned back to her partner.

But that wasn't the last she saw of Alexander

and Patrick that evening: no, not by any means. Around an hour later, Adelaide found herself confronted by her husband's aunt Margaret, a fierce woman in her eighties. Margaret accepted without comment the news that Charlotte had retired for the night and could not bid her good-bye, but she demanded to see her nephew. So Adelaide began weaving through the people left in the ballroom, looking for her husband. The ballroom itself was finally clearing out, but people were still crowding the hallways and reception rooms.

At the end of the first floor hallway, to the right of the huge marble staircase, was the room they called the Green Room. It had a huge, old grand piano that had been deemed too much trouble to remove. Adelaide did not find Marcel there, but she did find the two sons of the Earl of Sheffield and Downes.

As she paused in the doorway she heard a strong, sweet voice raised in song. One of the twins was seated at the piano, with his back to her, singing in a beautiful baritone. For a moment she just paused in pleasure. Young women were forced to take piano and voice lessons as part of the accoutrements of young ladyhood; it was rare to meet a gentleman with the same skills. And he did have a superb voice.

His brother was leaning negligently against a pillar off to the right; the singer himself was surrounded by a pale, fluttering group of debutantes who had somehow shaken off their

59

chaperones, Adelaide thought, her eyes sharpening a bit. Of course — the chaperones must have gone off to the marquee for a bite to eat, and the young women had gathered here. *Not proper*, she thought firmly.

Suddenly the little flock of three maidens convulsed into soft gales of laughter, but the male voice continued. And for the first time Adelaide actually heard what he was singing:

"The touch of her hand increases his flame,
Who conquer'd by charms a captive doth lie;
And when he but thinks of his true love's name,
He vows for her sake he could freely die:
Then she revives him again with a kiss,
He cries you undo me, undo me, undo me,
Had ever poor soul such pleasure as this?"

Adelaide's mouth fell open. He could "die," indeed! Why, that young heathen was singing bawdy tunes to debutantes.

She moved forward sharply, her skirt brushing the door portals. The nonsinging brother looked up at her from his pillar and surveyed her from under soaring eyebrows.

"Patrick," he said abruptly. "We have company. And I believe" — he pulled himself gracefully upright and walked over to her — "we have been joined by our hostess herself."

The girls swung around quickly, and little Barbara Lewnstown actually turned pink.

"Girls," Adelaide said in a faintly admonishing

60

tone. "Are you alone? Where's your mother, Barbara?"

Barbara answered, rather faintly. "Well, she went off with Sissy's mother" — she flapped her hand at Cecilia Commonweal behind her — "but it's all right, your grace. These are my cousins, you know."

Of course, she did know that, Adelaide thought, but she'd totally forgotten. She cast a stern eye on the handsome young man who had swiveled around on the piano bench and stood up, and now was looking sweetly at her. If this was Patrick, he was the younger one. My goodness, these boys are a devastating pair, she thought.

Patrick swept into an elegant bow, picking up her hand and kissing it. His eyes twinkled wickedly under his mop of silver-black curls. Despite herself, Adelaide felt a little feminine thrill.

"Your grace," said Patrick Sheffield, "may I sing you a song?" He threw her a glance full of mischief. "A most *proper* song, of course."

And without even thinking of Aunt Margaret, waiting impatiently by now, perhaps even beating her stick on the parquet, Adelaide twinkled back.

"Very short, and *very* proper," she said.

Patrick swung onto the piano bench and poised his large hands over the keyboard. His voice wound into the notes of a teasing, light song:

"You ladies who are young and gay,
Since time too swiftly flies away,

61

*Bestow your hours of leisure, bestow your hours
   of leisure
On courts, on gardens, springs, and groves,
On conversation's lawful loves,
And ev'ry harmless pleasure, ev'ry,
   ev'ry harmless pleasure."*

Wickedly, he accented *harmless pleasure* with an ironic deepening of his voice, so that even Adelaide couldn't prevent herself from laughing out loud.

"Enough!" she said, still chortling. "Girls, shall we return to the ballroom?" And she ushered the three young women before her, not missing the languishing look cast back by Miss Isabella Riddleford. I wonder which one she's after, Adelaide thought, and looked back herself.

The older twin, Alexander, was standing quite straight and watching them with a slight frown. His deep black eyes caught hers. Well, Adelaide thought, I certainly hope Charlotte went into the garden with the singer! This one is so moody-looking. One of Adelaide's friends had a husband who brooded and Adelaide felt tired just hearing about his woes.

She turned briskly and herded her charges into the ballroom.

"I didn't see the girl herself," said one young gallant, the Honorable Peter Medley to a friend the next morning in White's.

"I did," said his friend Justin. "She was

nothing special. None of the bounce her sister has. But did you hear what the Foakes twins got up to later? I heard that Alex actually decked a policeman and they knocked out three of the watch before they were hauled off to the police station."

Peter looked at him suspiciously. Since when did he know the future Earl of Sheffield and Downes well enough to call him Alex?

"Where'd you hear that?" he said.

"From old Beckley." Justin nodded across the room. Sure enough, Beckworth Cecily clearly had burning news to relate; he was surrounded by a small group of men whose faces mingled open amusement and condemnation.

So Adelaide's plans for the prince's ball came to naught. By four days later it was open knowledge that Woodleigh Foakes had ordered his sons onto ships bound for the Continent and the Orient. Just as the Honorable Sylvester had surmised, the heir (Alexander) was bound for Italy and the spare (as he was jocularly known) was bound for more exotic, if dangerous, travels in India. They weren't expected back for at least two years.

Adelaide kept silent, wondering if she should have dashed up the stairs and dragged Charlotte down to the ball. For a few weeks she was tormented by regret: What if she had? What if Charlotte had been seduced by one of the Foakes twins? What if they had come to the ball specifically looking for Charlotte? Finally her common sense comforted her: There were so many men in England with silver-black hair.

Then Campion brought her the succinctly worded report of a private investigator who wrote that the Saturday night Hookers' Ball was a regular feature of the Kent countryside. It was attended by nobles and gentlemen, but also by every other sort of person including, of course, prostitutes. And hearing where Charlotte had been, Adelaide felt sick but resigned. Most likely Charlotte was right: She had met a handsome footman in the twilight.

Besides, Adelaide had other problems. Charlotte's ball may have been a success but Charlotte herself was not. She spent hours in her room painting. She went to balls only when threatened with terrible punishments like the removal of her canvases. She hung listlessly around the edges of rooms full of her chattering contemporaries, and complained of boredom. She developed a cool, impenetrable glance that ranged over the assembled ranks of men and dismissed them all. It was a brave twenty-two-year-old who requested a second dance with her, since she seemed to have no small conversation and terrified empty-headed young gentlemen by asking them what they thought of events in France.

After a while, Adelaide forgot about the dark eyes of Alexander the senior and the velvety voice of Patrick the junior. And Charlotte presumably forgot about her tryst in the garden . . . at any rate, it was never mentioned between them again. Mother and daughter spent their time, if the truth be known, bickering over Charlotte's refusal to attend society functions, and her contemptuous air when she did.

Adelaide didn't understand that, to Charlotte, the young men she met paled next to the memory of *his* face; Charlotte didn't understand her mother's growing terror at the prospect of her daughter's marriageless future. She had taken to painting flowers, and she was happiest in her room, delicately copying the dusky gold shade of a lily.

To Charlotte, the future was clear. She wouldn't marry one of the silly boys she had met so far; she probably wouldn't marry at all. The prospect didn't bother her too much. What did bother her was wasted time and slow dances, tepid lemonade and too-tight dresses.

By a year later she too thought only rarely about the man she met in the garden. When she did think about the experience, she saw it as a lucky event that made her a woman overnight and taught her to see what she wanted. Without it, she'd have been herded into some man's arms by the end of her first season, Charlotte thought contemptuously. She'd probably be pregnant by now, and her husband would be romping at Ascot while she was left at home.

Charlotte stood back from her easel, looking at her latest picture, of a tawny tiger lily. The lines of the stem were not perfect, but the color was splendid. This, she thought, was a far better life.

Chapter 3

London, England
May 1801

The spring Charlotte turned twenty, her family gave up hope of her marrying. In the three seasons since she had made her debut she had done surprisingly well, considering that she rarely attended balls and had to be coaxed into attending garden parties and tea parties and rides in the park, the normal activities for gently bred young ladies.

But when she did come to a ball, she was never ignored. After her miserable debut year, she gathered a circle of gentlemen about her who applauded her wit. If they secretly admired her lovely curves, they quickly learned to keep silent. Even the most innocent of compliments, say a comparison of Lady Charlotte's eyes to stars, was met by a calm but freezing withdrawal.

"I can't understand it," the Earl of Slaslow gloomily told a friend, leaning in the corner of Almack's and watching Charlotte gracefully circle the floor. "I didn't even think that much of her in the beginning, but she . . ."

"I know," said David Marlowe, a mere younger son of a squire, destined for the clergy. "I know: She ignored your compliments, and piqued your curiosity, and now you are caught. Women!" David was disgusted. Clearly the little baggage was playing Braddon like a fisherman with a trout.

No one would honestly refuse Braddon's attention. Why, he was the best catch on the market this year, if one discounted the enormously wealthy, but terribly old, Duke of Siskind. And Siskind was just looking for a nurse to take care of his eight children, everyone knew that.

But here was Braddon, as glum as a trout on the riverbank, and this Charlotte *had* turned him down for a second dance, that was a fact. At this very moment, she was circling the floor for the second time with that old gossip Sylvester Bredbeck. And chortling with laughter at a story Sylvester was telling her.

"Why don't you write her a poem or something?" David suggested, nudging his friend.

"I did," Braddon said dismally. "It wasn't bad either; I pretty much stole it out of one of the old books lying around my library; *you* know."

David did. Not that he'd read any of those books, of course, but he'd had many a smoky game of piquet in Braddon's walnut-paneled library.

"It wasn't bad," Braddon insisted. "I said that her hair had pearls threaded on each strand, something like that, and that her eyes were suns and her teeth were crystals."

"Pearls — threaded on each hair," David repeated dubiously. "I don't know, Braddon. What'd she say?"

"She laughed." The earl crossed his arms over his chest. "She just laughed, and then she said thanks, and then later she accidentally sat on the poem." He looked mutinous at David's snort of laughter.

"Wilkins had copied the whole thing out, on parchment mind you, and he tied it with a ribbon and a flower. But she got up to greet someone, and then sat on it later and crumpled the whole thing, and she did *not* look sorry."

David looked at Charlotte with greater curiosity. A woman who crumpled the Earl of Slaslow's literary efforts (no matter how poor) really was quite different from the run-of-the-mill young woman in Almack's.

"The thing is," Braddon continued, lowering his voice a bit, "I could see living with her, you know? I have to get married — I mean, my mother is after me like one of those Furies in Greek drama, you remember them? Well, she doesn't have snakes for hair, but really, it's the same idea. She snaps at me every morning." Braddon shuddered slightly. "And my sister, Marge, is the same. You'd think she would be happy enough with her own four brats, but no, she's after me all the time to, to *spawn!*" he ended savagely.

David weighed the trouble of being urged to spawn against that of being a younger son whom no one would ever want to marry, given his complete lack of income. Still, he was free. He was in Almack's only because he was visiting his old friend; it wasn't him that all those hungry-looking young women kept eyeing.

And this Charlotte: She was beautiful, in her own way. She was wearing a rather plain gown, but even so, one could tell that she had a lovely bosom. Her hair was so black that it kept catching the gleam of the chandeliers overhead.

"I think you should do it," he said firmly. "Look around here. All these girls look alike. Now, if that one can laugh, and she can ride a horse — she can, can't she?" David paused anxiously. Braddon lived for his stables.

"She rides like a dream," Braddon said.

David cast another glance at him: Braddon really was far gone. "Well, why don't you pop the question, then?"

"You think so?" asked the Earl of Slaslow anxiously.

"Definitely," said his closest friend. "You could even ask her father now; I think he's in the card room."

"Oh, no," said Braddon, lounging back into the corner. "My mama's been dinning this whole thing into my ears for months. I go in the morning and send in my card, and then I see her pa, and then I see her, and the most I do is kiss her forehead, so I don't scare her off."

There was a little pause.

David was feeling sorry for the soon-to-be dowager countess. The new earl had a head as hard as brick; David clearly remembered trying to fix certain facts in Braddon's skull during their time at Eton, just basic ones, like the date of the Battle of Hastings. If you repeated things about eight times, they would stick for a matter of a few hours, long enough for an exam. It was always touch and go. Yet surely asking for a girl's hand in marriage couldn't be that difficult.

And that was how Charlotte conquered the biggest catch on the market. She rejected him just as quickly. When her papa summoned Charlotte for a private meeting with the Earl of Slaslow, Charlotte turned Braddon down flat, gently explaining that she liked him enormously, but wouldn't he be happier with Miss Barbara Lewnstown? Barbara and Braddon seemed so well-suited, given that she loved horses just as much as he did.

Charlotte's mother went to bed for a whole three days, and wouldn't speak to her daughter for two weeks. Braddon went away glum and unconvinced, and when he next glimpsed Miss Lewnstown at Almack's he gave a ferocious grimace and turned away.

By 1801, Charlotte had received solid offers of marriage from some eight gentlemen, only two of them known to be interested in her dowry. The other six wooed her for her green eyes and her slow, unhurried smiles.

No, Charlotte will never get married, her mother and father admitted, lying in the ducal bed on a Thursday evening.

"It's the painting!" the duchess said. "Oh, Marcel, she'll dwindle into an old maid . . . I'm so unhappy," she said in a burst, tears rolling down her face.

"Well," said Marcel uncomfortably. "Violetta married quite late; why give up hope for Charlotte?" Marcel was a large, quiet man whose French first name had been given to him by his romantic mother. It had caused him quite a bit of embarrassment in the past few years, especially in 1797 when republican France threatened to invade England.

"I think," he said, settling his wife's head firmly into the crook of his shoulder, "we should just loosen the reins a little. What if she doesn't want to go to parties? Let her paint." He thought of adding the fact that he was tired of arguments about balls, but he didn't.

The duchess wriggled her head against her husband's shoulder. He was a sweet man, but he had no idea of the daily vexations that greeted a woman who never married, the snubs and insults that were already being doled out to Charlotte.

"But what about when . . . where will she live?" Adelaide said despairingly. "Horace will inherit this house and the one in the country, and he'll want to start a family, and who's to say that he would want a maiden sister living with him, especially one who has a reputation for an unlady-

71

like interest in painting!"

"I'll tell you what," said her spouse comfortably. "The other two girls are settled. Winnie's husband will never lack blunt and Violetta's marquess is doing just fine. I'll turn that Cornish estate over to Charlotte, you know, the one that I inherited from Aunt Beatrice. It's not entailed, and it turns a pretty profit. With the land and her dowry, she'll be right and tight."

Adelaide thought about it. Their eldest daughter, Winifred, had married Austen Saddlesford, a madly wealthy American, and gone off happily to live in Boston, and Violetta had married the Marquess of Blass, and indeed, neither girl was hurting for money. And Horace would inherit all the ducal holdings; he wouldn't begrudge the Cornish inheritance.

Characteristically, she saw it from a slightly different angle than did her husband. He thought, kindly enough, that with the Cornish rents Charlotte could live comfortably and buy a house in London if she wished. But what Adelaide immediately grasped was that the Cornish estate — a little Elizabethan manor house and its land — would turn Charlotte from the very well-endowed daughter of a duke into being a remarkable heiress. And *that,* she thought sagely, would perk up interest in her daughter and what's more, would stop tongues wagging about her being an old maid. A great heiress just didn't fit the category, somehow.

One never knew; perhaps the right man *would*

come along for Charlotte, and now it wouldn't matter if he wasn't wealthy.

"Marcel, you are a wonder," Adelaide said gratefully, rubbing her hair against his shoulder like a silken cat.

So the season of 1801 opened on a rather different note for Charlotte. Ignoring all her protests, her father had signed over to her a quite vast amount of land in Cornwall.

"You might as well get used to the responsibility while I'm around to advise you," he said, signing the last papers with a flourish of his quill. The duke's thin, prunelike lawyer, Mr. Jennings of Jennings and Condell, shuddered delicately, inside of course. Jennings and Condell did not approve of women holding property of any kind and Mr. Jennings foresaw endless bother after the Duke of Calverstill passed away.

On her side, Charlotte quickly realized that owning a house made her very happy. *She* owned a manse in Cornwall; twenty-three people lived and farmed near the house, and some three hundred sheep grazed on her land, according to the manager's report. She read the latest reports over and over. The newspaper gained an interest that it never had before. When workers destroyed looms in the Cotswolds, she shuddered: What if riots spread to Cornwall?

As soon as possible, she promised herself, she would go to Cornwall. She could just imagine her mother's horror if she suggested such a thing

now (the trip! the dirt!), but perhaps in the fall
. . . with a chaperone, of course.

And the season was better because it seemed
to Charlotte that her mother was becoming more
comfortable with her rejection of eight worthy
suitors. Adelaide stopped looking at her with a
pained expression. They even began speaking
again without sorrowful innuendoes underlying
every conversation.

In fact, Charlotte didn't notice immediately
that her mother was no longer prodding her into
attending balls. One night she walked into the
dining room and realized the room was bare.

"Where are my parents, Campion?" she asked
the butler.

"I believe the duchess is attending a *fête de
champagne* given by Lady Bridgeplate, and I am
not cognizant of the duke's location," Campion
replied, holding out her chair with a flourish.
Charlotte looked at the table.

"What are we eating tonight, Campion?" she
asked absently.

Campion brightened. He loved to talk about
food, although this family simply didn't appreciate it as they ought to. *"Poulet à la diable, crab
rémoulade,* and *fraises à la Chantilly."*

"Oh," Charlotte said flatly.

She sat down and stared at the steaming
consommé that Campion placed tenderly before
her. The solitary life was, well, so *solitary* . . . Perhaps she should find a companion. She thought
of an elderly lady with a cap, and pursed her lips.

Perhaps not. Two old maids, she thought. She didn't feel bitter, but it did seem tedious.

Perhaps she had made an error. In the course of fending off eight marriage proposals, Charlotte had discovered that, in fact, she didn't have a wanton sexual response to each and every man who tried to kiss her. When the Earl of Slaslow offered his well-phrased and elegant proposal, she responded in dulcet tones; when he refused rejection and hauled her into his arms, kissing her fiercely, she didn't respond at all. Instead she stood with her mouth tightly closed and except for grinding his teeth against her lips, there was nothing he could do about that. So Braddon gave up and backed away, even pouting a little.

On the other hand, when the well-known fortune hunter William Holland — an impoverished baron but so good-looking! — pulled her against his chest, she did open her lips, and she did enjoy the kiss. She even felt a little swooning feeling in her stomach. But it was nothing like the raw emotion that had flooded her at the masked ball.

Now, three years later, she didn't remember the footman's face very well (for that was what she'd decided he was), but she definitely remembered her own reaction. And she'd grown rather tolerant of herself. While it was true she probably shouldn't get married, given her lack of a maidenhead, she had heard lots of stories about maidenheads that never existed, especially if one was active and rode horses.

Perhaps she should take more interest in the

whole process, now that her mother seemed to be relinquishing control. She even found herself wondering whether Will Holland had found the rich wife he needed.

Campion entered the dining room and removed her untouched consommé and gently placed a half chicken, *à la diable,* before her. Charlotte didn't like eating alone. It made her low, in fact. She liked painting alone: Her mother had turned over a large room on the third floor, which had good light in the morning and excellent light in the afternoon; she loved entering her studio, putting on her apron, and mixing paints.

At the moment she was copying paintings. One after another, she took down paintings from all over the ducal estates and carried them up to her room, keeping them for a month or two, even (in the case of the duke's only Rembrandt) for six months.

"Why, darling?" her mother had asked hopelessly that afternoon, looking at Charlotte's third copy of their sturdy Elizabethan ancestor, Sir Vigilant Calverstill. Adelaide looked back and forth between the two easels.

"Do you think his eyes are quite right, darling?" she asked. "He looks so — well, so piggy, in your version."

Charlotte smiled back at her mother lovingly. "I know, Mama. I had a problem with his eyes, and then I decided that it emphasized his corpulence rather well. He *might* have been a quite greedy man, after all. He certainly managed to

76

acquire a lot of possessions, didn't he?"

"But why copies, dearest? Why not make some more of your own pictures, perhaps some more fruit? I love your fruit, and the series of violets you did for Violetta's wedding were so splendid! I almost burst with pride," the duchess said.

"I'll tell you what, Mama," said Charlotte. "As soon as I've finished with Sir Vigilant here, I'll paint you a really beautiful bunch of flowers for your room."

"Do you know what I'd like, Charlotte?" asked her mother. "I would really like you to paint a picture for your great-aunt Margaret. It's getting quite difficult for her to leave her chambers now, and — I know!" she said with great excitement. "When Margaret was young she was known as Marguerite: I believe she was quite beautiful, and so everyone called her after the flower. You can paint her a vase of marguerites, and I vow she'll be so happy!"

And so Adelaide bustled off to find Campion and arrange for a boy to visit the flower market first thing tomorrow morning and bring home loads of daisies.

"She's not done with Sir Vigilant yet," Adelaide confided in Campion. "But having marguerites in the room will put her in the mood, so to speak. Who will you send? Fred? Well, Fred must be sure to tell the flower stalls that we shall be wanting marguerites every morning for at least six to eight weeks. *You* know how long it takes."

And indeed he did. The whole household revolved around the progress of Charlotte's paintings, although she would have been amazed to realize it. When she began a new piece Charlotte worked long hours and danced down the stairs, her face glowing. And when Charlotte danced, the house danced.

She always noticed if a footman had a toothache, for example, and sent him back to the servants' quarters immediately. She asked about the housekeeper Mrs. Simpkin's two nieces, who were growing up a bit unruly; she never forgot to inquire kindly about Campion's only son, who had been a chef-in-training over in France, but had to get out quickly when the Frenchies went crazy, and now he was doing very well for himself, training over at the Maison Blanche on Thurston Street.

But if a painting bogged down because a nose or an ear gained a misshapen air that didn't match the original, then the house hummed rather than sang. Housemaids tiptoed past Charlotte's studio on the third floor, and dust accumulated in the room because the servants never knew when she would be found standing in front of an easel. Once a tweeny entered the room at eleven o'clock at night to replace the candles, and accidentally walked in on Lady Charlotte, who sent her away with a sharpish remark. After that Mrs. Simpkin and Campion monitored the progress of pictures themselves, and regulated the household accordingly.

So Campion nodded sagely and smiled at his mistress. He'd take care of the marguerites first thing, and her grace shouldn't worry about a thing, he murmured. And then he reminded the duchess of her engagement at a *fête de champagne*. Adelaide dashed lightly up the stairs to get dressed. She didn't think of asking Charlotte, and the duke was out at his club.

Charlotte sighed heavily. Campion swum silently into the room and removed her barely touched chicken, suppressing his own sigh at the sight.

The Calverstill chef, Renoir, was *wasted* on the family, absolutely wasted. But Renoir would never know. When the family dined alone Campion always removed the dishes himself, and they invariably returned to the kitchen as if a rejoicing family of ten had surfeited themselves. It was part of his campaign to keep Renoir happy, and he knew that the underfootmen, Fred and Cecil (a ridiculous name for a footman), would never reveal that they too enjoyed *duck à l'orange* of an evening.

Charlotte wandered back up to her bedchamber rather disconsolately. She could dress and follow her mother to Lady Bridgeplate's *fête*, but it would look rather odd. And what if her mother had gone on to another party, something she was quite capable of doing? Charlotte would arrive and find herself without a chaperone, and Lord knows that would be bad for her reputation.

Her maid was down in the kitchens, so Charlotte pulled open the doors to her wardrobe and looked at the row of gowns. She hadn't done much about her apparel lately. She realized it was partly an act of pique, a way of telling her mother to leave her alone. But now she gazed with dislike at her dresses. They weren't exactly out of fashion (her maid, if no one else, would never let her wear something actually dated), but they weren't in the newest style either. And perhaps even worse, they were all naive pastels, the soft buttery colors of innocence and youth.

And I, Charlotte thought savagely, am not young! So why should I dress that way? She began ruthlessly pulling dresses off hangers and throwing them on the bed. When Marie entered the room some ten minutes later, never expecting to find her mistress in her chambers, she was dumbfounded to see piles of gowns piled on the bed, and her mistress gazing with a satisfied expression at four or five morning gowns left in her wardrobe.

"Mon dieu!" Marie breathed, wondering if Charlotte had suddenly gone mad. Her mistress, she privately thought, was already as odd as could be: Perhaps she'd decided to join those nudists who were emigrating to America!

"Marie!" Charlotte said, without turning her head. "I've decided to make a change. Tomorrow I shall go to Madame Brigette's and order a whole new wardrobe. Everything: from top to bottom."

Marie instantly grasped what was happening. Her mistress had finally woken up to the truth: A woman needs a man. At least, that was what Marie had confided over and over to her beloved, the second footman Cecil, when they were lying snug in Marie's room. Campion and Mrs. Simpkin, the housekeeper, didn't know *that,* of course, but Marie's French sensibilities did not require that she adhere to English morality. She and Cecil could not get married until she had sufficient money for a *dot,* but until then she saw no reason to deny herself or Cecil the pleasure of occasional company.

Marie's eyes brightened. "And your hair, my lady! Shall I summon Monsieur Pamplemousse?"

"Yes, Marie, that's a very good suggestion." Charlotte perched on top of the bed and looked into the mirror over her dressing table, unthinkingly crushing four or five layers of delicate dresses. She pulled her hair from its ribbon at her neck. "I think I shall have something entirely different . . . perhaps I shall cut my hair!"

"Oh, Lady Charlotte, I'm not certain," said Marie, thinking of the beauty of her mistress's silky black curls as they dried before the fire. "Men like such things, long hair," she said, her Gallic accent pronounced. Marie's parents had immigrated from France some ten years ago, when she was just a girl, but she tended to slide into a thick French lisp in moments of excitement.

"This short hair . . . well, it's very *new*, isn't it? Lady Marion Lamb cut all hers off, of course, and Pearl Clotswild, the American heiress, and . . ." Marie's voice trailed off. She was an avid reader of the illustrated gossip papers, and she knew that cropped hair was one of the most daring things a young lady could do.

Marie came around the bed and pulled Charlotte's heavy black hair off her shoulders. Together they stared into the mirror over her dressing table, Marie's tiny face gazing intently, her lips pursed. She twisted Charlotte's hair this way and that.

"Perhaps," she said finally. It was true that Charlotte's face sprang into high relief when it escaped from its mantle of hair. In the three years since Marie had become Charlotte's maid, her mistress had never let her spend more than ten minutes arranging her hair, and so Marie had finally taken desperately to threading a simple ribbon through the front, which at least held most of the weight off Charlotte's face. But the style didn't emphasize Charlotte's eyes. Now she saw they were a remarkable size, slightly almond shaped, and her eyelashes were as black as her hair.

"We shall see what Monsieur says," Marie announced. She had the greatest reverence for Monsieur Pamplemousse, about whom one heard the most riveting stories: he was the hairdresser to Louis XVI, he had escaped from the very shadow of Madame Guillotine, he was the hairdresser to Napoleon's beloved Josephine. Of course the English all abhorred Napoleon, but Marie reserved judgment. To her mind, Josephine was a model of feminine beauty and fashion, and her husband of rather less account.

"And as for Madame Brigette's, my lady," Marie said earnestly, "had you thought of perhaps visiting the establishment of Antonin Carême? Madame Brigette creates perfect dresses for young girls, but . . ."

"You are right, of course," Charlotte said, her voice rather bleak. She was not, and would never again be, a "girl."

She met Marie's worried eyes with a brilliant smile. "Actually, Marie, I never was much good at the girlish look anyway. It is time to try another style. I saw a woman in the park yesterday in one of those new high-waisted dresses, and no corset. Of course," she said, "I think the lady herself was probably not of the highest moral fiber, but the point is that the new French styles are rather charming, don't you think?"

Marie clapped her hands. "Oh yes, Lady Charlotte! Monsieur Carême is just the person to visit. And," she said shrewdly, "you have just the figure to neglect the corset. Perhaps . . . you might order one gown in gold? I have often thought that you would look splendid in a dress the color of the morning room curtains!" Charlotte was startled for a moment, and then smiled.

"I shall wear no more pink," she said. "Nothing rosier than a strong peach. And" —

more slowly — "no flounces, no ruffles, no embroidered flowers, no bows."

"Absolument, oui, oui!" Marie was almost babbling.

Charlotte looked up, smiling. "Now, Marie, would you like to take all these dresses away?"

Marie's eyes shone. Not that she would *ever* wear such outmoded clothes herself, but she could sell them for a tidy sum (in perfect condition as they were!) and she and Cecil would be that much closer to marriage.

"Thank you, my lady," she said, sweeping Charlotte a graceful curtsy. Marie flung a huge stack over her arm and half-staggered out of the room, blinded by underskirts puffing into her face. It took three trips and then Charlotte had the room to herself again.

She paced about, frowning slightly. Then she began to take down the china figures on the mantel, and all the knickknacks that had sat on her bedside table since she was five years old, and to place them carefully on her dressing table. The room was still too frothy: it was a girl's room, for a girl's dreams, all buttercups and daisies.

It will have to be changed, Charlotte thought, but I can do that tomorrow. She envisioned something cooler, perhaps even blue, the color of cornflowers. She had retained a horror of blue, based on memories of her debutante ball, but that was foolishness.

Charlotte went to bed without a thought for

the almost-finished third version of Sir Vigilant Calverstill, waiting on the third floor. Instead, she went to sleep thinking dreamily about herself, dreams in which she was waltzing with a man who had silver-shot hair, and she was wearing a silk gown of Persian blue, and he was gazing at her in adoration, desire stark in his eyes.

He bent his head and his lips brushed against hers, once, twice, three times, inviting, beckoning, promising. Charlotte turned restlessly in her sleep and woke up, her heart pounding. She stared into the dark for quite a while, thinking. Tomorrow morning she would definitely find out whether William Holland had found himself a wife. It's rather odd, Charlotte thought amusedly, to join the ranks of husband-seeking women so late. But it didn't strike her as an insurmountable task by any means. All she had to find were brains, given her new wealth. Brains, and something unnameable, Charlotte thought. Whatever that footman had. With a sigh she snuggled back into her covers and went to sleep.

Chapter 4

No one greeted Charlotte's determination to buy a new wardrobe with more joy than her mother. They visited Antonin Carême together, the very next day, and while Charlotte recklessly ordered dozens of wispy, high-waisted dresses, so light that the outline of her entire body could be seen through them, Adelaide watched happily from a comfortable chair.

In turn, Monsieur Carême was ecstatic. In Charlotte he saw a young lady with an exquisite figure and perfect bones: His dresses would dance out of the shop after this particular duke's daughter appeared at a few balls wearing his creations. Adelaide's eyes twinkled when she heard the price of a particularly elegant dress that Charlotte was considering. She estimated the price to be rather less than half the going rate, but Antonin was shrewdly correct to reduce the price, she thought. Without a corset, her daughter's body was revealed to have developed natural, luxurious curves. Men would swoon when they saw the way her breasts smoothly rose out of Carême's tiny bodices, looking perfectly shaped and utterly unrestrained. Women would order the same gown, hoping to duplicate the effect.

"She won't lose the top of that dress, will she, Antonin?" Adelaide asked with some anxiety.

Charlotte was standing in front of a three-sided mirror, wearing a startling gown. It was stark white and its only ornamentation was six or seven narrow black ribbons falling straight down the skirt, which seemed endless as it began just under Charlotte's breasts. And there was practically no top at all, Adelaide thought, wondering what Marcel would think when he saw the gown. It was the most starkly fashionable dress Adelaide had ever seen.

She cleared her throat. "Charlotte," she said. "You must have it. You will start a new fashion."

Charlotte turned around. "Oh, yes," she said happily. "I shall have it, thank you, *monsieur.*" And Monsieur Carême smiled, and ferociously beckoned to a girl hovering in the corner with his next creation reverently laid over her arms.

At forty-one, Adelaide considered herself far too old for the new fashions, but even she was talked into buying just a few morning dresses: pale, delicate gowns with the so-fashionable Greek key pattern embroidered at the hem. They are constructed, Monsieur Carême whispered confidentially, so that one might wear a light waist corset with them, should one desire. And Adelaide did so desire. Not for her, this naked look that Charlotte was taking up so quickly!

Still . . . Adelaide smiled, thinking with satisfaction of the cattish remarks that some dowagers had made to her recently about her youngest daughter being likely to "stay on her hands," and "never fall off the shelf." Nonsense. No one, she thought, looking at Charlotte's long slender legs and lily-white skin, would ever murmur to her again about Charlotte being long in the tooth. Not in these clothes!

That afternoon Monsieur Pamplemousse arrived and before Charlotte had time to think about it, her long hair was lying in little sheaves around her dressing room chair.

"Regardez," said Monsieur Pamplemousse excitedly. "You are an Incomparable!" He kissed his fingers. "Ah, my scissors are made of gold!"

Charlotte stared at herself in the mirror. Her hair was curling in artful abandonment and her head felt light, as if it was a balloon about to float away. Freed from all the hair, her lips looked larger and her cheekbones were immense.

"Lady Charlotte," said Marie earnestly. "You look more beautiful than I have ever seen you. You will start a rage!"

Charlotte smiled back at her in the mirror. Monsieur Pamplemousse was fussing about, showing Marie how to adjust a band around her mistress's head, if she would like, although — he pulled himself up importantly.

"Lady Charlotte must summon *me* for any important occasion." He was fully engaged for the following day, for the Duke of Clarence's ball, but he would make a special exception and arrive at Calverstill House at four o'clock.

"I do not wish my creation to be marred," he said, with a tremendous frown at Marie. Marie quailed and broke into French protests that Monsieur Pamplemousse ignored, flapping his hands at her.

"I must go, I must go!" he said in his marked accent.

Charlotte smiled to herself. It hadn't escaped her that Monsieur Pamplemousse didn't respond to Marie in French; in fact, although he dropped foreign words into his speech, they were not *all* French: he seemed to be using Italian as well. She looked at herself again. It didn't matter whether he was from the South Pole: he did have scissors of gold. She — Charlotte — felt beautiful, really beautiful, for the first time. To be honest, she felt exuberant. She was beautiful, and desirable, and exquisitely dressed. Why should she feel any shame? She couldn't wait for the Duke of Clarence's ball!

And that was why when Alexander McDonough Foakes, the new Earl of Sheffield and Downes, stopped in at his club on his very first evening back in London after three years in Italy, all anyone seemed to be talking about was a delectable heiress named Charlotte. Two gawky boys were practically threatening to duel each other over the question of which of them she had liked the best; his old friend Braddon Chatwin looked miserable when she was mentioned.

They settled down together in a quiet corner of the library, legs stretched out before a warm fire. Alexander fingered his brandy, listening absentmindedly to Braddon's tale of woe . . . he'd asked her to marry him; she'd said no; last night she danced twice with . . . Lord! why didn't he remember how boring all of this was! He didn't care who this arrogant little snip danced with. He looked at Braddon darkly.

"Cut rope, Braddon," he drawled. "She must be a complete twit. Who would turn down an earl? It's not as if you have seventeen children or something."

"What do you know about it, Alex?" Braddon said hotly. "You always have luck with women. . . ." but he trailed off uncomfortably. Suddenly Braddon remembered something awful, something he'd forgotten in the excitement of seeing his old friend stride into the club after three years.

Alex didn't seem to have noticed his pause, Braddon thought, stealing a peek over his brandy snifter. His heart quieted down. Alex *looked* just the same. He didn't limp or anything. Braddon shuddered slightly and took a huge gulp of brandy. What would Alex do with his time now? Why, all gentlemen did was box, and bet, and — and wench. Alex never liked gambling, and now he couldn't wench, apparently.

He cleared his throat. "Ah . . . so, are you back for good?" Braddon asked.

"Yes," Alex said absentmindedly, not even

looking up from his glass. "You know, my father died eight months ago, and I couldn't come back just then, but now I . . . Well, the estate takes some running, and . . ."

He looked up and fixed Braddon with his disconcerting black eyes. "I missed England after a while. Italy is splendid, but then Maria, my wife, died and so I decided to return."

"But . . ." Braddon was bamboozled. "I thought . . . everyone thinks that you aren't married, that Maria, ah, annulled your marriage."

Alex looked up, his eyes dark. "She did," he said briefly. "She remarried, and then she died. Of scarlet fever, a month ago."

"So you, you stayed in touch?" Braddon hazarded.

"No. But she summoned me when she was dying." Alex looked up again, and caught Braddon's gaping expression. Poor old Braddon! He always was a slow top.

"Enough of this!" Alex said, tossing off his brandy. "Didn't you say there's some sort of a ball tonight?"

"Yes," Braddon said, "but you can't go like that! You're not even dressed." He cast an accusing look at his friend's buckskin pantaloons. "Besides," he blurted out, "why on earth would you want to go? You always hated those things, even before —" and he caught himself again.

"I plan to attend the ball for the same reason you will, Braddon," Alex said gently. "I need a wife." He stood up and hauled the silent earl to his feet. They stood, eye-to-eye, in the empty library.

"Why?" Braddon asked bluntly.

Alexander turned and strolled for the door. "I have a daughter," he threw back over his shoulder. "She needs a mother. Come on, Braddon. I've got my coach outside; we'll stop by my house and I'll change and we can have some dinner. Then we'll go find ourselves wives."

Braddon followed him dumbly. *He* had a daughter? Everyone in London knew that his wife had annulled the marriage on grounds of impotency. *And* that Alex hadn't contested it. He'd never find a wife . . . well, of course he would, Braddon thought. Plenty of women wanting to marry earls; he could attest to that himself. But Braddon didn't understand, he just didn't. If Alex was impotent, how did he have a daughter? And if he had a daughter, why was his marriage annulled? And if . . . Braddon's head was reeling.

The carriage pulled up in front of Sheffield House. Black swags still hung on each window, although they were getting a bit frayed now, eight months after Alex's father died. Braddon trotted after Alex, thinking furiously. He couldn't work it out, and he couldn't get it straight without asking about the impotency business, and he wouldn't do that, not under any circumstances.

It did cross his mind that it might be a little sticky, bringing Alex around to Lady Prestlefield's ball. She was an awfully high stickler for morals and things like that; why she'd barred Lady Gwenth Manisse from entering her house one day, just because poor Lady Gwenth was so disastrously and famously in love with a married archbishop. But then, Alex was an earl and there were only about ten or so of them in the country. And what's more, he wasn't divorced, exactly, and how could you turn someone away from a party because they were — disabled, so to speak? Which brought Braddon around again to wondering about the problem of the daughter: Where did that daughter come from?

He'd better just forget it, Braddon thought finally, and pretend that he'd heard nothing about the whole annulment business. His head was aching trying to think it out. He'd get one of his clever friends, like David, to explain the whole thing to him later. If he just remembered not to mention any women, even that luscious little singer he'd just met at the opera, there wouldn't be any uneasiness at dinner. Well, particularly he must forget the singer, because she was Italian, or she said she was. Braddon brightened. Horses were obviously the trick! Nothing risky about talking about horses.

Braddon always had a remarkable ability for putting things out of his head (to the great annoyance of his mama, his tutors, and every logical person who came in contact with him, especially his personal secretary, his estate manager, and his butler). And so he thoroughly en-

93

joyed his meal, and had no idea how much he bored Alex by giving him a point-by-point description of each and every horse in his stables.

After dinner Alex excused himself and ran upstairs to get changed. But first he walked softly into the chamber adjoining his and tiptoed over to the crib. Nestled into the sheets, his daughter was curled on her side, her face resting on one hand, the other flung above her head. She looked so angelic asleep, not at all like the demon who had turned his life upside down in the last month.

He reached out and traced the shape of her arching eyebrows: *his* eyebrows. His heart thumped again with rage. How could Maria have kept her from him? He'd lost a whole year of Pippa's life. . . . Alex took a deep breath and pulled the sheets snugly up around her small round body.

In her sleep, Pippa didn't look sad; she was smiling faintly. She never had the nightmares the doctor forecast. It was only when she was awake that the loss of her mother showed. Damn you, Maria, Alex thought fiercely. If he'd known . . . well, Maria would still have died, wouldn't she? Someday Pippa would stop missing her mother. At least Maria had summoned him when she knew she wouldn't live. And now Pippa was here, and safe. He bent down and kissed her forehead.

"Don't worry, chicken," he said softly. "I'll be back by the time you wake up."

They arrived at Prestlefield House just a little after eleven o'clock, when the ball was in full swing. Braddon's fears regarding Alex's reception were for naught because Lady Prestlefield had just closed the receiving line when they entered the house and by the time they reached the ballroom she was energetically swinging through a country dance.

The Prestlefield butler's chest swelled out a bit with pride as he ushered in not one, but two earls. His voice boomed over the crowded ballroom: "The Earl of Sheffield and Downes, and the Earl of Slaslow."

There was no pause in the chattering noise that filled the room like an aviary. But everyone's eyes darted up the steps and saw the two young men descending into the room; and everyone's thoughts flew to tales they'd heard from Italy; and they all bent their heads a little closer to their partners, or longed agonizingly for the end of the dance so they could seek out better, more informed companions.

Charlotte didn't even hear the announcement, because she was busy being gloriously indiscreet on the balcony. In the month or so since she had unveiled her new wardrobe, she'd found that looking gorgeous made her *feel* gorgeous, and feeling gorgeous translated into feeling daring. In fact, she'd rather given up the idea of finding a husband. She was having too much fun just flirting.

At the moment she was leaning back against the balcony, smiling up at Baron Holland. His eyes were sparkling, looking back at her. He was standing in front of her, just a fraction of an inch from her thigh, and she knew he was doing it on purpose. He put his hands on the balcony railing on either side of her. Charlotte tapped his chest with her fan.

"Ho, ho, Will," she said. "Not too close."

"What am I doing?" Will complained. "I'm not even touching your sleeve." He leaned a trifle closer.

"I think you have an insect on your face," he said seriously, with just a tiny quirk at the side of his lips.

"Oh?" Charlotte said. "What kind of insect?"

"A bee," he breathed, very close to her lips now. "Do you want me to kill it?"

"I'm not sure," she said, smiling.

"Think of it this way," he said. "Your lips are honey and mine are the bee —" But wherever that rather strained metaphor was going, it was rudely broken off by Lady Sophie York, the daughter of the Marquess of Brandenburg.

"Charlotte!" she said, elbowing Baron Holland to the side. "Your mother is coming across the ballroom as if she were parting the Red Sea. You'd better go back inside and draw her fire; I'll stay with Will for a minute and you pretend you were just taking air."

Charlotte grimaced. She said, "Thanks, Sophie!" and slipped past Will's shoulder through the curtain, without even a farewell glance.

Sophie looked up at Will, her eyes wide and innocent. Even though he felt a little cross, he had to smile back. She was such a perfect little person — probably not much over five feet tall, and delectably shaped.

"Oh, Will," Sophie said mournfully. "Don't tell me that Charlotte's lips are as honey-sweet as mine. . . ." She looked utterly dejected.

Will looked at her suspiciously. He knew Sophie York by now. "Well, you know how it is, Sophie. I *did* adore you, but then I saw Charlotte and she's so tall, so willowy and statuesque, and somehow small girls just faded —" He stopped suddenly as a small fist punched into his stomach.

"Come on, Sophie! Give over!" he demanded, pulling a fragrant armful into the crook of his right arm.

"Your lips," he said, looking deeply into her eyes, "are sweeter than honey grown by Tasmanian bees."

She gurgled with laughter. "Are you sure I'm not the bee, Will? I did sting you, didn't I?"

"Tasmanian bees in the Alps," Will insisted, laughing back. He was thinking how much he liked these new French dresses. Sophie may be small, but her body was perfectly rounded, and he liked having her pressed against his side. His eyes darkened.

"Oh, no you don't, Will," Sophie said, seeing his intent. She nimbly turned out of his arms and pushed the heavy brocade curtain aside. "We had our kiss in Kensington, remember? Oh, surely you didn't forget, Will?" She pouted slightly, her eyes glinting. Will's groin tightened. He didn't think he'd ever meet such an alluring pair of women as Charlotte and Sophie, this side of the demimonde, that is. Sophie twinkled at him, and slipped into the ballroom.

Baron Holland stood for a moment, braced against the balcony. If Charlotte and Sophie were so lovely, why did they jointly make him feel like such an idiot? And more important, how was he going to get one of them to marry him? He knew in the pit of his stomach that he had to have one of these girls. Even if they had been poor. But luckily they weren't, he remembered cheerfully.

Sophie paused on the other side of the balcony curtain. Charlotte was just to her left, talking to her mama and a group of dowagers. Sophie smiled. Charlotte needed rescuing again. She drifted gracefully toward the group.

"Charlotte," she said in dulcet tones.

"Excuse me, Mama," replied her friend, turning gratefully toward Sophie.

"I feel a trifle *déshabillé*," Sophie complained, waving her fan before her perfectly arranged hair. "It's so hot in here, don't you think, your grace?" She smiled at Charlotte's mother.

Adelaide smiled back in spite of herself. Sophie's smile was entrancing, even though Adelaide wasn't entirely pleased with Charlotte's new friendship. She wasn't quite sure why. Sophie was perhaps a trifle wild, but everyone knew that she would never really step beyond the bounds of propriety. It was just that she seemed so *unlike* her serious, nonfrivolous daughter. But then, what was her daughter like? In the last few weeks Charlotte had become the toast of London. From being someone who had received eight offers of marriage in three years, she received more than that last week alone.

"Oh, Sophie," Charlotte laughingly chided. "You shouldn't say you feel *déshabillé:* That means you're only half dressed, doesn't it, Mama?"

Adelaide nodded. That comment was just the kind of thing that made her wonder about Lady Sophie. She knew for a fact that Sophie's French was flawless, given that her mother was French and she had had a French nanny. Whatever was the girl doing, suggesting she felt undressed? Really! Her sense of humor . . . it was a little *outré,* a little improper.

And Charlotte and Sophie went everywhere together now. The sight of Charlotte's shining black curls bent close to Sophie's strawberry-blond locks was common in Hyde Park; even more astonishing, Charlotte was actually painting Sophie: her first life portrait. Perhaps I am a little jealous, Adelaide thought.

Suddenly she started. "Oh, no!" Adelaide half-shrieked. "Wax!" The little gaggle of women jumped back, looking up. Sure enough, they were standing directly under a chandelier, and hot wax was dripping from the candles.

"Charlotte," Adelaide commanded. "And Sophie, of course," she added. "We are going to retire for a moment. Come, girls." And she plowed imperiously through the crowds, heading for the ladies' dressing room.

Sophie and Charlotte followed, rather more slowly. Sure enough, Adelaide did have a white waxy streak down the back of her gown. She would probably have to take the gown off and let the maids iron off the wax.

Charlotte's eyes were glowing. She was wearing one of her new gowns, made of dark green silk. She loved the way the fabric slid smoothly over her legs as she danced or walked.

"So, are your lips made of honey?" Sophie whispered to her as they walked along, automatically returning smiles and salutes. "And is that a honey bee you left back there on the balcony?"

"Oh, no," Charlotte wailed in mock despair. "Don't tell me that you are going to ruin another perfectly good flirtation! I *liked* that honey bee story!"

"I am not!" Sophie replied. "I thought Will was a lovely honey bee. And," she said with some indignation, "it's not fair to suggest that I ruined your flirtation with Reginald last week — all I did was ask how many times he adjusted his toupee while you were sitting out the dance with him. I am right, you know! It's a perfect indicator of desire. When his wife has a headache she'll learn to dread his fidgeting with his wig."

Charlotte laughed at her, half shocked, half delighted. How *could* Sophie say such outrageous things?

"I suppose," Charlotte replied, "that his hands are constantly on his head whenever *you* sit out a dance with him!"

"Naturally," Sophie drawled. "I should consider myself in very poor form if he didn't jiggle his wig at least every other minute. And you know," she said more reflectively, "maybe one of us should take him up seriously. He's not at all bad-looking."

They wove their way up the stairs, a laborious task given the throngs of gossipers positioned halfway up, still thinking about Lord Reginald Petersham.

"Of course, he's only a baronet," Sophie said.

"But he has a lovely forehead," Charlotte replied. Lord Reginald was blessed with a long, thin face, the kind she would quite like to paint, now that she'd graduated to painting real people. Still, she couldn't paint him without marrying him; unmarried ladies did not spend hours in a room alone with a man, even if he was posed on the couch and not allowed to move. And she didn't like his forehead enough to marry him for it.

"I don't know," Charlotte said with a sigh. "One could burn all his little hair attachments. I like bald heads. But . . ."

"Do you know who he'd be perfect for?"

Sophie said suddenly. "Your friend Julia!"

"Oh, Sophie! Julia's married!" Julia had made a very good marriage, in her first year. Charlotte still couldn't think about that season without feeling faint pangs of humiliation. While Charlotte sat out dances at the side of the ballroom, Julia energetically bounced her way into the heart of a red-coated major, who seemed on his way to becoming an admiral. They currently lived in Gibraltar.

"Why Julia in particular?" she asked.

"Because Reginald loves to listen; haven't you noticed? He likes the two of us not just because we're beautiful but because we *talk*. And Julia: Well, she talks more than both of us put together, doesn't she?"

Charlotte giggled. It was true that Julia could carry on a conversation with a brick wall. But Sophie had shocked her again. True, Charlotte thought that she looked well, and she knew that Sophie was beautiful, but to refer to it so carelessly . . . there was something uncivilized about Sophie York. She was so observant — and she never hesitated to voice her opinion, no matter how indelicate that opinion was.

By now they had reached the upper floor, and crowded after Adelaide into the ladies' parlor. Sure enough, Adelaide was turning her back to a maid, who had begun painstakingly unbuttoning the hundred-some buttons on her back. Charlotte groaned inside. They'd be here for hours!

Just then her mama looked up and caught her

eye. "Girls, will you help me, please? Sophie, if you would sit here and hold my bag, I would be very grateful." Sophie sat down with Adelaide's delicate little French reticule on her lap. There had been a rash of burglaries at *ton* parties lately, and Adelaide was not going to risk losing her favorite handbag.

"And, Charlotte, my dear, would you mind slipping downstairs and telling Sissy where I am? I told her mama that I would keep an eye on her, and I don't want her going into supper with just anyone. Prudence will be furious if that John Mason takes Sissy in to supper again."

"Yes, Mama," said Charlotte dutifully but not enthusiastically. Sissy, or Miss Cecilia Commonweal, was a problem; no one particularly liked her, and she had dreadful taste in men. Given a room full of eligible men, she would unerringly single out the only impoverished second son. And since Sissy's mother, who was a school friend of Adelaide's, had a weak heart and didn't attend many balls, Charlotte had spent rather too many dinners with a sullen Sissy, recently rescued from the attentions of yet another ineligible man.

Charlotte began to make her way down the staircase, struggling to see whether she could glimpse Sissy, by looking over people's shoulders. She didn't seem to be in the ballroom. She's probably kissing someone on a balcony, Charlotte thought scornfully, forgetting that she herself had almost done precisely that just ten minutes before.

Toward the bottom of the staircase she suddenly thought she spied Sissy's plumes. Sissy had taken to wearing an elaborate set of three or four dyed ostrich feathers pinned to the back of her hair that did make her a little easier to spot in a crowd. Charlotte privately thought the hairstyle was dreadful, like the nodding plumes on one of the queen's guard horses.

She was on tiptoe just three or four steps from the bottom, straining to see where those gaudy plumes had gone, when her right foot slipped out from under her, striking the person at the bottom of the stairs squarely in the lower back.

"Ooof!" he said, and *thump!* went Charlotte's bottom against the marble step. Tears came to her eyes as her back hit the marble stair riser.

The person she had struck turned around and squatted before her. Charlotte raised her eyes. She began to say, "I'm so sorry," but the words failed in her mouth.

He was larger than she remembered, and handsomer. His thighs strained through his thin pantaloons; she didn't remember his having such wide shoulders. But his eyes were precisely as velvety dark as she had remembered, and his hair was the same black-silver curls, falling over his forehead in the French manner. Monsieur Pamplemousse would approve, Charlotte thought idiotically.

Suddenly Charlotte realized she was staring. Her eyes flew to his and she turned faintly rosy. The man was staring back at her, his eyebrows slightly furrowed. Charlotte tried to think of something to say. Finally she blurted out,

"What are you doing here?" Instantly she felt acutely stupid. Of course he wasn't a footman! He was wearing formal dress, and besides, how could she have ever thought such a thing? He had an undeniable air of command and gentlemanly breeding.

His winged eyebrows flew up. "Where else should I be?" the man asked, still balancing on his heels.

Charlotte blushed again. "Oh, you know, at a masked ball," she said vaguely. "This time *I* knocked *you* over," she added.

Alex frowned again. What on earth was this beautiful girl talking about? Just his luck: He'd met the first interesting woman of the whole evening, and she was off her rocker. His glance drifted down. From here, he could see straight into her gown. She had the most beautiful, creamy breasts he'd ever seen. They were lavishly round, and soft, and perfectly shaped. His hand actually twitched. My God! He'd almost touched her right here. Suddenly he became aware of piping little voices around them, enquiring about injuries and calling for help.

He reached out a hand and brought her to her feet.

"Is your back all right?" Alex asked, ignoring her nonsensical comment about masked balls. Now he liked her even more. She was just the right height, tall, and when she raised her head her mouth was kissably close to his. Alex drew her over to the side of the hall and without even thinking, reached out to rub the middle of her back where she must have struck the stairs.

His hand instantly stopped. Her gown was so thin he could feel the rising swell of her bottom, and he was rocked by one of the most powerful surges of lust he had ever felt. He must be losing his mind, he decided. It had been too long since he had a woman.

Charlotte didn't even feel his hand on her back, or notice when he snatched it away. "Did you . . . do you remember me?" she asked, finally, looking straight into his eyes.

Alex frowned again. He'd never met her, that was certain. He looked at her carefully. She had a delectable, triangular face enveloped in soft curls: a perfect straight nose, and high cheek-bones. Her mouth was a natural dark red. Her eyebrows were exquisite: high and winged, a woman's version of his own. For a second, some memory stirred, but . . .

"I've never met you," Alex said, smiling at her. He wouldn't forget meeting a woman as beautiful as this.

Charlotte's mouth fell open slightly. He took someone's virginity, and he didn't even remember? What were men, anyway? Did he do that every week?

Alex took her arm again and led her toward the parlor to the right.

"You must have met my brother," he said conversationally. "We're twins." He looked down at her and smiled wickedly. "You are not the first to mistake the two of us."

Charlotte smiled back without thinking, and her heart gave a huge thump. "You are a twin?" she repeated. Her mind seemed to have gone numb.

"Yes," Alex said cheerfully, having figured out the whole problem. The girl wasn't insane; she was just thinking of Patrick. "Even our mother couldn't always tell us apart."

Charlotte looked up at him. She knew exactly who he was — well, she didn't know *who* he was, but she knew that he was the one. She even recognized the dimple in his right cheek and the shape of his lips. But he didn't seem to be pretending; he genuinely didn't remember meeting her. Charlotte's heart sunk. Her virginity had mattered so little that he didn't even remember taking it.

Her steps slowed. Where were they going, anyway? She had to get back upstairs, to her mother. She calmly took her arm out of his grasp and brought them to a halt.

"Thank you so much for helping me up, sir," she said softly. "I apologize for knocking you to the floor." Without waiting for his reply she turned and almost — not quite — dashed up the stairs.

Alex stood dumbfounded. One minute she was there; the next minute she was gone. He looked after her wildly. Who was she?

Suddenly he heard an anxious voice at his ear and turned to see Braddon. "What do you think?" Braddon asked. "Isn't she devastating?"

"Oh, yes," Alex said, grasping the whole situation in mere seconds. "I'm going to marry her. What did you say her name was?"

Chapter 5

Alex slept deeply, linen sheets pushed down to his waist, exposing a deeply tanned, muscular chest. He lay perfectly still, on his back with his arms folded behind his head. It was one of the few ways he and his twin brother, Patrick, could be told apart. Patrick slept in a tangle of arms and sheets, tossing and kicking all night long. When Patrick was small his restless sleep often landed him on the floor, where he would simply continue sleeping. But when Alex was a baby he slept so soundly that his mother used to tiptoe in and touch him, just to make sure he was still breathing.

It was almost eight o'clock when Alex awoke. The sun was casting bright, slanting lines below the curtains. He lay back, eyes closed, thinking about the previous night.

He and Braddon had headed off to a gambling club soon after his encounter with the daughter of the Duke of Calverstill. When Charlotte reappeared from the ladies' salon she was swept into a crowd of laughing, reproachful dance partners whom she had neglected while attending her mother. Alex watched her fending off their imploring gestures for a minute or so. My God, he thought, she *is* beautiful.

Charlotte's color was high: She knew the minute he entered the room. Knowing that he was watching made her feel hot and tremblingly excited. *Now* she could feel his large hand on her back, just touching her bottom as he rubbed the bruise on her back. She may not have noticed at the time, but now she felt as if her flesh were burning. Thinking of his touch brought on a flood of memories. She was filled with longing to feel his hands on her again, all over her, the way he had touched her three years ago. But at the same time, she felt punishing humiliation. He had simply forgotten the whole encounter; he didn't even notice who was in his arms that night. She could hardly think, torn between rage and desire, although none of the men surrounding her noticed her lack of attentiveness.

Thinking of the garden, Charlotte smiled at Will Holland so suggestively that he immediately dismissed all thought of marrying Sophie York. Charlotte was the one. He bent over her hand, beseeching her to allow him to take her into supper. Or — he looked at her wickedly — dance with him once more? They had already danced twice; a third dance would be akin to announcing an engagement. Charlotte laughed and shook her head reprovingly.

If Charlotte couldn't dismiss the gardens of Stuart Hall from her mind, Alex had no thought of his long-ago encounter with a young prostitute as he watched the lovely daughter of a duke joust with her suitors. His memories of the garden, in fact, were keen: the woman's long, silky hair and skin so white that her hair had to be red, the shape of her small breasts, upturned like champagne glasses, her soft, dusky eyes. But Charlotte had short black curls, eyes that sparkled with life and intelligence, and breasts that made you ache just to see their generous outlines. There was no similarity between memory and the duke's daughter, even if the possibility had occurred to him.

Suddenly Alex felt like a cloddish boy, standing by the wall, lusting after the reigning belle of London society. He pushed himself disgustedly into an upright position and turned on his heel. He knew where the Duke of Calverstill lived; why bother contending with the swarm of gnats surrounding the duke's daughter? Alex rooted a protesting Braddon out of the gaming room and summoned his coach. By the end of an evening spent gambling at Brooks, Alex was some six hundred pounds richer.

By three o'clock in the morning the candles were burning down in what Brooks called the Velvet Room. The room was hung in swathes of dark green velvet, designed to make day seem like night, to make the gamblers feel enclosed in a timeless space. But Alex had won a great deal of money, and although most of the gamblers would keep going until dawn, he was tired and a little bored.

His eyes flicked about the room. It was filled with aristocrats lounging in the armchairs that surrounded four gambling tables. Only the servant who was replenishing the wall chandeliers looked as crisp as he had at five o'clock when the doors of Brooks opened. The gamblers had loosened their elaborately tied cravats, or torn them off in pure frustration. They looked untidy and exhausted, feverishly throwing dice or clutching their cards.

"Well, my lord," said a drawling, heavily accented voice from the other side of the table. "You have done extremely well tonight."

Alex swung his head around and calmly met the eyes of Lucien Boch, a French marquis living in England. Boch had gambled outrageously, and lost.

Boch leaned forward, his hands squarely set on the green felt lining of the table reserved for the card game ombre. "You are so . . . *lucky*," he said in a soft, poisonous tone. Alex looked at him. Ombre was a game of skill, not luck. Boch had played carelessly.

"I trust, *monsieur*," Alex said evenly, "that you meant nothing by your comment. I would willingly grant that my winnings are the result of — luck."

There was a small silence. Boch's eyes burned with rage; he could hardly breathe he was so angry. His lip curled. "Ah, my lord," he finally said in response. "I would take my luck at cards any day over yours . . . at love."

The room had grown relatively quiet. Three of the four tables had fallen perfectly still, the players listening intently. Everyone knew that the sons of the late Earl of Sheffield and Downes had been sent out of England due to their propensity to settle arguments with their fists. Alexander seemed to have matured, but could any man allow an insult of this nature to pass unnoticed?

Alex's heart didn't even skip a beat. He had grown used to gutter insults in the year following his annulment. Still, he had thought to leave them behind, in Italy. Alex squarely put both his hands down on the table's green surface, leaning forward slightly. The two men were face-to-face, parted only by a small space. He smiled.

"Perhaps, monsieur," Alex said softly, "you are jealous of my success with women, and that is why you risk your life?"

Lucien stared back at Alex. He felt sick; he had done a terrible thing. Swept into the heat of gambling, he had thrown down a jewel that he kept always near his heart: It was the ring given him by his wife at their marriage.

"My lord," he said hoarsely, ignoring Alex's threat, which hung over the entire room. "I am a fool, because I lost to you my wife's ring. And she is . . . is no longer here, and I must have it back. Will you play me again?"

Alex drew back. Boch's eyes were desperate, black. Alex put a hand in his pocket and pulled out a delicately chased ring, graced with a sapphire.

"What does it say?" he asked, turning it over in the candlelight. The ring's sapphire caught the candles and flung back their light. It must be worth a thousand pounds, he thought.

"*Toujours à moi*," said Boch quietly.

"Forever mine," Alex translated. He suddenly realized that the entire room was dead silent. He looked keenly at Boch, whom he had just met that night. "How long have you been in this country?" he asked sharply.

Boch swallowed hard. "Eight years, my lord." His countess, Alex thought, did not accompany him. She must have fallen under the guillotine. He tossed the ring in the air, caught it, and placed it gently in front of Boch. "There, man, take it." He swept up the remainder of his winnings as a wave of male voices hit the air, and turned to go.

A hand stopped him. It was Boch, who had come around the table and stood before him, slim, tall, and dressed in black. "My lord," he said slowly. "I am a fool who is in your debt for life. But while I am stupid, I do not lack money. Please, let me buy the ring from you."

Alex realized Boch was not as young as he thought, probably around his own age, in fact. "I will not," he said briefly. Boch stood ramrod stiff before him. Oh, Lord, Alex thought. French pride: He quite liked the man too. "Care to join me for a brandy?" he asked.

Boch's lips tightened and then relaxed. "All right, my lord," he said sighing. "I gather that fools cannot buy themselves out of their idiocy."

Settled in the library with coffee laced generously with brandy, the two men did not mention love, rings, or wives, but talked amiably of the latest debates in the House of Lords. As an exiled Frenchman, Boch naturally had no part in government but he took a keen interest, particularly given the threatened grain riots.

"I am wondering," he said, "whether we could have prevented the recent events in France. If we had had grain machines, such as you are beginning to use here, could it have prevented the rage of the peasants?"

"But my understanding," Alex said delicately, "is that grain was not scarce, but the peasants were not allowed to eat any. In other words, that the food was being hoarded by the very rich."

"Yes, that is true," Lucien said in a brooding voice. "I told my father . . ." his voice trailed off. "We grew complacent, and that is a great sin. My brother, in particular, understood the danger. He bought land in England." Lucien looked up. "That is why I am not destitute, like the majority of my countrymen living in England. He was very intelligent, my brother. He came to England twice a year for several years, and slowly moved a good deal of our wealth into the house here."

Alex noted in silence that Lucien's brother was also dead. "Do you enjoy fencing?" he asked, changing the subject.

"I love it," Lucien said, his voice brightening.

"Would you like to have a match tomorrow?"

he asked. "Just before leaving Italy I began to learn the French method of fencing, and I would appreciate a chance to practice the art."

"I should be honored," Lucien said formally. "Tomorrow, at Breedhaven's?"

Suddenly Alex remembered Pippa. He couldn't meet Lucien for fencing practice while she was awake because she couldn't enter the all-male premises of Breedhaven's Fencing Emporium.

"I would prefer to fence at Sheffield House, if you don't mind," he said without explanation.

Lucien's eyes were puzzled. "Certainly, my lord," he said. Why on earth would a man want to fence at his own house instead of at the fencing court? He rose to his feet. He was an unusually tall Frenchman who came eye-to-eye with Alex. They would be good fencing partners, Lucien thought with satisfaction.

He held out his hand and Alex shook it without hesitation. "I will see you in the morning, my lord," Lucien said. He hesitated, and smiled. "I shall not bring my ring to a gaming establishment again," he said. "There are not many who would show your kindness." He bowed deeply. "I am truly thankful."

"Call me Alex." Alex had forgotten all about the ring incident in the pleasure of talking to a well-read man. Poor old Braddon certainly had grown boring over the past few years. He thought so again when he rooted Braddon out of one of the gaming rooms. Braddon was up fifteen pounds, and had been down as much as two hundred; he was also drunk and shaky on his feet.

"Steady," Alex said impatiently, as Braddon tottered toward the door. Lord! The man must be at least thirty, since Alex was thirty-one; why couldn't he hold his liquor yet? He watched pensively as Braddon wobbled into his coach. Was society life so boring three years ago? Of course, he had Patrick then. But still — what did he and his brother do all night? They gambled, and drank, and got into fights.

Alex's memories were interrupted by the sound of bare feet trotting unsteadily into his bedroom. "Papa!" shouted a little voice happily. He opened his eyes. Pippa was clutching the heavy gold brocade of his bed curtains, smiling widely.

He reached down and swept his little daughter up next to him. She giggled and clutched the black hair on his chest. Oh, Lord. He'd been trying to remember to wear a pajama top, given her propensity for joining him in his bedchamber in the morning. She looked small but she had a powerful grip and loved to pull hair.

"Hey!" he said with mock severity. Pippa nestled down in the crook of his arm and looked at him expectantly.

"Cocca," she said impatiently. "Me, me!"

Alex leaned over and rang the tasseled bellpull next to his bed. He hated the habit of drinking hot chocolate in bed. But then, he never thought to have a one-year-old child in his bed either.

Keating appeared at the door, silver tray in hand. Neatly arranged on the tray were two sturdy mugs, filled precisely to the midpoint with hot chocolate. When Pippa and Alex first returned from Italy and Alex deciphered what "cocca" was, the tray had held delicate Wedgwood teacups, brimming with truly *hot* chocolate. Now, after a series of mishaps, Alex philosophically drank lukewarm chocolate from a servant's mug.

Pippa sipped chocolate while she sang her morning song, something Maria must have taught her. Alex thought it was — or had been — an Italian children's song, but lord knows what any of the sounds were meant to represent. Pippa's language skills were none too good, although she said "Papa" very clearly.

Suddenly she clutched his arm, spilling some chocolate on the sheets. "No! No, Papa, no!" she said. She was escalating into panic, her small body starting to shake. Alex grabbed her chocolate, put it on the table next to the bed, and pulled her against his chest, whispering into her ear.

"Pippa, it's all right, remember? It's all right." He rubbed her back rhythmically. "Calm down, Pippa, you know Papa won't leave you. I promised, remember?"

Finally he looked up. There in the doorway, a look of horror in her eyes, was Pippa's new nanny, hired a day earlier.

"My lord," said Miss Virginia Lyons, and stopped.

Alex's flying eyebrows rose even higher. "Yes?"

"My lord, what is Lady Philippa doing here?"

Alex looked at her in some surprise. "Why shouldn't she be here?" he said. "I don't mind. And it keeps her from screaming."

Miss Virginia opened her mouth and stopped again. She didn't even know how to formulate an answer to such a basic question.

"Children," she finally said, "are to be seen and not heard, at the proper times, in proper places. The rest of the time they stay in the nursery."

"She screams in the nursery," Alex said. "I explained that to you yesterday. She screams so loudly that she can be heard in the basement — and the nursery is on the third floor. And she drums her feet against the floor. I can't have that," he said reasonably.

Alex frowned a bit at Miss Virginia. She was red in the face. He adjusted the sheets, pulling them a little higher. Thank goodness he had taken to wearing pajama bottoms since Pippa's arrival. He waved his hand dismissively.

"Miss Virginia, we are not yet receiving company."

The nanny was not ready to give up. "Lady Philippa must come with me now. She does not belong in a man's bedroom —"

Alex cut her off. "Miss Virginia, while I accept with some reservations the presence of my child

119

in this bedroom, I am not ready to extend the privilege to all the staff. Please. We will join you, in the nursery, after breakfast." He smiled amiably at Miss Virginia, whose face was fiery red now, and she backed out of the doorway.

"That was not kind of us," he murmured into Pippa's hair. Now that the menace (as Pippa saw all nannies) had disappeared, Pippa was humming happily and trying to grab her chocolate again. Alex settled her firmly against his side and handed her the scant third of a cup left in her mug. His own chocolate was stone cold. He finished it in one gulp, shuddering slightly.

"Come on, Pippa," he said, taking away her empty cup and ignoring her indignant wail. She liked to trail the last drops over his bedsheets. Like magic, Keating appeared with a large tub of steaming water. During the last month he and Keating had worked out a routine.

With a practiced hand Alex stripped off Pippa's nightgown and plopped her in the water. Ignoring the little waves splashing over the side of the tub, he scrubbed her clean. Then he smoothly pulled her squirming plump self out of the bath, handing her to Keating, who waited with a large towel. Pippa was fairly silent, meaning that she only yelled three or four times. And they weren't the terrified wails that disturbed the whole household, only loud yelps. Keating bore her off into the next room to get dressed, while Alex took a quick bath and dressed himself.

Too bad Keating couldn't simply be her nanny, Alex thought, remembering the embarrassed Miss Virginia waiting on the floor above. Pippa was gurgling away in the next room, while Keating sang a little ditty to her. Alex cocked his ear. It was clearly a seafaring song, and probably not fit for young — or any — female ears.

He sighed. Time to rejoin Miss Virginia. The last nanny had lasted only two days, worn out, she said, by screaming hysteria. *She* suggested that Alex send Pippa to a mental hospital for treatment; Alex only barely stopped himself from tossing her into the street without any baggage.

Pippa toddled into the room smiling widely. "Papa!" she said. "Papa!" Alex looked at his small daughter. She was perhaps a year old. Maria had died so quickly that he never found out exactly when Philippa was born. And the only way he could find out was to contact the priest, or ex-priest, whom Maria married after annulling their marriage, and that he refused to do. Besides, once he got the measure of the screaming child Pippa seemed to be, his only thought was to get her back to doctors in England.

But on their fourth day together, Pippa had stopped struggling against his arms and simply looked up at him. "Papa," she said softly. And with growing confidence, "Papa, Papa, Papa." Since then she only screamed when he wasn't either with her or in the next room. The minute he tried to leave, she split the air with riveting screams, or worse, lay down on the floor and had hysterics. It was, he guessed, the fruit of her mother's illness and death. Doctors varied from suggesting institutionalization to saying she'd grow out of it.

Alex's jaw tightened. He needed a wife. Men weren't supposed to be bathing infants or choosing nannies. Obviously he didn't pick nannies very well. Miss Virginia was the fifth in two weeks. He scooped up Pippa and headed to the nursery.

At two o'clock that afternoon, Campion was reigning over a quiet Calverstill House. The duke and duchess were visiting the new exhibition of Italian marbles. Charlotte had painted all morning and was just taking a bath and dressing. Baron Holland was due in a half hour, to accompany her to a picnic *al fresco*. The household had noted with discreet interest the frequency with which Baron Holland accompanied Charlotte. Not that they were in agreement about him.

The housekeeper, Mrs. Simpkin, was a strong supporter of Baron Holland.

"He's . . . he's so romantic," she said, patting her ample bosom. "He's a real gentleman, Mr. Campion, always so finely dressed."

"That's not the point, Mrs. Simpkin," said Campion severely. "The question is, is he a gentleman underneath? Why doesn't he have any money, think you? Because he gambles, most likely. And would he stop gambling once he had Lady Charlotte's money? I ask you!"

"We don't know that he gambles," protested Mrs. Simpkin. "Perhaps he lost his inheritance in a fire."

"Unlikely," said Campion. "Most unlikely, Mrs. Simpkin. Because, had there been such a fire, we would have read about it, wouldn't we? And we didn't. Therefore he gambles."

"He loves her," Mrs. Simpkin said illogically. "He loves her; I can see it in his eyes."

"His eyes!" Campion said with disgust. "There's another problem: They are too blue. No man has eyes that blue."

When someone thumped the heavy brass knocker that afternoon, Campion opened the door majestically, prepared to intimidate Baron Holland's manservant, who had to act as footman as well.

But at the door was a proper footman, a regular long-jawed type dressed in fancy livery from head to toe. Campion recognized quality when he saw it, and this was a quality servant.

"May I help you?" said Campion in his deepest voice (for Campion too was a quality servant).

"The Earl of Sheffield and Downes requests the presence of Lady Charlotte Daicheston at a picnic *al fresco* this afternoon," said the long-jawed one.

By this point Campion had taken in the elegantly hung, gold-embossed carriage that waited before the house. Of course, he ought to point out that Lady Charlotte was previously engaged, and send this footman on his way. But perhaps he should send a message upstairs first? An earl, after all. There weren't many of them.

Campion finished his calculations without moving one facial muscle. "I will ascertain whether Lady Charlotte is available," he said, closing the huge doors of Calverstill House.

The quality footman retreated back to his position, standing behind Alex's carriage. Quiet descended on Albemarle Square for five minutes. Suddenly the door of the carriage flew open and Alex, with Pippa rather precariously situated on his shoulder, descended and climbed the steps. He briskly banged the door knocker.

Campion was not at his post, so the second housemaid, a rather timid girl who had only recently been promoted to an upstairs servant, opened the door instead. She was no match for a real earl demanding to see Lady Charlotte. She curtsied so deeply that her knees knocked together, and fled upstairs.

"Lady Charlotte," she stammered. "He's here, now, here, downstairs, here, in the Green Room, here."

Charlotte looked up, startled. She was sitting in front of her dressing table while Marie put a few deft finishing touches to her hair. She was wearing a walking dress of rosy silk. It left her slender arms bare; Marie was threading a ribbon of the same color through her curls.

Charlotte had a good sense of who the Earl of Sheffield and Downes must be. Her heart was beating fast. Part of her yearned to race out to his carriage. But she had an engagement with Will Holland, and ladies do not break appointments on a whim. Marie's hands were trembling with excitement. The gossip columns were full of information about the handsome earl and his recent return from Italy.

Meanwhile Campion took the gasping housemaid's arm in a strong grip that promised retribution for her garbled message. Servants were *never* to be disturbed by anything that might happen in the household, as he himself had lectured the downstairs staff just a week or so ago.

Of course, in the Calverstill House nothing really happened to disturb a servant, but Campion rigorously lectured those under his command anyway. You never knew about underservants: They might quit at any moment and join a household full of unsteady characters or drunkards. His training was intended to prepare them to behave impeccably no matter where they found themselves.

With the steadying influence of Campion's hand on her arm, the second housemaid (whose name was Lily), pulled herself together and curtsied to Lady Charlotte. "The earl is downstairs and I put him in the Green Room," she said, fairly clearly. "And he's not alone. He has a small child with him."

Charlotte rose. Her heart was beating like a

trip-hammer. "Thank you, Lily," she said. "I shall see him myself." She descended the stairs, her mind whirling. He couldn't be married, could he? Her heart felt painfully large in her chest.

Charlotte paused in the door of the Green Room. It *was* he. He had his back turned to her, but she would recognize his broad shoulders anywhere. Her eyes swept down his back. He was wearing an elegant gray jacket, molded to his large body, and skintight pantaloons in dove gray, with high boots. Her eyes stopped at his feet.

Sitting between his feet was one of the plumpest, most enchanting children she had ever seen. The little face peering between the earl's boots had round cheeks and three or four dimples, and unmistakably, her father's flyaway eyebrows.

Charlotte smiled. The little girl's face darkened and she let out an earsplitting yell. Charlotte instinctively took a step backward, just as Alex swung about. He quirked an eyebrow at her, and then easily pulled the baby up onto his shoulder, patting her. "Shhhhhh," he said softly. "This is not a nanny; this is Lady Charlotte. Shhhhhh."

Charlotte cleared her throat. She was uncertain about what to say. She had never been introduced to the man; in fact, she only just learned his name from her butler. Nothing taught to her in Lady Chatterton's School for Girls had prepared her for this situation.

Then Alex looked up from soothing his daughter and smiled. His dark eyes crinkled at the corners when he smiled. Charlotte felt a warm glow that began in her belly and spread through her body.

He stepped forward and, holding his daughter firmly against his shoulder, ceremoniously thrust out his right leg and made a deep bow. Pippa gurgled with delight at suddenly being brought forward and back upright.

"May I present Lady Pippa McDonough Foakes, daughter of Alexander McDonough Foakes, the Earl of Sheffield and Downes?" he said solemnly. A bubble of laughter moved up Charlotte's chest.

"Lady Pippa," she said obediently, and curtsied.

Pippa giggled.

"Pippa," said her father, "pay attention. I would like to introduce you to Lady Charlotte Daicheston, the daughter of the Duke of Calverstill."

Pippa giggled again. She had an infectious giggle; Charlotte laughed back.

"I shall put you down now, Pippa. You can see that Lady Charlotte is not a possible nanny, so I don't want to hear any more yelps." Pippa seemed to understand; at least when Alex put her on the floor she simply crawled over to the sofa and began tangling the striped tassels that adorned its seat cushions.

Alex stepped forward again and stood just in front of Charlotte. She turned faintly pink. Her heart was beating so fast she was afraid that it was visible through her thin dress.

"Do you know," he said conversationally, "you are the first female I have ever met whom I always want to kiss?"

Charlotte's eyes flew up to meet his. She was *not* going to be the silent peahen that she was the last time they met!

She smiled wryly. "Dare I say that the feeling is not mutual?"

"No?" Alex said. Suddenly he bent his head and brushed his lips, feather-soft, across hers. Unthinkingly she parted her lips under that gentle persuasion. She felt his warm breath on her mouth, and for an instant the kiss deepened, and his mouth turned from pleading to commanding, from persuasion to demand. Charlotte's entire body relaxed; had he not instantly steadied her with large hands on her bare arms, she might even have toppled.

And that was enough to return her to sanity. Furious at herself, she drew back. Alex looked at the woman in front of him with wonder. He was only barely in control. This woman with her tossed black curls and rosy mouth moved him like no woman he had ever met. The only thought in his mind was to sweep her into his arms and carry her over to the sofa.

He noted with satisfaction that a pulse was beating wildly in her neck. Charlotte was not impervious to him either. "Shall I summon your butler to introduce us," he said calmly, "or is a mutual tumble on the staircase enough?"

Charlotte bit her lip, trying not to laugh aloud. "Sir," she said, but at that moment the doors to the Green Room swung open.

Campion's ample form appeared in the doorway. "The Baron Holland," he announced sententiously.

Oh, Lord, Charlotte thought. But Alex's head had jerked up at Campion's voice. "Will!" he positively shouted, and strode forward. Charlotte swung around to find the two men beating each other on the back. Charlotte glanced back and met Pippa's eyes, curious to see whether she screamed at every person who entered the room. But Pippa had simply returned to tangling sofa tassels, without a second look at Will.

Alex caught Charlotte's glance. "No, she distinguishes between the sexes: It's women she can't stand," he added hastily, "at the moment, of course."

Will Holland was trying to figure out what was happening. His carriage was outside, loaded with delicacies for a picnic *al fresco* with Charlotte. Moreover, in his pocket was nestled a small but exquisite circle of diamonds, once his mother's, which he hoped to bestow upon Charlotte. But here was Charlotte, unchaperoned except for a small child, with an old friend who he thought was still in Italy. And she looked — well, she looked *kissed*. Her mouth was rosy and her

129

cheeks flushed; Will's eyes narrowed in suspicion. The last thing he wanted was to be in competition with an earl, for God's sake.

Still, like the rest of London, he knew that Alexander's first wife had annulled their marriage on grounds of impotence. He had found it hard to believe, given acute memories of nights in the best London brothels, accompanied by Alexander and his brother, Patrick. Why he distinctly remembered opening the wrong door, in a very select establishment maintained by a woman known as Serena — and Alex definitely hadn't been impotent at that point.

"Lady Charlotte," he said easily, holding out his hand. "Are you prepared to join me for our picnic?"

"Oh dear," said Alex with mock sadness. "Now, that is precisely the occasion for which I arrived here. And Lady Charlotte has been explaining to me that she has a miserable memory, and so she accidentally promised to accompany both of us."

Charlotte stifled a giggle. "I think," she said with a reproving glance at Alex, "that I shall accept Baron Holland's invitation, as it was the first extended."

"Oh, no," Alex said airily. "Why, Will and I are old friends, aren't we, Will?"

Will nodded slowly.

"So we will all go together," said Alex swiftly. "I have two carriages outside with more than enough picnic food and a nanny. Why don't we all meet at the east side of Hyde Park, next to the statue of Eve? Will, perhaps you could accompany Lady Charlotte?"

Will nodded, his head spinning. Why on earth were they all going on a picnic together? And if Alex was competing for Charlotte's hand, why did he so carelessly hand her over to him? He had to know that the carriage was a perfect tête-à-tête.

For her part, Charlotte was furious. She wasn't as naive as Will Holland. She knew that she was outmaneuvered. After being so thoroughly kissed, she was unlikely to enjoy Will's company overmuch in the carriage. No doubt, that was what this Alexander — or Alex, as Will called him — had surmised.

Ha! she thought vengefully.

And so when they were in the carriage and Will put a gentle arm around her shoulder, she unresistingly moved closer and lifted her face for a kiss in an entirely natural gesture that made Will's hopes skyrocket. He kissed her skillfully, his tongue racing over her lips, parting them delicately.

Charlotte's mind remained entirely clear. She did enjoy it, to a point. But there was nothing there to make her knees weak, or to make her feel instantly flushed. Even when a hand descended to her curls and pulled her closer, she didn't feel a tingle in her stomach.

Will wasn't fooled either. Charlotte was not responding at all. He swiftly pulled back and smiled down at her.

"I think," he said, "that we should have a well-bred conversation, like the well-bred people that we are. Do you know, I think I saw your friend Cecilia Commonweal yesterday in the Pantheon Bazaar? She appeared to be buying fourteen ostrich plumes, dyed a violent purple. Do you think that is possible?"

Charlotte giggled and then caught herself. "Feathers are all the rage," she observed, not sure how possible it was to defend Sissy's fashion sense.

"Oh, really?" Will said saucily. "And will London soon be seeing Lady Charlotte dressed up like one of the king's best horses?"

To Charlotte's mind it was taking an awfully long time for their carriage to arrive at Hyde Park. In fact, Will had directed his coachman to drive around the park twice before stopping, since he had hoped to spend the time passionately kissing his future bride.

But there was no talk of marriage in the Holland coach. Charlotte and Will wrangled amiably over fashion trends and the latest excesses of the Crown Prince; the diamond ring that once belonged to his mother rested undisturbed in Will's pocket.

Chapter 6

When the coach finally stopped, Charlotte swiftly glanced around before lowering her eyes and pretending a modest uninterest in the whereabouts of the Earl of Sheffield and Downes. Clearly his coach had not yet arrived. Will's heart lifted. Perhaps Alex was giving him a chance, after all. He led Charlotte gently off toward the willow pond, leaving his man to prepare the picnic. For her part, Charlotte tried to keep her attention on what Will was saying, but her mind kept wandering away. She desperately wanted Alex — the earl, she reminded herself — to appear, and yet she was furious with herself for the wish. Why should she look for him? He didn't even remember her!

"Charlotte," said Will patiently, as he repeated himself yet again, "what *do* you think of the prince's gold heels?"

"Ah . . ." Charlotte looked up at him, hopelessly confused. "The prince's gold heels?"

"Yes," Will said. He looked at her expectantly.

"I'm sorry," Charlotte said humbly. "I haven't the faintest idea what you are talking about."

"I know," said Will with a wry smile. "That's

because I've been making up nonsense, and you have been very charmingly nodding and agreeing with whatever I say."

"Oh," Charlotte said with a little gasp.

Will firmly drew her over to a nearby bench. They sat down for a moment and watched two sullen swans trolling for bread. Japanese willows hung down over the pond, their branches trailing into the water like strands of wet hair.

Charlotte longed to be back in her calm studio, finishing her portrait of Sophie. She had posed Sophie — somewhat ridiculously, she would admit — in a bluebell wood, and it had turned into an endless task, painting bluebells stretching into the distance. Yet even if she was occasionally bored in the studio, at least there she was never buffeted by desire, or flushed with sudden humiliation.

Now she was on a picnic without a chaperone, escorted by a handsome young man who seemed to be in love with her, and she could not keep her mind clear. Will's tousled blond hair and blue eyes left her pulse unmoved. But all she had to do was remember that she would soon be seeing Alex and her body instantly responded, tingling from her toes to her fingers.

"Charlotte," said Will seriously, putting his hands on her shoulders and turning her toward him. "I would like you to do me the honor of becoming my wife."

"Oh," Charlotte gasped again. She had been refusing marriage proposals for weeks, and suddenly she had forgotten all her lines.

Will didn't wait for her to answer; he simply lowered his head and kissed her. Charlotte snapped out of her hazy state and began to feel distinctly annoyed. What was it about these men? They seemed to think they could just plaster their lips to hers at any moment they wished! She drew back sharply, rising to her feet.

"Baron Holland," she said calmly. "You and I have already discussed the subject of marriage and I refused your hand."

For an instant Will just sat on the bench and looked up at her. That was *before,* he thought silently. Before you cut your hair, before you changed your dress, before you became so irresistible. But how can you tell a woman that *this* time you really mean it? How could you say such a thing without revealing that you had been hunting her fortune and not herself, even if now you were not? He rose and took her hands in his. "Charlotte, I —" but whatever he meant to say was broken off.

Charlotte's eyes flew past his shoulders and a small but radiant smile broke over her face. Will stared down at her in stupefaction for a few seconds, then dropped her hands in resignation, turning around. Striding through the trees toward them was a chattering party of elegantly dressed people including Alexander Foakes, the Earl of Sheffield and Downes, who once again carried his small daughter perched on his shoulder.

Will looked down at his companion. Her face grew faintly rosy as she watched the earl approach. She seemed entirely unaware of Will's presence. The baron's shoulders drooped slightly. He was no fool. Charlotte was lost to him . . . unless . . . could she be aware of Alex's impotence? For a mad instant Will pictured himself telling her, comforting her as she threw her disconsolate self into his arms. Insanity. How on earth would you tell a gently bred young lady such a thing? Why, she probably didn't even understand the mechanics involved! And it would give her a hatred of Will.

He glanced at Alex. It seemed so unlikely, anyway. Alex's large, muscled body suited the current fashion for skintight pantaloons perfectly. Even from here Will found it extremely unlikely that he was incapable.

Damn it! Will felt a stab of pain in his chest. He had grown so used to the idea of hunting a young woman for her fortune that he had forgotten that real emotion could be involved. But . . . he glanced down again at Charlotte. Her lips were upturned in a welcoming smile; in her eyes was a look he had never seen before. Oh, the hell with it, Will thought. Even if her parents did send Alex packing (what parents would allow a girl to marry a man with an impairment like that?) she would never really be his.

And at that point Will, unbeknownst to himself, moved smoothly out of the category of fortune-hunter. He turned a corner that disallowed marriages made solely on the basis of money.

For his part, Alexander instantly noticed Charlotte's rumpled hair and pink face, and a swell of rage rose in his throat. How dare Will touch her, he thought furiously. How dare she kiss another man? Pippa, sensing the current of emotion pulsing through his body, clutched his hair and began to cry.

"Hey," Alex said softly, swinging his daughter down against his shoulder and smoothing her hair. "Shhhh, Pippa."

"Papa," Pippa sobbed, "Papa."

"Lord." Alex sighed, and waving his hand at the small band, said carelessly, "Will, do the pretty for me, please? I'm going to take this little fish bait for a walk." He set off without a backward glance.

Charlotte watched, nonplussed, as the earl rounded a bend in the path and disappeared. That was it? He just shambled off, like someone's groom? She felt a flush rise up her cheeks. By God, she wasn't just some easy maiden, ready to fall into his hands the moment he raised his finger.

"Well," said Baron Holland, "I should certainly like to 'do the pretty,' as Alex has it, but I'm afraid I haven't had the pleasure." He looked appreciatively at the lovely young woman who had just arrived.

The gentleman with her made a low and elegant bow. "I, sir, was the Marquis de Valconbrass but," he shrugged in a very Gallic fashion, "now I am simply Lucien Boch. And this is my sister Daphne."

Daphne sank into an elegant curtsy. She was very young, probably only sixteen, but she already wore her hair up in a chignon, indicating that she had been presented at Court. She looked, to Charlotte's mind, quintessentially French, with dainty features and a strong yet delicate chin. She seemed at once romantic and intensely practical. Her hair was so blond it looked like spun silver, and it shone in the sun. And her clothes were exquisite, from the tip of her parasol to the glimpse of rosy slippers peeking out from beneath her fashionable gown.

Baron Holland bowed as gracefully as the marquis. "Baron Holland, at your service," he said cheerfully, "and this is Lady Charlotte Daicheston, daughter of the Duke of Calverstill. It is a delight to meet you." He raised Daphne's hand to his lips.

Lucien shrugged, looking off in the direction taken by Alex. "Shall we return to the carriages? I believe the picnic is being set up in that direction."

Charlotte felt a bubble of laughter rising inside her. This was too ridiculous! She was on a picnic with a rejected suitor, who rather than sulking seemed perfectly ready to turn his attentions to Daphne; another possible suitor, if she could even call Alex that, considering his inattentive behavior; and a third man whom she had never seen before in her life.

"Sir," she said to Lucien, "since our host is so whimsical, why should we not be equally wayward? I, for one, would much enjoy a small walk before eating."

Alex recognized immediately the work of a master opponent when a good while later a happy band rounded the corner, walking toward the picnic laid out in the sun. His footmen had set out linen tablecloths of the palest gold an hour ago; napkins embossed with his crest were stacked next to silver tableware; the champagne was slowly warming in pools of melting ice. He was stretched out on the grass, his mouth irresistibly quirking with amusement as he watched Charlotte stroll slowly toward him, head turned appreciatively toward Lucien, her eyes shining with laughter at something he had said. Foiled, Alex thought. Hoist with my own petard! That will teach me to indulge in a fit of petulance.

He rose easily to his feet. "You see," he said with a welcoming smile, "our tempers are restored and we await you." He gestured at Pippa, happily picking grass, but Charlotte had to compress her lips to avoid laughing. Surely he had emphasized *our*, ever so slightly? There was a moment of silence as everyone arranged themselves on the linen.

"Aha!" Will said happily. "I see that my meager picnic has been supplemented by regal fare!"

Charlotte was trying to figure out why she

sank naturally into a place next to Alex. Remember, she told herself fiercely. Remember the way he treated you before. Do not make a booby of yourself again! Yet even the lightest touch of his hand on her arm made her shiver.

"Sir," she said, keeping her tone light and indifferent.

"I merely wanted to offer you a strawberry," said Alex with dulcet sweetness. He was stretched out on one side, propped up by an elbow. He leaned forward and handed her a strawberry.

"Ah, where is your daughter, that is, Lady Pippa?" Charlotte asked weakly.

The earl rolled back slightly and Pippa came into view on his other side.

"Should she be eating grass?" Charlotte asked.

"Probably not," Alex said in an unperturbed fashion. "Here, Pippa, you stop eating that grass. You're not a horse." He took the uneaten strawberry out of Charlotte's hand. "Eat this instead," he said, putting the strawberry into Pippa's plump hand. She looked at it with interest and smashed it against her face joyously.

"My goodness," Charlotte said. "She looks like a lot of work. Doesn't she have a nanny?"

"Oh, yes," Alex replied. "The nanny's over there." He nodded over toward a small grove of trees. His servants were decorously seated in a small group. Unlike their master, they were seated on benches, and rather than champagne, they seemed to be drinking ale. The one woman was unmistakably dressed in the uniform of a governess.

"Well, why is she over there and not here with Pippa?" Charlotte persisted.

"Pippa doesn't like her very much," Alex said. "I don't seem to pick governesses terribly well. She's had five of them in the last few weeks, but none of them seemed to take. Here, I'll show you the problem." He picked up Pippa and put her down between his body and Charlotte's. Pippa took one look at the woman to her left and broke into hysterical sobs. Alex hauled her back over his body with a practiced grasp. As soon as she was removed from Charlotte's vicinity, she gave one final sob and settled back down to picking grass. And eating it, Charlotte noticed.

"Why?" she asked simply.

"Her mother was gravely ill, for three or four weeks, I'm not sure how long. And Pippa was left with a succession of nannies — they kept leaving for fear of catching Maria's scarlet fever."

"Oh, poor thing!" Charlotte said. "And now she is afraid of women?"

"That's it," said Alex. "So you see," he added lazily, "I'm afraid the only thing left for me to do is to get married. She doesn't like nannies, or governesses. I think the only way she'll ever get used to a woman is if I marry one." He looked over at her, his black eyes dancing. "What do you think?"

"Perhaps," Charlotte said gravely. "Don't you think it's rather an extreme measure?"

Alex shrugged slightly. "You know how it is;

there comes a time in every man's life when he feels the chill of old age . . . the breath of the grave . . . the —"

"Oh, please!" Charlotte laughed. "You must be all of what? Thirty-five?"

"Thirty-one actually, but I must marry," Alex persisted. He had somehow drawn even closer. "Why, my aunt Henrietta has told me so many times. You see," he said, tickling her nose with a piece of grass, "the future of the Earldom of Sheffield and Downes lies in my hands."

Charlotte was biting her lip, trying not to laugh. "What about your twin brother?" she whispered. They were so close together now that there was hardly a need to speak out loud at all.

"Alas," said Alex. "Patrick is in India, and life is so uncertain. No, I must marry — for the good of the earldom, you understand."

"Hmmm," said Charlotte. "Such a sacrifice. How lucky I am not to be a man! I could never bring myself to it."

"No?" Alex asked. "Even if it was truly necessary?"

"Why ever would it be?" Charlotte said. "I have an independent income, and my brother, being a man, is all that is needed to carry on my father's dukedom. No —" she shook her head, her eyes shining with mischief, "I foresee a future without a husband. But," she said, patting the earl's hand comfortingly, "I can recommend some very nice women for you. After all, your requirements aren't very high — only that she be maternal — a widow with several children would be just the ticket. Let's see, there's Lady Doctorow. She's not precisely beautiful, but only the strictest critic would say she was *fat*. More important, she is very motherly, and she has five children already, so she is sure to like Pippa!"

"Oh, no," said Alex. "My wife can't have children already. No, Lady Doctorow is out."

"Well," Charlotte began, but she was interrupted by Daphne Boch.

"That child," she said rather sharply, "has fallen asleep with her face on a plate."

The entire party swung about. Pippa had indeed fallen asleep, her face lovingly pressed into a plate that had once held ice cream. Moreover, she still had strands of grass sticking to her face, mixed with mashed strawberry. In all, she looked so thoroughly motherless that Charlotte's heart turned over.

Alexander merely picked her up and looked about for a suitable cloth to wash her face. When he couldn't see one, he turned and in one smooth gesture, plumped Pippa straight into Charlotte's lap.

"Would you hold her for one second?" he asked with a charming smile. "I will simply trot over and see whether the nanny fell in the lake or what." Even from here Charlotte could tell that Pippa's young governess was having an excellent time flirting with the earl's four footmen and the baron's one attendant.

She looked down at Pippa, who thankfully had

not woken up and was now loudly sucking her thumb. He wasn't joking. Alex really was looking for a mother for Pippa, and she was apparently the current candidate for motherhood. She had a split-second urge to roll the dirty, rather damp child straight out of her lap. But then . . . Pippa was sleeping so sweetly, her face pressed against Charlotte's knee. She stayed put, torn between indignation and tenderness.

Alex seemed to be spending an awfully long time talking to his servants. She looked up to find the rest of the party gazing at her in horrified amusement.

"I am so sorry," remarked Daphne in her strong French accent. "Your beautiful gown will be quite ruined. And that gown was made by Antonin Carême, was it not? This earl does not exhibit good manners!"

Will gazed at Charlotte thoughtfully. Could it be that a crack was appearing in her enchantment with his handsome friend? Perhaps he could use the child as a wedge? But no. He sighed inwardly. Better to flirt with the accomplished Daphne and forget the dream of a witty, lovely Charlotte next to him in bed. Charlotte wasn't howling with indignation, and that probably meant that she didn't mind having that messy brat hurled into her lap.

Charlotte felt an embarrassed flush rise up her neck. Alex's maneuver was hardly subtle. She felt as if the whole party was judging her aptitude for motherhood. Lucien's sharp eyes noted her mortification and he rose gracefully and bent over her.

"May I?" He nimbly picked up the sleeping child and rolled her deftly into his arms. As Charlotte watched with surprise, Lucien tucked Pippa into the crook of his arm and smiled down at the group. "I shall take her for a walk, shall I not?" He strolled off.

Charlotte instinctively looked at Lucien's sister. Daphne's eyes filled with tears and she looked blindly off past the picnic debris, her face rigid. Will swiftly drew her to her feet. Having known Daphne for only one hour, he already knew that she would dislike showing emotion before relative strangers.

"Let's go for a walk as well, shall we?" he suggested casually. They walked off in a different direction, and if Daphne walked rather blindly, Will appeared to see nothing of it.

Charlotte sat alone.

Alex sauntered up, wet linen in hand, and stopped in surprise when he saw no child in her lap. He crooked an eyebrow at her.

"Lucien . . . he took her for a walk," Charlotte said slowly. Alex dropped to the ground beside her. Charlotte turned to him, her eyes perturbed. "Have Lucien and Daphne lived in England for several years?"

"I believe so," said Alex cautiously.

"And was he married before coming to England?"

"Yes."

"I think he had a child as well," Charlotte whispered. "How horrible!" One read of the fate of French aristocrats, of course, but it didn't seem so bitterly painful until one saw a father hold a child not his own.

Alex said nothing. He had come to the same conclusion earlier in the day. He and Lucien had fenced in the long picture gallery of Sheffield House, with Pippa ensconced in a makeshift crib at one end. Confronted with Pippa, his other male friends had either pretended not to notice her or complained (justly, no doubt) that she was an ill-handled problem and should be instantly consigned to a nursery.

Lucien said nothing about her either way, but during a break in the game he stooped over Pippa's crib and allowed her to teethe on the back of his knuckle. Not one of Alex's unmarried friends would have known to do that. He himself had only been a father for a month, but he was continually amazed at the revolting habits propinquity to Pippa had led him to — such as allowing her to chew on his hand.

"I instructed the servants to clean up," Alex said in his deep voice. "Shall we mimic the rest of the party and take a small walk?"

Charlotte hesitated only briefly before agreeing. They strolled silently for a while and then sat at the edge of the very willow pond where Will had earlier made his ill-fated marriage proposal. She and Will had naturally sat on the bench provided, but she and Alex just as nat-

146

urally sat on the riverbank. Charlotte didn't even consider the possibility of further damage to her gown. She sat primly, her arms wound around her knees, staring at the murky water.

Alex leaned back and put his head on his arms. He pretended to close his eyes but actually watched Charlotte through lowered eyelashes. She was sitting absolutely still. From his position on the ground he could see the slender curve of her back, leading up to her beautiful neck, and just a glimpse of long, curling eyelashes brushing her cheeks. There was no point in analyzing why he wanted her so much. He did, that was all there was to it. He wanted to run his tongue up that neck until she shivered with delight. And given that he needed a wife, the timing of this strange bolt of lust was perfect. Charlotte would make a splendid, decorative countess, a delightful bed companion, and sooner or later she would be an excellent mother to Pippa as well.

He cast a swift look around. No one was within sight. "I suppose," he said, "you must think me very odd to have tipped my child into your lap without notice." Alex swung about to sit before Charlotte. "In fact, more than odd: blasted rude. Is this dress a fabulous French creation?" His hand slid over the strawberry stains on her knee.

Charlotte had been thinking about the afternoon, and had decided that she did not like being embarrassed.

"Oh, no," she said sweetly. "I have no expectations whatsoever about your conduct."

"Touché!" said Alex appreciatively.

"Let me see," Charlotte continued. "You have entirely forgotten our first meeting, during which you — well, never mind that," she added hastily. "During our second meeting you touched my back in a most improper way, and on our third meeting you lied to Baron Holland, who apparently has some claim to be your friend, finagled your way into this picnic, left us abruptly before introducing your French friends, and finally thrust an unkempt child into my lap. I am much inclined to think," she finished primly, "that there is little you do that escapes remark, and thus for me to have expectations of civility would be past hope!"

Alex noted with appreciation that she said nothing about his hand on her knee. "You are absolutely right," he said humbly.

Charlotte looked at him. His hand slid a little higher up her leg.

"You are very provoking!" she said, shaking his hand off her knee.

He laughed. "I am out of my depth in two areas." His right hand captured one of hers and gently bent down her ring finger. "Number one, I have only been a father for a short period, and I don't feel entirely easy in the role, at least in front of people I don't know well."

"I would say the contrary, actually," Charlotte broke in. "I don't believe I have ever seen a man who is as easy with the role as yourself."

"Ah," Alex said hastily, "that is only because I

am suddenly forced to act as both mother and nanny and so I appear to be more accomplished than I am." He did *not* want to go into the reasons why he abruptly left the group before making introductions. How could one reveal that a perfectly well-bred peer in his thirties had been caught by a wave of jealousy so intense that he had to leave the scene in order to avoid giving an old friend a square right to the jaw?

"Number two," Alex continued, caressing Charlotte's middle finger before bending it down. "I didn't think to meet a woman I wanted to marry on my first evening back in England. It has taken me rather by surprise." She looked up at that and was met by a look of wry self-irony.

"Ha!" she said. "I know why you want to marry. You have found yourself burdened with a one-year-old child who loathes her nanny."

"Actually, you are unlike any nanny I have seen. Where is your tight cap?" He ran his free hand through her velvety curls. "And I regret to tell you, madame, that your mouth is far too soft to administer the necessary discipline!" His finger moved to her lower lip.

"Governesses," he continued, "always wear garments which cover their collarbones." His finger trailed over her chin and down to the base of her neck. "I am something of an expert after ushering some five governesses in and out of my house in the past few weeks. Governesses," he said softly, "never, never, never allow a man to see something as beautiful as this . . ." His finger swooped over her curves, falling into the delectable dark shadow between her two breasts and lingering there.

Charlotte drew in a sharp breath. She didn't move for a second, shaken by a firestorm of desire that began low in her belly and moved up her chest. Then she pulled back. This was exactly what had happened three years ago. She was about to be seduced on the grass, and this time in broad daylight! In fact, perhaps this particular earl made a habit of ravishing young ladies outside. She, however, was not a pullet ready for plucking.

"My lord," she said coolly. "I must beg you to curb the wandering tendencies of your hands. There are those who find such undesired caresses . . . distasteful."

Alex's eyes darkened. He leaned forward until there was hardly room between their faces for a breath of air.

"Are you such a one?" he said, his deep voice sending shaking tremors through Charlotte's knees. She kept prudently silent. Slowly, keeping his eyes fixed on hers, Alex lifted her right hand to his mouth and pressed her fingers against his lips. His lips opened and he delicately bit the tip of one finger. Charlotte's eyes fell, afraid that he would be able to tell how much his very touch affected her.

"Perhaps you are right," he said, with amusement in his voice. Her eyes flew back up to his. "Even Aunt Henrietta could hardly expect me to marry a . . . reluctant woman."

"Exactly!" Charlotte said, collecting her scattered thoughts and pulling her hand out of his. "I know just what your aunt Henrietta would like. A young damsel, just out of the schoolroom." She looked at him mischievously. "She will fall desperately in love with you on first sight and she probably won't mind your advanced age . . . much," she added with just a touch of doubt. "You are an earl, after all!"

"That's true," said Alex. "I should probably be wise to point out the coronets on my coach two or three times, in case she forgets my rank."

"Precisely," said Charlotte approvingly. "Now you're beginning to understand the situation, my lord. I'm afraid that those with white hair" — she glanced at his curls — "can't expect the same success in love that is enjoyed by younger men."

"And what should I do," said Alex in an oddly gentle voice, "if I don't like this girl as much as she likes me? You do see the problem, don't you? I'm afraid I have a tenderness for, oh, the over-the-hill sort of lady, the sort who has been hanging around ballrooms for three or four years . . ." his voice trailed off.

Red dots danced before Charlotte's eyes. No one! No one had ever insinuated that she was an over-the-hill, on-the-shelf sort of lady. "I should say that the problem, in fact, is that a more experienced woman may have too much force of mind to accept your offer, my lord," she said, her mind registering with approval the evenness of her voice.

151

Alex sighed loudly. Somehow he had again possessed himself of her hand and brought it to his mouth. "I am desolate, Charlotte. I had set my heart on this older lady — why, she must be all of twenty years old, Charlotte — and I'm quite sure that I wouldn't prefer a sixteen-year-old, no matter how docile."

Charlotte felt fiercely irritated. What a stupid conversation! She didn't even know this man, and here they were, talking about marriage. And he was insulting her. And he was mauling her fingers, which made it hard to think rationally.

"I feel sure," she said in a perfectly composed voice with just a drop of uninterest, "that when you actually come to making this painful decision, sir, you will find it to be far easier than you may believe at present."

Alex growled. She heard it: He growled. And when she looked at him in a rather bewildered fashion, he jerked her forward and up on her knees, and before she could squeak out a protest, he pulled Charlotte toward him so that their bodies touched from chest to knee.

In fact, had Charlotte struggled, the whole embrace might have become something more athletic than Alex had in mind. But instead her body betrayed her. She lifted her head as if he kissed her every day. And Alex's arms tightened in response to her unconscious invitation.

His lips descended fiercely on Charlotte's and, unbidden, her mouth opened. A warm tongue plunged into her mouth and withdrew, plunged

152

in and withdrew. Charlotte was instantly intoxicated, her body responding with fiery awareness to the push of his belly against hers, the hard strength of his hands molding her back.

Suddenly Alex's lips left hers. Ruthlessly he avoided her pleading mouth, running his tongue provocatively over her eyebrows, biting the sweet fullness of her bottom lip. Charlotte unconsciously pressed forward, begging silently for more. He pulled her even closer, molding her body to every inch of his. His hardness jutted demandingly into her soft curves. Charlotte gasped and without thinking, she reached up and pulled his mouth down to hers, bringing her tongue, somewhat hesitatingly but seductively, to touch his lips.

Alex shuddered, almost completely out of control. Somewhere in the back of his mind he knew that this had to stop. They were kissing in the open. Ruining Charlotte's reputation didn't seem a propitious way to start a marriage.

So, without saying a word, he rocked back on his heels, swiftly turned Charlotte about, and pulled her into his lap. Then he wrapped his arms around her from behind and willed his heart to slow down. She remained absolutely stiff for a moment, and then relaxed, collapsing against his chest.

Alex rested his chin on top of her fragrant hair. His fingers, willy-nilly, trailed down over the front of her gown. "Charlotte," he said, his voice deep as black velvet. "I will give you a week to accept my proposal. After that I'll probably have to snatch you out of your bedroom myself, just to keep my sanity."

Sensing her intake of breath, he folded his fingers firmly over her mouth. "No." They sat quietly for a moment and then he felt small even teeth biting his fingers.

"Oh, dear," he sighed. "I forgot I am marrying a woman who has already cut her milk teeth."

But actually Charlotte couldn't think of a single thing to say. She knew, with blinding clarity and acute humiliation, that she would have made love to this man right here, in the sunshine of Hyde Park, next to the Willow Pond; without a single protest. In fact, she'd probably make love to him anywhere he proposed. She shuddered slightly.

When he pulled her to her feet, Charlotte finally summoned the courage to meet his eyes. What she saw made her heart bound. Alex's arched eyebrows seemed to be flying even higher, but he didn't look ironic, or sarcastic, or jeering. Instead, his eyes were an intense, fierce black. He didn't look at her as if she were a hoyden, but as if she were a drink he would never tire of.

He didn't touch her, just ran his thumb over her eyebrows. "Do you know that we have the same eyebrows?" he asked. "Do you suppose it is this similarity that has driven me mad with desire both of the two times I've met you?"

Charlotte restrained an impulse to correct

him. They had met three times — but how could she possibly say, don't you remember? You ravished me in the gardens of a ball, three years ago. A large hand cupped her chin, forcing her face up.

"We're getting married," he said conversationally, smiling at her. He frowned when he saw the tiny crease between her brows. "Are you engaged? Already married?"

She shook her head.

"Then," he said with supreme confidence, "we'll get married by special license a week from today."

"No," said Charlotte.

"No?"

"No, my lord," she said, and turned to walk back toward the waiting carriages. Her body was still shaken by his kisses, but her mind was finally clear. Alex treated women like interchangeable coins. Had she not met him years ago, she would probably have been drugged today by the sweetness of his kisses and his incredible physical allure. But he had had the same effect on her three years ago, and yet he had walked calmly away from the encounter and promptly forgotten her. Even though he had taken her virginity. Obviously, what seemed to her a devastatingly erotic encounter had simply been business as usual to him. And the only reason he was asking her to marry him now was to get a permanent nursemaid for his daughter. She'd be damned before she'd marry someone just to care for his child, especially given that her husband would be out seducing women in a park every time she turned her back.

Her eyes were distinctly cool as she looked at Alex, walking silently next to her. If only he didn't make her heart turn over just to see him. Even now her body was fraught with desire walking next to him. She longed to walk closer, to run her arm up his arm, to . . .

What if she did marry him? They would share a bed. Unconsciously, she sighed out loud. But no. She steeled herself. Her father respected and loved her mother. She had to keep their example in mind. This earl was a strange man, abrupt, sometimes impolite. He would be difficult to live with. She wanted someone who would love her, even if she herself didn't feel a blazing physical desire for him. Desire was no basis for a marriage.

They walked silently back to the carriages. The rest of the party was already grouped there. Pippa seemed to be perfectly happy (and now clean); one of Alex's servants was playing with her under a tree. Daphne, on the other hand, was distinctly annoyed. One elegant slipper tapped under her light gown. The Earl of Sheffield and Downes had easy ways as a host that did not suit her French sense of propriety. And Lady Charlotte, she noted with some distaste, looked even more disheveled than she had an hour ago. English aristocrats! She would never understand them! No one would *ever* catch her looking as unkempt as that duke's daughter.

Alex, on the other hand, looked at Charlotte walking next to him and thought he had never seen any woman look so beautiful. Her lips were deep red and her short curls were tossed by his hand. The very arch of her eyebrows made him want to growl like a tiger and throw her over his shoulder. The sight of her steeled his resolution. No matter what she said, she belonged with him, in his bed, and that was where she was going to be. She had everything he wanted: true sweetness, even down to the delicacy of her downcast lashes, and a blazing passion he had never experienced in a well-bred woman.

His jaw tightened with resolve. He had simply moved too fast, that's all. Charlotte was a young, beautiful woman, courted by half of London. How could he expect to simply inform her that they would get married in a week? She had probably never experienced anything like the swell of passion they shared today. He'd frightened her. He had to go slowly, woo her, not ravish her on a riverbank.

Alex politely escorted his petulant guest, Daphne, to his carriage, and just as politely hailed Will good-bye as the baron escorted Charlotte to *his* carriage. He ignored the wintery smile with which Charlotte bid him farewell. His girl had got herself into a tweak, that was clear, but he could take care of that tomorrow. In the carriage he bent himself to coaxing Miss Daphne out of her disdainful mood. He succeeded so well — showering her in an artful downpour of compliments — that her tinkling laughter filled the carriage again and again. Daphne would have sworn that Alexander Foakes's attention was solely focused on her. But in fact Alex was brooding over the delicious moment when Charlotte pressed against his body. His wife. It had a devilishly good ring to it.

Chapter 7

In the following week London society was treated to the delectable sight of the handsome but disastrously ineligible Earl of Sheffield and Downes laying determined siege to the reigning beauty Lady Charlotte Daicheston. No one could quite determine how she felt about it. She laughed and flirted with all her suitors; she exhibited no particular inclination to favor the earl. Sharp eyes watched as she gave two dances to Alexander Foakes, and then two dances to another earl, Braddon Chatwin. And then she danced twice with Will Holland and, scandalously, three times with a man old enough to be her father, Sylvester Bredbeck. But everyone discounted that as pure mischief; he was a friend of her mother's.

The crowning question was, of course, had anyone told her? Charlotte's mother fended off dozens of gently worded questions designed to get at the heart of the issue: Was her daughter cool toward Alexander Foakes because she knew of his incapability, or was she innocently following her own instincts? Or was she, as some less kind people said, a wily young woman who, knowing that the fervor caused by the earl's courtship could only work in her favor, kept everyone guessing on purpose?

But the truth was that no one had told her. All London knew of Alex's impotence, but Charlotte had no idea. She had grown suspicious about his past marriage, given the sly remarks people had made about him in her hearing, but the remarks were vaguely malicious rather than informative. And impotence was certainly not something that would spring to *her* mind in terms of Alex: After all, she of all people could have attested to the opposite.

Her mother was torn. Had Adelaide not had the strong suspicion that Alex was the man with shot-silver hair who took her daughter's virginity three years before, she would unhesitatingly have told Charlotte the truth and warned — nay, commanded — her to have nothing further to do with him. But . . . what to do? Her daughter had not confided in her, and Charlotte's demeanor did not encourage Adelaide to broach the subject.

Marcel, on the other hand, had never been informed about his daughter's misadventures in the garden three years ago. And so he was violently opposed to the prospect of Charlotte accepting Alexander Foakes's hand in marriage.

"And so I shall tell him," he blustered at his wife. "And so I shall tell him, if he has the impudence to ask me for her hand in marriage! I will not have one of my daughters marrying a limp carrot, a —" He broke off, remembering that there are phrases which gentlemen do not repeat in front of gentlewomen even if the lady in question is his wife.

"I understand, Marcel," said Adelaide soothingly. "And I agree with you, darling, of course. But I think we should allow Charlotte to dance with whomever she wants."

"Don't be a peahen, Adelaide! She has no idea, has she?" Marcel swung around, his eyebrows furrowed.

"No," Adelaide admitted.

"Well, you have to tell her, that's all. I suppose it will be embarrassing, but she has to know the facts at some point. Blast it! You must have told Violetta and Winifred *something* before you set them off on their weddings, didn't you?"

"Yes," said Adelaide unhappily, "but —"

"You'll just have to do it, Addie. We can't have all of London chortling at our unknowing daughter. Half of 'em seem to think she's a fortune-hunter who doesn't care that the man is a . . . a limp rag, and the other half are laughing at her. I won't have it, do you hear?" He was alarmingly red in the face. "Do you know how many people have had the infernal impertinence to ask me how I feel, having my daughter courted by a floppy poppy?"

"A floppy poppy," Adelaide repeated, fascinated despite herself. "That's quite good — a floppy poppy."

"Lord! Don't repeat that, Addie. It's not at all

161

proper," her husband groaned. "Do you see what I mean, though? People are simply vying to create new nicknames for the man. Don't think I'm not sympathetic. I quite like him personally. He made a remarkably decent speech in Lord's the other day, about the corn riots in Suffolk. No one whispered about his incapabilities then! But the fact is, he's not a man that a father would want courting his daughter. No children, Adelaide. Have you thought of that?" He glared at his wife accusingly.

"Marcel," she protested, "I'm not suggesting that Charlotte marry the man; I simply don't want to broach this subject with her. After all, she shows no signs of favoring him over any of her other suitors. Why not let it be for the moment?"

"Because at any second he might win her over! You should have seen him in the House, Addie. The man has a silver tongue. And he's damned good-looking, I'll give him that. No one would think to look at him that there was anything wrong. Barring his problem, I'd say he was perfect for Charlotte."

"I see," said Adelaide. "You're afraid she'll fall in love with him."

"If she does, we're in trouble. You know how stubborn she is, Addie. Why, we couldn't even stop Winifred from marrying that American, and she was the most biddable of all our children. If Charlotte gets it in her head to marry him, she'll do it. And she won't pay any attention to whether he's capable or not."

He sat down heavily. "Except she won't be happy, Addie. She can paint all day long in that studio of hers, but it won't make her happy." Marcel reached up and pulled his wife down to sit on the bed beside him. "It wouldn't be right."

Adelaide snuggled against her husband's side, torn whether to tell him about Charlotte's experience in Kent three years ago. Better not, she decided. He would be absolutely furious and probably charge into Alexander Foakes's town house like a bull. At any rate, she was worried about that twin brother. What if it had been the other one — what was his name? Some sort of Irish name, she thought. Well, what if it had been the other twin in the garden? Could Charlotte tell the difference between them? She quailed at the idea of asking her daughter.

"There's one thing I don't understand, Marcel. Sarah Prestlefield told me — you know how malicious she can be — that Alexander Foakes has a daughter. In fact, she said that his daughter is with him practically every moment, and never with a nanny. She's apparently about a year old, and very ill-trained, and he carries her around town. *And* Sarah said she looks exactly like him! So how can this be if he's . . . well . . . incapable?"

"I don't know," Marcel said. "I hadn't heard about a daughter. But you know, Adelaide, this daughter might be anyone's. I gather that his first wife is dead now. So who's to say whether she

163

was the child's mother or not?"

"Well, how would that change things, Marcel? I don't understand. Either he can, or he can't. And if he can, then we shouldn't worry about Charlotte."

Marcel sighed. He didn't feel like explaining the intricacies of potency with wives as opposed to potency with courtesans. "Well, dear," he said uncomfortably, "there's a possibility that Alexander Foakes's incapability is not, ah, applicable in all situations."

There was a short silence. "Oh, dear," Adelaide said quietly. "This is all so unpleasant. And I like him, Marcel, I really do. Are you absolutely *sure*? Maybe this is all gossip."

Marcel shook his head. "Several of my so-called friends have taken great pleasure in assuring me of the accuracy of the report. His first wife, a woman named Maria Colonna, petitioned the Pope — she was Catholic, of course — to annul their marriage after one year, claiming that her husband was impotent. And Alexander Foakes did not contest the annulment. Apparently she was from a quite good family too, in Rome, and they all considered it a great disgrace. She died a few months ago, and he returned here. I suppose he came with this child, although no one has mentioned a daughter to me."

Adelaide tried to think it out. She had a separate problem. She didn't want to let Charlotte know that Alexander and his brother had come to her debut ball, and that she had seen them and not mentioned it to Charlotte. What if she were enraged? What if she thought her mother had betrayed her?

Marcel broke the silence. "They're betting on her in Brooks," he said heavily. "There are two whole pages devoted to bets on whether she'll take him or not."

He didn't mention the fact that there was another page devoted to whether a) the marriage would be annulled, b) Charlotte would take a lover within one year, or c) she would become discreetly pregnant, thereby giving Alex an heir, but not one that necessarily resembled him.

"It's an ugly situation, Addie. I cannot like it. Why don't you encourage her to take Braddon Chatwin? He's an earl as well, and while he may not be the brightest, I knew his father quite well. He was sound." To be *sound* was Marcel's highest praise.

"This Alexander is a loose screw, and it only makes it worse that he's flaunting a child. He was in scrapes all the time as a young 'un. Not that they were bad ones, I have to say. Just the usual jackanapes flummery that youngsters get up to. Champagne breakfasts with Cyprians, that sort of thing. He wasn't a libertine, but . . ." Marcel's voice trailed off as he contemplated the odd fact that Alexander Foakes was best known in his youth for amorous escapades.

"Perhaps he was in a riding accident," Marcel muttered, half under his breath. "But if this marriage goes through," he said with renewed vigor, "we'll end up with a miserable child, one whose name gets dragged through the mud. There's no pope in England, you know, to smooth over something like this. The scandal would ruin her. *And* it wouldn't be pretty for Horace either, when he came into the title."

"Oh, Marcel," Adelaide said with some irritation. "I do think you're blowing this out of proportion! There's no need to cut up our peace about it. For goodness sake, all Charlotte has done is dance a few times with the man!"

"Not true," said her spouse with asperity. "She's been on a picnic with him, and the talk is that she spent some time alone with him at that picnic. Of course, it's just servants' talk, most likely, but that's the news on the street. She will be ruined, if this goes on, and without even marrying him at all!"

Adelaide absorbed the news of the picnic, about which she knew nothing, in silence.

"I don't see why," she said stubbornly. "If he is incapable, why should anyone fault her for spending some time with him? I can't see anything wrong with diverting herself for a time with a . . . a floppy poppy!"

Marcel glared at her between jutting brows. "Don't repeat that phrase, madame! It makes you sound like a loose fish. Whenever have you found gossips to be logical?"

"Perhaps not logical, Marcel, but this is ridiculous. How can Charlotte be ruined by a man who hasn't the capability to ruin her?"

"That's as may be," Marcel said obstinately. "The fact is, everyone is watching her now because she's with *him*. They are simply waiting for her to misstep and they'll be on her like a hawk with a pullet. She must give him his marching orders, now."

"All right," Adelaide said finally. "I'll speak to her. But there's something odd about all this, dearest. Alexander is pursuing Charlotte as if . . . well, he's been so marked in his behavior that I would think it the most romantic match I'd ever seen, if there wasn't this problem."

"I know, I know," said her husband testily.

"So why does he want to marry her?"

Marcel frowned over this for a moment. His mind boggled at the idea that Alexander Foakes was lonely, or that he wanted Charlotte's dowry. Why, he had three times the blunt that Marcel himself had.

"It must be the competition," he said slowly. "Why, remember when I was courting you, Addie? All those coxcombs and Bingo-club boys that were buzzing around you. I didn't pay them any mind, of course, but when you accepted my suit it did add a certain sense of victory." He thought back, remembering all the sapskulls he had beaten to the punch when Adelaide accepted his hand.

"There was a squire — quite a good fellow, remember him, Addie?"

"Squire Noland," she said with a little smile.

"Well, he caused me a bit of worry," Marcel

said cheerfully. "My God, now I think of it, they were betting on me too in Brooks. I remember Glimflabber, we used to call him — what was his name? Something dreadfully pedestrian like Glassblower, but that wasn't it. Well, he strutted up to me right in the middle of Paul's and told me that you had graced him with a second dance, and I should just withdraw my suit at that very moment. Ha!"

Adelaide listened patiently. "It was Glendower, darling, not Glassblower."

Marcel turned to her. "You accepted me that very night, Addie. And it *was* rare to see Glendower so out of countenance over the announcement. He scuttled away the next time I laid eyes on him, and finally put it about that you'd only taken me because of my title. Sour grapes."

Adelaide rose, dropping a kiss on her husband's head. "I'll speak to Charlotte now."

Marcel caught her hands in his. "You tell her, Addie. This is not a request. I will not accept Foakes's marriage proposal if he makes one. And the only reason I'm not talking to her myself is ... is ... the delicacy of the whole situation. But I will *not* countenance the man as my son-in-law."

It was about ten o'clock on a Sunday night and Adelaide knew where her daughter ought to be — in her bed, drowsily thinking about her engagements the next day. But instead of heading toward Charlotte's bedchamber, Adelaide unerringly walked up the stairs to the third floor. Sure enough, candles were burning all around the walls of Charlotte's studio.

Charlotte was standing absolutely still, looking at a portrait on its easel in the middle of the room.

"Darling," said her mother. "May I come in?" She walked around to stand behind her daughter. "Why," she said, startled, "it's lovely, sweetheart. Truly lovely. My goodness."

Charlotte had finished her portrait of Sophie York. Sophie was posed on the branch of a broken-down tree, in the clearing of a forest. The ground was covered with bluebells, stretching into the distances of the forest glade. The folds of Sophie's dress were perfectly reproduced, her petite curves elegantly rendered by Charlotte's brush — but her look! Rather than looking dreamily into the middle distance, as peers invariably did in portraits, Sophie was looking straight at the beholder, a small smile hovering around the corners of her mouth. She appeared to be laughing at the very absurdity of sitting on a branch. And there was a twinkling invitation in her eye . . . in fact, Charlotte had made Sophie look rather less than a perfect lady, Adelaide decided. Something about the fullness of her lower lip, perhaps? But, of course, Sophie wasn't a perfect lady. That was what gave her mama so much anxiety.

"Oh, Lord," Adelaide sighed. "You aren't going to let Eloise see this, are you, dearest?"

"Oh, no, Mama," Charlotte said, smiling. "I think I'll keep it and give it to whomever Sophie marries, when she marries. Because she looks so enticing, doesn't she?"

Adelaide smiled back. "It's a very good portrait, Charlotte. It really looks like Sophie." She was rapidly rethinking what she had come to say. Why were she and Marcel so worried about broaching difficult subjects with Charlotte? These new young women . . . they knew so much more than she had as a young girl.

She retreated to the sofa and invitingly patted the cushion next to her. "Darling, we need to have a talk."

Charlotte sat down rather reluctantly. She had a fair idea of the subject her mother wanted to discuss. Lately she felt as if wherever she turned someone threw her a significant look and asked how she found the Earl of Sheffield and Downes. A small frown creased her forehead. There was something very odd about all this intense interest. People seemed to be so fascinated by Alex's pursuit of her. Comparatively speaking, they paid almost no attention to Braddon Chatwin's courtship even though he too was an earl.

She herself thought about Alexander all the time, day and night. She swayed alarmingly between exhilaration at his obvious attraction, and sharp feelings of mortification at the idea of accepting his hand. She felt as if her imagination had been taken over by a genie who alternately produced intoxicating images of an unclothed Alex and desolate images of her future self, relegated to the house while her husband was out seducing other women. Probably in her own garden, she thought glumly.

Adelaide didn't know where to start. "Your father and I have noticed," she said finally, "that the Earl of Sheffield and Downes is paying you rather pointed attention."

"Yes, he is," said Charlotte.

"We . . . we felt," Adelaide said stumblingly, "that you should know the circumstances of his previous marriage."

"His previous marriage," Charlotte echoed.

"You know that he was married before?" Adelaide asked.

"Yes, I met his daughter," Charlotte replied.

"Oh," Adelaide said flatly. She felt incapable of addressing the issue of the daughter. "Well, Alexander Foakes was married to a woman named Maria, Maria something. Your father knows her name," she added hastily. "After a year the woman petitioned the Pope for an annulment of their marriage. On grounds of impotence." She looked expectantly at her daughter.

"Impotence," Charlotte repeated. "What's that?"

This was what Adelaide had feared. She floundered into a tangled series of half-truths and euphemisms, none of which Charlotte clearly understood.

"Are you saying that he has no . . . no male part?" Charlotte asked sharply. "Because it's not true."

Her mother's head swung up. Too embarrassed to meet her daughter's eyes, she had been staring carefully at her folded hands. Now she looked straight at Charlotte. "And how do you know that?" she asked, rather grimly.

"He's the one, Mama." Charlotte's hands were twisting unconsciously in her lap. "He's the one from three years ago."

"Ah," said Adelaide. There was a small pause. "Impotent doesn't precisely mean that the organ in question doesn't exist, Charlotte. It simply means that it doesn't function . . . properly."

Charlotte had no idea what her mother was talking about.

"I can't do it!" Adelaide cried in frustration. "This isn't a proper conversation." Her eyes strayed to Charlotte's new portrait and she had a sudden inspiration.

"Perhaps you could ask Sophie about impotence? I'm sorry to be such a blunder-head, my darling, but these things are just not . . . not in my vocabulary. I explained the important things to your sisters because I didn't want them to be abominably ignorant on their wedding nights. My mother said nothing to me at all, and the whole event was quite a shock."

I bet it was, Charlotte thought grimly, thinking of the stabbing pain she experienced in the garden. It was a question that had perplexed her ever since. How do women put up with all that pain, every night?

"It's all right, Mama," she said soothingly. "Whatever the problem is, it doesn't matter. You see, I have made up my mind not to marry Alexander," she continued. "I have already refused his offer, and when it finally dawns on him that I really mean it, I'm sure that he will find some other woman to . . . ." Her voice shrunk into silence.

Adelaide looked at Charlotte sharply. There was a good deal more going on here than met the eye.

"If he *was* the one from three years ago," she said hesitatingly, "might it not be a good idea to marry him? After all, he . . ."

"No." Something about the closed tightness of Charlotte's face made Adelaide discard the subject.

There was a pause. Charlotte gathered herself together and gently drew her mother to her feet. "Don't worry, Mama. I'll ask Sophie about it, and you can reassure Papa that I do not intend to marry Alexander Foakes, no matter what his problem may be." Although, she added silently, I don't believe for a single moment that he has any impediment in that region!

Her mother hesitated at the door. "Charlotte, have you heard that Alexander has a twin brother?"

"Yes."

"Do you think that perhaps you might have confused the two men?" Adelaide persisted unhappily. She simply had to suggest it. "They are as alike as two peas, you know. Even people who know them well can't tell them apart."

"I can't believe you're suggesting this! You know what happened that night! How can you possibly think that I wouldn't recognize the man when I saw him?"

"But, darling, it was dark, wasn't it? And it was years ago, and wasn't he wearing a mask or something?"

"There's . . . there is just no possibility," Charlotte whispered. "I even recognized his smell, and the shape of his cheekbones, and the curve of his jaw."

"Sweetheart," her mother said softly, gathering her into her arms.

"It's him, Mama," Charlotte said. "It's he who doesn't recognize me!"

Adelaide stiffened. She had never even considered this possibility. In her reconstruction Alexander recognized the beautiful maiden whose virtue he had blemished, and pursued her (despite his affliction) out of loyalty, or desire, perhaps. But not recognize her daughter? Her beautiful, exquisitely beautiful daughter! She looked at Charlotte in pure amazement.

Even now, with tears stealing down her cheeks, her daughter was objectively one of the loveliest women she had ever seen. Her face had grown more slender in the past few years, accentuating her cheekbones, and her new short haircut emphasized her large eyes. But all the essential parts of Charlotte were unchanged. Her eyebrows, her sweet, flying eyebrows that she had even as a newborn baby — how could he possibly have forgotten those eyebrows?

A surge of rage swept over Adelaide that was unlike anything she had experienced before. She knew precisely how mother tigers felt when their young were threatened.

"That bastard!" she said through clenched teeth. "That absolute, unmitigated bounder. I'll have his head!"

Charlotte was shocked out of her misery. Her mother rarely expressed any strong emotion outside comfortable ones, like love for her children. The most agitated Charlotte had ever seen her was when the gatekeeper at their country estate gave his wife a black eye while in his cups. Even then she just marched up to the gatekeeper and told him that if she ever heard that he had drunk more than three tankards of ale at one sitting he'd be fired on the spot. But now she was actually panting with rage.

"Mother." Charlotte put a hand on her arm.

Adelaide looked at her fiercely.

"There's nothing to be done about it, Mama," Charlotte persisted. "In fact, one could think that I made a very lucky escape. I . . . I don't know that I would have resisted him if I hadn't met him three years ago, and then I wouldn't know that he is such a —"

"Libertine!" her mother snapped.

"Whatever he is," Charlotte said shakily, "he's forgotten that he ever met me. And he can't find out that he did, Mama! You must see how humiliating that would be for me." She wiped away the tears that kept tracking slowly down her cheeks, willy-nilly. "He says he wants to marry me. But he didn't even try to find me before. I think it was probably just a moonlight frolic for him," she said, with a tone of acute self-disgust. "I just keep thinking, *why*. Why did I let him take me into the garden? I thought it was so magical. I thought it was . . ." She turned away and rested her forehead against the cool wall of her studio. "What a silly, stupid little fool I was! Captured by moonlight and drunk on lemonade, ruined by a man who thought so little of it he doesn't even remember the event! It meant nothing to him, nothing to him and everything to me. . . ." Sobs racked her body as she rocked back and forth, face caught in her hands.

Adelaide stood rock still, unable to think of anything to comfort her weeping child. Silently she drew Charlotte back to the settee they had just left. They sat quietly until Charlotte's tears finally stopped falling and she caught her breath.

"I think you should marry him," Adelaide finally said quietly.

Charlotte raised her tearstained face. *"What?"*

"I think you should marry him," Adelaide repeated. "We need to think calmly, darling. We have been thinking with the heart, and not with the head. The fact is that men do not take sexual encounters very seriously. Oh, not your father," she added as Charlotte's eyes widened. "Your father is remarkable.

"But, Charlotte, the majority of my friends

176

have watched their husbands . . . well, have known that their husbands were bedding one female or another. Why, dearest Georgina has had to inure herself to all manner of affronts."

"You mean Julia's mother?" Charlotte asked, fascinated despite herself. "Squire Brentorton seems like such a kindly man."

"He is, darling, he is. But he's a man, and there aren't many who set store by their wedding vows. John truly loves Georgina, but he just doesn't see it the same way she does. At least he hasn't set up a mistress, or anything of that nature! And he never sleeps with women of our class, which is a great boon, believe me. Why do you think that Sissy's mother pleads a weak heart so often? She simply can't stand to watch her husband swan around the ballroom with that piece of muslin he's set up on Mayfair Street."

"What?" Charlotte gaped.

"I think her name is Melinda, something ridiculous like that; she's a major's widow, supposedly . . . but it's common knowledge that Nigel Commonweal spends most of his time at her house, and while she doesn't get invited to the best houses, she does seem to finagle invitations to most of the large balls. Prudence just doesn't have the backbone to ignore it, not that I blame her. I have been terribly lucky with your father; I have never been confronted with anything of this nature."

"You don't mean that Papa too . . ."

"I don't think so," Adelaide said. She sighed.

"No, I'm fairly sure he has not. But if he has not, darling, then he must be one of perhaps five men in the *ton* who don't occasionally sleep with ladies other than their wives. The important point is that these men don't necessarily dislike their wives. Men simply see sexual acts rather more . . . flexibly than do women."

"I cannot like it, Mama," Charlotte said, frowning.

Adelaide had to smile. On the surface, Charlotte looked to be entirely her daughter, but occasionally she was so like Marcel it made her heart melt. Just so would Marcel announce that he disliked a certain social impropriety.

"No woman likes it," she replied simply. "Well, that's not true. There are also women in the *ton* who occasionally . . ."

Charlotte's eyes widened again. "Who?" This was just the kind of gossip that abruptly ceased when she sat down with a group of dowagers. As an unmarried girl, she was far too innocent to know such things, they said.

"That's not the point," Adelaide said with a glimmer of a smile in her eyes. "The point is that while Alexander may have forgotten a brief encounter in the garden, he seems to be ardently pursuing you now and perhaps you ought to marry him —" She broke off, frowning. "But I forgot; I forgot all about his . . . problem."

Charlotte waited patiently until it seemed that her mother was not going to elaborate. "It seems rather dismal to marry a man *knowing* that he will be unfaithful to you, Mama," she finally observed. "Surely Sissy's mother never thought that her husband would establish a friendship with a major's widow."

Adelaide was trying to work through her tangled thoughts. "If he . . . if he is unable, then he would not make such an attachment. Although the condition doesn't make Alexander a good prospect as a husband either," she added, remembering Marcel's adamant objections.

Charlotte bit her lip. She was thoroughly perplexed. "*What* condition, Mama?"

Adelaide took a deep breath. "Your father says —" She broke off. Then she spoke abruptly. "Impotence is when a man . . . when his member becomes soft rather than stiff. Such a man *cannot* get married, Charlotte, because he and his wife would have no children. Do you understand?"

Charlotte nodded. She had a fair idea of the mechanics of sexual ingression, less, it must be admitted, from that night in the garden than from inadvertently seeing two horses mating a year ago.

"It's not right," Adelaide added. "It's not right that Alexander is pursuing you, given his limitations."

"He is quite, ah, stiff, Mama," Charlotte said weakly. "I mean, I noticed, because he kissed me and —"

Adelaide interposed, her eyes slanting away into the corner of the room. "The fact is, darling, that apparently a man can be quite capable up until the last minute, or something of that nature," she said hurriedly. "I can't say I understand it completely. But an impotent husband cannot have a child."

"But — he has a child," Charlotte said in a puzzled tone. "Pippa looks exactly like him."

Adelaide groaned inwardly. This was precisely the subject she didn't want to discuss.

"The child might not be, well, she could be his child but not his wife's, if you grasp my meaning."

"Nonsense, Mama. He told me that Pippa is distressed because when his wife was dying, the child was left with a succession of nannies. He was telling the truth."

"I don't know, darling. I don't understand about the child, and your father doesn't either. But the fact is that his wife annulled the marriage on the grounds of impotence, and he didn't raise a whisper about it. In fact, he must have agreed with her assessment, or there would have been an examination."

"An examination," Charlotte whispered. "You mean by doctors?"

"Oh, Charlotte," her mother said in agony. "You'll simply have to forget about this man! Everyone is talking about him and anyone who marries him will have to face the harshest scrutiny . . . can you imagine? What if he *is* capable and you had a child who didn't resemble him? What would everyone say then? No, no," she said with decision. "I don't know why he is even trying to get you to marry him. He will have to settle for taking his brother's child as heir, that's all."

Charlotte absorbed in silence the news that all London was talking about Alex. Her heart was wrung by the idea of people laughing at him. Did he know? He must know. He showed no signs of distress. And no signs of worry about his . . . capability, she thought slowly. In fact, even remembering the moment when he jerked her body against his, at the picnic, made her feel flushed.

"He wants to get married because his daughter won't accept a governess," she said softly, looking up at her mother. "He was quite honest about it."

Looking at her daughter's miserable face, Adelaide felt a sympathetic pulse of sadness. Alexander was devastatingly handsome, with his dark hair and eyes. She took her daughter's hand comfortingly in hers.

"Your father thinks he may have had a riding accident, dearest."

Charlotte thought about this for a while.

Her mother cleared her throat. "You do see, darling, that his suit is impossible? You are far too lovely to become a mere governess. I want you to fall in love and — to be able to make love. And to have children." She stroked her cheek lovingly. "You children have been the greatest source of joy in my life. I would hate to see you unable to experience that."

Charlotte nodded silently.

"Perhaps you could direct Alexander to speak to your father," her mother prompted. "Marcel could make it quite clear that he would never accept his suit, and the man could look for a nursemaid elsewhere. Really." She frowned. "I dislike him more for pursuing you for that reason than I do for any disability he has."

"It's not that reason alone," Charlotte said, almost inaudibly.

"I am sorry, darling," her mother said, instantly understanding. "But there's nothing to be done about it."

"I would prefer to tell him myself."

"Yes."

There was a short silence.

"You will have to be very resolute, Charlotte. Perhaps it would help if you kept your mind fixed on what happened three years ago."

"Yes," Charlotte said.

"I meant what I said about your father, dearest. We have shared, well, life together for almost thirty years. I know that you can find a man who takes his private life seriously. If he loves you, he will," Adelaide added firmly.

Charlotte looked at her numbly. She felt instinctively in the pit of her stomach that if she didn't marry Alex, she would marry no man. But why bring that up with her mother? Her parents' point of view was quite clear. And even if she refused Alex's hand for a different reason than they would — she didn't countenance this question of impotence overmuch — her mother had merely confirmed her sense that Alex's inability to re-member their encounter three years ago signaled an unhappy future. She did not want to end up like Sissy's mother, huddled at home while her husband circled the ballroom with other women. Even the idea of seeing Alex smiling down at an-other woman, whether she was married to him or not, made her sick to her stomach.

"Mama," she said seriously, "I want you to promise that you will not discuss with Papa what happened three years ago. I know that he won't accept Alex's suit. But I insist that I tell Alex my-self."

Charlotte had no clear idea why she was so in-sistent about personally refusing Alex's pro-posal. In the back of her mind she knew that if her father spoke to Alex, Alex might never speak to her again. Even the thought wrung her heart. How would she get through an evening knowing that his deep voice wouldn't appear at her ear at some point? How would she be able to dance without the knowledge that at some point, his large hands would grasp hers, might even circle her waist if there was a waltz? If she were com-pletely honest, in the week since the picnic at which he asked her to marry him she had lived for the moments when he approached her.

Charlotte went to bed feeling numb, cried out. She had promised her mother that she would in-form Alex at the first opportunity that her par-ents would never accept his suit.

"I can't just spit that out in public!" she had

said dully, huddled on the couch in her studio.

"I know," her mother replied. "All we ask is that you end his courtship as soon as possible. We are only trying to guard your own reputation and happiness, darling."

That night, for the first time in a week, Charlotte did not go to sleep dreaming of velvety dark eyes and hands that tantalized and persuaded. She stared at the ceiling until glimmers of dawn crept through her new chenille curtains. Finally she turned over and fell dreamlessly into sleep.

Chapter 8

Charlotte didn't wake up until almost two o'clock in the afternoon. Her maid tiptoed in and out several times, trying to decide whether to pull the curtains and wake up her mistress. But she looked so white lying against the linen sheets, her face distressed even in sleep, that Marie finally decided that her mistress must be getting ill and should be allowed to sleep as long as possible.

When Charlotte awoke she lay still for a moment as details of the conversation with her mother dropped back into place in her mind. Finally she stretched, pulling the bell cord next to her bed. Somehow the situation didn't seem so tragic in the light of day. She swung her feet out of bed and stared absentmindedly at her toes.

Perhaps she didn't have to give up Alex entirely. She would explain the situation — her mind nimbly evaded the question of how *that* was going to be aired — and they could continue as they were, with the understanding that marriage was not an option. Charlotte really felt quite pleased with this idea. Wiggling her toes happily, she pictured herself circling the floor in

Alex's arms. Maybe she would even go in to dinner with him at the next ball. So far she had made certain she was engaged for dinner before he even appeared (he invariably attended any ball late, just before the doors closed in the case of Almack's).

When Marie appeared, followed by a puffing footman with a large tub of hot water, she was surprised to find a faintly pink, smiling Charlotte humming and darting about the room.

"I'm going to the theater tonight, Marie," Charlotte said. "I believe I shall take a ride now, and then I'll go to Blackwell's and see if I can find a new novel." Not that she really had any time for reading, but she was between paintings. Who should she paint next? Her mind wandered off into a pleasurable daydream that involved Alex sitting on the couch in her studio. She would lean over him to rearrange his arm . . . what the imaginary Alex did then made her cheeks turn from pink to rosy. Marie stared at her in amazement.

"And after the bookstore," Charlotte added hastily, "I would like another bath, Marie. Would you send a message to Monsieur Pompelmousse, please? If he could attend me at some point this evening, I would be grateful."

Two baths in one day! Marie mentally shook her head. She herself found a semiweekly wash-off to be more than enough. As her mother had often told her, too much water caused water on the lung.

"What would you like to wear tonight, my lady?" she asked.

Charlotte stretched out luxuriously in the large tin tub. "I think I shall wear the white and black gown. You know the one."

Marie nodded vigorously. It was her favorite of the dresses Lady Charlotte had bought from Antonin Carême, although she had yet to see her mistress wear it. Marie looked speculatively at Charlotte. She was wearing that dress for an engagement at the theater? Something important was going to happen tonight.

Marie's assiduous reading of the gossip columns had gleaned two interesting facts: The Earl of Sheffield and Downes apparently came to balls only to dance with Charlotte, and there was something very sniffy about his previous marriage. Ah, well. Marie was no great believer in condemning a man for behavior during a previous marriage. Unless — her eyes widened a bit — he *killed* his first wife! But no. The papers said very clearly that she died of scarlet fever. Just like Marie's own aunt.

She bustled about pulling out gossamer stockings, silk underclothes and her mistress's crimson riding costume.

"No, not that one," Charlotte said suddenly, looking up from her bath. "I'll wear the gray costume."

Now Marie knew that something was happening. The gray riding habit was one of her mistress's new purchases. It was the color of a mourning dove and fit like a glove, with black braid trim that gave it the air of a Russian soldier. It was exquisite . . . but also rather uncomfortable. If Charlotte was wearing that riding costume, she was expecting to meet someone on her ride. Marie glanced at her speculatively. If only the duchess knew her daughter was making assignations in the park!

In fact, Charlotte was not engaged to meet anyone in particular on her ride. But she had woken with blood singing in her veins, and she was simply not allowing herself to think about the cause. She felt like looking her best, she reasoned. If the Earl of Sheffield and Downes happened to be riding in Hyde Park when she was there . . . well, she would be friendly but cool. There was nothing wrong with wanting to look her best.

Charlotte stretched a long, elegant leg out of the bath and looked at it meditatively. Then she sat up energetically and, balancing herself carefully with hands on both sides of the light tin tub, stepped out of the bath.

"Marie, will you send one of the footmen over to Lady Sophie's, please, to ask whether she would like to join me in the park? Thank you."

Marie, having laid all her mistress's clothing on the bed, whisked over to the door. Any opportunity to take a message downstairs meant that she got to see Cecil, and perhaps even to snatch a kiss behind a door.

"I'll be back immediately, my lady," she said.

Then she ran down the back stairs.

Alone in her room, Charlotte finished rubbing herself with cream, faintly scented with orange blossoms, and paused in front of the mirror. For some reason, ever since she woke up this morning her belly felt fiery. Even the sight of her own curvaceous self — the body she had lived with for twenty years! — seemed exotic, exciting. She tried to look at herself as a man might, but gave up. She'd lost some weight recently, but oddly enough her breasts seemed to have grown larger. When she looked at the tender weight of her breasts, all she saw was a honey-colored male hand curving around them . . . Charlotte shivered all over, and turned away from the mirror.

She managed to dress herself almost completely before sitting down and waiting impatiently for Marie to return. What on earth could be taking her so long? Finally she pulled her bell cord, and downstairs Marie gasped and pulled away from Cecil's hard chest.

"Go, go!" she said quickly, her French accent intensified by excitement. Lady Sophie only lived a few streets away, so he could be there and back in a flash. Marie dashed up the servants' stairs and slowed to a walk just outside Charlotte's door, quietly slipping inside.

"I am sorry, my lady," she said, beginning to fasten the hundred or so buttons that made the gray suit so form-fitting.

Her mistress was sitting in front of her dressing mirror, absentmindedly staring at herself.

189

"That's all right, Marie," she said.

Marie smiled a bit. She was very lucky and she knew it. Charlotte was never bad-tempered, and even when she was irritable she rarely snapped at Marie. Whereas Marie had a friend working for a certain young lady who had not received an offer so far this season, and *she* regularly had to dodge hairbrushes and combs, and recently her mistress had even thrown a jar of cream at her!

There was a discreet knock and Marie stopped brushing Charlotte's hair and opened the door, just a crack. It was Cecil, looking very formal.

"Lady Sophie York would be pleased to join Lady Charlotte in approximately one hour," he said, rather loudly. Then he whispered wickedly, "And Mr. Cecil would like to take a certain French miss into the laundry closet for a ride!"

Marie rolled her eyes indignantly, shutting the door.

Charlotte was looking rather amused, for some reason. She couldn't have heard Cecil, Marie reassured herself.

"Lady Sophie will ride in an hour, my lady," she said.

"Hmmm . . . was that Cecil?"

Marie's hands got even busier, arranging and rearranging Charlotte's soft curls.

"Yes, my lady."

"He's quite handsome, isn't he, Marie?" Charlotte asked mischievously, picturing the large blond giant who often accompanied her on rides in Hyde Park.

"I don't . . . know," her maid said hurriedly.

"He's *very* English-looking," Charlotte persisted.

"There! You look lovely, my lady. *Ravissante*," Marie said.

Charlotte twinkled at her in the mirror. Marie only slipped into French in moments of strong emotion.

Sophie was waiting for her by the time Charlotte's mare delicately pranced her way to a stop before the marble steps of the Marquis of Brandenburg's town house. She ran down the steps lightly, dressed in a crimson riding costume that was just as form-fitting as was Charlotte's. Sophie's groom threw her up onto her fidgeting horse, a sprightly, slender mare she had named Erica.

"Erica!" her father the marquis had said in disgust. "Such a pedestrian name for a lovely animal."

But Sophie just smiled at him and sent her groom to fetch Erica. Nothing he said, her father gloomily thought, had ever had any effect on her actions; what made him think that he could influence the name of her horse?

Now Sophie looked appreciatively at Charlotte, whose gray costume was perfectly complemented by her midnight black mare.

"My God! We make an exquisite pair, don't we?" She gave Charlotte a wicked smile. She loved to embarrass Charlotte by pointing out the obvious, but she noticed with interest that Charlotte didn't turn a hair today.

"Do you think we ought to bring two of our grooms, rather than one of yours and one of ours?" Sophie twisted about to look at the two grooms mounted behind the girls.

"Why on earth?"

"Sweetness," Sophie teased, "their liveries don't match. And when two dashing high fliers like ourselves are taking the air, shouldn't we be accompanied by matching grooms?"

Charlotte shrugged, sending a slanting grin in Sophie's direction. "I personally think that all eyes will be on me," she said impudently. "And if there is anyone left to look at you, I don't think they'll notice the grooms."

"Oooooh," Sophie replied. "My sweet Charlotte is growing some thorns. All right, then. *On y va,* Philippe," she called to her groom. The marquis — who insisted that his title be spelled in the French way — was more than a little proud of his wife's French background. He employed only French servants, insisting that they provided a nobleman's house with an extra touch of refinement. After growing up her whole life surrounded by French servants, Sophie slipped easily into either English or French.

Sophie and Charlotte ambled along the crowded London street together. After meeting noses and snorting a few times, their mares pranced neck to neck, one occasionally tossing her neck and indicating a wish to bolt. The street was thronged with London's rich and poor inhabitants: Orange sellers slipping past well-breeched swells, their hands sliding gently over rich fabrics, perhaps removing a watch chain or a wallet. Children dashed into the crowded street every other moment, running between carriages and horses, recklessly tossing their lives into the hands of people who, for the most part, didn't give a tinker's monkey for the life of a London waif.

"My mama," Sophie said with a sideways glance at Charlotte, "is somewhat perturbed about tonight's entertainment."

"Really?" Charlotte said politely. "I believe the play is quite unexceptional: Shakespeare, isn't it?" Sophie's mother had grown up in a French convent, and she had notoriously strict ideas about propriety.

"That's not the problem. The problem is that where you go, along comes the earl, and . . ."

"Which earl?"

"You know which earl! The Earl of Sheffield and Downes, of course. Every wit's favorite target."

Charlotte's heart sank. Sophie had been kept at home with a cold all the past week and she hadn't had a chance to speak to her; if she too knew about Alex's supposed impotence, then her mother was right. All of London was discussing the man's ability.

"I don't like it," she said fiercely, staring between her horse's flicking ears. "How can people be so vulgar!"

Sophie cast her a curious glance. "Is it true, then?" she asked.

"How on earth would I know?" Charlotte answered. "It took my mother about an hour to become clear enough so that I could even understand what she was talking about."

Sophie listened silently. The virtues of having a French nanny were that talk of male properties was not uncommon in the Brandenburg nursery. Not, of course, that the marchioness, Eloise, had any notion of that fact.

"Perhaps you could ask him?" she asked, her face alight with devilment. Charlotte looked up sharply. There, edging down the street on a huge black stallion, was her sometime suitor, Alexander Foakes himself. Charlotte's heart instantly started beating so quickly she felt as if the buttons on her riding costume must burst.

"Lady Charlotte; Lady Sophie," Alexander said easily, reining his horse to a stop just to the left of Charlotte. He doffed his hat. He was wearing a gray riding coat and top boots, and looked every inch the gentleman. Charlotte looked at him somewhat wonderingly. How on earth did she ever fool herself into thinking he was a footman?

"Sir," she said, inclining her head. Sophie contented herself with an impish smile. She liked this suitor of Charlotte's, with his stormy black eyes and huge body. Not for her, someone so large and moody-looking, but he was perfect for Charlotte, she had to admit. Naturally, only *if* all

194

those rumors were untrue.

"Won't you join us, my lord?" Sophie asked.

Alex hesitated, looking down at Charlotte's downcast face. He only had to see her to become aflame with desire. Even now, the one thing he wanted to do was sweep her off her horse and carry her . . . where? Into his house, his bad angel quickly said. Charlotte's eyelashes were so dark and thick that they cast shadows on her cheeks.

This was ridiculous. "I am sorry to say that I cannot," he replied, watching Charlotte's enchanting profile. Surely a tiny sigh escaped her lips when he said that?

Sophie looked a silent question.

"I have been informed by my man that if I do not make my way to Schultz this afternoon he will leave my employ, and that would never do."

Sophie giggled.

"You see the problem, don't you Lady Sophie?" One flying eyebrow rose even farther. "I would be vexed beyond all bearing if Keating decided to leave me. Ah, the life of a dandy. Schultz will take all afternoon to fit me for one coat, and then it will take all evening for me to shrug myself into another one, and a good two hours to achieve a proper waterfall with my neck scarf." He sighed deeply.

Despite herself, a small smile curled around Charlotte's lips. She stole a glance at Alex. His coat was close-fitting but by no means could it promote him as one of the dandy set.

"Alas," she said sweetly, "I fear that with such

a *low* collar as the one you are sporting today, sir, and such a plain neck cloth . . . dear, dear. Indeed you must rush to Schultz's. I would recommend some lemon-yellow pantaloons."

"My goodness," Alex said appreciatively, bending dangerously close to Charlotte and looking straight down into her dark eyes. "Do you know, I believe you are the very first young lady who has had the temerity to mention my unmentionables, let alone criticize them?"

Charlotte flushed slightly. It was true: No proper lady would be caught discussing pantaloons in the company of a gentleman. Alex stared down at her, his eyes burning into hers. Suddenly his horse tossed his head and he reined back sharply in order to avoid bumping into Charlotte's mount.

Sophie noticed with satisfaction that if Charlotte had turned pink, Alexander Foakes also seemed to be a little overheated. Alex met her eyes, and a rueful smile touched his lips for a second. The man could not be impotent, Sophie decided. In fact, she was going to do everything in her power to further a marriage between her closest friend and this particular earl.

"Charlotte and I were just discussing the Shakespeare play we see tonight," Sophie said airily. "*King Lear*, I believe. Are you familiar with the play, sir?"

"No, but I am much looking forward to seeing Kean in the role," Alex replied, his smile turning into a positive grin.

Charlotte turned her head from Sophie to Alex, a rather bewildered look in her eyes. She wasn't even aware that the two knew each other. Sophie had been at home most of the week; when had they met?

Alex doffed his hat again, remarking gravely that he hoped to have the pleasure of greeting them that evening, and rode away. His whole body protested, riding down the street away from his delectable love, especially given that her riding costume emphasized every lovely curve. His eyes darkened as he imagined picking up Charlotte and putting her on his library table, tossing up her elegant skirts, uncovering . . . His horse curvetted in protest as his hand involuntarily shortened the reins. For God's sake. He rode a bit faster. The tale about Schultz was flummery: In fact, he had to be home before Pippa awoke from her nap.

He was extremely irritated as he threw the reins to a waiting groom and strode into the front hallway of Sheffield House. Instantly he paused and cocked an experienced ear. No piercing screams meant that Pippa had not yet woken up. Alex walked into his library, only to be greeted by his desperate-looking secretary, Robert Lowe. Alex's desk was piled with papers and had been for days; his secretary seemed to tag behind him everywhere, asking for signatures. Alex grimaced, remembering his ordered life before Pippa's arrival.

Meanwhile he sat down at the desk and

quickly began working through the largest pile of papers, tossing them in the direction of his secretary with instructions about how to respond. Suddenly he stopped in astonishment. Before him was a sheet of newsprint, clearly one of the scandal sheets printed daily, with an arrow pointing to a paragraph.

> *Last night Lord L —— was caught with Lady D ——.*
> *If Mrs. B —— will still continue flirting,*
> *We hope she'll draw, or we'll undraw the curtain.*

"What the devil is this piece of rubbish doing here," Alex said in a deadly voice, his dark eyes pinning his secretary to the chair.

"I just thought," Lowe said miserably, "I thought you might want to consider a suit for libel . . . anyway," he finished in a rush, "I thought you should know." Alex's eyes sharpened and he returned to the sheet he still held in his hand.

> *A certain earl had better stop a-knocking.*
> *It takes a stiff rapper to enter a duke's locker.*

Alex swore and violently crumpled the sheet, throwing it to the ground. His secretary trembled.

"Out!"

Lowe left, clutching a sheaf of papers to his chest, bowing reflexively as he went. He felt ill.

The whole house knew (thanks to Keating) just how perfidious his master's first wife had been, *and* they knew quite well that he didn't have any problems with his "knocker," given the satisfied ladies — well, women — who had occasionally graced the master's bed since his wife left. Although there haven't been any in England, Lowe thought.

Meanwhile Alex leaned against the mantelpiece in the library, his face savage with rage. God damn her, God damn her! Maria, with her soft wails and shrieking complaints . . . he shook with disgust even thinking of her.

Finally he took a deep breath and forced himself to calm down. After all, his ex-wife was hardly responsible for insolent verses printed in a London scandal sheet. He could easily have refused the annulment if he wished. It had seemed a heaven-sent way out of a horrible situation, Alex thought, his mind drawn back to feverish nights in Rome during which Maria would scream incomprehensibly and regularly throw objects at his head. In a period of two months he had had the windows in their bedroom replaced four times, to the great amusement of the household servants.

He still remembered the awed sense of joy he felt when Maria confessed — in a moment of calmness — that she was in love with a priest and wanted to annul their marriage. He had, in fact, been on the verge of volunteering for the dragoon guards, even given his position as heir to the earldom. Hang his father! Patrick would make a better earl than he, any day. He would have done anything, anything to get away from his Italian wife.

Alex flung himself into the big armchair next to the fire, thinking moodily of his first meeting with Maria. He had barely been in Italy for a week, and he attended a *concerto* at the Palazzo Barberini with some count; he could barely remember his name now. Count Rossi-Ferrini, he thought. And there she was. She looked exactly like the girl he had met in the gardens of Stuart Hall, the girl he had spent two fruitless weeks searching for. True, she didn't have red hair, and he was certain that the garden girl, as he had taken to calling her in his head, did. And she didn't smell as sweetly clean and innocent as that girl did. Odd, given that Maria was a well-born Italian maiden and that girl was training to be a prostitute. But their faces were the same shape, a delicate triangle, and they both had intriguingly full lower lips.

Fool that he was, he assumed that Maria and he would share the same passion that he and the garden girl had . . . what an absolute jackass, he thought, his lips twisting cynically. Once married, Maria had to be compelled to any sort of physical intimacy. When they finally did share a bed it was abundantly clear that far from being the innocent, convent-raised girl her family had represented her to be, she was no virgin. After that the marriage rapidly disintegrated, spiraling into a series of screaming tirades on her part and longer and longer absences on his part. He took trips into the Italian countryside, stopping at any *taverna* he saw, drinking local wine until he fell off the bench. By the end of a year his Italian was fluent and his tolerance for alcohol (never slight) had doubled.

But he was miserable. He was going to the dogs and he knew it. Then, just as he was on the verge of joining the Third Dragoon Guards, the papers signed and the only task remaining to inform his wife, Maria came to him and begged him to release her from the marriage. Release her! He would have done anything to wipe out their wedding. Oddly enough, they made love that night for the first time in months, rather tenderly, as he remembered. Unfortunately, it was also the night that Pippa was conceived.

Within a month her powerful family had arranged everything. Alex had one sticky and uncomfortable interview with three black-gowned bishops who asked him politely: *"Lei avrebbe per caso un problema?"*

"Sì, sì," he responded earnestly. He may not have had the problem they thought he had, but he had no trouble labeling Maria a problem. And he was free. Maria set off with her priest, now ex-priest he supposed, carrying with her all the household silver, jewelry, and every piece of furniture she could put her hands on. She even took a miniature of his mother, presumably to sell it since she could have no attachment to the picture.

In the first joyful breath of liberty he didn't care, thinking that the marriage was over and he would never again have to wake up to Maria Colonna in his bedchamber. But in fact he was still not entirely free. The debris from that dreadful marriage kept washing up on the shores of his life. The miniature of his mother showed up in a secondhand store in Naples. At one point Maria's feckless brother tried to blackmail him. And now ribald verses. Personally, he didn't give a hang what the papers printed about him. But Charlotte's father, the Duke of Calverstill — that would be another story. To tell the truth, he himself would never allow Pippa to marry a man with a reputation like his own.

His thoughts were broken by the sound he was unconsciously waiting for in the back of his mind. Little footsteps padded down the stairs, stumbling slightly but recovering, he knew, because Keating tightly held Pippa's hand.

"Papa!" her little voice shouted a greeting as Keating pushed open the heavy double doors to the library. "Papa!"

Alex stood up and walked around from the back of the armchair, crouching down on his heels and opening his arms in a huge bear hug. Pippa toddled as fast as she could toward him, leaving Keating standing at the library door. As Alex scooped her little body into his arms, his heart melted. So what if he couldn't have Charlotte? He had Pippa. He'd try harder to find a proper nanny. Miss Virginia had left after three days. She was the first nanny who hadn't quit; Alex's housekeeper had fired her. Apparently she became very close to two of the lower footmen in the week she spent in Sheffield House, and that intimacy resulted, naturally enough, in a whole brace of footmen sporting black eyes.

"Papa, *fwore*," Pippa shouted. Shouting seemed to be Pippa's normal mode of speech. *Fwore* mean *fuori:* outside, Alex translated. Pippa only had ten words that he had been able to decipher, and he couldn't afford to ignore the ones she spoke in Italian. But she was adding them every day. Yesterday she said *kiss* very clearly, and this morning (before breakfast), *cake*.

"All right, love," Alex said, the corners of his mouth curling upward. "Let's go to the park." He banished the fleeting image of Charlotte's tight riding costume from his mind — but he did scoop up Pippa and stride quickly toward the hallway, shouting to Keating to have Bucephalus, his horse, readied once again. Keating handed Pippa up to him once he was seated on the massive stallion. Mrs. Turnpike, his housekeeper, emerged from the house looking anxious. She hated these excursions to the park with Pippa balanced on a great prancing horse. She wrung her hands in her apron, but stopped herself from saying anything. There was no telling with the earl. One day he was right as sunshine, and the next he would snap your head off.

Alex and Pippa paced gravely up and down the

aisles of Hyde Park. Now that he had read the *Tatler* riddle, he was able to see a clear influence in people's demeanor. No one would ever snub him; he was an earl, after all. But older women bowed more stiffly than they were wont to, and men bent a sympathetic eye on him. The sapskulls! Alex's chiseled face became even more forbidding. To tell the truth, some of his acquaintances avoided him, not due to the scandal, but from pure fear.

But more looked curiously at Pippa and then whispered behind their hands. Alexander Foakes's daughter was his spitting image. In fact, if Pippa hadn't been wearing a lemon-yellow dress she would look quite simply like a younger version of the earl. More than one member of the *ton* circled around the walks in order to drive a carriage past the pair again, or turned carelessly at the head of a walk to return toward them. Who was she? Who ever heard of an annulled marriage that produced children?

"The only annulment *I* ever heard of," reported Lady Skiffing, "came about when young Lord Sybthorpe was married practically at birth to his father's second cousin's daughter, or some such relation like that, and then it was clear by a few years later that the bride was stark-raving mad. So she had to be removed to an asylum, and he ended up marrying that consummate tart — what was her name? Barbara Cullerson, I think. Out of the frying pan, into the fire!" she finished triumphantly. "There were no children from that marriage either," she added, "not that it signifies, of course."

"Well, I know that when Miss Filibert — you must remember her, dearest Lady Skiffing, she was the one with such horribly gaping teeth — at any rate, when Miss Filibert eloped with her music teacher, or was it with her dance instructor? I vow, I have quite forgotten. At any rate Lord Filibert had that one annulled. They had only spent three hours alone together, and so . . ." Lady Prestlefield trailed off suggestively.

"The real question is," Lady Skiffing said in lowered tones, "who is that child?"

"Yes." Lady Prestlefield pursed her lips thoughtfully. The two ladies were sitting in a baroach, barely wide enough for them and their petticoats. They could hardly ask the Earl of Sheffield and Downes to join them, not that he would ever join two old ladies anyway.

Suddenly Sarah Prestlefield laid a hand on her friend's whip, signaling her to bring the baroach to a stop. "Look!" she breathed through scarcely opened lips.

At the top of the drive Alexander Foakes had encountered the two reigning beauties of the London ton, Charlotte Daicheston and Sophie York, and Lady Charlotte seemed to be scolding the earl. It was hideously vexing to be so close and not be able to hear. Lady Skiffing coaxed her horses to a slow amble and they drew closer without the three young people noticing.

"It is not a question of convenience," they

heard Charlotte say as they got close enough. Her eyes were flashing magnificently; she really was a lovely girl, Lady Skiffing thought. "That child is not safe!" Charlotte continued.

Well, there all of London agreed with her, of course. The two ladies exchanged significant glances. They had both given their spouses an appropriate number of children who were housed and cared for out of sight. Out of sight *and* out of danger, one might add. It chilled the bones to see a young thing perched on top of a great beast like that black monster of the earl's.

Charlotte had no thought about the proprieties of children in the park. The sight of a smiling Pippa wiggling vigorously within her father's arm and drumming her heels on the back of a jittery stallion awakened all the maternal feelings she had buried three years ago. She slipped off her own horse, Jamaica, handing the reins to her groom.

"Give her to me," she said deliberately, standing close to Bucephalus's hugely muscled shoulder.

Alex looked down at her in amazement. What the devil? Pippa was perfectly safe with him.

"Bucephalus is very sedate, Lady Charlotte," he said with just a slight edge to his tone. "He's as calm as a cow, I assure you."

"Nevertheless," Charlotte replied, "Pippa is not safe. I shall walk to your house holding Pippa and you may follow. It's not far."

Alex's eyes crinkled with amusement. His girl

had revealed she knew where he lived. She remembered Pippa's name. She was showing maternal feelings. No matter that it made him feel like a bear with a sore head to have his decisions about Pippa questioned.

He shrugged. "You do remember what she's like with women?"

"She will be fine," Charlotte said firmly. She reached up her arms, and Alex dropped his daughter straight into them.

Pippa took one look at Charlotte's face and opened her mouth to emit a titanic scream. Charlotte immediately put her down at the edge of the walk. Then she waited for a few minutes. When Pippa took a breath, Charlotte said, "I'm the not-nanny, Pippa. Don't you remember me? I'm *not* a nanny."

Pippa's mouth closed as she thought about that. "My name is Charlotte — the not-nanny," Charlotte hastily repeated. "Now, I am going to pick you up and carry you so that you can see your father on his horse, would that be all right?"

Pippa didn't say anything, but she didn't scream either. Charlotte swiftly gathered up the little girl and held her against her shoulder, so she faced backward and could see her father. Pippa gurgled approvingly. Charlotte started walking.

Sophie was still sitting on her horse, stunned. One minute they had been on their way home and the next Charlotte was biting at the man she might well marry, and then she was carrying off

207

his brat. Sophie slid off her own horse, giving Alex an admonishing look. He looked like the devil himself, about to burst out laughing.

When Sophie caught up with Charlotte, she peered about the baby's round bottom and many petticoats. To her relief, Charlotte didn't look furious anymore, just amused.

"Have you had anything to do with babies?" Charlotte asked, quietly enough so that Alexander Foakes, pacing behind them on Bucephalus, couldn't hear her.

"Never," Sophie said. "I'm an only child, you know."

"Well, this one is rather wet," Charlotte said. "And she's much heavier than she looks."

"It's only about four more streets," Sophie said encouragingly. "Why don't I take her for a while?"

"She won't agree." Charlotte grimaced. "Pippa is terrified of women."

Sophie cast her a sidelong glance. Charlotte was reflexively cuddling the child, her hand smoothing the soft curls at the nape of Pippa's neck. Sophie smiled to herself.

They left the bronze gates of Hyde Park behind them and set off down Hurston Street. Alex lived in Grovesnor Square, only three streets from the entrance to the park. Sophie held up her skirts as they picked their way through rubbish and crowds of people, the odd little band of grooms, horses, and one earl, still mounted, attracting not a little attention.

"Well, Charlotte," Sophie said, *sotto voce,* "if you don't marry Alexander Foakes after this, the gossips will probably have an apoplexy."

"Whatever do you mean?" Charlotte raised her head. She had been rubbing her cheek on the baby's round head and whispering nonsense to her, and Pippa seemed to like it, since she was giggling.

"Lady Skiffing's baroach just drove by and believe me she didn't miss a single detail. You're holding Foakes's child, and he is on a horse behind you, with a face like thunder. *And* she had Sarah Prestlefield with her, and even my mama, who claims Lady Prestlefield as a close friend, says she's the most fiendish gossip in London. Lady Prestlefield always announces that whatever tattle she knows is *certainly* untrue, and then she repeats it. You should have seen her bonnet peeking out from the side of the carriage, Charlotte!"

Charlotte didn't know what to think, so she just concentrated on crossing the street. Alex, riding in the street next to the sidewalk, had also seen Lady Prestlefield's poked bonnet emerging gracelessly from a baroach. He grinned, the last fragments of his ill humor disappearing. Perhaps gossip and Charlotte's soft heart would take care of his marriage problem for him.

At that moment one of London's many street sweepers, a little boy of about nine years old, darted into the street just before Bucephalus's foreleg. The boy alone would never have upset his horse, Alex later thought, but he was followed by a burly fruit seller from whom he had just snatched an apple. The boy slipped in front of Bucephalus; the fruit seller directly collided with his shoulder. And just to his left a hackney coach driver narrowly missed the fleeing boy by jerking up the reins of his two poorly fed, irritable mounts. They both reared in the air to a tremendous jangling of reins and hardware.

It was too much for Bucephalus. He and his master had been out twice today and so far he had been given no opportunity to stretch his legs. And he had had a very uncomfortable walk as Pippa drummed her feet and pulled his mane. He trumpeted loudly and reared straight in the air, his front hooves pawing the air.

"What the devil!" Alex said furiously. He reflexively shortened the reins and leaned forward with his other hand to grab Bucephalus's bridle. Bucephalus, a well-trained horse, thudded back down to the ground immediately. But Alex straightened only to meet the amused eyes of his beloved, who had paused on the sidewalk to watch.

Alex stared at her for an instant. He knew she would be wild in his arms; he sensed it when he kissed her in the park. But now she looked as demure as if butter wouldn't melt in her mouth. His mouth twisted in a rueful grin and he jumped off Bucephalus, throwing the reins to Charlotte's groom.

"Let me take that plump pullet," he said easily,

when he reached Charlotte and Sophie on the sidewalk.

Charlotte had been very pleasantly thinking that she must be getting used to Alex, because her heart was beating normally, and she felt absolutely like herself. But when he reached out his arms and took the child, his eyes twinkled down at her in such a way that all her newly found calm fell to pieces and she felt a blush creeping up her cheekbones.

Sophie, never one to miss an opportunity, nipped back and signaled to her groom to toss her back up on her horse. *"Au revoir,"* she said gaily. "I must return to my *maman* now. No, no, I'll be perfectly all right with Philippe. Charlotte, I will see you tonight." She bowed her head politely to Alex and edged off into the crowded street, followed by her groom.

At first Charlotte felt paralyzed with shyness, walking next to Alex with all of London doubtlessly watching them. But Pippa, who spent the time on Charlotte's shoulder trying to get Alex's attention, now turned her head, laid it lovingly on her papa's shoulder, and proceeded to flirt wildly with Charlotte. Charlotte laughed out loud. Alex remained prudently silent.

They walked past the road to Grovesnor Square and into Albemarle Square, where Charlotte lived, before she really even noticed. At her step she held out her hand coolly.

"Sir."

Alex inclined his head. "Forgive me for not

bowing. I'm afraid if I bow the wet patch on my shoulder will become apparent."

Charlotte giggled despite herself. Alex caught her wrist in his free hand, pulling her hand up to his mouth. Rather than kiss the back he put her palm to his lips. Charlotte paled. The joyful glow she felt in her belly that morning spread tinglingly through her body.

"I shall see you tonight," Alex said in a velvety deep voice, his eyes on hers.

Charlotte didn't trust herself to say anything, so she drew her hand from his, nodded silently, and walked up her stairs. At the top she stopped, struck by a sudden thought. She turned about, her eyes pleading.

"You won't get back up on that horse, will you, my lord?"

Alex looked at her and then at Pippa.

"No," he said. "No, I won't take Pippa on Bucephalus again."

He smiled at her in such a way, Charlotte thought as she slipped past Campion at the door. It made his eyes crinkle; it spoke of . . . oh, kisses. Kisses and more.

Chapter 9

Eloise York, the Marchioness of Brandenburg, slowly descended the stairway of her husband's town house, irritably smoothing her elbow-high gloves. She was displeased, she thought. Highly displeased. Eloise was a woman who understood her own consequence. She had an acute sense of propriety, a quality of which she was very proud. And somehow, through the cruelty of God, she had been given a wanton, silly chit for a daughter. When she was Sophie's age she dressed only in white and bent her head docilely whenever a parent entered the room. She never met her father's eye until she married. But Sophie! Had there been a moment when she didn't boldly meet her mother's eye *and* refuse to do whatever small thing her mama requested?

Take this afternoon, for example. When she, Eloise, had announced that they were to attend a tea party given by the Honorable Lydia Bingley, Sophie flatly refused, saying that she had scheduled an appointment with her tutor in Portuguese. Eloise couldn't even think how many times she had pronounced that a young lady need only study how to find a husband. But

Sophie obstinately kept refusing offers of marriage, and learning new languages.

The marchioness took a large, calming breath. Her eye skittered over her ensemble. At least *she* looked perfect. A trifle old-fashioned, perhaps, but she did not approve of the new French fashions. She felt sure her own dear mother — so stern and unyielding in her moral convictions — would forgive her disloyalty to French garments. No, she would never accept these waistless dresses. *And* she would never exchange her sturdy corset for one of the newfangled light corsets. Not that Sophie appeared to be wearing even a light corset! There wasn't room under that nightgown she was pleased to call a dress. Eloise's eye kindled again.

She had reached the entranceway and stood there impatiently, one slipper patting the marble floor under her wide taffeta skirt. Where *was* Sophie? The girl insisted on visiting the theater — Drury Lane too, where all the world was sure to see her — and since she apparently planned to attend the theater half-naked, she might as well present herself on time.

George emerged from the library, and Eloise cast a sharp eye over him. She knew what he was doing. Tossing off a bit of brandy, no doubt. Well, Shakespeare was difficult, and he'd been good enough to change his plans when she realized just how much attention they were going to receive tonight. Drat that girl! She didn't even know what made her feel the more annoyed —

that silly chit upstairs, dressed in a transparent napkin, or her sillier friend Charlotte, entertaining the courtship of a thoroughly ineligible earl. A shame, that's what it was. A real shame. If there had been any other impediment, she would have advised marriage. But with no chance of children, there was no point to marrying. No, it was the twin brother who was the really interesting target now. As soon as he emerged from wherever he'd gone — Borneo, wasn't it? or China — she intended to make Sophie marry him. It was *his* child who would inherit the title, obviously. Goodness sakes, she thought a bit complacently, if I were Adelaide I'd get my daughter away from Alexander Foakes as fast as might be.

There was a whisper of silk and Sophie was standing beside her. "Lud!" her mother said peevishly. "I didn't hear you coming. Undoubtedly because you aren't wearing enough clothing to wake a mouse. You *are* wearing a petticoat, aren't you?" Luckily Eloise turned away before seeing Sophie's grin. In fact, Sophie was wearing a petticoat, but it was made of the finest chenille, and she had dampened it as well.

Her father loomed up behind her shoulder as their butler helped Sophie into a velvet evening cloak. "No antics tonight, girl," he said, his eyebrows curling fiercely.

"Oh, no indeed, sir," Sophie responded demurely, twinkling up at her father.

Despite himself, George relaxed. His wife always took things so seriously. Perhaps she was blowing all of this gossip business out of proportion.

It was only when they entered their box, George ushering his daughter and her beautiful friend, and then his wife, to their seats, that he realized just how correct his wife actually was. It had been quite a while since he heard a true hush fall on the audience at Drury Lane. But it fell like a cool snow over all the upturned faces, and was instantly replaced by a rising tide of whispering voices and shuddering fans. Lord, he thought. It was going to be a long night. He couldn't stand Shakespeare in the first place — he didn't care how many ballads they added; it made him deuced sick to his stomach. And now he foresaw a very ugly interval as well. Probably be swamped by beaux, he thought gloomily. Well, looking at his daughter and Lady Charlotte, seated in the front of the box, certain to be. And then there's that earl. Bound to be here; it looked as if the whole world had decided to see this blasted play on the same night.

Charlotte sat quietly in the front of the box, trying not to furl and unfurl her fan too many times. She was wearing Antonin Carême's white gown with the black ribbons. Somehow since she bought it — was it only a few months ago? — it seemed to have got smaller, or her bosom got significantly bigger. She felt as if she were falling out of it. And the white! Why didn't she notice how delicate the fabric was when she ordered the gown? Even now she fancied she could see the pink of her leg through the cloth and her petticoat, which was itself made of handkerchief cloth.

She looked over at Sophie and a small smile crept to her mouth. Sophie might be petite but she wasn't small on top, and she too was wearing a very daring empire-style gown. The bodice was made of midnight blue fabric and appeared to be about two inches at the widest spot. Sophie caught her glance and impudently winked at her.

"Don't you love making an uproar?" she murmured behind her fan. "I vow, Charlotte, if I didn't love you so much anyway, I would insist that we become friends, because we must sit together. If only out of kindness, so the gossips don't gain a crick in their necks by turning from your box to mine!"

"Oh, Sophie!"

"Of course they are really all looking at you, not at me. I am only gaining celebrity by association," Sophie said sadly. "Oh, where is an earl for me?" She rolled her eyes up to the heavens. "Send me a notorious lover — please!"

"He is *not* my lover!"

"Oh, yes? After you walked down the street holding his child *and* looking at him with your heart in your mouth? Then you are leading him astray, and woe betide the woman who leads that particular man into a blind alley." She nodded down to their right.

Charlotte watched, fascinated, as Alex strode

into the Sheffield box, bowing gravely to his acquaintances. He appeared to be accompanied by a small party; she recognized the Marquis de Valconbrass and his sister. She felt a sudden stab of jealousy as Alex escorted Daphne to a place at the front of the box.

Sophie's strong, small hand descended on her wrist. "Stop watching him, Charlotte!"

Startled, Charlotte settled back in her chair, fanning her suddenly pink face.

"Pooh!" Sophie said. "I can't trust you for a minute! Even a fourth part of French blood would have stopped you from being so obvious."

Charlotte glared at her fiercely. Sophie wrinkled her nose at her. "Don't you grump at me, Charlotte Daicheston!" She lowered her voice. "You want him, don't you?" Startled, Charlotte nodded. "Well, you can't have him if he isn't capable," Sophie said practically. "It would never work out."

"I don't think, I mean, I think he is," Charlotte said equally softly.

"Well, you have to find out," Sophie said. "You have to *know*, and then you can go ahead and accept him. I assume he has proposed?" She waited, one eyebrow raised.

Charlotte nodded.

"What a woman! You have two earls after you, and what else — a score of mere counts and barons, and a few lowly sirs."

Charlotte laughed. She was keeping her eyes fixed on Sophie in order to avoid meeting the eyes of all the people who seemed to be staring in her direction. And to stop herself from stealing another glance at Alex.

The noise of tuning fiddles finally stopped and the director of the Drury Lane Theatre walked out before the red velvet curtain. There was a faint dimming of the audience's chatter.

Charlotte's mind wandered as the director talked on, boasting of the wonderful changes he had made to *King Lear* . . . now fit for a modern audience . . . fit for modern propriety, love of gaiety, blah, blah. She kept her eyes fixed on the railing in front of her. She had the strong sense that Alex had no plans to attend the theater until Sophie dropped the name of the play they were seeing. She had never seen anyone in the Sheffield box except Alex's aunt, Henrietta Collumber.

At the moment she felt as if he must be looking at her. Every nerve in her body signaled that his eyes were on her. The blood was not dancing in her veins — it was racing. Insanity, Charlotte said to herself. Insanity! And just how was she supposed to ascertain whether Alex was impotent or not? She raised her head as the curtains of the theater swung open. Willy-nilly her eyes slid to the right. Alex was sitting perfectly easily, his long legs stretched out before him and crossed at the ankles. He actually had his back to her, and his head was bent close to Daphne Boch's smooth blond locks. It wasn't jealousy Charlotte felt; it was hatred. She jerked her eyes away. The last thing she wanted was for Alex to catch her glaring at his — friend.

She straightened her back. Two could play at that game. She leaned forward slightly and glanced about the theater. There was Braddon . . . but Braddon wasn't really anyone to make Alex jealous, unfortunately. Her eyes slid over a number of men whom she might summon in an instant, and then her eyes brightened. Will Holland, looking like a great blond giant, was sitting in a box down to the left. He raised his head and she threw him a slight smile, an enchanting, beckoning smile. Unfortunately that was the moment when Alex finally allowed himself to throw a glance over his left shoulder at the Brandenburg box. He stared for a moment, his eyes hard. Damn it!

Will's reaction was about the same. He had spent the last week setting up a useful flirtation with a rich tradesman's daughter, and she wasn't even too unattractive. But looking up at the unbelievably sensual duke's daughter, her black curls deliberately tousled as if she just emerged from bed, he felt all his resolution of the last week fade away. Perhaps Charlotte's parents had warned her away from Alex. He cast a sapient eye at his old friend, who appeared to be whispering into the ear of that French miss, Daphne Boch.

If he went up to Charlotte's box during intermission, it might spoil the game with Miss van Stork. And she wasn't bad; he might never find another heiress this bearable. Chloe van Stork sat quietly next to him. She had russet curls, not a bad color, and a slim body, he thought. Her clothing was abominable — she was wearing some kind of thick stuff that looked durable. He shuddered slightly. She was probably even wearing one of those huge old corsets made out of whalebone, given the stiffness of her upper back. Nothing could be further from Charlotte's gossamer French gowns.

Suddenly Miss van Stork turned her head and looked straight at him. "Are you going to go?" She nodded up toward the Brandenburg box. Will gaped at her. She has lovely white teeth, he thought irrelevantly.

"I saw that woman — it's Charlotte Daicheston, isn't it? — I saw her smile at you. I think she would like you to visit her box."

Will just stared back, nonplussed. Chloe van Stork turned her attention back to the stage, where two tumblers and a juggler had just left, clearing the way for the play itself. Will studied Chloe's calm, serious profile, trying to figure out what she felt about Charlotte's smile. Did she even understand what conclusions would be drawn by society if he disappeared from her father's box and reappeared next to Charlotte? He felt strangely reluctant to drop the flirtation now, when it seemed to be bearing fruit. He had had dinner with Chloe's parents and herself that evening, and this was the first time he had accompanied them to a public event. He'd be a fool to let a golden fleece slip through his fingers because Charlotte Daicheston whimsically decided to smile at him.

Suddenly Chloe turned back to him. "Go! Go!" she said fiercely. Will gaped again. She waved her hand impatiently. Feeling like a chastised puppy, Will courteously drew himself to his feet and bowed to her and her parents, murmuring something about greeting some acquaintances. A few minutes later he appeared in the Brandenburg box, to the great satisfaction of the audience. There was a rustle of chatter. This was going to be an even more interesting evening than anyone had anticipated.

Charlotte sweetly held out her hand to him, and even the stiff marchioness greeted him kindly. To her mind anyone was better than that abominable earl. Will pulled up a chair and sat just behind Charlotte, whispering a few quips that made her laugh. She laughed overmuch, he thought, given the quality of his jokes. He looked over at Sophie. She had her delicate eyebrows raised and was looking rather amused. Will felt suddenly impatient.

He looked down at the box he had just left. Really, Miss van Stork had a very sweet, upturned nose, especially given the fact that her father's nose was rather large. The candlelight was catching her hair, making its red highlights gleam. She looked at the stage, not at him. He wouldn't mind going back, he thought. Except she had shooed him out of their box as if she knew that he was just fortune-hunting . . . Well, of course she does, a voice said in the back of his mind. Look at her! She's an intelligent woman, dressed like a dowdy in the midst of London's most elegant women. She knows you only want her fortune. I wonder why she's wearing that gown, Will thought. He caught himself. What the devil was he doing? He was sitting next to the most beautiful women in the *ton* and he didn't even feel like being amusing. He couldn't think of a single seductive metaphor. He was thinking about a frumpy woman in a corset. Charlotte's pearly shoulder gleamed next to him, a soft expanse leading the eye irresistibly down to the creamy mounds rising from her slight bodice. His breathing quickened. Will banished the thought of Miss van Stork, sitting alone in her box. The hell with it! Didn't he vow to stop fortune-hunting?

Down in his box Alex's fists curled with rage. He had risked one more look at Charlotte only to find his old friend Will Holland hovering behind her and leering down at her breasts, unless he was grossly mistaken. He turned to Daphne Boch and leaning intimately over to her, complimented her fan. Daphne looked at him a bit ironically. She had no particular aversion to flirting with this so-handsome earl, even if he was really just interested in that tall beanstalk of an Englishwoman.

The play was starting, trumpeters blowing an earsplitting entrance, signaling the presence of the king — King Lear, that is. Charlotte's thoughts were tumbling over each other, but she felt calmer now that Will had joined their box; as if he were camouflage somehow. She didn't feel so naked, so certain that everyone in the audience knew that her eyes kept straying to the right.

Slowly she was drawn in to the story of an old king gone foolish, demanding that his daughters swear they love him more than anyone or anything else in the world or they would inherit no money, no land, no part of the kingdom. She didn't pay much attention as the two elder sisters hysterically barked their inability to love anyone beside their father, even with their husbands standing right beside them. That was life, life in London anyway. People would do anything for money. Look at Will. She'd summoned him from a tradesman's box, unless she was greatly mistaken. Charlotte's eyes wandered down to that box. A young woman sat in the front, staring directly at the stage. From where she was sitting, almost directly above her, Charlotte could see that her hands were clenched into fists in her lap. She studied her profile for a second, but then her attention was jerked back to the stage.

The king's youngest daughter was flouncing about, refusing to answer her father. Or perhaps she said something he didn't like? Charlotte started to listen, her ear first rejecting the old musical lines as too difficult. Then they suddenly fell into place and became easily intelligible. The audience calmed, listening intently, and when the first act ended and a buxom Spanish singer began singing of cherries and lemons, there was a moment of silence before chatter rose into the rafters.

Charlotte looked back into the box below. There was something she liked about that tradesman's daughter's face.

"Will," she said softly, turning her head a bit. She gave him her most charming smile. Will visibly softened. Really, Charlotte thought. Men are such boobies. "Why don't you ask your friend to join us?" She nodded down toward the woman in the box. "It must be most uncomfortable down there alone with just her parents for company."

Will's spine grew suddenly cold. He didn't want Chloe laughed at, or mocked in a way she didn't understand by seasoned society women. His mouth tightened. Charlotte put a hand on his sleeve. "I would truly like to meet her, Will."

Will's deep blue eyes met hers and he relaxed. He had never heard of Charlotte Daicheston doing anything shabby or cruel . . . so why not? He stood up and a minute later reappeared in the van Stork's box. Chloe's parents courteously moved out of the way for him, although he knew that unless they were totally impervious they must be seething at the affront dished out to his daughter when he went to another woman's box.

He stooped next to Chloe's chair. "Would you like to join the Brandenburgs?"

Chloe turned astonished eyes on him. Her eyes are blue, he thought, as blue as mine. "Why?" she said bluntly.

Will couldn't think of a good lie. "Lady Charlotte requested it."

Chloe's eyes darkened. "It's not like that," Will said urgently. "Charlotte is not that kind of person."

Chloe looked down at her hands involuntarily twisting the dark twill that her mother insisted her dresses be made out of. How could she go up to that box and sit with this beautiful woman he carelessly called Charlotte? She longed to be home, perhaps adding up a column of figures for her father, or watching her mother pack up boxes of shirts for the poor.

Her mother leaned forward suddenly. "It's acceptable to us, dearest," she said in her Dutch accent. Chloe stood up. She hardly had a choice if her own mother was ready to condemn her to be laughed at by a bunch of . . . of peacocks! Tears stung her eyes but she walked steadily out of the box and down the red carpeted corridor. People were pacing up and down the corridor, defeated by Act One of the play and simply waiting for intermission. Chloe walked with her head down, certain that they were all staring at her.

When they reached the top of the stairs, Will pushed open a door adorned with an elaborate coat of arms. The door led to a brief corridor which was very dark since the entrance to the box proper was hung with heavy curtains. He stopped for a moment in the velvety darkness. His hand pushed up her chin and a voice said "Courage!" And then a mouth touched hers, very lightly. Chloe gasped. There was a brief instant of silence and then she heard Will's voice again, sounding rather surprised. "Let's try that again," he said, and she felt rather than saw his head descend. His lips touched hers and then she jumped as his tongue smoothly slid into her mouth. Chloe jerked her head back.

"No, don't," Will said rather thickly, dropping his arms around her back and pulling her against his chest. This time his lips were forceful, demanding, and she opened her lips as if she knew exactly what she was doing. Even through her whalebone stays Will felt the little shiver that traveled over Chloe's body. His breath was warm against her lips and then, he couldn't help it, he took her mouth again, unable to believe how a simple kiss affected him. His hands moved down her back. "My God," Will finally said roughly. He turned Miss van Stork sharply about and pulled open the curtains leading to the box, half-pushing her through them.

They emerged just as Act Two began. Will pulled Chloe down on a chair, allowing silent, smiling nods to serve as introductions for the moment. Chloe was surprised: Both Charlotte Daicheston and Sophie York were watching the stage intently, completely ignoring the rustling audience around them, even though many of those people were looking only at the two women. She would have thought people like them — people whose names were always in the gossip columns — went to the theater only to see and be seen. But Charlotte, in particular, was so absorbed that her knuckles were white on the box railing. Chloe turned her own attention to the stage. The king, or ex-king now, was hulking about his eldest daughter's house, demanding to keep a hundred armed men.

Charlotte felt a certain amount of sympathy for Goneril, the king's eldest daughter. Who would want to keep a bunch of feckless soldiers about? Look at the problem her father had with their hundred or so servants, and they weren't even armed. The footmen were always in brawls of some sort or another, and Campion had a separate butler's fund just for use in bailing the servants out of prison. Still, it was heartbreaking to watch the old king divested of all his trappings, all his kingliness . . .

For his part, Will couldn't keep his mind on the play at all. He felt absolutely astonished. Chloe was watching the play, her chest quietly rising and falling as if nothing at all had happened in the corridor. Whereas he was distinctly uncomfortable in his tight pantaloons. Even sitting with his legs crossed wasn't helping, given the proximity of Chloe's round arm. At least her dress didn't cover every single inch of her body. He looked speculatively at the part of her arm that was visible. Her skin was a flat, creamy white, and her wrist so delicate that he felt as if it might snap at any moment. He shifted his legs again. This was not the right thing to be dwelling on at the moment.

By the time intermission finally came around, Alex, for one, was thoroughly bored. Shakespeare was one thing. For God's sake, they had acted *King Lear* themselves when he was a schoolboy at Eton. But this wasn't *King Lear.* This was a stupid, adulterated muck-up. He couldn't believe his own eyes when the Fool started dancing an Irish jig. It was clear already that this Cordelia was not going to die, not if the theater manager had anything to do with it — and he already had had entirely too much to do with the whole play. Who were these new characters, for example? And some had definitely disappeared. He knew damned well that Gloucester used to have a bastard son, because that was the role *he* played at school! He felt nothing but relief when the curtain finally fell on the end of the third act.

Without conscious thought Alex smilingly raised Daphne from her seat and suggested a stroll in the corridor. Daphne showed no sign of surprise when they headed directly for the stairs leading to the next level of boxes.

"I would be happy to meet Lady Charlotte again," she finally said, tired of walking next to a silent companion. Now they were not being watched by the entire audience, the earl seemed to feel no need to speak to her at all.

Alex came to a halt. "Am I so obvious?" he said with a charming, ironic smile.

"*Oui*," said Daphne. "You do not hide your feelings so well. But then, that is not an English trait," she said meditatively.

Alex began walking again, albeit more slowly. "And Lady Charlotte?" he asked.

"Well," Daphne gave a very Gallic, dismissive shrug. "She too has no ability to disguise herself."

They arrived at the Brandenburg box, only to find that the hallway outside was filled with men trying to jostle themselves into a position to get through the door to the box. A little hush fell when Alex and Daphne appeared, however, and as if by magic the gentlemen pulled back slightly. Alex walked gently through the crowd. The footman guarding the door doffed his hat and Alex and Daphne disappeared through the door, pulling it decisively closed behind them.

They emerged into the glare of the theater slightly blind after the silky darkness of the corridor. The marquess — or marquis, to use the preferred spelling — of Brandenburg turned around sharply. He had distinctly told Jones not to allow any more men into the box. There were already more than enough young bucks in here, breathing down his daughter's low dress. He groaned inwardly when he saw who had breeched the footman's defenses. Lord! This would make Eloise breathe fire.

But the Earl of Sheffield and Downes was

bowing pleasantly enough and introducing the lovely Frenchwoman who accompanied him. The marquis's eyes brightened. He had a distinct tenderness for all things French and this young lady, he saw at a glance, was as distinguished as his own wife and far more beautiful. So Alex walked forward without Daphne, who was laughing kindly at the marquis's rather worn jokes. It was pleasant to hear her own language at least. People had no idea how difficult it was to set up a flirtation in a foreign tongue, especially one as graceless and unnuanced as English.

As Alex slipped between chairs there was a sudden flurry at the front of the box. Sophie York rose with a twirl of flimsy skirts, laughing up at the four men surrounding her, each of whom had attempted to help her stand.

"Now!" she said gaily. "We are going to take some air. You" — she emphasized her choices with a tiny rap of her closed fan — "you, and you. Will you accompany me?"

The three beaux she had chosen stumbled over themselves to clear a path through the Heppleworth chairs scattered around the box. As Sophie passed Alex she raised her head, nodding a greeting.

"My lord," she said demurely. He could swear that the small smile trembling on her lips was a conspiratorial one. An answering gleam lit his eyes. Sophie continued out of the box, a little startled despite herself at Alex's sensual appeal.

231

Charlotte *was* lucky, she thought almost wistfully. Then she emerged from the corridor, causing something of a riot, and all thought of Charlotte flew from her mind.

With one eye Alex noted with interest that Will was talking quietly to the young woman sitting beside him rather than hanging over Charlotte's bosom. He cast a minatory glance at the young bravo who had his hand on the back of the chair Sophie had just vacated, about to sit down, and the man snatched his hand back as if the chair burned, sinking his red ears into a high starched collar. Alex smiled at him kindly and sat down himself. For a moment Charlotte didn't turn her head. She knew, of course, that he was there. She knew the minute he entered the box.

Alex stretched out his long legs, ignoring the loud reaction of those theater patrons who had not left their seats, hoping to see precisely something like this. Lady Charlotte Daicheston and the Earl of Sheffield and Downes, seated side by side! Sarah Prestlefield, who had just entered the Brandenburg box to greet her dear friend Eloise, felt a glow of satisfaction. This was such an interesting tangle. The only shame, thought her scandal-loving soul, was that Charlotte's parents weren't at the theater. She would love to see the so-calm Adelaide put out by her daughter's obvious penchant for the Ineligible Earl, as everyone was calling him.

Finally Charlotte could not pretend to be listening intently to the flimflam of the young man on her right any longer. She turned to Alex, an involuntary smile lighting her eyes.

"My lord."

"Lady Charlotte."

There was a small pause. Alex wanted, very badly, to lean over and kiss Charlotte's neck. Then he would pull her to her feet, walk to his carriage, and rip that bit of muslin she called a dress right off her. His eyes darkened and he felt himself growing hard. Damnation.

"What do you think of the play?" he asked, nodding toward the now empty stage.

Charlotte considered his question. "I liked the first two acts very much, but the third act was flimsy. . . . Would a mad king really wander about the moors with only his Fool? And why did that monkey suddenly appear?"

"Yes, the monkey." Alex scowled. "Didn't you read Shakespeare at school?" he asked.

"Of course. But there were many plays they wouldn't allow us to read, and then there were always blacked-out parts in the plays we were allowed to read."

"Blacked-out parts? What about this one?"

"We didn't get to read *Lear* at all. Although I'm not sure why. It seems lighthearted enough, too light."

"Lighthearted! The third act is supposed to be bitter . . . terrifying. Do you remember when the king sang a little jig about being mad as the wind and the snow?"

"I didn't like it."

"Those lines are supposed to be howled, not sung — brilliant lines, spoken by a man who is howling mad: mad as the wind and the snow."

Charlotte considered this in silence. "The verse too . . . it hops and leaps," she said. "For instance, the king's speech about old age was brilliant, but then that man, what is his name? Reginald — he seems to be speaking prose, not verse."

Alex shuddered. "That's because Reginald is an adornment that this ass of a stage manager decided to give to Shakespeare's play. There's no Reginald in the original."

"How lucky you are," Charlotte said regretfully. "We were so shortchanged at school."

"Well, couldn't you read the plays now?" Alex could never figure out what gently bred ladies *did* all day long. Men took care of investments and met their estate managers and gave speeches in Parliament, as well as boxing, gambling, and wenching. But what did women do? He remembered his mother counting the linen and carrying around food to the poor, but that was it.

"Oh, no," Charlotte replied absently. "I work in the mornings and I never seem to have time for reading these days."

"You *work?*"

Charlotte caught herself. She never talked with men about painting; they immediately fancied her as a watercolorist, painting sweet little wreaths of flowers onto paper handbags.

Charlotte looked up into Alex's face, a hint of

a smile glimmering in her eyes. "Do you know that they wouldn't even let us read all of *Romeo and Juliet?*"

Alex cast his mind back. They hadn't acted the play at school; he couldn't think of anything off-hand that might need censoring.

Charlotte continued. "My friend Julia Brentorton — she's now married and lives abroad — figured out that they excised precisely ten lines, all from Juliet's epithalamium, you know, her soliloquy before Romeo climbs up the rope ladder to her window."

"Of course!" Alex said, startled. "For he shall lie upon me like snow on a raven's back, like day on night . . ."

Charlotte colored. She would look like snow if she lay on top of Alex's chest; his skin was the color of dark honey. She jerked her thoughts away.

Alex was more interested in Charlotte's mention of work. "What kind of work?" he asked bluntly.

Luckily at that moment Sophie reappeared, followed by a flock of admirers.

"Charlotte, dearest," she said in her half-laughing, mischievous tone that drove all the men behind her mad with desire, "this play is simply not Shakespeare, is it? But Lord Winkle has a delightful suggestion . . . that we eschew the second half and go to Vauxhall instead."

"Oh," Charlotte said rather stupidly, her eyes instinctively meeting Alex's. What she met there made her feel feverish. She knew without question that her mother would forbid an excursion to Vauxhall in company with Alexander Foakes. Vauxhall had far too many dimly lit pathways and shadowy arbors.

"What does your mother say?" she finally asked, looking up at Sophie.

"She doesn't like it, but she has agreed." Sophie bent over, ringlets brushing Alex's cheek. "I think my father fancies that he has an *amour* with Miss Boch," she said softly, "and my mother would like to leave the theater."

Charlotte rose immediately. She felt as if she had been ridiculously naive before the conversation with her mother. It would never have occurred to her that the marquis might try to fix an interest with a young lady, even if she were French. She never would have given a second thought to a lively conversation between them, or guessed that the marchioness might dislike watching her husband laugh genially at Daphne's French witticisms.

Will looked questioningly at Chloe van Stork, who had watched all the traipsing around the box with rather wide eyes. She looked at him quickly and then down at her hands. Will thought he would rather like to lure Chloe into a dark avenue and kiss her again. He thought of her soft lips under his.

"Shall we join them?" he asked, his tone smooth as honey.

"Vauxhall," Chloe said. "My mother would not like it."

But when Chloe appeared at the van Stork's box, flanked by her huge blond cavalier, her mother surprised herself by nodding agreeably. Katryn cast a loving look at her serious daughter. There was pink in Chloe's cheeks and her eyes were shining. She had watched Chloe in the Brandenburg box and felt a little guilty. Chloe looked like a crow, surrounded by gaily fluttering gowns. Perhaps she was too prudish in her notions of dress. She certainly didn't want Chloe to marry one of the solid, plump Dutchmen who thronged into her husband's workrooms. While this Baron Holland was undoubtedly a fortune-hunter, her shrewd assessment was that he was also an honorable man. *And* she was starting to think that he and her daughter might even make a genuine marriage.

"Will you be properly chaperoned?"

Will explained that the Marquis and Marchioness of Brandenburg would accompany the party.

"Yes, go, daughter," she said, and nodded at the Baron. He bowed politely to Chloe's abstracted father. Her father was properly dressed, an elegant evening coat straining across his plump stomach, but he looked distracted, as if he was thinking of his work.

"Ah, humph," her father said in farewell. A small smile lit Chloe's eyes and she dropped a kiss on his bald head.

She put her hand on Baron Holland's arm, ignoring the secret tingle that she felt at his touch.

She felt as if she were in some kind of dream. What was she, plain Chloe van Stork, doing going to Vauxhall with Charlotte Daicheston? In the last months the gossip columns had anxiously chronicled every move Lady Charlotte made. She knew with absolute certainty that her own name would appear in the *Tatler* tomorrow morning. Chloe shivered a bit with excitement and looked up at Will Holland.

His bright blue eyes looked almost black . . . it must be the lighting in the corridor, Chloe thought. He drew her quickly down the stairs and toward the carriages. Finally she was almost running to keep up.

"Sir," she gasped, pulling him back slightly.

Will turned his head, completely surprised. He was feverishly thinking of getting Chloe into the carriage and kissing her again; he didn't remember ever being so obsessed that he forgot the normal social graces.

"I apologize," he said. And then it just came out of his mouth: "I wanted to kiss you again, in my carriage."

Chloe's eyes widened. She knew that Will Holland was only courting her for her money. Why on earth was he so eager to kiss her? It must be part of his courtship routine. Will felt her infinitesimal withdrawal and cursed inside. He tucked her hand back into the crook of his arm.

"I'll tell you what," he said firmly. "We will amble toward the carriages and I won't touch a hair of your head: how's that?" He turned rather anxiously to look down into her blue eyes.

But she surprised him again. Chloe's eyes were dancing, unmistakably enjoying his discomfort.

"I should enjoy that," she replied.

Will looked ahead again. Enjoy what? What would she enjoy? Ambling? Or him not touching her? He drew her hand closer to his side and consciously controlled his walk. Chloe smiled to herself. They proceeded toward the carriages at a snail's pace.

Chapter 10

By the time all the carriages met at Vauxhall and the group had reassembled and found each other, they were around twenty persons. Charlotte felt a moment of annoyance. She hated large parties where you never got to talk to anyone seriously, and you spent all your time shouting over someone's shoulder. Besides, Alex was behaving in a most offhand manner, strolling on ahead with a group of men. The men had all lit cigarillos and were talking loudly of a boxing match scheduled for the coming week. She found herself walking next to Chloe van Stork, walking toward the brightly lit pavilion. Charlotte studied Chloe's profile again and felt a quickening of interest. Yes: This was the person she wanted to paint next. Chloe was very beautiful, even though she didn't know it, but more interesting was the painfully honest look she had. As if she would always blurt out the truth and would never gain the smooth social apparatus that Sophie was probably born with and which she herself had painfully acquired in the last three years.

"Miss van Stork," she said.

"Yes, my lady," Chloe replied.

Oh, Lord, Charlotte thought. "Please do call me Charlotte," she said. "Why don't we sit over here?" She steered Chloe toward a large table, away from the smaller table where a group of beaux were already clustered, looking expectantly at Charlotte.

Chloe sat down, wondering where in the world Will had gone. He had behaved (to her secret disappointment) like a consummate gentleman in the carriage, and then she seemed to lose him on the walk. The party itself was also unexceptionally proper. The marquis appeared to be a little drunk to her inexperienced eye, and the marchioness frigid with annoyance, but there was nothing remarkable in that. She had noticed that *ton* marriages seemed invariably strained. Probably, she thought, it was all that alcohol they drank. It frizzled your brain, her mother said.

Lady Charlotte seemed to be staring at her in a very peculiar way. Probably she was entranced by the novel idea of sitting with a bourgeois cit. Chloe raised her stubborn little chin.

"Why are you regarding me so . . . intently, Lady Charlotte?"

Charlotte's face glowed. "That's it! That's exactly the look I want!"

Chloe looked confused. The woman must be mad as a hatter. How odd that the papers hadn't mentioned it.

"No, no," Charlotte said hastily. "I'm not making any sense, am I? I paint, you see. I've just started painting people — well, I have painted Sophie, that's all. And I'd like to paint you." She paused. Chloe van Stork was looking at her doubtfully.

Charlotte gave her a deliberately charming smile. Unlike Will, Chloe didn't unbend an inch. Charlotte leaned across the table. "I don't dabble with paints." She broke off. "May I call you Chloe?"

Chloe nodded silently.

"I really paint. And I work at it like the devil," she said frankly. "I'd like to paint your portrait, in profile I think. Yes, that would be best." Charlotte narrowed her eyes, unconsciously chewing on her lower lip. "Do you think that you could possibly sit for me? A portrait takes a long time, about six weeks, but I wouldn't need you every day. I work from about eight in the morning to one; any time you could give me would be wonderful."

Chloe was staggered. Everyone knew that society belles didn't do a single thing all day long. They sat around and counted their pearls. She gulped rather gracelessly, staring at the exquisitely chic woman on the other side of the table. *She* worked like the devil at painting?

"I suppose so," she finally replied, hesitating. "I would have to ask my mama."

"Of course. Perhaps she would like to accompany you? She probably wouldn't want to just sit in my studio, but I know that my mama would much enjoy some company," Charlotte said, recklessly ignoring the duchess's elaborately planned mornings.

Chloe tried to imagine her mother having a leisurely tea with the Duchess of Calverstill and totally failed.

"I doubt it," she answered uncertainly. "She is frightfully busy, most of the time." Then she could have bitten her tongue off with embarrassment. Charlotte's mother probably lay about on a daybed most of the day. Charlotte might think she was being critical.

But an insult had never occurred to Charlotte, who had been trained to run a large household and knew just what an enormous amount of work it was. "Yes," she said absently. She was still staring at Chloe's face. She reached across the table and tucked a strand of hair behind her ear. Chloe's maid had pulled her hair ruthlessly into a tight circle of braids, but small ringlets were starting to fall out.

From across the large vine-hung arbor scattered with tables Will saw Charlotte tuck up Chloe's hair and he frowned. She wasn't planning to transform Chloe, was she? The way she herself changed? He didn't like it. Chloe was Chloe, and he didn't want to see her in one of those flimsy French gowns, leaving all the men free to gape at her bosom. He walked over and loomed behind Chloe's chair, frowning at Charlotte.

"Miss van Stork," he said with deliberate formality. "Would you like to join me for a stroll?

We might look at the mechanical train."

Chloe sat perfectly still for a second. It really was ridiculous, the way her heart leaped into her throat when she heard his voice. He was a fortune-hunter, nothing more. She had read all about his pursuit of Lady Charlotte, for example.

"All right," Chloe said coolly. She nodded at Charlotte, giving her a rather sweet smile, and walked off with Will. Charlotte watched them go, smiling slightly. She had no delusions about how long Will would be a single man. He was well and truly caught, she thought. She shrugged a bit and met the brown eyes of the young man seated to her right.

"Lady Charlotte," he said. "Would you like to take a walk with me?"

Charlotte felt truly annoyed. She disliked walking into shadowed passageways with strange young men. In her experience they invariably tried to kiss you, certain that their masterful lips would conquer all resistance. Vauxhall was surrounded by pleasure gardens and ivy-hung walks that were only dimly illuminated at night by Chinese lanterns and strings of lights. Her eyes met Sophie's and Sophie twinkled at her sympathetically. She herself was busy fending off three men with a similar mission. Meanwhile the marquis had managed to talk Daphne Boch into going to see the fireworks, and the marchioness was staring straight ahead, a pinched look about her mouth. Charlotte wanted to go home. Alex was nowhere to be seen, and what was she doing with him anyway? Not that she *was* with him, considering that he sauntered off the moment they arrived. She felt cross, humiliated and rather tired.

The young brown-eyed gallant was standing next to her, politely holding out his arm. She looked up at him appealingly. "My lord, I find that I am quite exhausted. Would you be so kind as to escort me back to my home?"

Happily enough, the Honorable Peter Dewland evidenced no sign of libidinous fever at the idea of being alone in a carriage with Charlotte Daicheston. He simply nodded. Charlotte made her apologies to the tight-lipped marchioness. Sophie had disappeared into the flower-scented night, escorted by all three bravos. Alex was nowhere. Charlotte put her fingers lightly on Peter's arm and they walked off toward the carriages.

They were about halfway to the carriage park when a particularly lovely burst of fireworks lit up the sky. Charlotte had been so busy trying to pick her way over the ill-lit brick walks without stubbing her toes that she hadn't paid much attention. But now Peter Dewland said in a rather boyish and charming way, "I say, Lady Charlotte! Just look at that!"

A scarlet serpent curled around a large tiger lily, flaming for a moment and falling into broken pieces.

"Oh, how lovely," she said.

"My brother would love this," Peter said, still

watching sparkling fragments crumbling into blackness.

"Why didn't he join us?" Charlotte asked. "Is he too young?"

Peter colored and looked down at his companion, worried that he was boring her. But she looked genuinely interested.

"Quill is my older brother — he hurt his leg in a riding accident," he said. "He has to stay in bed all the time now, unless one of the footmen carries him outside. But it hurts quite a lot to be moved and so . . ." his voice trailed off.

"Oh, dear," Charlotte said in a small voice. Here she was, fussing over a silly thing like her ineligible beau deserting her, and this boy's brother was permanently bedridden. "You know, you can buy some fireworks here. You could buy them and set them off in your back garden, and then if your brother could come to the window, he could see them as well."

"Oh, Lady Charlotte, that's a lovely idea," Peter exclaimed. "Do you know where the fireworks are sold?"

Charlotte nodded back toward the huge, lit-up pavilion they had walked away from. "I believe they are back there."

Peter hesitated and then turned to go. "I will buy some tomorrow, Lady Charlotte, and I shall tell my brother that it was your suggestion."

Charlotte laid a hand on his arm. "Oh, no! We have to do it tonight, don't you think? And mightn't I help with the fireworks?" A sudden

246

thought struck her. "I'm not sure that the marchioness would wish to join us, however." She could not accompany any man to his house without a chaperone, no matter how good the cause.

"My mother," Peter said with his appealing near stammer. "My mother would be happy to chaperone us, I feel sure. I believe she knows your mother quite well."

Charlotte took this with a grain of salt. It was amazing how many members of the *ton* said they knew her mother quite well; Adelaide had never been much good at repulsing people. Still . . . Charlotte was struck with the determination to set off fireworks for Peter's injured brother.

"Let's go!" she said gaily. They started back towards the lit pavilion, walking rather less carefully. A slight breeze set Charlotte's black ribbons dancing around her slender white dress. Alex, who was standing at the edge of the pavilion, staring out in utter fury, recognized the gown in an instant. His eyes narrowed, even as he felt a flash of happiness in his belly. God almighty, this woman would probably drive him mad. Who was she with, out there in the dark, anyway? The marchioness had told him that Charlotte had returned home; why was she coming back? He had pretended to himself that he was angry because she had left the party without saying good-bye to all her friends. Inside he knew that he was furious because she didn't bother to say farewell to him. He had gone to order a banquet of delicate sandwiches to be brought to their table, only to return to find his girl (as he invariably thought of her in the last week) gone, and all the rest of them wandering around in the dark somewhere. Only the grim-faced marchioness was left, staring into the darkness. He quickly found her a rum punch and was contemplating murder when he saw Charlotte's billowing ribbons returning to the pavilion.

And now . . . he was quite happy and didn't bother to analyze his change in mood. Alex strode out in Charlotte's direction. My God, it really was dark out here. No wonder there were so many thefts and rapes and what have you at Vauxhall. He felt a sudden flash of alarm and quickened his stride. He had almost reached Charlotte and the young gentleman accompanying her. One look at Peter, even in the dim light, reassured him. *This* one wasn't going to pull any fancy tricks in the dark. Alex pulled to the side, pressing into the hedge. Charlotte and her escort walked on, not even noticing him. Alex waited until Charlotte was almost past him and then he reached out and caught one of her floating black ribbons, pulling it sharply back toward him.

She swung about fiercely, jerking the ribbon out of his hand. Her eyes flashed at him for an instant until she recognized him, and then some other emotion touched her eyes . . . he wasn't sure what. He caught another ribbon.

"Sir," said the young gallant in a rather

strained manner. "The lady would prefer that you not touch her garments."

"Do you, Charlotte?" Alex said, gently pulling the ribbon towards him. Charlotte perforce walked a step closer to him. "Do you prefer that I don't touch your . . . garments?"

Charlotte raised her chin, meeting his eyes. "Certainly, my lord. I am not certain but that you have damaged my gown already."

Alex's eyes smoldered down at her. He tugged a bit more on her ribbon, and Charlotte stepped forward again. There was only a hairbreadth between them now. Peter, standing behind Charlotte, couldn't see Alex's hands, so he let them slide from the ribbon and spread them wide on her front, his fingers fitting snugly under the rise of her breasts. Charlotte drew in her breath, sharply.

"I'm just checking for damage," he said with a lopsided grin.

Charlotte couldn't think of anything to say. "We're going to buy fireworks," she finally said, retreating a step. "Lord Dewland's brother is unable to leave his bed and we thought to buy some fireworks and set them off in his backyard."

Alex's eyes shifted from Charlotte's face to that of Peter Dewland, who was standing off to the side, unsure what to make of the earl's antics.

Suddenly Peter's face looked familiar. "Is your brother Quill?" Alex demanded.

Peter nodded.

"What a fool I am," Alex said, looking

thunderstruck. "I've known Quill for years," he explained to Charlotte. "We were at school together. I was very sorry to hear of his accident."

Peter looked at the earl doubtfully but Alex continued, his tone brisk.

"Right you are!" Alex said, turning Charlotte around. "I think I know exactly where to buy fireworks."

By a half an hour later, Alex had rounded up those fragments of the party that were round-upable. Will seemed to have taken Miss van Stork home, leaving a message for Charlotte that Chloe would wait on her at nine o'clock in the morning. Alex heard that in silence. Before the evening was over he intended to know exactly what his beloved planned to do with a city miss at that unfashionable hour in the morning. His two French friends had also gone home, Daphne desperate to get away from the marquis's increasingly familiar commentary. And after hearing their plans and receiving Peter's assurances that his mother would act as chaperone, the marchioness bundled her sodden husband into a carriage and took him home. A few gallants sniffed at the idea of pleasing an invalid and wandered off into dark pathways to find a willing courtesan, of whom there were many at Vauxhall. So Sophie and Charlotte, with a reduced contingent of about five men, not including Alex and Peter Dewland, set off, bringing with them a perfectly marvelous collection of fireworks.

When Alex found that the only fireworks officially sold were simple rockets, he threw his peership around — backed by a noble number of coins — and ended up with one Mr. Glister, a fireworks director at Vauxhall, and a few of his "spessial works," as he called them. "I'd as lief do it myself," Mr. Glister kept explaining anxiously, "you might as well take a finger off as look at these. They'll take the nose right off your face."

It was only when the carriages pulled up in front of Peter's darkened house that Charlotte felt a twinge of anxiety. She had been relieved to find that Peter lived in a respectable area, two houses down from her great-aunt Margaret, as a matter of fact. But when Peter ushered them in his mother greeted them cheerfully; it seemed that she and her husband, a viscount, were having a game of chess in the library, and had sent most of the servants to bed. And Charlotte did fancy she had seen Viscountess Dewland with her mother, so that was all right.

Mr. Glister disappeared into the backyard to set up his "spessial works," and Charlotte happily accepted the glass of champagne someone put in her hand. Ever since that disastrous night three years ago, she hardly drank any alcohol. It hadn't taken long for her to figure out that the lemonade she and Julia drank so enthusiastically had been spiked with spirits. But now . . . She measured Alex's large body, leaning carelessly against the mantelpiece. Alex was listening to Peter's father prose on about the extraordinary efforts of Bow Street Runners to catch tollhouse thieves. Maybe it was the champagne. Little fingers of excitement kept darting up her spine. She was terribly glad that she hadn't gone home. And when Alex looked up and met her eyes she couldn't stop herself from giving him an entirely intimate, shameless smile. Alex's eyebrows flew up and he pushed himself into an upright position.

Viscount Dewland kept babbling on about the Runners. Alex let his eyes range suggestively over his beloved's face. Her glorious mop of curls was even more disheveled than usual, the effect of wind rather than art. She was heartbreakingly beautiful, with her arching eyebrows and huge green eyes. He felt himself hardening in a way that was simply not acceptable, given the skintight pantaloons that passed as fashionable evening wear. Still . . . his eyes drifted lower to her soft breasts, rising out of that white dress as if they were begging for kisses. God! This would never do. He politely disengaged himself from Viscount Dewland and walked over to Charlotte. Her own eyes hadn't strayed below his chest, although he damn well wanted them to. On the way he picked up another glass of champagne. Alex stood a whisper's breath away from her, his eyes glinting a dangerous, sensual message. Charlotte felt a familiar heat creep up from her knees. Why did he do this to her? She only had to be next to him and she wanted to do *that* again.

"Lady Charlotte," he said gravely. "Shall we

check how the redoubtable Mr. Glister is doing in the garden?"

She tensed. It was a moment of decision: Should she go into the gardens with him? She looked about rather wildly, but no one seemed to be paying any attention. Then she caught Sophie's eye and Sophie winked deliberately.

"Oh, Charlotte," she called across the room, her clear voice arching over the chatter. "Don't you think someone should venture out and see what is happening? We cannot intrude on Lady Dewland's hospitality too long."

Alex offered Charlotte his arm. Still she hesitated. What was he going to *do* out there in the dark? Hadn't she sworn to herself that she wouldn't go outdoors alone with him again? She did want his kisses, the heavy, drugging feeling of desire that swept over her when his lips met hers. But she didn't want to . . .

"It's a beautiful night," she said, smiling back at Sophie. "Why don't we all go into the garden and see if Mr. Glister could use some help?"

Alex held out his arm. "Lady Charlotte?" And then, quietly, "Coward!"

Charlotte gasped, and looked up at him. His eyes were dark with desire but there was an unspoken smile there as well.

She grinned back, feeling quite daring. "Sir, your penchant for the outdoors makes me justly wary."

Alex responded to the grin, not to the words. What on earth was she talking about? So he

253

kissed her on a picnic — well, not that it mattered. She was absolutely right; his fingers were itching to push down her gown and pull a rosy nipple into his mouth.

"Come on," he said almost roughly. They walked out into the night. The Dewlands' town house had a large formal garden stretching behind it. Charlotte felt a little ashamed of her doubts about Peter. The Dewlands were clearly an old and well-established branch of the nobility. Her sister Violetta was so nimble about things like this. She could immediately place any member of the *ton,* and discuss his or her antecedents and claims to nobility . . . but Charlotte had never bothered to learn. She spent no time reading *Burke's Peerage.* How could she? It was extremely difficult as it was to meld the life of a marriageable young woman with that of a part-time painter. Her mother kept warning her that she would have trouble once she was married. "How will you know how to organize a party going in to dine?" she had asked. Charlotte had thought briefly of the boring shuffling and re-shuffling that prefaced a dinner party, especially when a sticky question of precedence came up. To be honest, the question of marriage had seemed so remote, she would never be organizing her own dinner parties, so why worry?

The whole party flocked out of the large double doors leading from the drawing room to the garden. Alex handed Charlotte the glass of champagne he carried in his hand. Charlotte heard Sophie squeal with delight as the smell of roses drifted over the garden, her three gallants jostling in an attempt to be the first to pick her a perfect rose. Alex led Charlotte to a perfectly unexceptional bench, in clear view of Lady Dewland. She felt a tiny pulse of disappointment. Didn't he want to pull her off into the darker paths leading to the back of the garden? *Not* that she would have permitted such a thing, of course. She sipped her champagne and then bent her head back, feeling soft curls brush the back of her neck. It was now so late that it was possible to see a few stars in the sky, even given London's ever-present haziness.

"Did you read the piece in the *Gazette* about coal dust?" she asked suddenly. "The writer argued that coal fires are not only obscuring the air, but actually making people ill, especially babies."

Alex looked down at her curiously. He hadn't thought that society belles read anything but the gossip pages.

"I thought he argued the case too strongly," he said. "There's no scientific evidence linking coal dust and mortality. I should think that many of those babies die of malnutrition."

"Why do they cough so much then?"

"They could have colds . . . pneumonia. I thought his point was interesting, but without better information we could not ban coal fires as he proposed."

"But, Alex," Charlotte protested, not even realizing that she used his first name, "he said that autopsies have found babies whose lungs are *black* inside!"

"Well, then why are most of those babies only found among the poor?" Alex rebutted. "They could have died from anything!"

"You know as well as I do that only the children of the very poor are autopsied." Charlotte was keeping a tight rein on her temper. She drank some more champagne.

"Yes, but I have seen very few babies among my friends who have a constant cough, as he was describing. And if I had," Alex said, "I would take Pippa to the country immediately."

"That's just it," Charlotte said patiently. "Children of nobility spend most of the year on country estates. We're only in London for the season — half the year at the most. Whereas poor children breathe this air all the time." She waved her hand at the sky. "I spend a lot of time thinking about light," she said, "and you have no idea how different it is here than in the country. It's hardly even *light* in the city." They lapsed into silence.

Alex looked down at Charlotte with a new respect. She had just argued him into a standstill. A small frown creased his forehead. Why did she spend a lot of time thinking about light?

He'd bet she wasn't thinking about light at the moment. Her head was thrown back, exposing a lovely white column of neck, and she had her eyes closed. Just so would she look when she rode on top of him, her curls tossed back in abandon.

"What are you thinking?" he said, his voice roughened by that thought. He trailed a finger down her forehead, over her small straight nose and stopped at her lips.

Charlotte opened her eyes. "The smell of roses," she said. "They smell so warm. Why should a smell be hot or cold? But they smell warm."

Alex thought about this for a minute. "I suppose," he said rather doubtfully. "Hot chocolate smells warm."

Charlotte laughed, a lovely, joyful sound, he thought. "That's not it! I was thinking of flowers. Freesias smell cold, for example."

"Hmmm." Alex trailed his finger over her chin and down to her collarbones. He leaned closer and took a loud sniff. "You smell . . ." he paused provocatively. She giggled. He was so close that she could feel his warm breath on her cheek. "You smell warm," he said finally. "Very warm. Also faintly like orange blossoms."

"Very clever," Charlotte said approvingly.

"I met a girl once, in a garden, who smelled like lavender, and so far that has been my favorite scent." He leaned so close that his lips were almost touching hers. Then he gave another exaggerated sniff. She giggled again. "I think . . ." His lips were touching hers now, whisper-soft. "I think that orange blossoms are my new preference."

Charlotte was trembling slightly. But Alex drew back. He couldn't kiss her here, in full view of Viscountess Dewland, not to mention Sophie's band of gallants. In the moonlight his eyes were black as jet, blacker than night, Charlotte thought. She felt like a hypnotized rabbit, unable to pull her eyes away from his. Alex stood up and pulled her to her feet. He seemed to feel no such weakness, she thought with a faint pulse of humiliation.

"Let's check how Mr. Glister is doing with the fireworks, shall we? Your mother will be worrying about you soon."

Mr. Glister had set up camp at the bottom of the garden. "So as I won't show a burned patch," he earnestly explained. "Because these here gardens are very nice, very nice indeed, and I wouldn't want to show them any indig— any indignity, no."

The footman standing behind him rolled his eyes. Charlotte suppressed a smile. Alex had taken her hand as if it were the most natural thing in the world, and while he talked to Mr. Glister about the technical problems of setting up large fireworks without a platform, Charlotte simply relaxed and thought about her hand in his. His hand was so large. Her fingers were trembling and she was afraid he might notice, so she rubbed her thumb against the base of his wrist. He responded in a most gratifying way, instantly tightening his grip even though his voice never faltered speaking to Mr. Glister. Charlotte, on the other hand, was unable to think of anything but his fingers, which had started a slow, sensual massage of her hand. She tried to look pleasantly interested in the fireworks, although in fact she didn't hear a word Mr. Glister said.

Finally Mr. Glister said, "Aye, sir, aye, it'll be just a wee bit of time now. Why don't you tell all them up at the house to look out of their windows. And the wee sick bairn as well."

Alex tucked Charlotte's arm into his and smilingly turned her back toward the house. This was no better, Charlotte thought frantically. He was holding her so tightly that she could feel the warmth of his long body walking next to hers. She felt as if her body were on fire. How was she going to disguise this? If he guessed, he would think she was a wanton tart. Ladies don't feel like this, she knew that for certain. Her mother was not talking about the kind of raging desire Charlotte felt when she mentioned marital pleasure.

Suddenly Alex paused. They were sheltered from sight, standing in a line of apple and plum trees leading to the front gardens. He dropped her arm and simply stood next to her.

"Do you know," he said conversationally, "I don't think I can go back out there in the light for a few minutes?"

Charlotte looked up at him, her eyes confused.

"Why ever not?" Instinctively she swayed a little closer to him. He swiftly grabbed her wrists and pushed her back, giving a bark of laughter. Charlotte felt consumed by embarrassment. He thought she was a trollop. She swallowed hard.

Alex looked at her downcast head and cursed silently. Then he reached out and pulled her into his arms. Why not? It's what he had wanted to do ever since he saw Charlotte that evening. Her soft body melted into his. He could feel every curve, from the luscious weight of her breasts pressing against his chest to the slim flatness of her waist. God. This was doing nothing for his ability to rejoin the party.

"Charlotte," he whispered into her small ear. She was still holding her head down, but she must be able to feel his body as clearly as he felt hers. But did she know what she felt?

His tongue ran around the delicate pink whirl of her ear and her whole body trembled in response. Alex let his hands slide down her back.

"Charlotte," he said again, lingeringly. "Do you know what you are doing to me? I feel like some kind of satyr from a classical play — the kind of play they never let you read in school." His hands had reached that delicious spot in her back where her bottom swelled gently. "There was a good reason for not reading those plays too. Satyrs are hairy, lusty beasts, after all, and there's no telling what young women might think, reading about them." He couldn't help it; he pulled her against his body again. "They might even run into the woods looking for them. . . ." His tongue traced a burning path down her neck. "Oh, God!" he said aloud, putting her away from him.

Charlotte looked up, totally bewildered. His eyes were black as ebony as he stood back, running his hand through his hair. In the moonlight the silver gleamed coldly. Charlotte reached up and touched a strand.

"Has your hair always been this color?" she asked.

"It turned this way when I was seventeen," Alex answered, staring down at Charlotte. Was she untouched by the desire he felt? He grabbed her wrists, roughly. "Don't . . . don't look at my hair, Charlotte."

She was looking at his hair because she felt too shy to meet his eyes. And when she did, what she saw there made her feel dizzy with excitement. Alex smiled a little, to himself. His girl wasn't unaffected, no. He was right about her. She would be wild in his bed and intelligent at his table. He couldn't do better for a wife. She wasn't at all like Maria, although . . . he looked closer. She did have a triangular face, as did Maria, and her lower lip was wide and generous, just like Maria's. But that means nothing, his mind hastily assured him. Hundreds of women have those features.

Now he had to calm them both down so that he could saunter out there under the lanterns and tell the party to expect fireworks. He moved farther back and leaned against a tree. He could tell she had no idea what was going on.

"My lord," she said tentatively.

Alex crushed a pulse of disappointment. What

had happened to "Alex"?

"Shall we join the others?"

He stayed perfectly still, leaning easily against the apple tree. "I can't," he said simply.

She looked at him, her eyes wild with speculation.

He sighed inwardly. For one thing, this meant she probably had no idea why he was an ineligible marriage partner. Her mother seemingly hadn't got around to explaining it to her yet. But he didn't want to think about that particular problem.

"Charlotte," he said, his voice velvety smooth and deep. "Come here."

She looked at him and did nothing.

"Charlotte."

She walked over and stood just before him. Deliberately he reached out and put his hands against her cheeks. Then he slowly allowed them to slide down her body, over the swelling mounds of her breasts, down to her slim waist, right down to her thighs . . . as far as he could go without stooping. She shivered and he saw her tongue nervously touch her lips, but she didn't move.

"Why did you do that?" she asked, finally.

"Because it was fair," he answered obscurely. "Now —" he took her hands in his and placed them on his cheeks. "You do the same."

Charlotte stared at him, her green eyes large. She won't do it, he thought. She's a gently bred lady, for God's sake. She's probably about to run back to the house screaming. But there was something scornful about his look that steeled Charlotte's backbone. Just as deliberately as he had, she drew her hands down over his cheeks. They were prickly with a growing beard, his face shadowed by small hairs. Her fingers drew slowly over the tiny hairs' sharp edges; she wondered what they would feel like against her lips. Watching her Alex felt himself growing even harder, if that was possible. *This* was a great idea, he thought, remaining absolutely still.

Charlotte's fingers trailed down, down the strong brown column of his neck, down over muscled shoulders and chest. Then she pulled her hands away.

"Oh, no," Alex said in a curiously deep voice, recapturing her hands and returning them to his chest. "You have to keep going."

Charlotte blushed. He kept his hands on her wrists, flattening her hands against him, and slowly, slowly drew them down his body. Charlotte felt herself flushing scarlet. Her heart was racing. When he reached his crotch, he stopped. Charlotte gasped. Under her right hand was a huge, swollen . . . it pulsed slightly against the palm of her hand. Alex looked down at her, his eyes an enigmatic black in the moonlight. She pulled her hands away from his, turning away. As she was about to run back to the house Alex grabbed her shoulders from the back, pulling her against his chest.

His lips were warm on the back of her neck. "You see," he said so softly that his breath hardly

263

lifted the tendrils of hair on her neck. "You are driving me stark-raving insane." He punctuated each word with a kiss. "I don't remember ever feeling this . . . mad."

Despite her embarrassment, Charlotte felt a little smile lurking at the edge of her lips. She relaxed against him. He crossed his arms over her chest and rested his chin on the top of her head.

"Alas," he said with mock seriousness. "Even this prudent embrace is not going to help me. Why don't you go warn the group that the fireworks will arrive soon? I shall make my way back to Mr. Glister and offer him some more help."

He didn't say it, but obviously if he stayed with Mr. Glister it provided an alibi for their time in the fruit arbor, Charlotte thought. Her heart felt curiously light. She skipped forward, out of his arms, and turned around. Alex looked like an enormous dark shadow, leaning against the tree. She took a step forward, leaned forward and pressed her lips against his.

"I knew that all those classical plays had much to offer," she said softly against his lips. "I could become quite interested in reading . . . about satyrs, for example." She turned in a flurry of black ribbons and half flew back to the lights of the house.

Alex cursed again, out loud this time. Damn but these pantaloons were uncomfortable! He grinned and strode back toward Mr. Glister. She was *his*, now. Tomorrow he would go to her father and tell him so.

Thirty minutes later Alex loomed up at Charlotte's left shoulder as glorious bursts of light cracked and scattered, drifting with the wind in drops of green and gold light. His hands rested lightly on her shoulders and he pulled her back against him. Charlotte snuggled there, feeling curiously content after all the fierce emotion of the past few hours. Up at the window a lean white face watched as a red poppy formed and seemed about to be eaten by a rearing stallion. Sophie, standing in the circle of her three gallants, peeked at Charlotte. She looked so happy, so glowing. Sophie hoped the viscountess didn't notice Alex's hands on Charlotte's shoulders.

For her part, Charlotte was content just to lean against Alex. She didn't give a thought to Viscountess Dewland, or the footmen, or anyone else who might see them. She had just discovered that her bottom was snug against the top of Alex's legs, and although there had been nothing disturbing there a minute ago, even as the poppy flew into a hundred brilliant scarlet sparks she felt . . . well, she felt. She grinned happily.

Chapter 11

The next morning Chloe van Stork sat up straight in bed at seven o'clock and rang her bell vigorously. Today she was going to begin sitting for her portrait! After her bath she looked dubiously at the row of drab gowns hanging in her wardrobe. Finally she chose a simple white morning dress. Probably it didn't matter anyway. Her school friend Sissy had had her portrait painted in costume, as Cleopatra. And when Chloe admired it Sissy told her that the costume didn't really exist, and her mama would never allow her to wear something like it until she was married. Chloe had stared at the gold snake curled around Sissy's waist, whose head ended somewhere just under Sissy's right breast and heartily agreed with Sissy's mama, although she would never have said so.

"Well, miss, so you will not be helping us finish the collar bands today?" her mother said ponderously. But Chloe could tell she was pleased. After all, why did Katryn send her daughter off to an enormously expensive school if she didn't want her to move in high circles? In fact, her mama was well near ecstatic, although she would never

266

exhibit such an extreme emotion in front of her husband, who emphatically disliked the idea of Chloe joining the aristocracy. But from the moment Katryn van Stork realized that their only daughter was going to be very pretty, if not beautiful, she had been planning and scheming for that very thing. So she beamed at her buttered muffin and kept her mouth shut.

Just then their terribly starchy footman entered the breakfast room and bowed. Mrs. van Stork jumped. He moved like a snake, this Peter.

"Flowers for Miss van Stork," Peter intoned.

Just as if he were announcing a funeral, Katryn thought crossly. Chloe's eyes widened. Peter was holding what appeared to be five or six bunches of violets, fresh with dew. They looked as if they had been picked no more than ten minutes before. Peter paced around the breakfast table while Chloe waited impatiently. He bowed again, at her chair, and she finally snatched them from his hands. Peter walked out, his eyes searching the ceiling for an answer to why he was working for a wealthy cit instead of a great lord. Because they pay more, he thought practically.

Chloe plucked the card from among the violets, her fingers trembling a little. Then she half laughed in surprise. They weren't from Will — or Baron Holland, she hastily corrected herself. Instead she was holding an elegantly printed card that read *Charlotte Daicheston* across the bottom. Written in handwriting that looked almost male was a note: *I am very much looking for-*

ward to our appointment. Do let me know if another time would be better for you. And it was signed *Charlotte,* in a sprawling, confident hand.

"Who is it from?" barked her father from his end of the table. "That jackanapes who ate here last evening?" He had missed all the implications of Baron Holland's brief attendance of Lady Charlotte at the theater, but he thought he knew the smell of a fortune-hunter when he saw one. Although he had to admit that the baron was a good deal more bearable than most of the dissolute, useless aristocrats he saw wandering down the Strand. He seemed to know *something* of commerce, for example, which is more than one could say of the majority of Tulips his daughter met.

"No, Papa," Chloe said, her eyes dancing. "It is a note from Lady Charlotte Daicheston."

"Humph," her father said. "That woman's got herself into the papers again."

"Oh? May I see, Papa? That is, if you are quite finished."

"Finished? I don't read the gossip pages, miss!" His family tactfully ignored the issue of how he knew about Charlotte Daicheston's presence in the papers as Chloe scanned the gossip pages.

"Oh, Mama," she gasped. "Apparently Charlotte and her friends arranged to have fireworks set off for a poor sick man last night, after we left Vauxhall." Chloe didn't even notice her use of Charlotte's first name, in her excitement. She

268

personages such as a real duchess. But Charlotte led her nimbly up the grand flight of stairs and off to the left.

"This is the morning room." Charlotte threw open a pair of delicate, tall doors. Chloe found herself on the threshold of a pale gold chamber, hung with chambray curtains that swayed in the light breeze. Sunshine was pouring in and the furniture was comfortable rather than elegant. Six or seven women, some clearly servants, were seated around a large table sewing. Charlotte's mother rose and moved toward them. She was a surprisingly tall woman with a very sweet smile, who took Chloe's hand and asked about her parents. Then she begged them to excuse her.

"We are trying to finish a score of boys' shirts that are desperately needed at Bellview Orphanage," she said apologetically. "Otherwise I would accompany you up to Charlotte's studio. But I am sure you will be fine." She gave Chloe a distracted smile.

Chloe smiled back. "I left my mama finishing a set of shirts — for adults, not children."

"It *is* endless," Charlotte's mother said rather helplessly. "I feel as if we sew and sew, and everywhere I see people wearing only rags."

Charlotte and Chloe curtsied and they continued up the stairs, past the next floor. The stairs got suddenly smaller and steeper, going up to the fourth floor.

"This is really the nursery floor," Charlotte said over her shoulder. "But there aren't any children now, obviously, and so my parents turned the nursery into my studio."

They paused in the door of a large room, painted white. All around the walls were candelabra, large ones, small gilt fragile-looking ones, a pair covered with seashells. Chloe's mouth fell open. There was a hideous, large candelabra designed to look like tree branches, and even one that must have been in the original nursery because it depicted Noah's Ark with candles sprouting from several of the animals' heads.

"Oh," Charlotte laughed. "I completely forgot how odd this room must look. You see, I need light more than anything else. So we put up all the extra candelabra we had in the attic, and then we sent one of the footmen down to the Strand with instructions to buy anything he could find. And this was the result."

Chloe looked around slowly. The lights had been affixed to the walls every foot or so, and each one had stark white candles in its holders.

"The footmen put in new candles every morning," Charlotte continued. "I get hideously irritable when they burn down, because if one goes out it changes the light, and finally Mrs. Simpkin — our housekeeper — decided that the candles burn first here. They are changed every morning and then they go into other rooms, like the bedrooms. London is so dark with coal dust that I can only work until around eleven o'clock in the morning with natural light, and often not even then."

Chloe nodded. She had never seen so many wax candles in one room. Her mother was no nip-cheese, as she said, but even so they used wax sparingly and tallow dips in all the bedrooms. She walked slowly into the room. Posed before a large set of windows was an easel. When she walked around and stood in front of it she was transfixed. The picture was a laughing version of the young woman, Sophie, whom she had met the night before at the theater. Sophie was so *alive*, as if she might dash off the canvas. She didn't look at all dreamy or posed, like the portraits exhibited in the Royal Portrait Gallery each year.

"I brought it out," Charlotte said, "so you could see my work. Ah, do you like it?" Chloe's little face was like a barometer, Charlotte thought. You could see each expression register clearly. At the moment she looked appalled, hopefully not because of the painting.

Chloe turned her head quickly. Charlotte actually sounded a bit anxious! "It's splendid," she said stumblingly. "But . . . why would you want to paint me? She's so dazzling, and I am quite ordinary."

"That's nonsense, of course," Charlotte replied. "You are very lovely, as you probably know. But that doesn't matter. If you hadn't agreed, I was thinking of painting Campion, our butler. What I want is a look, not a face. See — if you look at Sophie here, what I tried to do was catch *Sophie* herself, not just a beautiful set of features."

Chloe looked hard at the painting. "Oh," she finally said. "She's very, um, alluring, isn't she?"

Charlotte beamed. "Yes. And that's Sophie too, in person." Chloe thought about the hungry eyes of the men surrounding Sophie York the night before.

"Yes," she said. "But there's something more. . . ."

"It's a joke to her," Charlotte said. "She is provocative, but not *really* seductive: What I mean is, she's untouched, herself." Charlotte strongly wondered if she should be so explicit with a young, chaste girl. But Chloe was only the third person to see the painting, not counting Sophie, and the first who had bothered to ask her anything about it.

"I see," Chloe said slowly. "It's around the mouth, isn't it? She looks — well, like the goddess Diana. Not that I know what Diana looks like," she added in some confusion. "But as a goddess, she's supposed to be incredibly beautiful, but rejected all men, isn't that right?"

"I never thought," Charlotte replied with interest. "I'm not sure I'd agree . . . I thought of the picture more as someone who plays with fire she doesn't understand — *yet*."

"Ah," Chloe said. Now she understood perfectly. Only two days ago she would have unhesitatingly classed herself with Sophie, except she didn't even play at being seductive. But last night an emotion she didn't know she had blazed into life when Will Holland kissed her.

She turned back to Charlotte without saying anything, but Charlotte instantly realized that Chloe was no demure, unawakened maiden. Chloe said so little that one was in danger of classifying her as naive. Charlotte was growing more interested in this portrait every moment.

"What would you like me to do?" Chloe asked politely.

Charlotte led her over to a comfortable divan. "I should like you simply to sit. There is no need to fix your head in one position, or not move. I am going to spend the next couple of hours making a whole series of sketches of your head in profile and from the front. Then, as I told you last night, I will work on it myself for a while, and hatch a plan. And then I will ask you to come back for another sitting, probably next week."

Chloe sat down, feeling self-conscious. Charlotte quickly pulled a huge chef's apron over her head and sat down before her with a large pad of paper in her lap. She started sketching, the quick, sure movements of her wrist the only thing Chloe could see. At first Charlotte asked her a few questions, but Chloe could see that she didn't really want to talk. So Chloe fell easily into silence and started thinking about Will. Will last night . . . in the corridor . . . in the carriage, in front of her house.

Charlotte's hand trembled. What in God's name was happening to Chloe? The self-contained, earnest little girl she'd met the night before had transformed into a passionate woman, glowing at every pore with sexual interest. Could it be that she, Charlotte, was the naive one? She simply didn't *see* the world as it was until Alex came along and . . . Charlotte scowled violently. She wasn't sure she liked this new world, full of roving husbands and maidens feverish with desire. But — perhaps it was *Charlotte* who was feverish and she was writing the emotion onto the face of a sedate little Dutch maiden? Charlotte looked down at the sketch in her lap, and at the sheafs that had fallen like snow around her chair. No. Her pencil didn't lie. It never had. The thought steadied her and she began sketching faster, trying to capture Chloe's restraint, the quality of extreme self-control that was so fascinatingly balanced by glowing sensuality.

Charlotte had fallen into a rhythm by an hour or so later. And she was getting somewhere. Bits of certain sketches had something she wanted. She'd caught a look in Chloe's eyes, for example, somewhere in a page on the floor. And she had a beautiful, calm chin and throat tossed off in coal, not pencil, also drifting about the floor. The portrait was beginning to tumble itself together in her head, when there was a sudden interruption. A sharp knock sounded on the door of the studio.

"What the *devil!*" Charlotte said in a completely unladylike manner, jumping to her feet.

Chloe's mouth fell open for the second time since she entered the studio. She had never heard a lady swear like that.

Charlotte was furious. Chloe had only relaxed about ten minutes ago. Her shoulders had been strained and unnatural for forty minutes. Everyone knew not to enter this room during working hours.

A large dark hand gripped the door and swung it open. As soon as Charlotte heard a voice telling Campion that no, he wouldn't wait and be damned with him, her heart flip-flopped. It was Alex, genially dismissing Campion's protests. He must have followed the butler right up the stairs, because normally Campion would never have permitted an unchaperoned man to enter the upper floors of the house.

Charlotte straightened her back, her mouth tight, as Alex entered the room. She was ready to give him the lecture of his life when she realized he wasn't alone. In front of him trotted Pippa, her plump legs moving her surely toward the lovely heaps of paper she spied in front of her.

"Stop her!" Charlotte shrieked. Alex managed to catch the big, starched bow on the back of Pippa's dress as she was about to dive into a pile of paper. Charlotte ran about, gathering papers while Alex held back his howling daughter. Chloe rose from the couch.

"How do you do, my lord?" she said in her quiet way. "You met me last night; I am Chloe van Stork."

"I remember," Alex said, smiling warmly. "Are you having your portrait painted?" He had instantly grasped the connotations of the candelabra and the easel.

"Well, not yet," Chloe replied. "Lady Charlotte is still making sketches."

"Oh, please!" Charlotte said. "Do call me Charlotte." She was still picking up paper, watching Pippa out of the corner of her eye. She wouldn't put it past Alex to let go of his daughter. She finally managed to gather all the sketches together and place them securely on the mantelpiece, weighed down by a candlestick. Meanwhile Alex, carrying Pippa, who was squealing, although a bit more quietly, walked around to see Charlotte's easel. Charlotte couldn't help watching him out of the corner of her eye.

He stood absolutely still. His only movement was to drop Pippa gently to the ground. She immediately scooted off and started trying to climb a chair. Still he stood. Charlotte was feeling more and more peevish. Perhaps he couldn't even think of a pleasant compliment. Finally he raised his head and looked straight into her eyes.

"Why bluebells?"

"Why . . . what do you mean?" Charlotte responded confusedly.

"Why bluebells — why not rabbits?" His mouth quirked. He walked over to her. "You *are* going to hang on to that picture until Sophie marries, aren't you? I can't see it joining the stodgy members of the Brandenburg portrait gallery, somehow. So rabbits — fertility."

"Rabbits, fertility," Charlotte repeated stupidly.

278

Chloe cleared her throat gently. "It's an Italian custom, isn't it, my lord? In the Renaissance, Italian brides were given pictures of themselves with rabbits playing in the background."

Charlotte smiled involuntarily. He *got* it! Her portrait was precisely a bride picture: a woman on the cusp of learning something. Alex's huge hands grasped her shoulders.

"Your portrait is quite splendid. You know that, don't you?"

She looked up at him without responding.

I wonder why he's called ineligible, Chloe thought to herself, watching the lithe, beautiful couple. They were standing very close to each other, and from what she could see of Alex's face, he was within a hair's breadth of pulling Charlotte into his arms. Chloe felt suddenly embarrassed. The naked passion on Alex's face made her own face feel hot. She turned away.

"We have to go to Italy," Alex said without pausing. "We'll go to Florence and see the Leonardo portraits . . . and Rome, the Michelangelos —"

Chloe wouldn't have been so embarrassed if she could have seen Charlotte's face. Even as Alex listed the places Charlotte most wanted to visit in the whole world, her irritation grew. She woke up cross this morning, aching inside for something unknown. And with Charlotte's annoyance grew the conviction that she would *not* marry Alex. What she felt for him was raw sexual desire; obviously that was not an emotion that a

279

lady cultivated, let alone married someone for. In fact, she had thought with satisfaction of the moment when Alex would ask her to marry him again, and she would politely, but coolly, refuse him. And now he was simply *assuming* that she would marry him! The gross arrogance of it galled her to the quick. Her face darkened even more.

Alex was no fool. He broke off his list of Italian cities and stared at her, his eyebrows flying even higher.

Charlotte opened her mouth and then closed it again. She could not tell him exactly what she thought of him and his assumptions in front of Chloe and Pippa. Besides, she had been aware for some time that Pippa was precariously perched on the settee, trying to throw her fat little leg over the back. From there she would certainly fall down and hurt herself. So she simply turned about and swept Pippa off the settee.

Pippa opened her mouth to scream and then settled. Charlotte smiled at her hugely. She might not like her papa, but she certainly liked this small, independent spirit.

"I'm the not-nanny, remember me?"

Pippa gave her a small, cautious smile. Charlotte tucked her into the crook of her arm, so she was sitting up and could see where they were going.

"Miss van Stork," she said courteously. "Since our sitting has been interrupted, shall we join my mother in her morning room and have some tea?"

Alex's heart sank. Not only was his love looking like a black thundercloud and cross as a termagant, now she wanted to join her mama. And from what he understood from the Duke of Calverstill this morning, the duchess was likely being talked into the idea of meeting him at this very moment.

He cleared his throat. "Ah, your mother is busy."

Charlotte swung around. "And how, pray, would you know?"

"Your father told me," Alex said, rocking back on his heels and looking absolutely imperturbable. Charlotte stared at him for a moment in frustration. What was going on here? Suddenly the light dawned. Alex must have met her father and asked for her hand in marriage this morning. And somehow he talked his way out of her father's absolute refusal of the idea. So now her father was relaying whatever story Alex came up with to her mother. Charlotte threw Alex a brooding look.

"Hmmm," she said, nonplussed for a moment.

"I should leave now," Chloe interjected. She really didn't enjoy all this strained conversation, especially as she had no idea what was going on. "My mother was very clear about the fact that she needed me to return this morning."

Charlotte turned to her, her face falling. "Oh, but surely . . ."

Alex intervened. He took Chloe's hand and smiled at her genially. "We all know what mamas are like when they want you to return on time," he said. "I promise not to interrupt your next sitting with Charlotte."

Chloe looked at him silently for a minute. My goodness, but this man was confident. She couldn't deny his incredible attractiveness, but was there no chink in his assurance? Well, he was a man and a peer of the realm, and handsome, and rich, she thought with some resentment. Why should there be?

"Of course," she replied hastily, aware that she had been mute too long. Chloe withdrew her hand and turned to Charlotte. Then she gave an involuntary smile. Perhaps the earl's comeuppance was at hand. Charlotte looked as mutinous as a mule, in her mother's term. Chloe smiled with genuine warmth, and curtsied to Charlotte.

"Oh, Lord," Charlotte said. "Here we are, curtsying and addressing each other formally. Are you sure you want to do this, Miss van Stork? We're going to be locked up in this room with each other for almost six weeks — you'll *have* to call me Charlotte."

Chloe twinkled at her. Little fits of temper didn't bother her, given that her father indulged in them all the time. "Oh, no, Charlotte," she said, holding out her hand. "I am looking forward to this portrait, even if I can't see it until I get married!"

"Oh, I let Sophie *see* her portrait," Charlotte said. "She just doesn't understand it yet. Her only comment was that she thought her teeth were too large." They shook hands with total understanding.

"I'll see you tomorrow morning, then," Charlotte said resignedly. "Let me show you out, please." Charlotte went first, still holding Pippa, who laughed madly and tried to swipe all the pictures off the wall as she descended. Chloe came next and Alex followed. He was feeling rather vexed. Why was Charlotte glowering at him? Surely she didn't think he was playing fast and loose with her when he kissed her last night? Didn't she expect to marry him? What kind of person did she think he was, anyway, some kind of castaway who would kiss a girl — the way they kissed — and then fly the coop? His first proposal two weeks ago, and her rejection of it, didn't even enter his mind.

Charlotte saluted Chloe at the door and then turned around briskly. Without missing a step she dumped Pippa into Alex's arms.

"She's wet," she said.

"Oh," Alex replied. He made such a funny picture, an elegant gentleman holding a child whose beautiful white dress was becoming more soggy by the moment, that Charlotte almost burst out laughing. Only a hint of darkness about his eyes stopped her. Alex turned to Campion, who was waiting patiently.

"Will you call Keating, my man, please?"

"Certainly, my lord." Campion bowed deeply. "Would you like me to bring the child down-stairs?" The entire household was riveted with interest in the Earl of Sheffield and Downes; Campion knew that Pippa would be eagerly welcomed by Mrs. Simpkin and the other upper servants. Keating was being feasted royally at this very moment, he had no doubt. There was no one in the house who didn't know that the earl had spent forty minutes alone with the master in his study, and that they had emerged on most amiable terms. And there wasn't a single lobcock too stupid to draw the right conclusion about what had happened in that study.

"Yes, thank you," Alex said. He handed over Pippa, who miraculously didn't scream but just patted Campion's face. Alex and Charlotte watched Campion carry Pippa off as if he bore wet children around the house every day.

"She's a bit better," Alex said in a distracted tone. "She hasn't had a true howl in two days."

"Yes, well," Charlotte said. Just like the rest of the household, she knew exactly why he was here, and she didn't want any part of it. Not now. Not when she still had the residual headache she'd had all day. Not when she was feeling so cross and prickly that she might burst into tears. She just couldn't — wouldn't — cope with an-other marriage proposal at the moment.

So, rather than walking into the Blue Room, or one of the other salons off the entrance hall, she held out her hand graciously.

"It was very nice of you to visit, my lord," she said loftily.

Alex walked over until he was standing just in front of Charlotte, casting an admonishing look at the two footmen on attendance in the hallway. They instantly disguised the curiosity that decked both their faces and stood poker-straight against the walls. Alex kept walking forward until Charlotte receded a step and another step. He glanced at one footman, who quickly pulled open the door to the Chinese Salon, as it was called. Alex briskly took Charlotte's arm in his hand, swung her about, and walked her into the room. The door swung to behind them with a quiet click.

Alex immediately dropped Charlotte's arm and turned around to face her. "What makes you think I would leave my child to the mercy of that muffin-faced type you call your butler?" he said, affably enough.

Charlotte stared at him. She hadn't thought about the fact that she had tried to say good-bye to him *after* seeing his child carried down into the servants' quarters.

"My lord," she said, "I am not . . . fit for this conversation this morning. I have a headache." Charlotte dropped gracefully into a couch, feeling rather like a fraud, but also doing a good imitation of her great-aunt Margaret. Margaret was invariably ill with something, and she much enjoyed her own infirmities.

Alex stood before her, looking absolutely collected, Charlotte noted with some irritation.

"Perhaps you would like me to go down on my knees?" he asked. Charlotte saw the amusement lighting his eyes and glared at him.

"No."

"Good," Alex said. An undefinable suggestion of fury hung around him in a way that was making Charlotte most uncomfortable. She raised her chin defiantly. No one could force her to marry, not even an earl of the realm. Her head throbbed painfully.

"Perhaps you would like to commence now?" she asked defiantly.

Alex stared down at her. This wasn't going the way he pictured. He thought the interview with her father would be the most difficult part of proposing to Charlotte Daicheston. He had dreaded the explanations, the discussion of his first, horrible marriage — for God's sake, he never even wrote his own father with the details. But the duke had been genial enough, listening carefully, asking a few sage questions, nodding here and there. And at the end he shook hands with Alex and said he had his blessing, and Alex had thought that was it. If he pictured anything, it was Charlotte melting into his arms, madly grateful at the idea of becoming his wife. Swaying toward him, the way she did last night. In fact, he had counseled himself not to allow the whole proposal to get out of hand — he wasn't going to take his wife's virginity in a drawing room! Somehow after the discovery of Maria's perfidity, and after finding out she had bedded practically every man in Rome before turning eighteen, the idea of virginity and wedding nights had become very important. No graceless coupling in coaches for him. Yet he thought that he and Charlotte were so mutually fraught with desire that he even considered a special license. But Charlotte's father had rejected that idea.

"It's going to have to be big," he had said shrewdly. "We'll have to put on the romantic wedding of the century, in order to cool the gossip. And you" — he looked at Alex from under his bushy eyebrows — "you'll have to make a baby as soon as possible."

Alex nodded. He had no worry about that. In all he and Maria probably only made love ten times, and he had Pippa as a result.

But now — Charlotte was looking as testy as a cobbler with a sore head and he was losing all inclination to ask anyone to marry him. What did he need a wife for? Maria's screaming diatribes should have been enough to warn him off women forever. And Pippa was doing better. . . . The silence between them grew and grew.

Alex looked down at Charlotte again. With a faint pulse of alarm, he realized that her face was as white as her gown and she was leaning her head against her hand. He sat down next to her.

"You really do have a headache, don't you?"

Charlotte nodded miserably. Each nod made her head pound. Alex got up and went out into the hall. She heard him talking quietly to one of the footmen.

"I've sent him off to tell Keating to make you a special brew," he said, reentering the room. "Here — bend your head this way." He gently pulled her over until she toppled against his shoulder.

"This is most improper," Charlotte said, rearing her head.

"Hush. No one can see us." His hands pushed aside the curls at the nape of her neck and he started a slow light massage. Charlotte turned her face to the side and rested it against his shoulder. She could feel solid muscle under her cheek. It was oddly comforting, somehow. And his big hands were surprisingly tender . . . She closed her eyes.

There was a knock and Alex swiftly pulled Charlotte to a sitting position, smiling at her wan look. Campion brought in a tall glass on a silver tray.

"Here, swallow this."

She eyed it suspiciously. It looked vile — yellow and frothy.

"I *hate* egg drinks."

"Drink it anyway."

She did. It wasn't as bad as she suspected. Worse, she thought gloomily. The footman took the empty glass and bowed his way out of the room. Alex pulled Charlotte back onto his shoulder in a companionable sort of way. Charlotte closed her eyes again.

"There was liquor in that drink, wasn't there?" she asked drowsily, after a bit. "I don't like liquor. . . ." Her voice trailed off and Alex could tell she had gone to sleep. He patted her satiny curls back into place. An involuntary grin twisted his lips. How many women go to sleep when an earl comes to propose marriage? He thought of all the voracious glances he intercepted every time he attended Almack's. Patrick used to twit him, saying that all he'd have to do was dance with a girl twice and she'd be ordering wedding livery.

Well, this was a good story for Patrick. He looked down at his sleeping nonfiancée. A not-nanny, not-fiancée, he thought wryly. Charlotte's hair curled riotously, twirling around his hand. He pulled up a soft ringlet and let it spring back into a silky corkscrew. The way she was lying he could see only her profile. Long, curling black lashes lay on her white cheek — a bit rosier now, he noticed with satisfaction. Keating's headache remedy had enough liquor, as she called it, to heat an ox. Even watching her sleep Alex felt his body stir appreciatively.

That was enough. She didn't want to marry him, did she? Why not? Perhaps she had heard the story of his first marriage. That must be it, he thought, somewhat relieved. She must think that he had bought off her father somehow and was going to turn her into an unpaid nursemaid. Now he did remember his first proposal. She hadn't said much, just no. Alex shook his head. They needed to have a straight talk when she woke up. He leaned his head against the back of the divan and closed his eyes. Within seconds, the only sound in the room was the gentle breathing of two sleeping gentlefolk.

Outside the two footmen looked at each other in wild surmise. They hadn't heard anything — any words, no matter how muted — for a long time. What was going on in the Chinese Salon? Cecil thought he knew. He smiled widely and thought about Marie. He had tried to talk her into doing it in one of the public rooms in the house. Lord knows, they'd been in every linen closet. But she had always said no.

"Those rooms are formal and dangerous," she had insisted. "Why, we'd be put out without a shilling if we did anything so outrageous!"

Cecil had it all worked out. Sunday mornings the family was at church, and so were the servants. He simply had to wait until he was on rotation to stay in the house, or switch with one of the other footmen, and she could plead a headache.

"No," she had kept saying. But now he'd tell her that her very own mistress had done the same. Cecil stood quietly at his post, waiting for someone to emerge from the Chinese salon, an optimistic glow in his eyes.

Chapter 12

Charlotte opened her eyes some twenty minutes later. Her headache was gone and she had a delicious sense of warmth. Even her irritability had vanished. I'm drunk, she thought, feeling her head reel slightly as she sat up. Alex was sleeping soundly. At least he didn't sleep with his mouth open. At that moment he opened his eyes and stared at her wordlessly. A glimmer of a smile lit her eyes. Still without saying anything he pulled her over against his side.

"Sleeping together," Alex finally said in a tone of mock disgust. "Just like two old men on a bench in the sun."

"Would you like some tea?" Charlotte smiled. "Just to keep you awake, of course."

Alex hated the stuff. "Lapdog brew," he said. "Just the thing for an old gager like myself."

"Would you prefer sherry? Or something stronger? I suspect," Charlotte said primly, "that Keating's special drink has made me tipsy, and so I shall drink some tea to ameliorate the situation." She walked to the door and pushed it open. Cecil's face fell when he saw her. She looked perfectly groomed and composed: The mistress had not been doing anything untoward in that room. He trotted off to bring a tea tray.

Charlotte turned around. Alex was comfortably sprawled on a hideous Chinese settee chosen by her mother at the height of the rage for things Oriental. The arms were sleeping lions, their eyes picked out in red lacquer. But Alex . . . he was beautiful, Charlotte thought with an inner sigh. He was wearing an exquisitely cut coat of dove gray, which contrasted ruthlessly with the untamed masculinity breathing through his muscled thighs. Her resolution was weakening.

Alex raised his heavy-lidded eyes and said abruptly, "We need to talk." Charlotte nodded and sat down next to him.

Upstairs the duchess was becoming worried. Surely her daughter had been unchaperoned far too long. She walked quickly around her chamber a few times. At first she couldn't believe it when Marcel told her he had reversed himself and now approved the match. But when he detailed all the awful details of Alex's first marriage, she agreed. Adelaide sighed. Now if only Charlotte could bring herself to discuss what had happened three years ago. . . .

Marcel walked into her bedchamber through the connecting doors leading to his own chambers.

"Time to go, dearest. We'll be late. You know that I hate to be late."

"Oh, Marcel." Adelaide turned an anguished

face toward him. "We can't go anywhere. Why, Charlotte and Alexander Foakes are still closeted in the Chinese Salon . . . don't you think we should join them? They've been together, unchaperoned, for over forty-five minutes!" She yanked on the bellpull vigorously.

"Nonsense," her husband replied. "Charlotte's a grown girl. She won't get up to any tricks. Besides, Campion told me that she had a tea tray and a light lunch sent in. Does that sound like a seduction to you? Now, it's time to go." He firmly swept his reluctant wife toward the door.

"But what will he think of me?" she wailed. "We can't simply leave them there unchaperoned!"

"Listen, Addie. You told Charlotte all about the reasons why I originally forbade the marriage, didn't you?"

"Yes."

"Well, then, Alex obviously needs some time to explain about his first marriage and the annulment, and all the rest of it that I told you."

"Perhaps we should just say good-bye?"

"Nonsense," Marcel said again. "We'll leave word with Campion."

Marcel followed his wife down the stairs, ready to push her out the door if need be. He knew as well as anyone that leaving his daughter unchaperoned would be considered a piece of great folly in some circles. But he was playing a deep game, he thought proudly. Not for nothing was he considered a wily poker player. He liked this earl. In fact, he liked him more than he had liked any of Charlotte's other suitors. He fancied Alex had the right combination of strength and intelligence to cope with Charlotte's painting and general stubbornness. But he shrewdly reckoned that Alex had quite a job before him convincing Charlotte, and so he had told him, straight out. Women didn't like to marry men with reputations of this sort. Now, if Alex had had a reputation for whoring and the like, he wouldn't see any problem. But a reputation for being a limp lily — no. Charlotte had her pride, as much as the next woman.

Alex had listened to him silently, his black eyes inscrutable. But Marcel fancied his point had sunk in. Now, what he, Marcel, would do in this situation would be to *convince* her. Yes, *convince* her. And that might take a while, he thought with an inward grin. Under no circumstances was Marcel going to let Addie bounce into the room and ruin the mood. Down in the hallway he dismissed the footmen and told Campion to keep an eye on the place. (Campion immediately understood the master's vague direction meant keep inquiring eyes away from the door to the Chinese salon.) Then Marcel triumphantly bore his wife off to a musical luncheon.

Back in the Chinese Salon, Charlotte sat bolt upright beside Alex.

"Why don't you want to marry me?" he asked, finally. Startled, she swung her head to look at him. He looked so handsome, and almost —

could he be a little anxious? Charlotte's resolution wavered again. But no. She marshaled her reasons: He really only wanted a nursemaid, *and* he had forgotten their encounter three years ago. Which meant that he would be out propositioning girls in gardens whenever she turned her back.

"Can't I just refuse?"

"No," Alex said indomitably. "Not when you kiss me the way you do." A faint blush crept up Charlotte's cheeks. Oh, God, he did think she was a shameless wanton. If she mentioned what happened three years ago, he'd probably just walk out. Irrationally, she didn't consider the difference between Alex walking out and her refusing his proposal.

A little silence fell.

"Let me guess," Alex said in a somewhat softer voice. "You heard the rumors about my being incapable, and —"

Charlotte shook her head frantically, eyes fixed on the couch cushion.

"You didn't hear the rumors, or that isn't the problem?"

"I didn't . . . I mean, I did hear, my mother told me, but I knew. . . ." She bit her lip. She felt as if she must be crimson by now.

Alex gave a bark of laughter. "You knew," he said. "You're — remarkable, Charlotte." He reached out a lazy finger and stroked her neck.

"Don't!"

He withdrew his hand as if it had been burned.

There was another silence. Then: "I'm waiting, Charlotte." His tone was grim.

Charlotte raised her eyes to his, pleading for understanding. "I know what *ton* marriages are like," she said in a near whisper. "I don't want one like that. I —" She broke off suddenly as a brisk knock heralded the entrance of a tea tray. Campion brought it himself, beaming avun- cularly at the couple as he deftly set up a small table.

"I have brought a small luncheon as well, Lady Charlotte. The duke and duchess asked me to give you their regrets, my lord, and tell you that they had an unavoidable appointment. However, they would very much like you to join them for dinner. If you need anything further, perhaps you might summon me with the bellpull, as we have had to place the footmen elsewhere." Campion bowed his way out of the room.

Very clever of the duke, Alex thought, instantly appreciating Marcel's hand in all this unwarranted privacy that was being accorded to him and Charlotte.

Charlotte busied herself with the tea tray and tried to think what it was she really wanted to say.

"Do you love me?" she asked bluntly.

"Love you?" Alex was completely startled. His first impulse was to say "Yes, of course," and press a kiss on her lips. But he wanted this marriage to be different from his first, he reminded himself. To begin without lies.

"No," he finally said, deliberately. Charlotte's

body was rigid. "But, and this is a fair question, Charlotte — do you love me?"

Charlotte opened her mouth but Alex kept talking. "You see, I don't think that love is something that happens the way writers pretend. All those lines like 'who ever loved, who loved not at first sight' were made up by poets, not by real people. I thought I loved my first wife the minute I saw her," he continued slowly, almost as if he was talking to himself, Charlotte thought. "She looked so much like a girl I met before, here in England. She looked innocent, beautiful . . . like a girl who had been living in a convent.

"So I told her I loved her, and she told me she loved me, and we married two weeks later to the great rejoicing of her family. But do you know why they rejoiced so much?"

Charlotte shook her head.

"Because no one else in Rome would have married her." Charlotte just looked confused, so Alex smiled at her, a lopsided, self-condemning smile. "She had slept with a good many of the Roman gentlemen who danced at my wedding, you see." Charlotte's eyes widened. Alex shrugged. "More fool I."

"I'm sorry," Charlotte said rather lamely.

"I thought a good deal about love at first sight in the following year. Our life together was hell. She didn't love me, and I found out within a week or so that I didn't love her either. Love, I think, is something built on trust — and trust comes only with time. Do you see what I mean?"

Charlotte nodded. She was having a hard time putting together Alex's turbulent black eyes, talking about his wife's infidelity, and the fixed idea she had that he himself would be unfaithful once they married.

"Do you believe," she half whispered, "that trust is a matter of . . . of not being with other people after marriage?"

Alex nearly smiled. So Charlotte was thinking of adultery when she talked of a *ton* marriage! Perhaps her father had a wandering eye.

"I think that fidelity between a man and woman is the only basis for marriage," he said firmly. He took her hand and started a slow seductive massage of her palm. "I would never betray you with anyone." He pulled her palm against his lips. "As a matter of fact, I don't think I would have energy left for anyone else." Alex leaned closer, his breath warm on her cheek.

Charlotte pulled back again. "You told me that you were looking for a nursemaid," she said weakly. Why did all her reasons seem so nonsensical now? She felt like an idiot.

Alex simply pulled her against his body, a strong hand pushing up her chin. "Do you think I want to do this with a nursemaid?" His voice was oddly hoarse, Charlotte thought. She gulped and shook her head like a mesmerized rabbit.

"Or this?" He bent his head and brushed his lips across hers. His lips caressed hers, slowly, enticingly, asking for something. . . . Charlotte began to tremble.

"Was there anything else you wanted to say, Charlotte?" Alex asked, a little unsteadily. "Because I don't mean to silence you." His breath is sweet, Charlotte thought.

"Are you sure you don't remember meeting me before?" she gasped, before the last rational thought fled from her mind. Alex withdrew slightly and looked down at her.

"Sweetheart, I didn't ever meet you." His mouth swooped down on hers again. "How could I forget this loveable forehead? Or your eyebrows?" He punctuated each phrase with a kiss. "Or" — his voice was deepening into velvet — "your eyelashes? They lie so inky-black against your cheek. Or your stubborn little nose?"

Desperately, Charlotte pulled back. "Are you absolutely sure?"

Alex finally realized that the question was truly important to her. His eyes searched hers. "I am quite certain," he confirmed. "I could never have forgotten you. As soon as I saw you at the ball, I knew —" he broke off. But Charlotte guessed: He knew he wanted her. He just didn't remember that he'd already *had* her. A single tear trailed down her cheek.

Alex brushed it away tenderly. "Does it matter, Charlotte? Really? Isn't the first time we met just part and parcel of the myth of falling in love at first sight? Why not pretend that you never met me before the ball, and to hell with the past?"

Oh, God, Charlotte thought despairingly. Another tear followed the first.

Alex's eyebrows clamped together. What was going on here? Why did it matter when he met her? He searched his memory again . . . but he knew it wasn't any good. Before coming back from Italy he'd probably only been to seven or eight *ton* parties in his life. And Charlotte didn't even come out until the year he left for Italy. He stared down at her, his body painfully aroused just by the sight of her, even when she was crying.

Charlotte made an effort to get ahold of herself. Think rationally, she told herself. Don't be a widgeon! So he doesn't remember you. He probably forgot all about making love at the masquerade ball because he thought the girl was a trollop, and that's not the same thing as sleeping with a lady. But now he's saying that he won't run around seducing women in gardens. He's *promising*. And adultery is what you were afraid of.

She gave a broken, tiny smile that lit Alex's heart. "I'm sorry to be such a wet goose," she said. "I never cry!"

"Aha!" Alex said. "You see, I am making the right decision. You will be a lovely mother for Pippa, because that's the *only* thing she knows how to do well." Charlotte smiled.

"But Charlotte," Alex said seriously. "We need to sort this out. The fact is, darling, that you undoubtedly met my brother Patrick. We look like a matched set of pistols, my father always said."

And, in response to her questioning look, "all black with silver trim." Her smile peeked out again. That's twice, Alex thought. "Our own nurse couldn't tell us apart . . . she used to complain dreadfully when we would play tricks on her, which we did up to a few years ago. If Patrick were here, in England, he would clear up the whole mess. But since he's not, we simply have to forget it."

Charlotte nodded silently. Of course, he was absolutely wrong. She could never, never have mistaken Alex's endearing dimple for anyone else's, or the bullish set of his shoulders, or the arrogant way his eyebrows flew up. Those weren't even characteristics that were attached to one's face. She had a painter's eye, and she looked past faces, at mannerisms, all the time. Maybe some time after they were married she would feel more comfortable about mentioning something so intimate. And then she could tell him and perhaps he would even laugh.

Alex sensed it as her body relaxed. He pulled her back into his arms, his hands ruffling her soft curls.

"So, will you marry me?" he whispered against her neck. "Because I think I could easily love you . . . and perhaps you will love me . . . and I can watch you paint, and we can even have another baby like Pippa, but with your lovely mouth."

Charlotte nodded shakily against his shoulder.

Alex pushed her back, his eyes laughing down at her. "Did you say something?"

"Yes," she said. "Yes, yes, I will marry you."

"Ahhhh," Alex said, seizing her again. "Now you are my fiancée: Do you know what that means?"

Charlotte shivered. Was he thinking of doing something here? Here, in her mother's Chinese salon? His lips were tracing a pattern down her neck that made her feel short of breath. Meanwhile his hands slid from her neck down her back, making her body instinctively bend toward his. Their knees knocked together awkwardly and Charlotte giggled. Alex gave her a mock glare.

"I'll tell you right now that a good wife *never* laughs at her husband!" he growled.

Charlotte felt light, giddy with happiness, emboldened by his dancing eyes. She put her slender hands against his cheeks and slowly drew them down, over the strong brown column of his neck, down his hard chest, just as she had during the fireworks.

"I like everything you've taught me so far," she said wickedly.

"Oh yes, my lady?" Alex whispered back. His eyes shone with mischief. "And how low will you go?"

Charlotte snatched her hands away, giggling furiously.

"My turn!" Alex announced. He put his large brown hands on her cheeks. His palms almost covered her whole face, they were so large. And they felt intriguingly hard. Charlotte turned her head slightly and kissed the edge of his hand.

"No fair distracting me," said her fiancé sternly. His fingers ran delicately over her face, pausing at her mouth. One rough finger traced the outline of her generous lower lip. Charlotte suddenly opened her mouth and small teeth bit down on his finger. Alex grinned. He stopped grinning when a warm tongue touched the tip.

"You taste like honey," said Charlotte, staring at him, her eyes bemused.

Alex smiled slowly and pulled his finger from her mouth, quickly bending his head down and replacing his finger with his tongue. Charlotte gasped. Two tongues met, at first discreetly questioning, but then Alex's kiss changed. His mouth settled over hers with intent, demanding, forcing her mouth wider open. His tongue took on a wicked rhythm, coercing, mastering her. Charlotte found herself clinging helplessly to his shirt front, her head thrown back, completely vulnerable to Alex's onslaught. Her heart was beating like a wild bird's and she had instinctively closed her eyes . . . until his mouth withdrew. Then her eyes flew open. He was grinning at her.

"Now, where was I?" Alex murmured. He put his hands back on her face and drew them past her determined chin and languorously down her neck. Charlotte felt as if her lower belly were on fire. Even her fingers were trembling, she thought dazedly. She watched his black eyes as if they were the only objects in the world. Alex's fingers trailed over her collarbones and down the smooth, smooth skin of her chest. He reached the small ruffle which adorned the bodice of her morning gown. His fingers slid inside. Charlotte didn't know what to think. More than anything she wanted him to cup her breast, but his fingers slipped sideways, along the ruffle. They reached her armpits and Charlotte tensed. She was frightfully ticklish, but somehow, his caress didn't seem to make her ticklish. . . . The pressure in her lower stomach increased.

Alex's hands lingered on her slim sides, inside her dress, for an instant, and then suddenly his right thumb ran over the light cotton of her bodice and touched her nipple. Charlotte jumped. His left thumb did the same. Charlotte gasped and nervously licked her lips. At this Alex almost groaned. He didn't know how long he could prolong this particular game. Flames were licking at his groin; the only thought in his mind was to push Charlotte back against the arm of the couch and . . . and what?

He was the one who wanted a virginal bride. He looked at Charlotte. She was lying back against the couch, her head thrown back, moist lips apart as his thumbs rhythmically stroked her small, straining nipples. She was his; he knew that as clearly as he had ever known anything. But he didn't want to take her now, in her parents' house. He wanted to say vows that meant something, and then make love for the first time in the shadow of those vows.

"No," he whispered. And then he leaned forward anyway. "No," he said again, his breath warm against her skin as he pushed down the white chambray and took her rosy nipple into his mouth.

Charlotte instinctively arched her back and moaned. Alex's left hand rubbed her other breast, roughly now, and his teeth feathered over her nipple, nipping and sucking. Charlotte felt boneless, limp. The fire in her lower belly had been replaced by a feeling of wetness and aching, open longing.

"Alex," she gasped, her voice breaking. But Alex had momentarily lost control. Charlotte's breast was so sweet, so perfect: surprisingly heavy for such a slender body, and yet not too large, just right for his hand. He had her whole bodice pulled below her breasts now, the little cap sleeves slipping almost down to her elbows. Her breasts were silky white, with just a delicate pink circle around her nipples . . . and her nipples! They were a deep crimson, swollen, begging. Alex took a deep breath. He felt intoxicated. He had never been so wildly aroused. My God, he was close to taking his own fiancée on a damned uncomfortable Chinese couch full of knobs.

"No," he said hoarsely. He took his mouth off Charlotte's breast but his hands couldn't seem to stop caressing her. She opened her eyes and looked at him, a look drugged with desire. Alex looked back in wonder. She was everything he wanted: sweet, intelligent, chaste, *and* wanton.

She seemed to be so wholesome and yet she was wild . . . even as he looked Charlotte reached out and pulled him forward.

His lips met hers softly but then, as if she just remembered how to kiss, her mouth opened, moistly welcoming. And Alex couldn't resist; his tongue drove savagely into her, an erotic assault that vanquished an already subdued victim. Charlotte moaned and arched forward, pressing her breasts against his hard body. Alex pulled her around and onto his chest. His mind had gone blind again; his mouth savaged hers and his hand slid seductively up her stocking, pushing her dress aside as if it didn't exist. He was raw, hungry with the need to touch her. Charlotte half sobbed with excitement. The place between her legs was heavy, throbbing, scalding with liquid warmth. His fingers reached the ruffled legs of her pantaloons and didn't stop, slid inside the loose cotton legs.

"Alex," Charlotte whispered, shuddering. "I don't know. . . ."

"It's all right, darling." Alex's voice was raw, strained. He slid his fingers into the place between her legs and Charlotte almost jumped out of her skin. Her hand involuntarily gripped his arm like a vise.

"No!" she said fiercely. But his fingers moved languorously into her hot, wet warmth. Stabbing shocks of desire traveled all over Charlotte's body, especially her legs and stomach.

"No . . ." she said again, her tone wavering a bit.

Alex leaned forward and silenced her with his mouth. His fingers suddenly moved from being gentle and soothing to being hard and sure. Charlotte couldn't help it. Her hand fell from his arm; she tore her mouth from his and moaned out loud. Alex's heart was racing and he had an erection that would take a week to subside, but he felt ecstatic. Not only had he talked sweet, sweet Charlotte into being his wife, but she had a natural passion to match his. The tales he had heard so often from men in the *ton*, about wives who lay like unhappy sticks, the unpleasant matings endured on both sides only in order to have children, flashed through his mind. Charlotte's mouth was open, her lips crimson and swollen from his kisses. She was breathing in small, fast pants. He moved a finger into her tight, wet canal and she shook visibly, moaning again, her head moving restlessly from side to side.

Alex leaned over her, his left hand caressing her breast, his mouth taking hers again, stifling her imploring moans as she strained forward against his finger. It was all Alex could do not to jerk down his breeches and drive into her. The only thing stopping him . . . well, the only thing stopping him, he thought, was himself. Charlotte was completely lost, her breath coming in catches and starts, sensation racing through her body.

Suddenly her body stiffened and she grabbed his shoulders with a fierce grip.

"Alex!" she cried, and "Alex!" Alex devoutly

hoped that no one was in the hallway. Charlotte's body convulsed into a hundred starry, shattered pieces. Prickles of sweat broke out all over her body. Alex grimly hung onto the last of his self-control as her lovely body convulsed against his, ragged moans escaping her lips.

There was silence in the Chinese Salon. Alex looked up at the ceiling and prayed for mastery of his body. He hadn't felt this close to disaster since he was an adolescent, for God's sake. Charlotte would undoubtedly be wrenchingly embarrassed when she realized what had happened. He had to resume control of his aching, throbbing erection. Finally he looked back.

Charlotte was leaning against her corner of the divan, looking not embarrassed, but stunned.

Alex leaned over and caressed her face.

"What *was* that?" she finally said.

"What?" Alex said. He didn't understand her question.

"What happened to me?" She looked straight at him, her slender eyebrows flying toward her curls.

Alex couldn't help it; he grinned. "You had an orgasm. In France they call them *la petite mort* — the little death." Charlotte looked thoughtful.

"Will it happen again?"

Alex almost laughed aloud. "I promise," he said. "I promise."

Charlotte thought about this while she pulled up the sleeves to her morning gown and shrugged her skirt down to its proper position.

Then she reached past Alex and took a cucumber sandwich from the lunch Campion brought.

Alex concentrated on thinking about horse racing. Horse racing bored him to tears and so it had become his private instrument for bodily control. Wonder crept through him. His betrothed had just had an experience that many women *never* had, and she was coolly eating a sandwich. His eyes narrowed and he looked closer. Charlotte's hands were trembling. In fact, as he watched, a tear snaked down her cheek.

Alex sighed. Miraculously the uncomfortable bulge in his pantaloons disappeared. He grabbed a cucumber sandwich for himself and slid over to sit beside his teary betrothed.

"Actually," he said meditatively, "it won't just happen again; it will be much better next time. Because this time I gave *you* pleasure, but next time we'll give each other pleasure."

Charlotte started. She hadn't thought about him at all.

"Is there something?" she asked.

"Oh, no. If you even touch me, I'll detonate," Alex said cheerfully. "You see," he continued in a silky voice, "my body is clamoring to leap on top of you and *ruin* you, as they say, and it is only my great gentlemanly control and sense of honor which is keeping me here, eating this dry sandwich." He put it back on the tray and frowningly selected another. "What I ought to do is kiss you in the carriage and then stroll into my club

wearing these deuced uncomfortable pantaloons, and it would put 'paid' to all the rumors
about my capabilities."

Charlotte looked at him from under her lashes.
His dark eyes slanted over to meet hers, the message in them undeniably seductive . . . and
amused. Suddenly Charlotte giggled. It was
rather funny, although not exactly as he thought.
He didn't want to ruin her by going any further
on her mother's Chinese divan, but he already
had ruined her.

She touched his sleeve, still feeling a bit guilty.
"Thank you," she said. At that Alex looked really
startled, even shocked.

"What's the matter?" she asked.

"Only one woman ever thanked me before —"
He broke off, taking a bite of his sandwich.

"Have you had many lovers?"

"Hundreds . . . thousands . . ." Alex waved his
sandwich in the air. Charlotte made a little moue
of disapproval. He leaned over and looked into
her eyes. "A gentleman never discusses his other
conquests," he said. "But since you will be my
last conquest, I might as well tell you that I don't
remember ever being as aroused as I have been
this afternoon . . . not in my whole life, and with
all those thousands of women."

Charlotte blushed.

"We stopped," Alex said, "because I want to
make love to you for an hour, two hours, on a
comfortable bed." His eyes glinted wickedly at
her. "And I want us to be married. You'll be

wearing my ring, and you'll be mine, and no one else's. And I want your first experience to be the beginning of a long series of nights and days together."

"Days?" Charlotte repeated, mystified.

"Days," Alex affirmed with a decadent smile. "My bedchamber has large windows, and I am going to lay you on my bed with the midday sun pouring in on us, and" — his voice was a thread of a whisper now — "I shall feast on your body for the whole afternoon."

Charlotte felt she must be cherry red.

"Damn!" Alex said in a conversational tone. "I'm reaching my limit. I shall have to go take a cold bath." Charlotte giggled.

Alex reached out and put a companionable arm around her shoulders, his hand playing with her curls.

"So, will you marry me? Shall I tell your father you agree?" he asked.

Charlotte looked up at him, her heart almost bursting with love for his wild black eyes, his flying eyebrows, his ironic sense of humor . . . the Alex of him.

"You are not always right, you know," she whispered to him, her eyes shining.

"Oh?" His right eyebrow soared up. "I assure you, no one has *ever* said I was wrong about anything!"

"Maybe there is love at fifth or sixth sight," Charlotte said sweetly. She wound her arms around his neck. "Maybe love is a matter of

311

thinking the other person is beautiful, intelligent, and funny, and even wholly . . . desirable. Maybe —" but Alex interrupted her, his mouth descending on hers again.

The silence in the Chinese salon was only broken by the door opening a short time later as a rather disheveled but very happy earl and an equally happy but composed-looking future countess walked out.

Chapter 13

Three days before her wedding Charlotte nervously put the finishing touches on her portrait of Chloe van Stork. Chloe sat patiently on the couch, as she had for weeks, but Charlotte could tell that she too was excited. Chloe had not looked at the portrait in progress. She wanted it to be a surprise, she explained somewhat childishly. Finally Charlotte made herself put down her brush. She was so jittery at the moment that she might wreck the painting just out of nerves. It was so odd to be finishing the portrait and getting married at the same time. It felt as if she were putting away her old life . . . no, that was silly. Alex had already set up a magnificent studio for her in his house. He had put it next to his study so he would know she was nearby. Charlotte smiled a secret, silly grin. She wiped her brush carefully and put it down. Later the servants would clean up all her paints and take them over to Grovesnor Square. To our house, she thought.

"Would you like to walk around and see your portrait, Chloe?"

Chloe started in surprise and jumped up.

She's such a nice person, Charlotte thought affectionately, looking at Chloe's earnest little face and clear eyes. The two young women had become good friends over the eight weeks it had taken to complete the portrait. Charlotte squinted at her portrait. Was it there? Chloe's deep-down honesty? She thought it was. The other side to Chloe, the mercurial gleams of desire which seemed so clear to Charlotte two months ago were rather dimmer in the final portrait. Perhaps because Chloe herself had lost that yearning look she had after the night of *King Lear.* The night before Alex proposed to me, Charlotte thought with a little, irresistible smile. She couldn't stop smiling when she thought about him.

"Two more besotted idiots I've never seen!" her great aunt Margaret, a formidable lady at her best, had declared. Lady Margaret had a swollen toe and was feeling particularly testy during the formal dinner given by the Duke of Calverstill to celebrate his youngest daughter's engagement to the Earl of Sheffield and Downes. "We'll see how long that lasts," she said, rather spitefully. But Margaret really was fond of her youngest niece, and this Alexander seemed to be a decent sort. She had liked his father — Old Brandy Balls, they called him when she was young. He would have been horrified to find his son plastered with a nickname like the Ineligible Earl, that was certain.

In Charlotte's studio, Chloe clapped her hand

to her mouth. "It isn't me!"

Charlotte looked startled. "Yes it is, Chloe. It looks just like you."

"No," Chloe breathed. "It's far too beautiful." A smile lit the corners of Charlotte's mouth.

"You're a raving beauty, my dear." She put an arm around Chloe's small shoulders. "You'll just have to get used to that fact." Charlotte had chosen not to place Chloe in a fashionable setting, like a ruined temple or a flowery meadow. Instead, she was sitting on the divan, just as she had in real life. Its slightly worn surface was unchallenged by Chloe's heavy twill dress, the same dress she often wore to sittings.

"Don't you think it would be a nicer picture if I wore a new dress?" Chloe had asked rather dubiously, when Charlotte announced her intention. "After all, Sissy is in an Egyptian costume —"

Charlotte broke into this comment. "Don't even mention that vulgar portrait Sissy commissioned! Poor Lady Commonweal was cut up about it for weeks. Cleopatra indeed! Sissy has *no* sense of dress."

Chloe thought about defending her school friend and then decided to keep quiet. Sissy did have awful taste in clothing, there was no getting around it. Chloe fancied that she herself would have good clothes sense, if her mother would ever let her choose a dress made in a current mode. But now that Baron Holland had dropped his suit, Mrs. van Stork said quite frankly that she didn't see any reason to spend a huge amount of money outfitting Chloe. If she found another beau, then they'd see about it. But Chloe thought agonizingly that she didn't want another beau. She wanted Will, and only Will. But Will had not only disappeared from her life; she hadn't seen him at the theater — even if from afar — for over a month. She was getting over him, she promised herself. Any day now she would stop crying herself to sleep.

She certainly didn't look like a weepy miss in Charlotte's portrait. In the end Charlotte had posed Chloe in three-quarters profile. Against the background of her dark dress and the dark couch, her porcelain white skin and deep blue eyes gave her an otherworldly beauty, an unquestioning look of serenity.

"I don't usually feel like that," Chloe said in a rather small voice.

Charlotte pulled her over to the divan. "Now that the portrait is finished, I want to know what is going on," she said. "Where is Will? I haven't seen him in weeks!"

"I don't know," Chloe replied miserably. "I don't have any idea."

"Hmmm," Charlotte said. "It's not like Will to miss the prime part of the season."

"I know," Chloe said in response to her unspoken comment. "He has to find a rich bride, doesn't he?"

Charlotte was touched by the obvious distress in Chloe's eyes. She nimbly avoided the question.

"Did you turn him down?" Charlotte asked.

Chloe's eyes fell to her hands, pleating and repleating the folds of her heavy skirt. "No," she half-whispered. "He didn't ask me."

"Well, do you think your father might have warned him off? Because, poor thing, he *does* need to marry a fortune, after all. He might lose his estate, from what I hear. And all because his father was so addicted to racehorses. It's a shame."

Chloe shook her head. "I don't think so. My father actually liked him — he said that Will, Baron Holland, had a better head for commerce than the average flimsy nobleman — oh, Charlotte, I'm sorry. I didn't mean to insult you . . . or anyone." Her voice shrank to a whisper. "The truth is, the baron must have decided he just couldn't go through with it, that's all. It's one thing to have to marry a fortune, but it's another to contemplate marrying someone, especially the daughter of a cit. I think he just couldn't bring himself to propose to me, and so he went to the country."

Charlotte gave her a swift hug. Then she got up and pulled her portrait around so that it was facing the couch.

"Chloe van Stork," she said firmly. "Look at my painting." Chloe looked. "Do you really think that Will would be able to resist the idea of marrying this woman?" Chloe looked, but she didn't see the delicate appeal in her own blue eyes, the effortless nobility of her high cheekbones and narrow shoulders, the tempered hint of sexual passion in her full red lips.

"Yes," she said.

"Well, you're wrong." Chloe absorbed this in silence. "Will is coming to our wedding," Charlotte added.

The Earl of Sheffield and Downes was marrying with more pomp and circumstance than had been seen in London for years. The invitation list to the wedding was rigorously controlled, winnowed down to peers and special friends of the bride or groom. That alone ensured that every person with any claim to being a member of the *ton* was dying for an invitation and so far only two invitations had been declined. Charlotte couldn't move outside the house without being mobbed by reporters from *The Tatler* and the *Gazette*; there was even a semipermanent gossip column in the *Tatler* dedicated to speculation over her wedding dress, honeymoon, and future life (childless or not?).

"Now," Charlotte said practically. "What are you going to wear to the wedding?" Chloe shook her head. To be honest, she hadn't decided yet whether to attend the ceremony. Her parents had firmly declined their invitation, although they were inordinately pleased to have been invited. If she attended the ceremony, she would have to be chaperoned by Sissy and her parents. But she hadn't thought to wear anything special. What did it matter? Will clearly wasn't in London. Now her heart began to beat quickly.

She would see him in three days.

"Oh, no!" Chloe said in agony. "It's too late to get a dress . . . I'll have to wear one of these." She plucked at the heavy twill again.

"No," Charlotte said. "No, indeed. You see, my mama has been thinking about nothing but my trousseau for weeks — well, ever since Alex proposed. And that means my room is simply filled with gowns, more than I could wear in a year. *And* it means that there are seamstresses on the premises: They've been here for the last month, sewing upstairs. Let's go. We'll pick out a dress and they can alter it by tomorrow."

"No, no," Chloe gasped. "You can't do that! I won't let you . . . why, you will need those clothes on your honeymoon!"

Charlotte smiled impudently as she looked back at Chloe, all the while dragging her irresistibly to the door. "No, I won't. Alex says I won't need any clothes at all." That silenced Chloe, and Charlotte bore her off upstairs.

On the day of Charlotte's wedding, London-folk began to gather at Westminster Abbey at five in the morning, the better to see the gentry filing into the chapel. By early afternoon, they had formed a cheerful, rather polite little mob, who raucously commented on the attire of each and every guest — even old Lady Tibblebutt was applauded as she tottered from her carriage, and told in no uncertain terms that she wasn't in her dotage yet; a particularly kind bystander even offered to make her as happy as a butcher on Sunday until the crowd booed him down.

Thus it was a true compliment when even the sauciest of apprentices fell into a hush of approval as Miss Chloe van Stork descended from Sir Nigel Commonweal's carriage. Diamond drops fell from her ears. Her blue eyes shone. But what made the reporters frantically thumb their commentary books was the irresistible combination of her magnolia-white skin, russet hair, and a daring green gown that could only have been designed by Antonin Carême. Monsieur Carême was quite the man of the day, given that it had been leaked to the press that he designed Lady Charlotte's wedding gown. Speculation was ripe about the style of the wedding dress. Miss van Stork's gown was a classic Carême: made of a floating, lightweight fabric, it seemed just barely to cover her bosom, and it clung softly to her legs. But would Charlotte Daicheston want to wear something so bold for her wedding?

By a quarter to four the footmen who stood at the doors of Westminster Abbey had checked off almost all the names on their lists. Few had dared to be late, for fear they would be caught in the press of carriages surrounding the abbey. The crowd outside had reached a fever pitch of excitement. The groom was here; everyone saw him go in, looking not at all nervous.

"Well, it is the second time for 'im, in't?" a certain Mall Trestle said.

"So it is, so it is," said her friend Mr. Jack, genially. "Now what's going to make that 'un nervous ain't the wedding, it's the night!"

"You're a card, Jack," Mall said rather sourly. She preferred to think of the earl — such a handsome brute he was! — as having no problems in that area.

"Well, where's the bride, then? Maybe she's piked," Jack said helpfully.

"Loped off? She never," Mall said in disgust. "Who'd leave a bloke like him, an earl an' all, and even if he's got a floppy poppy, what's she care anyway?"

Jack frowned. It offended his sense of propriety to think of a woman who didn't care of such things.

"Now, Mall," he started heavily — but just then a shiver ran through the crowd, a chattering wave of voices, as if a flock of starlings suddenly landed on a pasture fence. The bride had arrived.

Charlotte sat absolutely still inside her father's carriage. She felt giddy; she couldn't stop smiling to herself. Her mother, on the other hand, had already started to cry, sitting on the opposite seat. But Charlotte didn't make much of this; her mother had wept straight through both of her sisters' weddings. Adelaide gave a loud sob.

"Mama," Charlotte protested, half laughing. "We're here; we're at the church."

Marcel pinched his wife's arm lovingly. "Now, you remember what we talked about, Addie," he said in a low voice. "You can cry all night if you want to, but no more crying now."

Adelaide drew herself together, shuddering a bit. Marcel thought it imperative that she not cry in case it was interpreted as dislike of the match. But who could dislike this match, she thought. Dear Alexander and Charlotte: They were so much in love.

First the duchess emerged from the ducal carriage, looking properly regal. She walked into the church on the arm of her maternal cousin, the Marquess of Dorchester. Then from a following carriage came one of the bride's sisters and her husband, the Marquess of Blass. Another sister and the bride's brother followed: the papers had reported that they came all the way from America for the wedding. And finally the Duke of Calverstill himself stepped down from his carriage and stood by the door.

When Charlotte appeared in the door of the carriage and was tenderly assisted to the street by a liveried footman, there was a moment of pure silence, an odd thing in the midst of London's noisy, crowded streets. Then the crowd spontaneously howled its approval.

Antonin Carême had outdone himself. Charlotte's dress was quintessentially French, constructed in the empire style. But it was made of heavy, heavy silk, not of Carême's usual light fabrics. It had a classic small bodice, caught up just under Charlotte's breasts. But the skirt was impossibly narrow, rather than light and floating.

The heavy silk fell and fell; it made Charlotte appear to be all legs and bosom. In the back there was a tiny train, the weight of which gave a dip and sway to Charlotte's walk. And, most surprisingly, woven into the creamy silk, sewn so tightly that they seemed part of the woof and the weave of the fabric, were small emeralds. Charlotte looked deliriously beautiful. Emeralds shone in her hair, and sparkled from her dress. Carême himself had shed tears when he attended the final dressing that afternoon. His future was assured; he wept because he was sure he would never dress such a lovely bride again.

Charlotte had a moment of panic, walking under the heavy stone archway that marked the entrance to Westminster Abbey. What if Alex had changed his mind? What if he didn't want to marry her after all? But there he was, standing far off, at the top of the abbey. She took a deep breath and began the long walk to the altar.

The organ music became light and joyful, announcing the entrance of the bride. And the *ton* gasped as one when they saw Charlotte.

Alex stood at the front of the church, his eyes fixed on Charlotte. He had never seen such a beautiful woman in his entire life. It took all his control not to bound down the aisle and sweep her into his arms. He stayed rigidly still. Lucien Boch, who was acting as best man in the absence of Alex's brother, Patrick (still traveling in the Orient), drew in his breath sharply. Alex glanced at him.

"You are a lucky man," Lucien said simply. "The stars shine on you."

Alex smiled. Lucien had a wonderful ability to shrink complexities down to a succinct truth. Indeed, the stars were shining on him. Everything he had ever wanted was being delivered into his arms — and as an extra bonus, Pippa was in the front row, quietly nestled in the arms of a nanny found by Charlotte. In the weeks before the wedding Charlotte had even managed to tame Pippa's fearful reaction to strangers.

Charlotte was nearing the front of the abbey. She hadn't yet had the courage to look up and meet Alex's eyes, although she could feel him looking at her. The duke gave his daughter's hand a squeeze.

"All right?" he said roughly.

"Yes." A look that has passed between fathers and daughters ever since weddings began passed between them. Charlotte leaned forward and gave him a fleeting kiss. The duke put her hand into Alex's and turned around, rejoining his wife.

Charlotte raised her eyes. Alex was smiling down at her so tenderly that her heart turned over. The archbishop cleared his throat and they both faced the altar.

Afterward Charlotte could only remember bits and patches of the ceremony. The vows — the vows sunk deep into her mind and soul. To have and to hold, in sickness and in health, till death do us part. And the moment when Alex looked at her solemnly, repeating everything the priest said, and then his eyebrow flew up and he said, "With my body I thee worship." And after the service when the trumpets carolled joyously from the choir loft, and Alex pulled her into his arms and kissed her as if he would never let her go. And, finally, when they started back down the aisle and Alex stopped and picked up Pippa in the first row and she held out her arms and said, "My not-nanny," and Charlotte carried her down the aisle, Pippa's small head of soft curls nestled on her shoulder, to thunderous applause.

It was agreed by all that the wedding of the Earl of Sheffield and Downes to Lady Charlotte Daicheston was the most romantic ceremony in recent history. Only the truly petty murmured anything about ineligibility or past marriages. Lady Skiffing was seen to wipe away a tear, and later allowed as how it had been a very touching occasion. Lady Prestlefield boasted loudly about how the *dear children* had met in her very own house.

There were, of course, those men who looked at the creamy expanse of Charlotte's bosom, the shadowed cleft between her breasts, and prayed fervently for the moment when the bride would tire of her incapable husband. But they said nothing. And there were women struck by so fierce a stab of jealousy, seeing Alex's adoring expression, that they could have tripped the bride as she walked out of the church. But they didn't. The wedding was a huge success: It did exactly as Charlotte's mother and father had planned. It established Charlotte and Alex as a pair to be admired, courted, and imitated; it cast the rumors about his previous marriage far into the past.

Indeed only a proper paperskull could have watched the newlywed couple dancing at the ball given by the Duke of Calverstill after the wedding and not realized that the night was going to be a long and passionate one. There were many sighs as Alex swept Charlotte about the room in their first dance as a married couple, their bodies moving as one, his strong arm pulling her closer as each bar of music passed.

"How long do we have to stay here?" Alex's eyes were twinkling wickedly at Charlotte.

"Be still!" She couldn't not giggle.

"This is *it*, the limits of my control. Over two months of extreme torture . . . and you want me to stay here and grin at my old cronies and your great-aunts?"

"Why torture?" Charlotte pretended to take offence. "Didn't I kiss you good night every night?"

"Yes . . . for as long as it would take to fry an egg!"

"No, longer," she protested. "By that measurement, last night you could have fried up eggs for a regiment, isn't that true?"

"It wasn't long enough," Alex said against her lips. "I can't take it, Charlotte. I feel insane with desire. I feel crazed. What if I lose my mind, strip off my clothes, run into Hyde Park naked, and end up in Bedlam?"

Charlotte chuckled, her eyes dancing. "If I thought that was going to happen I might insist we stay here until midnight."

"Shhhh, Charlotte!" Alex quickly retorted. "If these old ladies knew how desperate you are to see me naked, there's no telling what would happen to your reputation!"

"I am an old married lady, Alexander Foakes."

"So you don't think that married ladies have sought my naked self?" Alex gave her a mocking leer.

"I'm a married lady, a married countess," Charlotte said softly. "And I am *very* interested in your naked self." Alex's eyes darkened and he swung her around in a circle, putting his face against her soft hair.

"I won't answer that," he finally said, in a rough undertone. Charlotte smiled to herself and relaxed her body against his. Her breasts pressed softly against his hard chest. Alex drew in a deep breath and struggled for self-control, a common problem of the last few months. Lord, if only all those scandal-brewers knew how close he was to the opposite problem. Priapism, he fancied it was called. A constant, painful erection.

Chloe stood in the midst of a group of young ladies, watching the newlywed couple dance. Her eyes were wistful, even if her face was perfectly composed. The same couldn't be said for her friend Sissy, who was openly gaping at Charlotte and Alex. In fact, Sissy was frantically deciding that she *would* marry Richard Felvitson, even if he *was* a younger son and declared absolutely ineligible by her mama. Look at Charlotte! She was marrying an "Ineligible Earl" — and look how happy she was! Unaware of Sissy's reckless thoughts, Chloe struggled against the knowledge that her throat was tight with tears.

Charlotte's dress had worked its magic for Chloe. Her dance card was full; in all, five gentlemen had requested the honor of taking her in to supper. But if Baron Holland was here, The Dress — as Chloe thought of it — hadn't affected him. When Chloe first walked into the church she thought she caught a glimpse of his tousled blond curls, off to the left on a side aisle. But even when she craned her head to see him again she couldn't find him. And if he was attending the ball he hadn't bothered to ask her for a dance. Charlotte and Alex's dance ended and the ball proper began.

Peter Dewland bowed politely before Chloe and she gave him a shy smile. Ever since she met Peter in Charlotte's box, the night of *King Lear*, she had liked him. He seemed to be as quiet as she was, and he never bothered her with inappropriate comments or by trying to kiss her. They found their places in the country dance and by the luck of the draw they were one of the first couples to dance lightly down the arch of joined hands, twirling, whirling their way down the set and back up the other side, finally stopping at the bottom of the ballroom. They talked for a while, and Peter told Chloe all about the fireworks she had missed by leaving Vauxhall so early.

"Would you like some lemonade?" he asked, aware that the dance was drawing to a close.

"Yes, I would." Chloe smiled up at him guilelessly, unaware that furious blue eyes were surveying them both from a foot or so away.

Peter smiled back warmly. He really liked Chloe; she reminded him of his younger sister, Bess. "I'll return immediately."

Six feet of hard muscled body loomed up at Chloe's right shoulder. She turned her head quickly. It was Will. His eyes were just as blue as she remembered; bluer than the sky on a blistering day in July.

"Oh, it's you," she said lamely.

"Yes, it's me," Will snapped back. "What in God's name have you done with yourself?"

"Why, what do you mean?"

Will's eyes narrowed. "It was Charlotte, wasn't it? She's fitted you out like some kind of French tart. You look awful. What are you doing — trying to marry an earl?"

It was a particularly unfortunate remark since at that moment Chloe's next dance partner appeared: Braddon Chatwin, the Earl of Slaslow.

"There you are, Miss van Stork. No, you can't dance this one," he said genially to Will. "She's mine for the next *and* for supper."

The look of bruised hurt in Chloe's eyes faded to cool ice as she nodded at Will and took Braddon's arm. Then she deliberately turned and smiled up at Braddon.

"Shall we take a small walk on the terrace before dancing, my lord?"

Braddon Chatwin's friendly face lit up. "I'd be delighted to, Miss van Stork. I'd be delighted to." As they wove their way off toward the terrace, all Will could hear were Braddon's repeated protestations of delight. He cursed silently. What was the matter with him? He'd been waiting and waiting to see Chloe, and then when he saw her he behaved like a dunce, a mean-spirited, nasty sapskull.

When Braddon and Chloe glided to a pause at the end of their waltz, Chloe smiled at him with an effort. She was having a hard time maintaining a smiling front, given Will's unwarranted attack. She didn't know what to make of it. Why was he so angry about her beautiful gown? Chloe had no idea how delectable she looked in the gown; the way every man in the room was practically salivating just to see her. Will saw those men looking at Chloe in the gown, or rather looking at the parts of her that were hanging *out* of the gown, and it made him feel like a bull set loose in a field of dogs. He saw red.

Even as Braddon dropped his arm from Chloe's waist, Will grabbed her elbow. She jumped in surprise.

"You again," Braddon said, rather less affably than he had before. "I was about to escort Miss van Stork —"

"Nowhere!" Will snapped. "She's busy."

"No, I am not!" Chloe said sharply, struggling to free her arm from his punishing grip. "I'm not going anywhere with you, you —"

Will's temper grew. "Yes, you are! If you want to go out on the terrace again, you'll go out with me!" Braddon Chatwin looked from one to the other with a sense of regret. Pity: He really liked Miss van Stork. He had been on the cusp of seeing her as the answer to his mother's prayers. Oh, well, he reminded himself. If he wasn't the brightest man in London, he had been told several times that he was very *sensitive* for a man. And what a sensitive man would do in this situation, clearly, was to make himself scarce.

"Miss van Stork, your servant," he said. "Will." He bowed regally (she was giving up an earl for a baron, after all) and left.

Chloe raised her chin stubbornly. "Baron Holland," she said coolly, summoning the self-control acquired during years of attending the best schools without having the best background. "Is there something you would like to say, excluding further commentary on my apparel?"

Will stared at her, nonplussed. "Yes." He pulled her through the open French windows and onto the terrace. Chloe looked about quickly. They were well chaperoned; several matrons were sitting at their ease in the cool evening air.

"Well?" she said, in a tone of acute uninterest, pulling her arm from his. Rather than looking up she inspected her arm as if she thought to find bruises already appearing. There was a little silence. Will was cursing himself again. For years he had had a deserved reputation for being a lady-killer. He knew to a pin how to compliment a woman, how to turn a teasing, merry moment into an erotic question. And how to ask a woman to marry him. Lord knows, he'd asked three so far. So where had all his skill gone? He felt like a young buck trying to make the acquaintance of a duchess.

"Perhaps this is not a good time," he finally said. At that Chloe looked up, her eyes briefly meeting his, and then she looked back down again. "I apologize for insulting your gown, Miss van Stork," he said with deliberate formality. "I was, naturally, driven only by jealousy." But he said it so lightly that it sounded like a mere excuse. Chloe nodded in response.

"Shall I escort you inside? I am sure your next dance partner must be looking for you."

A faint pink rose in Chloe's cheeks. She was struggling not to cry as she never had before. She nodded silently again. Will took her arm and gave her without another word into the arms of her next partner. Thankfully the dance was a rousing cotillion, and Chloe didn't have to say anything and only smiled punctiliously at her partner when she bumped up against him in the movements of the dance.

The evening progressed. Chloe thought she'd never been to a more horrible ball in her life. Will, savagely aware of every man who took Chloe into his arms, flirted outrageously with the wife of Captain Prebworth. And everyone knew that Camilla Prebworth was no better than she should be, Chloe thought miserably. She tried not to watch, but somehow she just kept seeing Will's large blond head wherever she looked. Perhaps she should plead a heartache and go home? But then . . . then she wouldn't see Will again tonight, and he might disappear into the country. Wasn't it better to see him from afar than not to see him at all? She argued with herself back and forth.

Watching Charlotte and Alex wave good-bye from the top of the ballroom stairs only fed her heartache. They were so happy, so obviously in love. Alex looked at Charlotte as if she were the moon and the stars . . . you wouldn't catch him saying that his wife looked like a French tart, Chloe thought furiously. And then she blinked back tears again. It was probably just that Charlotte was naturally aristocratic, being a duke's daughter, and Will thought she, Chloe, was too low-born to wear a gown like this. First she felt like throwing up, and then like slapping him in the face.

Chloe and Braddon Chatwin had an extremely animated supper, given that Will was feeding

333

Mrs. Prebworth pieces of chicken with his fingers, a mere two tables away. Chloe flirted with Braddon in a way that shook that earl to the bottom of his toes. Luckily for him, he kept his head by assuring himself that his sensitivity had not been wrong, and Miss van Stork didn't really mean for him to grab her up and take her off to meet his mama this very moment.

Chloe had never been so wretched in her life. She was flirting with a big, clumsy person. He might be an earl, but he was the most ponderous man she'd ever met. All he seemed to be able to talk about were his stables. And meanwhile Will was practically kissing Mrs. Prebworth right there, in front of the whole *ton!* Finally she'd had enough.

She raised her eyes endearingly to Braddon. "My lord, I find myself suddenly quite tired — although I have most enjoyed our supper," she added hastily. "Will you escort me back to Lady Commonweal, please?"

And so when Will risked another glance in the direction of Chloe and that confounded Braddon, as he had taken to thinking of his old school friend, there was no one there. The table had been taken over by a chattering flock of matrons, escorted by one bored husband.

"Damnation!" he swore, jumping to his feet. Mrs. Prebworth raised her eyebrows, laughing.

"Did the bird fly the coop?" she asked.

Will sat down again. "You saw through me?"

"Not that I don't appreciate your attention,"

Camilla Prebworth assured him. "But I felt as if someone was being murdered to the right, you looked over so often. Well, go find her," she said. "And if you see my husband, will you tell him where I am?" She was a bit tired of being the target of so many gossips' eyes. Maybe it was time to take herself and her beloved, long-suffering husband home.

Will jumped to his feet, smiling down at her. "Thanks," he said briefly. He strode out of the supper room at top speed.

As soon as he entered the ballroom he saw her. Somehow his nerves seemed to be attuned to Chloe's presence. He could instinctively pick her out of any crowd. But what in God's name was he to do now? The Commonweals were making unmistakable gestures of leave-taking. Lady Commonweal was clucking about, gathering her shawls and pillboxes; Sir Nigel Commonweal was holding his wife's wrap while his eyes scanned — far too ardently! Will thought wrathfully — Chloe's bosom. But it was clear that someone was holding up the party. That tiresome girl of theirs must be missing, Will thought. What was her name? Something like Bessy, except that was a dairy maid's name. Even as he watched, Lady Commonweal urgently directed Chloe off toward the salons while her husband headed out to the terrace and the gardens beyond.

Will moved quickly along the side of the ballroom, twisting among groups of chattering girls, delicate French chairs holding matrons wearing little starched caps, the occasional gallant broodily leaning against the wall. He had to see her; he had to talk to her. Tomorrow would be too late. Then, suddenly, there Chloe was before him. She was working her way along the same wall, rather than heading straight out to the salons, as he had guessed.

Chloe looked at him guardedly, her beautiful eyes shadowed.

"She isn't back there," Will said with a toss of his head. Chloe frowned. "Bessy, or whatever her name is, the Commonweal girl," he added. "She must be in one of the salons."

Chloe nodded a chilly thank you and turned around, working her way back to the doors leading to the great hallway. Every nerve tingled, telling her that Will was following just behind. At the top of the ballroom steps she didn't allow herself to look behind her. Instead she set off resolutely down the hallway toward the Green Salon, as she had heard Charlotte call it. She pushed the door open cautiously. Surely Sissy couldn't be foolish enough to be sitting out a dance in a closed salon! That alone was enough to ruin a girl's reputation. The room appeared to be empty, lit only by candles that were beginning to burn low.

Suddenly a warm, utterly male body came up sharply behind hers and pushed her through the doors, which shut behind them with a little click. Will wrapped his arms around Chloe and held her there, her back pressed against his chest. She didn't struggle; that must mean something, he thought.

"I missed you," he said. Chloe stared straight ahead. She had her emotions under fragile control. The only thought in her mind was that she mustn't respond to anything he said because he would accuse her of being a tart again. Then his head bent and she realized he was dropping kisses on her head and rubbing his cheek in her hair.

"Sir," she began primly.

Will kissed her ear. "Yes?"

Chloe wrenched herself out of his arms, walking forward and only turning around when she reached the back of a chair. "Just because I look like a tart doesn't mean you can behave as if I am one," she said fiercely.

Will gulped. "I didn't mean that! I just meant that your dress . . . well, it's so revealing, or it reveals so much of you. . . ." His hands nervously sketched a shape in the air. Chloe glared at him.

"It's no more revealing than what the other *ladies* are wearing!"

Will wondered what she meant by emphasizing *ladies* but ignored it. He walked toward her. "You are not like the rest of the ladies —" he began.

She interrupted him. "I knew it! Because I'm not a lady you think I shouldn't be wearing this dress!" The tears that had threatened to fall all day welled up and overflowed. She ran to the door, but Will was there, quick as lightning.

"How can you even say that?" he demanded furiously. "I meant nothing of the sort! You are every inch a lady," he continued more softly, "from your beautiful hair to your delectable toes. I acted like an idiot because, well, I liked your old clothes because you were my undiscovered diamond, my jewel that no one else knew about. And I know I acted like a madman when I first saw you this evening. But everyone was looking at you, and all the men were saying you were a diamond of the first water. It was a fit of insanity. You see . . . I'd got into the habit in the last month of thinking that you were mine, and no one else's."

Chloe stood stock still, her face pressed against his shirt by the strength of his arms around her. "Where have you been?" she asked, her voice muffled.

"Working," Will replied. "I've been organizing the sheep farmers on my land. We have started a weaving guild, and just last week a new flock of fancy sheep were delivered. You see, I've decided to make a fortune rather than marry into it."

A hand pushed up her face and Will kissed the tears from Chloe's cheeks. She looked at him gravely. She didn't know what to say. What about *her* fortune?

"I want to marry you, Chloe. But I want you on my terms . . . with my own money, and not for your fortune."

Chloe nodded, her eyes filling up again.

"Why are you crying, dearest?" Will asked.

"I didn't know where you were . . . and I thought you couldn't bear the idea of marrying me." She hid her face in his shirt again. Will kissed her neck.

"I want to marry you. And so does virtually every other single man out there and quite a lot of the married ones as well. Can you wait for me?" He looked at her anxiously. Chloe just barely stopped herself from smiling at the ridiculousness of his request. "At most it will be a year before the wool starts making a profit — and the moment it makes a profit, I will be pounding at your front door."

Chloe did smile at that. "Oh, Will," she said. Will looked down at her. His composed, unfailingly neat beloved looked like a ragamuffin who'd been in a storm. He had ruffled her smooth hair when he kissed her head; her cheeks were tearstained and pink. But she looked exquisitely happy, and not even the abrupt and furious entrance of Lady Commonweal, who had found her daughter cannoodling on the balcony and now found Chloe cannoodling in a closed salon, could take away the light in her eyes.

Her hand lost in his huge one, Chloe listened as Will talked Lady Commonweal into a better mood, flattered Sissy, and arranged to escort Chloe home himself. Will's hand felt different — it was no longer a smooth, dancing man's hand, but a hand toughened and callused by two months' work. Chloe smiled blissfully and, characteristically, said nothing.

Chapter 14

The new Countess of Sheffield and Downes perched on the edge of a huge bed in the finest hostelry in Bournemouth, feeling unwontedly nervous. Charlotte looked at her hands. They were trembling slightly. The problem was that her husband was about to appear. And then they would make love, again. It was the *again* that was making her clutch the bedcovers. Oh, why hadn't she been more blunt with her mother, asked her a few more questions? For her part, Adelaide had avoided the subject entirely, simply patting her daughter on the shoulder and cheerfully remarking that since Charlotte knew all about marital relations they didn't have to talk about it.

Charlotte was unsurprised by Adelaide's wish to drop the topic. For one thing, Charlotte had a very clear memory of the pain that was involved. No wonder her mother didn't want to discuss it. Charlotte flinched at the thought, involuntarily pressing her thighs tightly together. She could only suppose that women got used to it as the years passed. Her eyes softened. She did love all the *other* things that Alex did. She thought dimly about the Chinese salon.

But what was really terrifying was her growing conviction that Alex would think something was wrong with her. The blood — and the pain — she hadn't thought about that for years. Then suddenly, about a week ago, it all came back to her. What if she *was* ruined, physically? She stared down at her toes, just peeking out from beneath her lace peignoir. Antonin Carême's idea of a trousseau was thoroughly French. She was barely dressed, Charlotte thought. There was no use hoping that Alex would be uninterested: He had spent the last two hours in the coach sitting on the opposite seat. Because he was feeling like a satyr, he said.

She got up and put on the large flannel robe she wore after bathing. It probably looked ridiculous, given that creamy silk trailed below its hem, but Charlotte didn't care. It made her feel safer. She tied the cord tightly. And knotted it. Marie had brushed out her hair, giggling significantly the whole time, but even she had left some twenty minutes ago. Maybe Alex had fallen asleep, Charlotte thought with dawning hope. Maybe she would be spared tonight?

But even as her shoulders relaxed, the heavy wooden door swung open and there he stood. Her husband, Charlotte thought. She couldn't help a tiny smile at the sight of him. Alex was so splendid-looking. He had taken off his cravat at some point, and his white linen shirt was open at the top. He didn't have his jacket on either, and her eye instinctively followed the line of his skintight knit pantaloons as he walked across the room toward her. Even a nitwit would have noticed that he was expecting a good deal more pleasure out of this evening than she was. The last trace of color drained from Charlotte's face.

Alex swallowed a grimace. By God, he had wanted a virgin bride, but now he saw what one looked like, he wondered why anyone would desire such a thing. Gone was his laughing, teasing betrothed, who would kiss him good-bye until his blood raged with desire and then run teasingly up the steps to her own room. Charlotte's pinched white face looked pitifully small.

"Sweetheart," Alex said, sitting down next to his wife on the bed. "Who's been telling you old wives' tales? It doesn't hurt that much."

Charlotte digested this in silence. She could hardly say, at this point, that she knew all about the pain and he was wrong. She buried her face in his shoulder. Alex pulled Charlotte into his arms. What in God's name was she wearing? She looked like a fuzzy white ghost. He started to kiss whatever parts of her face he could pry off his shoulder. Charlotte burrowed closer. Alex put butterfly-light kisses all along the rim of her dainty pink ear. Then he put out his tongue and ran it gently along the swirling shell.

A muffled voice emerged from his shirt. "Have you made love to many virgins?" Alex's eyebrows flew up. Did she think there was anything special to it? What *had* her mama said to her?

"Hundreds," he chuckled. Charlotte shivered. "I'm fooling, Charlotte," Alex said. "I made love to one virgin before you." That *was* me, Charlotte thought. "And she didn't seem to find it objectionable; in fact, I think she quite enjoyed it," Alex added. At that Charlotte clamped her mouth together. Clearly this was not the time to clarify their past relations.

Alex's hands had started to move over her shoulders and back in a manner that was less comforting than seductive. "Don't worry," he whispered. "I'm your husband and you are my wife. You may feel a moment or two of pain, but believe me, Charlotte, after that the pain will be gone forever. And there may not be any pain at all. We'll make love tonight, and tomorrow, and the next night, and every night for thirty years, and we will get better and better together." Alex's lips were trailing down her neck now, burning her skin. Charlotte forced herself to relax. She lay passively in Alex's arms rather than flinching away from him. His mouth trailed up her throat and pushed up her chin. She looked up at him.

Alex's heart missed a step. She was incredibly beautiful, his bride. Soft black curls framed a face so delicate that it looked like a Botticelli painting. Alex took Charlotte's face in his hands and covered it with passionate kisses, kissing her dark, questioning eyes, her winged eyebrows, the petal-soft curve of her cheeks, her small determined chin. She seemed quieter, he thought, less like a bird struggling to escape from his hand. He lowered his mouth gently onto hers, teasing her, begging her to open her mouth the way he had taught her.

Charlotte was having an internal battle. Alex's soft kisses were awakening all those trembling, stabbing feelings that made her sleep so restlessly in the last two months. She would awake gasping from a dream in which she begged for something . . . she wasn't sure what. Something only Alex could give her.

But some part of her also held back. Don't do it, a small voice advised. It will hurt; he will find out that there's something wrong with you; it will ruin everything! Yet even as Charlotte's mind struggled, her body responded. Alex was kissing her so sweetly, so tenderly. Almost unnoticed, her mouth slid open and she drew in his tongue. A corresponding stab of fiery desire mounted in her stomach. Charlotte's hands crept up to Alex's neck, and her fingers entwined with his thick curls. The kiss was deceptively innocent, like all the kisses they shared in the last two months. Fear flew from Charlotte's mind along with memory of pain. This was nothing terrifying, simply one of the feverish kisses Alex often gave her. He would finally tear himself away, gasping out loud. Momentarily she forgot that there was more expected this night.

So when Alex pulled back, looking down at his bride speculatively, he was happy to see her cheeks delicately flushed, her eyes dreamy. *This* was his Charlotte.

"I think we should have some champagne," he said. "I didn't get to toast the bride, after all." Relief showed in Charlotte's eyes. He wasn't going to jump on her and . . . penetrate her.

"Oh, yes!" she said, a little too quickly. Alex chuckled.

"Would you believe me if I said that next week when I ask if you would like champagne you will toss your wine glass to the side and leap on top of me?"

"No," Charlotte said, fascinated despite herself. Leap on top of *him?* What did he mean?

Alex uncorked a bottle of Dom Pérignon. He was having less trouble than he thought stamping down his raging emotions. It must be all the practice, he thought with a touch of self-mockery. Or, more likely, he just didn't find the idea of a frightened bed partner arousing. He carried two slender glasses back to the bed.

"At some point tonight we have to toast my father," Alex said, grinning at Charlotte. As soon as he had left her immediate vicinity, she had grown stiff and nervous again. "He laid down this champagne before he died, and what with the embargo because of Napoleon we would probably have to toast each other in brandy."

Charlotte wrinkled her nose. She had found out that the main ingredient in Keating's headache remedy was brandy. And she still couldn't quite reconcile the memory of her absolutely wanton behavior, sprawled over her mother's Chinese divan, with her sense of self. She could

345

only suppose that she had been totally inebriated.

"Now," Alex said. "I don't suppose you learned any drinking songs when you were in that prudish boarding school of yours, did you?"

Charlotte stared at him in fascination. "What do you mean?"

"Drinking rounds? No, of course not," Alex said to himself. But Charlotte wasn't stupid. She heard a way out, and she seized it.

"I would like to learn one," she said. She sipped her champagne.

"Right," Alex replied. He couldn't stop grinning tonight. This had to be the craziest way to seduce one's own bride that had ever occurred to a man before. "Now, this is one of Patrick's favorite songs." Alex began singing in a rich baritone. Charlotte listened, fascinated.

"Last night a dream came into my head,
Thou wert a fine white loaf of bread;
Then if May butter I could be,
How I would spread,
Oh! How I would spread my self on thee!"

Charlotte's cheeks turned hotly pink at the end of the verse.

"Now you have to drink," her husband prompted. Charlotte obediently sipped her champagne. "Not like that!" Alex protested. "A proper swallow, or I won't sing the next verse!"

Charlotte giggled and took a huge swallow. "Now," Alex said, "the audience has to pay the singer to continue." Charlotte looked surprised. "With a kiss." Charlotte obediently leaned forward and pressed a kiss on his lips. Alex smiled at her and began the next verse. *"Lately when Fancy too did roam . . ."* but he broke off in a strangled choking fit. Alarmed, Charlotte quickly pulled her feet up onto the bed and slid over to sit right next to Alex.

"Are you all right?" She pounded him on the back. Alex kept his head down to hide his smile.

"No," he said in a melancholy tone. "I'm afraid the singer wasn't paid enough."

Charlotte giggled despite herself. She took another drink of champagne and set down the glass. Then she put a kiss on Alex's ear. When he didn't move she daringly put out her tongue and slid it around the inside of his ear, just as he had with hers. Alex shuddered and surged at his bride. His mouth closed hotly over hers, taking her mouth in a drugging, passionate kiss that sent her melting into his arms. Her mouth was entirely open to his assault, to the fiery, demanding rhythm of his tongue.

Then he pulled back abruptly. Charlotte gasped. Alex smiled and tucked one of her curls back behind her ear. Then he sang again:

> *"Lately when Fancy too did roam,*
> *Thou were, my dear, a honey-comb;*
> *And had I been a pretty bee,*
> *How I would suck*
> *Oh! How I would creep, creep into thee."*

347

"Drink," her husband prompted. Charlotte giggled again. She couldn't help thinking of Will Holland telling her that he was a honey bee. She took a drink.

"Is Patrick's favorite song well known?" she asked.

"Tolerably. Why?" Charlotte smiled into her glass as Alex refilled it.

"I think someone once quoted part of this verse to me."

"Huh!" Alex snorted. "I hope it wasn't the last line." Charlotte chortled a bit. Alex looked a bit sulky at that revelation: Could it be that he was jealous? Alex frowned for a moment and then forgot his jealousy. He gave his beloved a mock glare.

"My payment."

"Oh," Charlotte leaned forward, entirely willing.

"No." His large hand pushed her back. Charlotte's left eyebrow flew up. Despite himself, Alex stared at her eyebrow in fascination. Could it be that they had a shared ancestor, somewhere back in the middle ages?

"My lord," Charlotte prompted in dulcet tones. "Your *payment?*"

"That white thing — off with it!"

Charlotte, who was relishing the glowing warmth that was spreading throughout her body, readily undid the knot at her waist and slipped off her bathrobe. She had the enormous satisfaction of seeing her husband's eyes widen for a moment. He swallowed hard. Charlotte grinned at him impudently.

"The next verse?" she asked.

"Just a minute," Alex said, his voice suddenly raspy. "I need a moment to recover." Charlotte was wearing a creamy silk nightgown of the type he wouldn't have thought proper ladies ever wore. It had wide lacy straps over her shoulders — but the unique part of the gown was that one of the lacy straps continued straight into the silk. It wandered over Charlotte's left breast, and Alex could clearly see a small rosy nipple peeping at him. It seemed to wind around the back, and curved to the front just below the waist. But because Charlotte had her legs tucked under her, he could just glimpse a bit of curly dark hair through the lace. Oh, God, she wasn't wearing anything under the gown.

Alex's arousal had reached an excruciating point. He tore his eyes away from Charlotte's waist, taking a deep breath, and readjusted his pantaloons. It would be heaven to take them off, but he didn't dare frighten her at this point. Still, he looked up and caught her looking at his hands. Instead of looking like a hypnotized deer, she was looking distinctly interested, it seemed to him.

"The next verse?" Charlotte demanded. Alex cleared his throat.

"You sound very tired," his wife said. "Maybe I could . . . give you some energy." To Alex's utter surprise, Charlotte closed the inch or so between them, so her side was touching his. She swung her legs over his. Then she leaned back on her hands and smiled at him enchantingly.

"Charlotte," Alex said hoarsely. "If you want me to keep singing, you can't torment me like this." His eyes kindled a blaze in Charlotte that made her simply arch one delicate shoulder, delighting in the way the silk draped over her full breasts. Without conscious volition, Alex's hand reached out and almost roughly traced the enchanting, heavy weight of one breast. Charlotte's eyes darkened but she didn't push him away. She let her breast stay in his hand and somehow found her voice in the midst of the raging feelings surging through her body. She felt like shamelessly pressing herself into his arms, but instead she said:

"My verse!"

Alex made a strangled noise and pulled his hand back from her breast. He grabbed the two glasses of champagne on the side table and took a gulp from his glass, handing her the other. After he gave her an admonishing look, Charlotte also drank.

"All right," Alex said finally. "But — for this kind of ballad a singer cannot be as uncomfortably dressed as this particular singer is." He stood up, swinging Charlotte's legs off his knees while continuing to talk in a conversational tone. "You know what I mean, Charlotte. That Indian snake charmer we saw at the Palladium — what was he wearing?"

Charlotte wasn't paying any attention. Alex drew his white shirt over his head, the action emphasizing his muscled chest. His skin was a golden honey-brown. She trembled with longing. She would like to run her fingers over his muscles . . . Alex noted her bemused expression with relief. He pulled off his boots, and finally hauled his knit pantaloons and underwear down to his ankles and stepped out of them. Charlotte's eyes widened but she couldn't stop lookiing.

Alex grinned. "He was wearing a white nightshirt, Charlotte!" She just stared at him. "Would you like me to pull on a nightshirt?"

Charlotte shook her head no, then yes.

"Too late!" her husband said cheerfully, sitting down on the bed. Charlotte's stomach felt as if it were melting. He was just going to sit there, stark naked, with all the candles burning? She instinctively crossed her arms over her breasts. She would *never* sit around naked, in the light, no matter what he thought. She had conveniently forgotten all of Alex's whispered stories about how he planned to make love to her in full sunshine.

Alex pretended not to notice the arms clamped over Charlotte's breasts. He handed Charlotte her glass of champagne again, and she reluctantly unwrapped one arm in order to take it. Then he cleared his throat self-importantly.

> "*A vision too I had of old,*
> *That thou a mortar were of gold;*

351

Then could I but the pestle be,
How I would pound,
Oh! How I would pound my spice in thee!"

Charlotte was trying to cope with the feeling of melting, liquid fire that seemed to be invading every limb of her body. Was Alex going to "pound" into her? It even . . . it even sounded pleasant. Never one to miss an opportunity, Alex took one look at Charlotte's flushed cheeks and trembling lips and smoothly removed her glass again. His body came down on hers with crushing force, suddenly pressing Charlotte back onto the bed. She gasped but her hands came up to his neck rather than pushing him away. The sensation of his body intimately pressing into hers engrossed all her attention. Instinctively she arched her hips slightly and pressed against him.

Slowly! Alex thought. Slowly! He took Charlotte's mouth, lingeringly kissing her in a tormenting, seductive rhythm that made her writhe under him. Her lungs felt as if they didn't have enough air; her legs were trembling. Charlotte moaned, her breath coming in short pants. Still Alex prolonged the kiss, his hand abruptly descending onto her breast. His thumb rubbed Charlotte's nipple through her silk gown and she arched against him again. She clutched his shoulders with her hands.

Alex was almost mad with desire, and yet in the back of it all he felt ecstatic. This was it —

heaven, the closest he'd been to heaven since he made love to his girl-in-the-garden. And this time was so much better than the garden, because it was *his* Charlotte who lay under him, her head thrown back, sweat glimmering on her throat, her red lips opening in shattered moan after moan. God, he knew she would be a fiery lover.

Then rational thought deserted him. Charlotte's hands fluttered from their snug circle around his neck and slowly found their way down his naked back to the curve of his waist where his muscled buttocks flared. Alex groaned as her hands curiously swept down as far as they could go, finally sliding to the side and coming back up. He grabbed her hands and held them over her head, rubbing his lips across hers.

She opened her eyes. "I want to touch you too," she whispered. Alex almost lost his control on the spot.

"No," he said huskily. "You're driving me mad, Charlotte. Next time." He caught up both of her wrists in one of his huge hands and dropped his other hand down to her waist. Then he began slowly to haul up her nightgown, watching her eyes for signs of fear. All he saw was dazed, innocent longing. In fact, Charlotte didn't even notice what he was doing. Her body felt as if it weren't hers anymore. Her breasts felt heavier, prickly, alive. Her legs had become a pool of liquid fire. The only thing she could think about was pulling Alex on top of her . . . feeling him rub his heavy weight against her again. Her stomach twisted with longing. She whimpered, and opened her eyes.

"Alex," she whispered, *"please!"*

Her nightgown was at her waist. Alex's hand dipped into the sweet enclosure between her thighs and a shudder of sweat broke out over his body. She was ready . . . she was more than ready. On her part, Charlotte let out a half shriek as his finger sunk into her warm depths. She sobbed out loud, her breathing labored.

Alex positioned himself over her, rubbing himself against her. Charlotte's eyes were fastened desperately on his, her body taken over by a throbbing, aching need. Alex slid slowly inside her, rigidly controlling every movement. He was planning the slowest, most gentle first time that any woman ever experienced. He went about a third of the way in and then began to withdraw. But Charlotte whimpered and clutched his shoulders with a heartfelt "No . . ."

Alex looked down at her. Charlotte's face was wild with desire, transformed. He leaned down to kiss her and her mouth opened vulnerably to his invasion. She arched against him again, and he burst free. For the first time in his adult life Alexander Foakes completely lost control.

He plunged into Charlotte's incredible warmth, ramming his way into the narrow canal that clung moistly and seemed to part for him. Dimly he noticed that Charlotte seemed to be lucky enough not to have a maidenhead. But he was lost, driving into her again and again. And yet, she was *with* him. He knew, even as he knew that if she hadn't been with him, there would have been nothing he could do about it. He had waited too long for this moment.

For her part, Charlotte was having a hard time not shrieking. But there was no pain, just unbearably sweet, unbearably piercing pleasure. With every stroke her body instinctively rose to meet Alex's. And she felt a rising sense of tension that wasn't helped even when her body ground against his.

When Alex came up on his knees, putting his large hands under her hips and pulling her up to meet his punishing strokes, she couldn't stop herself; she started to cry out with every drive of his hips. Alex reached down and ripped her negligee apart at the neck, grabbing her breast and bringing it to his mouth. It was like throwing gunpowder on a raging fire. With the next thrust of his hips Charlotte screamed out loud. Her body convulsed sweetly around Alex's and he plunged into her madly, driving himself home with her. His deep, growling moan came seconds after the explosions in her body began to cease. And then his heavy body, damp with sweat, settled onto hers.

There was a moment of silence. Alex was trying to collect himself. He'd made love in gardens, in a carriage, to French courtesans and to a Danish princess, but he had never experienced shared passion like this in his entire life. Charlotte was still trying to catch her breath. Her mouth kept curving into a smile of pure happiness. She snuggled her cheek against Alex's curls. Her whole body was caught in a wave of lassitude; her eyes started to close immediately. But she couldn't just go to sleep, she thought languorously.

"Alex," she finally murmured into his neck. "I didn't know . . . it was wonderful, so wonderful." There was a little silence. Alex lazily kissed the top of her head.

"I have never felt anything like it," he admitted. Charlotte almost drifted off into sleep. Then she remembered what she wanted to say.

"It wasn't at all like the other time," she whispered. "No pain . . ." Her eyes fluttered shut and she fell straight into sleep. She didn't notice that her husband's body had suddenly become rigid on top of her.

With utter disbelief Alex rolled away from his sleeping wife's side, staring at her incredulously. A black, black emptiness pressed down on his heart. By God, it had happened again. Charlotte was *no virgin,* just as Maria had been no virgin. No wonder she felt no pain; no wonder she wanted to touch him! Someone else, another man, had probably told her to say that, had taught her how to touch a man and arouse him. His stomach heaved. Charlotte looked so innocent, so unbelievably innocent, curled into a snug ball, her cheeks still flushed with pleasure, a small smile hovering even in her sleep. Why shouldn't she be happy, for God's sake? She'd fooled him. He was the loser again; fooled by a woman into thinking she was a virgin. She must have been laughing every night in the last couple of months! He thought with loathing of the nights when he had left her house, raging with desire. He had been such a simpleton he hadn't even visited a whore to satisfy himself, thinking it would be disloyal to her. *Disloyal!* By God, he had a whore of his own.

His stomach heaved again and Alex made it to the chamber pot just in time, regurgitating all the wedding supper he and Charlotte had lovingly shared in a private dining room downstairs. His mind was black, burning with rage, his body twisted with self-loathing.

In the bed Charlotte sat bolt upright, startled out of her sleep by the noise Alex was making in the corner of the room. Instantly she scrambled off the bed, running over to the corner in her bare feet.

"Sweetheart," she said softly, rubbing her hand along Alex's bent back. Then she let go and turned to snatch a towel from the chair. She brought it back just as Alex straightened up. He grabbed the towel from her and rubbed his mouth. Slowly Charlotte realized that something was wrong besides Alex's stomach. He was looking at her in such a way. . . .

"What's the matter, Alex?" she finally asked timidly. Something about his glance made her clutch her ruined nightgown together at the neck. His eyes raked her body, conveying utter disgust and rage.

"The matter is," he said in a grating, ice-cold voice, "that I only just found out that I married yet another whore, and I am finding it a difficult sop to swallow."

Charlotte stared at him in utter bewilderment.

"You were no virgin, were you?" he advanced on her menacingly, his eyes black with rage.

"No," Charlotte said tremblingly, "but —"

"God damn it!" Alex turned away from her abruptly. His fingers were shaking with the urge to hit her, but he had never hit a woman, not even Maria. "Aren't you going to scream back at me?" he demanded. "Maria was another whore like you, but at least she proudly stood up for herself! But then she didn't enjoy herself as much as you do. Or did you fake that whole performance, those little cries, the way you faked being so afraid? God, I should have known the minute you responded to me like that. No lady acts the way you did. I never *heard* of a lady begging for it, panting, the way you did!"

Charlotte was shaking all over. He was right — or no, he was wrong; she wasn't a whore. But voices clamored in her head, rules learned almost unknowingly from Lady Sipperstein at Lady Chatterton's School for Girls. Ladies don't wiggle their bottoms; ladies speak only in quiet voices; ladies *never* display too much exuberance or any strong emotion. Lady Sipperstein always said that Charlotte wiggled too much when she walked. Alex was right: she wasn't a lady. It didn't take much imagination to think of what Lady Sipperstein would think of a woman who screamed out loud and begged. . . .

Color stained Charlotte's cheeks. Her eyes filled with tears as she looked down at the floor. She was the picture of guilt.

"Why did you do it?" Her husband was walking toward her again; through her tears she could dimly see his large form looming down on her. "Why did you do it?" he hissed, emphasizing each word. "Were you so desperate for a husband? Or was it just that I was the best on the market? Why not poor Braddon? Didn't he seem like a better risk? Poor Braddon. He's such a block that he probably wouldn't have ever realized that you were just another slut, no virgin. He would have been perfectly happy with his tainted bargain. My, my," he said savagely, "I think you made a mistake. Because *I* already married one slut, and so I'm pretty familiar with the breed."

Charlotte couldn't even take in his words by this point. She clapped her hands over her ears, her whole mind and body protesting against the hatred that vibrated in her husband's voice.

"No!" she said loudly.

"Aha! Now the screaming is going to start, right? Let me give you a hand!" Alex picked up a jar that stood on her dressing table and flung it violently against the wall. It smashed, glass tinkling to the ground. Charlotte watched, mesmerized, as white cream slid down the wooden boards. Her heart was thumping in pure terror. Maybe he would kill her, she thought. She had read about such things in the papers. And the law would say he was justified. Because he had been tricked into marrying a woman who wasn't pure.

A drop of strength infused Charlotte's body. If she was going to be killed by an irate husband — some part of her mind couldn't even believe this was happening to *her* — she was not going to let him think he had the right to do it.

"I am not a whore," she said in a small but even voice. She didn't want to look at Alex but she made herself. She raised her head and met his eyes, flinching at the loathing she saw there. "I only slept with *you,* once before."

Alex's eyes narrowed. What kind of story was this? Did she think he went about deflowering virgins in his sleep and wouldn't realize that her story was just hogwash? "I *never* slept with you before," he retorted, utter contempt gracing every word. "And as God is my witness, I will *never* sleep with you again." He suddenly reached out and wrenched Charlotte's night-gown from her clutching hand, ripping it the rest of the way to the floor.

"You should be able to market your wares pretty well in London," he said calmly, surveying her body with steely eyes. Charlotte hardly heard him, only thinking that he seemed to be re-gaining self-control. "Yes, I think that you will be able to do pretty well for yourself among the younger set. I can see it now, the beautiful countess —" Suddenly Alex broke off. "Damnation!" He just remembered that if Charlotte did have affairs with men, it would be put down to his impotency. He felt as if a twining black snake had curled around his throat and was choking him to death.

Then Alex had an inspired idea. He wanted a nursemaid; now he had one. No reason Charlotte should live in London. Forget the trip to Italy — they had nothing to celebrate. No, he would take his new nursemaid to the country, in fact, farther than the country. He had an estate in Scotland. They would go there, and the new whore he married could earn her keep. Then he'd go back to London and leave her in Scotland. Maybe he would visit once a year.

He looked at her. Charlotte was staring at the ground, silent tears slipping down her face. For a moment he had a flash of pity, but he ruthlessly thrust it away. Just so had Maria cried and begged forgiveness for her past. Just so had she promised never to dally with another man again, protested that his skill in bed was so great that she would be happy to stay with him all her days. And only two weeks later he had walked in on her and his head footman, energetically performing in the matrimonial bed. Alex's fists curled. This time he would handle it better. His wife would live in Scotland, and he in London. She could raise his illegitimate daughter, and he would never have to see her again. And damn anyone who wondered why his wife lived in Scotland. He would set up a mistress and squelch all the rumors about his potency — in fact, maybe he would sleep only with noblemen's wives. Since he was an arrant cuckold, why not do the same to others?

His eyes fired with purpose. Alex took Charlotte's arm roughly and pushed her over toward their luggage, piled in the corner.

"Get packing," he said coldly. He rang the bell for Charlotte's maid. "We're leaving. Tell Marie to wake up Pippa and Miss Helms."

Charlotte looked at him numbly. "I didn't sleep with other men!" she protested. "I only slept with you, once, years ago!"

Alex hardly listened. He strode out of the room without looking back. Two minutes later there was a gentle knock and Marie entered, her eyes wide with shock. In an instant she took in the picture of her sweet mistress, still clutching the remnants of her beautiful gown, sobbing uncontrollably. At least he didn't seem to have injured her, Marie thought practically. Well, well. Her mistress must not have had the virginity he wanted — or maybe she just didn't have a maidenhead. Men are blockheads about such things.

She averted her eyes and began swiftly packing their bags, guessing that Charlotte needed some time to collect herself. A few minutes later, Charlotte was still motionless in the center of the floor. The door flew open and Alex stood there, flanked by his man, Keating. Marie shot a quick look at Charlotte. She didn't seem to have noticed the men standing in the doorway. Marie darted over and stood protectively in front of her mistress. Keating's eyes just as swiftly slanted off to the corner. He's a good man, Marie thought with approval.

"Get my clothing out," Alex rasped at Keating. He jerked his head at his wife. "She can go in the third carriage."

Marie swallowed. There was a serious breach between them, that was certain. The third carriage was the servants' carriage. It followed the master's carriage and the carriage carrying Pippa and her nanny. What would the servants do, having the mistress sitting among them? A look passed between her and Keating and she closed her mouth. Keating was clearly staring at her in a warning fashion, and the last thing she wanted was to be dismissed and leave her mistress alone with this — this madman! She shielded Charlotte until both men exited, lowering her eyes submissively as his lordship left. The great gallumping bastard, she thought after the door closed behind them, Keating hoisting a pile of clothing and trailing a few cravats. Well, thank goodness her Cecil had been chosen to accompany Charlotte to Italy. Cecil would sort out the footmen. They would all have to ride pinion, that's all.

But Marie's fears were for naught. When she finally emerged, around an hour later, Alex's coach was long gone, taking with him four footmen and his secretary. Keating had found the time to organize all the servants. The footmen, Cecil told her, were to ride outside, six hanging on to the back and the normal two in front. Keating would sit with the driver. Which would leave Charlotte and Marie alone in the servants' coach. Marie nodded. She felt heartsick, unable even to look at Cecil with much affection. What monsters men were. And what a monster her mistress had married! Marie knew, with a deep heartfelt certainty, that Charlotte was a virgin. Why, she'd been terrified when Marie prepared her for bed earlier that evening. Marie shook off her thoughts, giving Cecil a brooding look, and started back to the inn.

A strong arm caught her around the waist.

"Here you!" a beloved voice said into her ear. "It's not my fault that the master is a raving madman. We're all *for* her, you'll see." Marie nodded. She headed into the inn. She had left Charlotte sitting in a tub of hot water. When she got upstairs the water had cooled, but Charlotte was still sitting there, for all the world like an infant child, Marie thought. She finally managed to poke her mistress into some clothes. Charlotte had stopped crying, but her white emotionless face shook Marie more than her crying had. Women who looked like that . . . it wasn't good. She'd seen that look before, when her own mama miscarried a baby.

Just then a loud screaming echoed in the

hallway. *"Sacrebleu!"* Marie said, startled into French. It was Pippa, protesting her forced awakening at the top of her lungs. At that Charlotte walked away from Marie, who was still buttoning up her traveling gown in the back. She opened the door and said calmly. "Oh, Miss Helms." Pippa's nanny Katy looked back up the stairs, her hair bundled wildly on her head. "I'll take Pippa." The countess reached out her arms. Katy hesitated, and then walked back up the stairs. Pippa caught sight of Charlotte, and gave an urgent sob.

"My not-nanny," she wailed.

"Here, darling," Charlotte crooned, cuddling her in her arms. "Let's go downstairs and get in the coach, shall we? Mama will sing you a song, and you can go back to sleep again."

"Papa!" Pippa whimpered. "Want Papa."

"He can't be here right now," Charlotte said soothingly. "But Mama is here, and I'll sing you a song about a frog, shall I?"

On the stairs, the two other young women, Marie and Katy, looked at each other in surprise. Charlotte had never called herself "Mama" before. Yet Pippa seemed to accept it without a tremor. She cuddled into Charlotte's arms, catching her breath but not sobbing anymore.

Charlotte looked up at Marie. "I'm sorry, Marie. We seem to have changed our plans. Would you mind bringing my brush to the coach, please? You can do my hair there. I think we had better follow his lordship now."

Marie went back into the bedroom to pick up the last few things strewn around the room, bundling Charlotte's ruined nightgown into a bag. She didn't want to leave it in case the servant who cleaned the room decided to sell the story to the gossip columns. Lord knows, all this upset would be fodder enough for the papers.

But, in fact, no word of the changed plans of the Earl of Sheffield and Downes reached London. Under Alex's instructions, Keating handed out a good deal of gold and a strongly worded threat to each and every inn employee. He doubled the yearly salary of the eight footmen who accompanied them to the inn. He paid the captain of the ship that was to take them to Italy triple fare to keep silent about the disappearance of his passengers, and capped the money off with a threat as well.

So while Charlotte's mother and father thought she was aboard a ship for Italy, in fact she and Pippa were rattling slowly north. The two coaches Alex left behind were each pulled by two horses instead of four, so the little cavalcade didn't travel very far in any given day. But that was a blessing, Charlotte thought. Because Alex's coach was far, far ahead of them, and they didn't have to worry about him.

In fact, as each day passed and her husband presumably drew farther ahead, Charlotte deliberately slowed down their journey. They took three-hour lunch breaks while she and Pippa rolled happily in the grass. They stopped at any town that took her fancy and she sketched the church steeple, or gave a chortling Pippa a bath. In short, she and Pippa got to know each other, and she grew calmer, gathering strength for the moment when she would have to encounter her husband again. She felt more composed as each day passed. She had a fairly good sense of what lay ahead. Alex had decided to dump her in Scotland. The prospect didn't bother her too much. Let him think what he wanted. She was no whore; she had slept only with her own husband.

But she would never, ever allow him in her bed again. Even the ecstasy, which she allowed herself to remember only in her dreams, wasn't worth the acute sense of shame and horror that had followed both of her sexual encounters with Alex. She didn't foresee a problem in that respect: Alex had clearly said he would never sleep with her again. So Charlotte planned for a solitary future in Scotland. Perhaps her parents could visit her next summer. There wasn't much she regretted about leaving London, although she already missed Sophie acutely. And her mother. More than anything, she would like to sob on her mother's shoulder. But it wouldn't change anything, Charlotte counseled herself, as she rose from another tear-filled night.

By the time the two coaches crossed the border into Scotland, the young, innocent girl who had bumped into Alex on the stairs at Lady Prestlefield's ball was long gone. In her place was an utterly collected, assured countess who was approachable only when she played with her little girl.

"She's a proper lady, hain't she?" asked a red-haired urchin to his mother.

"Aw, she's a Sassenach, and don't you forget it!" she replied roughly. "Look at all her uppitty-ness! That sort never let down their hair. They're not like us."

Staring at the beautiful, somehow icy English countess, the little boy nodded. She wasn't much like his chubby, beloved mum, that's for sure. He clutched her around the waist in a sudden hug.

"Oh, Rickie, do give over!" She pushed off his arms. Just then a little girl hurled herself at the countess, crying loudly. And the exquisitely dressed Englishwoman bent down and swung the babe into her arms, smiling at her tenderly. Maybe they weren't *so* different, Megan thought. Megan hauled her own son up for a hug and they stared together as the beautiful countess walked off, her head bent close to her little daughter's ear.

Chapter 15

Alex arrived at Dunston Castle, his estate in Scotland, some ten days before Charlotte and her small entourage. He had spent the trip either sitting alone in his coach or riding on Bucephalus, which he greatly preferred. In either situation he cursed the fact that in his rage he had consigned Charlotte to the servants' coach. Why hadn't he left her in his coach, where he could have railed at her to his heart's content? Then, slowly, a feeling of mingled distaste and shame about his own behavior crept into his heart, and he was glad that his wife was out of sight. But out of mind she was not.

Surges of rage still attacked him when he thought about Charlotte's deception, but he began to regain an ability to analyze. One day he realized that he was allowing his still vibrant anger about Maria's betrayals to cloud the situation with Charlotte. And after that perception it was only two days until he sat bolt upright in the morning, Charlotte's voice echoing in his head.

"I didn't sleep with other men! I only slept with you, once, years ago!"

And then there was Charlotte talking about

sex: "I didn't know . . . it was wonderful, so wonderful . . . it wasn't at all like the other time. No pain . . ."

So Charlotte wasn't quite the arrant betrayer that Maria had been. No, she had slept with only one man, years ago — and she thought it had been him. It cast an ugly light on why she agreed to marry him, but that didn't matter, Alex thought, consigning dreams of love to the fire. He was no idiot. It was clear what had happened. Charlotte had slept with Patrick, and due to the unlucky fact of Patrick being out of England when the two of them met, she believed she had lost her virginity to him. Alex swallowed hard. He and Patrick had shared women in the past . . . but never a wife. It was a hard thing to contemplate. Still, if one had to marry under these circumstances, wasn't it better that the other man had been one's twin?

He thought about this for the last few days before Charlotte arrived, calming his intense irritability by casting fishing lines into foggy Scottish streams and pulling out trout that no one wanted to eat. So he threw them back. He spent hours staring at the gray-green water as it rippled slightly in the wake of his line.

Probably the most surprising part of the last three weeks, he finally realized, was how much he missed Pippa. For months he had been the primary person in her life — and then, in a fit of petulant rage, he drove off and left her in a carriage with a nanny and a stepmother she barely knew. And he *missed* her now, missed her with a deep visceral ache in his belly. He found himself wondering in the middle of the night how she had gone to sleep the night after he left without him twirling the curl on her forehead and telling her to have sweet dreams. If nothing else, the Pippa ache told him that his scheme to bury Charlotte in Scotland wasn't a good one. Unless he buried himself as well.

No, Alex thought grimly, he'd accept his wife. He would bring her back to London. They could rub along pretty well together, now that he had given up his rosy illusions about falling in love with the woman he married. They would have to go to bed together, because he needed an heir. (That he was using the necessity of an heir as a justification, given the likelihood that Patrick would have a child, was just barely hidden from Alex's consciousness.)

He shook his fishing line irritably. Where the hell was Charlotte? For the last two nights his mind had filled with the alarming stories he'd recently heard about raiders lurking on the Scottish border, waiting to jump on unsuspecting English travelers. God, why had he been such a hot-headed, arrogant brute? What if Charlotte and Pippa were robbed, taken for ransom — or worse? Even as Charlotte's carriage stopped, a mere two hours from Alex's estate, and the occupants ambled into a flowery meadow for a leisurely lunch, Alex tortured himself by imagining a far crueler fate.

So when the two travel-stained carriages finally trundled through the huge stone walls marking the entrance to the courtyard, Alex glimpsed them from his study window, and just barely controlled himself from bounding down the stairs and pulling his wife and child into his arms. Instead he stayed next to the window, rigidly braced against the sill. There came his wife, nimbly stepping down from the third, rather shabby servants' carriage. Then the second carriage opened and Pippa half-tumbled out, running over to Charlotte and holding up her arms. Alex couldn't know that this had been the arrangement for the last two hours only; that normally Charlotte rode in Pippa's coach. Pippa had tormented her nanny for the last hour, demanding her mama. He saw Charlotte laughingly swing Pippa up into her arms, and Pippa wind her little arms around Charlotte's neck and nuzzle her. This was what he had wanted, wasn't it?

Time to go downstairs. Alex walked down the twisting stone steps from his study, mentally bracing himself. He had forgotten, in the intervening weeks, just how much Charlotte's beauty moved him. Even just the sight of her trim bottom as she bent over to pick up Pippa sent a stab of lust to his groin. Well, all the better, he reasoned, pacing calmly toward the entrance. She *was* his wife, after all. Maybe he could keep her too busy to roam to other men.

He walked into the courtyard. Servants were

pouring out of the door, lining up for their formal introduction to the new countess. Charlotte was standing, Pippa in her arms, looking slightly amused. Her expression didn't change when she saw him. She merely inclined her head a fraction of an inch and said, "My lord."

Alex looked at her thoughtfully. He inclined his head in response.

"Charlotte." There was silence in the courtyard. Pippa, who had been watching the horses over Charlotte's shoulder, twisted her little self around. Alex smiled at her and held out his arms. But rather than say "Papa" in her lovely Italian accent, or struggle to get down and run to him, as she had to Charlotte, Pippa took one horrified look, twisted her free arm around Charlotte's neck and burst into loud sobs.

"Sweetie," Charlotte said, "I told you Papa would come back. You see, Papa is here, and he missed you, and he loves you very much. He didn't leave forever. Do you remember what I told you?"

There was no answer. Pippa just buried her face more tightly into Charlotte's neck. Alex felt a burning red creep up his neck. His own daughter was rejecting him in front of some thirty servants, all of whom were craning their necks to see what was happening. Alex walked over to the two of them, his body rigidly disguising his impulse to pull Charlotte into his arms and kiss her until she lost that distant look.

"Pumpkin," he said, his deep voice calm and

persuasive. "I missed you very much. In fact, I thought every night about how much I wished that I had never left you. But here I am, and I would very much like a hug from my own pumpkin."

Pippa raised her tearstained face. "Papa?" she asked. Alex stooped down, ignoring the fact that Charlotte drew back slightly as he came close. He rubbed noses with Pippa. She giggled and held out her arms. "Papa," she said. "Papa!"

The Italian accent was gone forever, Alex thought. But the warmth of his daughter's small chunky body clinging to his was all that mattered. "I love you, Pumpkin," he whispered into Pippa's neck. He forgot all the bystanders.

Charlotte stared at her husband. It was the old Alex, the premarriage Alex, the loving father she had seen before their wedding night. A sense of relief filled Charlotte's heart. Besides her own heartbreak, she had worried fiercely about Pippa. How could Pippa cope with the death of her real mother, if her newfound papa decided to just ride off and leave her in Scotland? But perhaps his plan wasn't quite so draconian as she had imagined. Alex and Pippa snuggled together, seemingly oblivious of their audience.

Suddenly Alex swung up his head. His eyes ranged over the assembled servants. "This is your new mistress, the Countess of Sheffield and Downes." He gave all the servants an arrogant stare; he didn't want them to slight the new countess, having seen her descend from the servants' coach. And wait until they heard stories from the footmen who arrived with her. Inside he groaned, but his face remained haughty and confident. Then he smiled suddenly. "And this is my daughter, Lady Philippa."

There was a resounding cheer and a flurry of clapped hands. Alex held out his free arm to Charlotte. She took it lightly and he led her to the front of the line and began making painstaking introductions to the primary servants of the estate.

For her part, Charlotte was delighted with herself. She felt *nothing.* After all the agony of the last three weeks, she looked at Alex, her husband, and she felt nothing: neither attraction nor acute rage. She felt a twinge of pity because he looked singularly drawn and tired. But seeing him didn't sway her resolution one tiny bit, she was happy to find. Even as she smiled and chatted with the servants, she inwardly gloated about the fact that his alarming effect on her, the inner weakness that made her shake every time he so much as touched her finger, was gone. She was holding his arm and she felt — nothing.

Finally Charlotte had met all the upstairs servants. She liked the butler enormously; judged that one of the upper housemaids would probably have to be replaced; made a mental note to have the housekeeper's records checked. Then she smiled generally at the mass of unnamed servants and dropped Alex's arm. Side by side they walked up the four stone steps and into the front hall.

"My goodness," she exclaimed as they entered the echoing stone entrance.

"I inherited it through my great-grandmother," Alex said cheerfully. Now that he had Pippa in his arms and Charlotte didn't seem to be looking at him as if he were a monster, he felt as if the world was manageable once again. As soon as he had the chance, he would simply explain to Charlotte that she had originally slept with his brother, but that he — Alex — had magnanimously decided to forgive her for the lapse. He smiled to himself. This was the right way to behave. His mother would have approved. His father — no. His father would definitely have cast Charlotte off, or left her entombed in this Scottish castle in the back of nowhere. But he wasn't like his father. He would have a marriage based on magnanimity, even if not on love. In fact, Alex was practically glowing with virtue.

Unfortunately, his wife didn't seem to have noticed. She was wandering about, touching the tapestries that lined the wide room. In fact, she seemed to be frowning over how dusty they were.

"Well," Charlotte said, meeting his eyes with no apparent self-consciousness. "I shall be in my chamber until supper, my lord. Mrs. McLean will show me the way, I am sure." Charlotte smiled at the plump housekeeper, waiting by the stairs. "What time do you serve supper in Scotland?"

Alex looked back at her, one eyebrow unconsciously raised. His new wife was very cool. "At eight o'clock," he said.

"My lord," Charlotte repeated, and curtsied. Alex started. Of course, his parents used to salute each other that way, but Charlotte had never curtsied to him before, except in the midst of a dance. Slowly, he bowed.

Then suddenly Charlotte approached him, and his heart raced. But she merely stooped and brushed Pippa's cheek with her lips.

"Mama!" Pippa said, and for a moment she managed to hook her chubby little arm around her mama's neck, bringing them so close together that Alex could smell Charlotte's orange-blossom scent.

"No, sweetie," Charlotte said lovingly to Pippa. "You stay with your papa awhile. There's my good pippin." Then she turned to Alex, and all the warmth fell from her face like magic, leaving not hostility, but a calm detachment. "Whenever you wish, return Pippa to her nanny. She is quite fond of Katy now."

An icy chill crept up Alex's spine. No, Charlotte didn't look at him as if she were angry. She looked at him the way he had seen a hundred society dames look at their husbands: not enraged, not even speculative, simply flatly uninterested. But very, very polite, he thought, as Charlotte curtsied again and began climbing the stairs with Mrs. McLean. Without thinking he tightened his grasp on Pippa until she gave a squawk of protest.

"All right, chicken. Let's go see the kittens in

the stable, shall we?"

Charlotte walked up the stairs slowly, hardly hearing the details Mrs. McLean was pouring into her ear — the difficulty of finding good servants, what happened to six pieces of the best china Tuesday last, the need for new linen. She wasn't as impervious to Alex as she had hoped. When Pippa pulled her close she had caught Alex's spicy male smell, and against her will her knees weakened.

Charlotte oversaw the transfer of her clothes out of the bedchamber adjoining the master bedroom and into one far down the corridor next to the nursery (the servants accepted without comment her wish for better light), directed the arrangement of her paints in one of the four corner tower rooms that was currently unused, and personally inspected Pippa's new nursery. After scanning the room, Charlotte ordered another layer of carpets laid on top of those already present. Pippa still spent a good deal of time crawling on the floor, and she didn't want her to catch a creeping influenza from the damp, cold stone that made up the castle floors.

Then she ordered a bath and lapsed into the steaming water, exhausted to the bone.

"Marie," she called out from behind the screens that protected the bathtub from the cruel drafts which circulated in every room. Marie was muttering to herself in French as she hung her mistress's gowns in the great wardrobe. She didn't approve of Scottish castles, practically hanging off into a cloud of mist, this one was. The damp! And what were they to wear? She had packed the mistress — *and* herself — for Italy. And Italy this was not!

"Marie!" Charlotte called again.

"I'm sorry, my lady." Marie's annoyed little face appeared between a gap in the screens. "Would you like me to ring for more hot water?"

"Yes, I would, thank you, Marie. And would you please send a message to the earl, telling him that I intend to retire for the night and will simply have a tray in my room? I am exhausted."

Marie didn't think much of hiding in one's bedroom; she thought Charlotte should go out there and battle her husband. But looking at Charlotte's white face, she had to agree. Perhaps it would be better to take up cudgels tomorrow, when Charlotte had slept and looked her best.

"Of course, my lady. Should I instruct Mrs. McLean to call a seamstress to the castle tomorrow? I'm afraid that we must have those wools that we bought in Glasgow made up into dresses as soon as possible. You and Pippa will be down with colds in no time flat in this weather."

"That's a very good idea, Marie. When Pippa returns to the nursery, will you ask Katy to send her in with me? I should like to have supper with her, please."

Marie bustled away. She sent for more hot water, and had the fire in the fireplace built up so high that sparks flooded up the chimney like fireflies caught in a draft. The room was warming up, Charlotte thought. Thank goodness, this room was considerably smaller than those making up the matrimonial suite down the hall. Out of the bath, she sat in a comfortable chair by the fire, so tired that she couldn't even move. When Pippa was brought in she seemed just as drowsy, so they sat together in the big chair and Charlotte told her a story about a horse who could fly, called Peggy. Pegasus seemed a mouthful for a one-and-a-half-year-old girl.

After a while they had supper on a tray and Pippa was so tired that she didn't even try to toss any food into the air. She just sat quietly on Charlotte's lap and opened her mouth docilely as Charlotte popped in bits of food.

Finally Charlotte toppled her into Katy's arms and, pulling on a nightgown, crept into her warm bed. Marie built up the fire one more time and left. Charlotte lay awake for a while, staring at the fire as it danced in the grate, casting twisting shadows on the old stone walls. What was going to happen to her and Alex? More important, perhaps, what did she *want* to have happen? Now that they had met again, and all the hysterical fear she had that he would say something horrible, call her a disgusting name in front of Pippa or the servants, had died down, she felt at sea. All her energies had been directed toward controlling what she had thought would be a dreadful reunion, with Alex shouting insults. Indeed, she had simply forecast an Alex as enraged as he had been three weeks ago, on their wedding night.

Despite herself, Charlotte's eyes filled with tears. Maybe it *was* her fault. Maybe she should have summoned the courage, before they got married, to detail exactly when they had met before. Instead, she had taken the coward's way out, and believed her mother when she said no one would ever know she wasn't a virgin. Alex was right in one regard: She had lied to him, at least by omission. Because he had thought she was a virgin, and she wasn't. Charlotte sniffed. She had cried enough in the last three weeks to sink a boat, she thought with a twist of wry irony.

So what did she want? She wanted . . . she wanted what she couldn't have. Alex *before*. An Alex who had never said such awful things to her, who had never thought such ugly things about her. Tears brimmed over again. But Charlotte was so tired that she couldn't even cry long; she slipped into sleep between one sob and the next.

Meanwhile Alex dined in the same cold, regal splendor as he had for the last two weeks. He had sent his secretary back to London as soon as they arrived, with instructions to return with warm clothing. So Alex sat at one end of the vast table alone. The dining room in the castle was a monstrosity, designed to be full of men at arms and barking dogs. The ten footmen ranged along the side of the wall merely looked silly; in the old days, Alex thought, there were probably thirty or forty servants dodging around many tables. And it was bitterly cold, summer or not. Alex looked around in acute dislike. What was he doing here, in this drafty fortress? His old nurse would have said that it was at the back of the north wind, it was so chilly.

He pushed away his food halfway through supper. Hell, he had a wife, didn't he? Why not talk to her? He was tired of eating alone. He walked upstairs, brushing past his surprised butler just as McDougal ushered in the fish course. In his room Alex paused. Should he knock on the adjoining door? Does one knock on one's own wife's door? After finding Maria in bed with the footman, he always knocked on her door. Thinking of that, Alex sharply pushed open the door to the adjoining chamber. But it opened to the same slightly dusty, empty magnificence that had been taunting him for the last few weeks. The bed hangings were moth-eaten. He had thought of having them cleaned for Charlotte, but forgot about it. Alex quickly pulled his own bedroom door shut, realizing that all the heat from his fireplace was escaping into the cold damp next door. So where the hell was his wife?

He opened the door and bellowed down the corridor.

"McDougal!"

Silence punctuated the faint wail of wind in the corridor. He shouted again.

"McDougal!"

Then he heard panting steps winding up the stairs.

"Yes, my lord," puffed his rotund butler.

"Where is the countess?" His narrowed eyes dared McDougal to be impertinent.

McDougal's face didn't shift a muscle. "She is in the north bedroom, my lord, being as she is wishful for more light." He bowed and exited precipitously. McDougal had heard an unexpurgated version of the events in Bournemouth from the countess's own maid, Marie, and he didn't want to witness an explosion of the new earl's temper. Foakes seemed all right when he visited here some four years ago — in fact, they had all been pleasantly surprised given that he was an Englishman — but that was before he inherited. And turning into an earl could have a perishing bad effect on a person's temper, McDougal knew.

Alex turned down the corridor to his left, wondering where in the deuce the north bedroom was. More light, ha! In a bedroom with that name? He judged he was roughly facing north, so he headed all the way up the corridor and grabbed the first door handle he saw. A wave of warmth greeted him as he opened the door. He walked inside and closed the heavy wood behind him, leaning against it. The room seemed to be empty. He was in a small bedroom that he didn't remember even seeing on his last visit here. There were windows on two sides, hung with thick red velvet curtains. Finally he walked over and looked in the bed, the only place he couldn't see from the door. And there was his wife. She was tucked under the covers, fast asleep.

For a moment or two Alex just stared at her. Charlotte's hair had grown from its fashionable short cut; soft, dusky curls spilled down over her collar and lay rumpled behind her raised hand. From what he could see, she wasn't wearing a temptress's gown tonight; there was a white ruffle framing her face. Annoyed at himself for even thinking about her nightgown, Alex plumped down on the bed and shook Charlotte's shoulder, rather roughly. She woke silently and stared at him, her eyes black and shadowed by the only light, coming from the fireplace. Then she gasped and instinctively pulled back.

Alex didn't move, but he was startled. Was she so afraid of him that she thought he might hit her?

In fact, Charlotte was shocked to see him. Her traitorous mind had spun her into a dream in which Alex was begging forgiveness and kissing her breasts at the same time, and she had been falling into a swooning whirlpool of desire — and then here he was; sitting on her bed. Staring at her with an arrogant eyebrow raised. Her heart thumped in response to a flood of scorching desire: to touch him, to reach out and pull him down to her, to kiss him sweetly, to tell him she . . . And just as quickly, Charlotte's blood cooled. She was never going to be lured into acting like a whore again. That much she would grant him: She responded to him in a way that no lady ever would. Well, she *was* a lady, she reminded herself. Just because one's husband had a sensual mouth that made butterflies skip in one's stomach was no excuse for losing control.

"What are you doing here?" she asked, her voice as smooth as butter and about as warm.

"Looking for my wife," Alex responded. He was determined not to get angry. After all, he just wanted a little companionship, and that was his marital right. There was no need for them to have an argument about it.

"Why?"

"Why not? It's lonely sitting down there at a table built for Scottish giants, all by myself."

"I am very tired, my lord," Charlotte said evenly. "We traveled a long way today, and I would be grateful if you would allow me to return to sleep."

"You traveled all of three hours," Alex retorted. "I asked Keating when I was trying to figure out why it took you ten days longer than me to arrive here." He reached out and trailed a finger down his wife's delicate cheekbone.

She flinched away from him and his eyes narrowed.

"We need to talk about our future," Alex said. "You see, I have decided to take you back. Under a few conditions, the primary one being that you never sleep with another man beside myself. You will do nothing to taint the reputation of my name. In return, I will not repudiate you for having slept with my brother."

"I did not —" Alex raised his hand, cutting

Charlotte off. "Apparently you lost your virginity to my brother. However, no matter how unfortunate the joke on both of us — had you waited a few months, I suppose you could have married Patrick — we are the ones who are married now. And I think we should make the best of it." He paused, but his wife didn't seem disposed to say anything. She stared at the bedspread, her face shadowed.

"I will share your bed," Alex said with deliberate cruelty, "whenever I please. However, let me repeat, no one else must share that bed with you, or I will banish you to this godforsaken place, and I shall not summon you back to London until one of us is on our deathbed."

Then Charlotte realized that, in fact, they did need to talk. She pushed herself up in the bed, resting against the backboard so she didn't feel so vulnerable. Then she folded her hands in her lap, just as her mother did when she argued with her father.

"My lord," she said composedly, "it seems I must remind you of your own words in Bournemouth. You said that you would never sleep with me again."

"Well, perhaps I won't *sleep* in this room. The bed is a trifle small for my taste, after all." Alex's eyes devoured the gentle swell of Charlotte's breasts, even muffled as they were in folds of white cotton.

It was Charlotte's turn to narrow her eyes. This man seemed to think that he could do anything he wanted: be a monster one day and expect to seduce her the next.

"I refuse."

There was a moment of dangerous silence.

"You refuse? Exactly what do you *refuse?*"

"I refuse to sleep with you, no matter how euphemistically you might want to phrase it. Surely," she added with deadly irony, "as a *whore* I should have the chance to choose my own clients."

"That's just what you don't have," her husband responded, his eyes gleaming coolly at her. "I'm your husband. I can *have* you, whenever — and wherever — I please. And I think I please to have you here, in this bed."

Charlotte thought about this for a moment. She knew that Alex had the right; she simply thought he would never want to exercise it, given the utter disgust he exhibited on their wedding night. Finally she gave a little shrug. He had probably realized that he needed an heir. But she'd be damned if she would let him seduce her again and then savage her with insults.

"All right," she said. She reached under the covers and pulled up her nightgown to her waist, pushing down the covers. Then she lay back and closed her eyes. Despite her calm exterior, Charlotte was absolutely pulverized with terror. She had just done the boldest, most mad thing she had ever done in her life. Here she was, totally vulnerable. The cool air brushed her thighs and she shivered. Sex like this was going to hurt, she knew it intuitively. Her legs seemed to have turned to a shaking mass of jelly.

Alex was staring at her incredulously. Silence descended on the room, broken only by flurries of crackling sparks from the fireplace. After a while Charlotte opened her eyes.

"Have you changed your mind?"

Alexander Foakes was slowly finding that he was more angry than he had ever been in his life.

"No," he breathed, with a harsh smile. "No, I haven't changed my mind." Charlotte closed her eyes again, terrified by the look on Alex's face. For some reason this was making him look more enraged — if that was possible — than he had been on their wedding night.

"What's the matter?" she asked, opening her eyes again.

"What's the matter," Alex repeated, his voice grating. "My wife lies there like a dead turnip and asks me, 'What's the matter?' "

"I don't know what you want," she said, just a little shakily. "Why are you complaining?"

Alex didn't reply. She is trying to get revenge, he realized suddenly. She's angry about the things I said in Bournemouth. He stretched out his hand and ran it up the long, sleek line of Charlotte's thigh. Then he reached under the nightgown and ran his hand up her waist, over the silky ripple that was her ribs, stopping at the beginning of a womanly curve. The intoxicating weight of her breasts made his blood beat furiously. If he couldn't seduce his own wife, then he didn't deserve his earlship.

But by a half an hour later, he was ready to throw in the title, coronet and all. It wasn't that Charlotte wasn't aroused: He *knew* she was. Her nipples . . . well, all of her was ready. But he felt about as interested in proceeding as she seemed to be. What had happened to the girl who strained forward to meet his touch? His conscience told him the answer to that. Revenge or not, she was winning. Alex just didn't have the appetite to make love to a woman who lay there passively, eyes closed, betraying only by tremors that what he did moved her.

"Open your eyes," Alex finally said, wearied to the bone.

Charlotte's eyes popped open. Alex was sitting on the edge of the bed, hunched over, head in his hands.

"What's the matter?" Charlotte asked again. She was genuinely bewildered. Wasn't this what he wanted? His voice had resounded endlessly through her mind in the last weeks — scorning her, *hating* her, because she responded too much, because she "begged," he said.

Without answering Alex hoisted himself up and began to leave the room. But he was stopped by Charlotte.

"Why are you leaving?" she demanded. "I don't understand you," she said, almost to herself. "You called me a whore because I didn't act like a lady. You said you would never sleep with me again, because you found out that I lost my

389

virginity with you — whether you want to acknowledge it or not — before we were married. And when I do act like a lady, you still look at me in utter disgust. What is it?" Charlotte was working herself into a fine rage now. "If you want an heir, make yourself an heir! Use my body; you said it was *yours*. I'm not stopping you! I am behaving *like a lady!*"

To her surprise, Alex gave a genuine, if brief, bark of laughter. "Ladies don't shout," he observed. But he sat down on the bed again. He looked at her seriously.

Charlotte's body reacted with a shock of alarm. It was the first time all evening that she had felt in genuine danger. When he looked at her like that, her body grew hotly attentive. And he wasn't even looking at her seductively; it's just that his eyes were dark and tender, like the old Alex, she thought wistfully. The before-Alex, who still liked her and didn't think she was a whore. The thought gave her a burst of renewed fortitude. This was what he wanted. She had behaved just as a lady should, no matter how difficult it was. So why did it bother him now?

"I'm sorry," Alex said heavily. "I'm sorry I called you a whore. I realized, a few days later, that you had only lost your virginity to a man you thought was me. I didn't understand it at the time, and I was so enraged that I couldn't . . . I couldn't control my temper."

"It *was* you," Charlotte persisted. "It was you, three years ago in —"

Alex raised his hand, protesting. "I really don't want to know the details," he said, shuddering a bit. "For God's sake, it's hard enough for me to accept the fact that my bride slept first with my brother: I definitely don't want to know on what back step he did it!" His mouth twisted ironically. "We share many things, but your virginity . . . I'll leave it to him."

Charlotte felt sick. He would never believe her; she could see it in his eyes. And so he would always think those ugly things of her. She closed her eyes again. Maybe it would be better to stay here, to live in Scotland. She didn't know if she could bear to see Alex every day, knowing that he despised her. Even after all his brutal talk, his face was still so dear. It was just too painful. A tear escaped under her closed eyelids.

Alex looked at his wife somberly. She was sorry, clearly. He had no real belief that she would ever sleep with another man. No, Charlotte was a true, loyal person. He picked up her hand and kissed the palm.

"Shall we try again?"

Charlotte wet her trembling lips with her tongue, and Alex felt an immediate lick of fire in his belly. She had the most enticing lips, his wife. They were a deep, dark cherry color, with the promise of passion. Passion she had displayed, he thought. He just had to figure out how to get her to reveal it again.

"Ah, what do you mean?" Charlotte enquired. Something about the way Alex's eyes were looking at her was setting off alarm bells. Little nerves woke up in her legs; her breasts suddenly longed to be touched.

"Let's make love again," Alex said, moving up the bed so he could bend down and brush his lips across hers. "I'm sorry I went insane afterward. I never experienced anything so wonderful, and I simply exploded when I found out I wasn't the only one. But that's in the past now. We should think about . . . about making an heir," he said with a deep chuckle.

Charlotte dismissed a pang of disappointment. Of course he wanted an heir. It was natural.

His mouth was just a hairbreadth from hers now. She could feel his warm breath, and then his tongue ran across her lips like liquid silver, icy and warm at the same time. His hand started to run slowly up, under her nightgown again. Maybe it wouldn't be so bad to kiss him back, Charlotte desperately reasoned with herself, even as her body began to tremble with desire.

Alex raised his mouth and looked deeply into her eyes. "Please, darling," he whispered, and Charlotte's resistance fell into a hundred splintered pieces. She wound her arms around his neck and raised her mouth to his, her lips already slightly parted, evocative of surrender. And Alex instantly took the implicit invitation, jerking her against his hard chest, driving his tongue into her mouth. His hand slipped naturally to cup the tantalizing weight of her breasts. And when he heard her sharp gasp, it filled his heart with pleasure. His Charlotte was back — more than back. By now he was stretched out beside her and when he began removing the studs from his shirt, Charlotte tremblingly ran her hands over his chest, her fingertips lingering on his nipples. Little jolts of fire ran up her limbs when his eyes widened with obvious pleasure. When she experimentally lowered her head and put her tongue on his chest, he moaned out loud and Charlotte's belly ignited into a fevered, flaming ocean.

Some time later they were both naked, their bodies glowing in reflected firelight, flushed skin meeting flushed skin, frenzied kiss following kiss. Alex's hands wandered all over Charlotte's body, igniting every inch. But it wasn't until Alex poised himself over her, bracing himself on his forearms, and began deliberately, tormentingly rubbing himself against her that Charlotte felt herself truly losing control. She shut her eyes tight, not even opening them when Alex's tongue teasingly ran across her eyelids. Alex was concentrating, thinking dimly of holding himself under strict control and making it up to Charlotte. He didn't notice that her closed eyes signaled distress. He pushed into her a little way. Then he withdrew and circled her again, luring, calling. Charlotte's hips involuntarily lifted, pressing against him. Despite herself, her eyes flew open and she wreathed her arms around his neck, silently pleading for what she could not bring herself to say. And still Alex teased . . . breaching her a little farther, pulling back until she was ready to scream. And then, just when Charlotte was about to explode with longing and frustration, Alex drove into her forcefully. Charlotte's mind went blank and she cried out; and Alex — who had been counseling himself sternly about not losing control — immediately lost all control. He rammed into her again and again, evoking fluttering cries from his wife.

But something wasn't right. Slowly Alex pulled his consciousness back from his mindless plunging into the hot, tight warmth of Charlotte's body. Now he saw that tears were seeping out beneath her closed eyelids. Even as her body arched to meet each stroke, she wept. He stilled his body instantly, forcing his throbbing manhood to lie quiescent inside her.

"Darling," he whispered. "What is it? Does it hurt?"

Charlotte's eyes opened, huge, tear-drenched. He kissed away the tears, but she turned her head away.

"What is it, Charlotte?" Alex's strong hand pulled her chin back, so he could see her eyes.

"I can't, I can't not," her breath caught on a sob.

"Can't not what?" Alex prompted.

"I can't stop myself." More tears flooded out now. Alex gently withdrew himself and pulled a handkerchief from the table, blotting Charlotte's tears.

"What are you talking about, sweetheart?" he finally prompted when it appeared she wasn't going to continue.

"You said, you said that no lady acts the way I did." Charlotte was crying hopelessly now, her voice broken by sobs. "You said that you had never heard of a lady p-panting, or begging for it, the way I did."

Alex's heart stopped. Had he really said anything so cruel? God, he couldn't have. In a fit of stupid rage he might have ruined the most wonderful thing that had ever happened to him.

"Charlotte," he said fiercely. "I was an idiot, do you hear me? An idiot. I was off my head, insane with jealousy. I wanted to hurt your feelings, and so I said the cruelest thing I could think of, but I didn't mean it. I didn't mean it," he repeated desperately as Charlotte kept crying.

"I just can't stop myself," she finally said in a ragged voice. "You were right. I'm not a lady; I'm a . . ." but she couldn't bring herself to say the ugly word, tears welling up in her eyes again.

"Oh, God, Charlotte," Alex groaned, pulling her into his arms. "Please, please listen to me. If you withdraw from me now, because of the stupid, cruel things I said, it will be the death of me. I will have destroyed the one thing I dreamed of: a passionate, loving relationship with my wife.

"Listen to me, Charlotte!" He bent commandingly over her, forcing her to meet his eyes. "Do you think I sound like a whore when I almost shout every time you touch me? When I am panting, and grunting, and making every ungentlemanly noise I can? Do I repulse you? Do I?"

Charlotte shook her head numbly.

"How does it make you feel when I moan at your touch?" Alex asked, more quietly.

A slight smile touched Charlotte's lips. "Like a queen," she said.

"I want to be king, Charlotte, king in my own house. Please, darling, please let me be king and you be queen. Nothing you could possibly do when we make love could ever disgust me. It was just rage speaking, not my genuine feelings."

Charlotte's lips quivered. "But what if you get angry at me again?" She drew in a shaky breath. "I know you're right; I don't behave like a lady. And I would rather not risk your rage again."

Alex rolled over to lie on his back. This was a facer. He *had* ruined everything. He hadn't trusted her; well, now she would never trust him. And that was the end of his dream of an erotic marital union, born of the encounter in the garden years ago, and nurtured stubbornly even during the awful years with Maria. It was over. He stared up at the stone ceiling, his mind hollow.

Then he felt a warm naked body press against his side, and a tousled curly head pressed against his chin.

"Shall we try again?" At first he didn't understand her whisper, and then he remembered his question. He had asked it only an hour or so ago, but it felt like a century. He turned his head slowly. His wife was looking at him, her beautiful dark eyes no longer brimming with tears.

Charlotte pressed her fingers against his mouth. "If you promise to trust me," she said shakily, but oh so sweetly, "I promise to trust you. If you believe me, I will believe you about this. I will never sleep with any man other than you in my life, as God's my witness, and if you will promise never to reproach me with my behavior when we make love . . . well, I will simply resign myself to behaving like a harlot — at times."

The gleam of amusement in her eyes evaporated as her husband rolled over, grabbing her in his arms and entering her with one swift, almost brutal stroke. Charlotte spontaneously cried out, her body throbbing with joy, her hands clutching his shoulders.

The night was very long. Alex left the bed only to pile more wood on the fire. They made love and slept; Charlotte woke up to find that a burgeoning presence was demanding to enter her body. Her immediate welcome made Alex's breath catch and he buried his face in her throat, hoarsely stating that he didn't deserve her. But when his wife started to tickle him in unusual places . . . well, his mind couldn't concentrate on its well-deserved self-reproach. He retaliated, and they finally went back to sleep, replete.

Except that Alex woke up again, some two hours later. Charlotte was deep in the sleep of the utterly exhausted next to him. He swore to himself that he wouldn't wake her, but then he irresistibly drew off her coverlet and looked at the elegant lines of her body. She was *his,* all his. And when Charlotte awoke, languorously returning to the world, she first shrieked in disbelief, and then in utter, abandoned pleasure. Alex's dark head was between her thighs and his tongue forced streaks of mindless bliss to rocket through her body.

So the night was long, but it was not, as wise men say, without its rewards. Morning light first slanted below the velvet curtains around six in the morning. In time the lines of warm sunlight crept closer to the end of the bed. They found the Earl, and the Countess, of Sheffield and Downes sleeping the sleep of the just, the exhausted, the newly married, and the thoroughly sated.

Chapter 16

The next two weeks were long remembered in the history of Dunston Castle, Scotland, the seat of four successive Earls of Sheffield and Downes. In fact, the castle's butler, Mr. McDougal, confided to his wife that there'd been nothing like it since the third earl, the present earl's father, he punctiliously explained, brought a young woman up to stay for a week. She was no better than she should be, obviously, and the antics they had to put up with!

There was the time they found the dining room door locked, for example, just as Mr. McDougal was about to bring in a flaming tart, himself being just an upper footman at the time. The tart was ordered special, McDougal recalled, the cook not being used to fancy continental dishes that had to be set on fire. And wasn't she in a tizzy when the whole thing had to be brought back to the kitchen, blackened and frizzled?

And there was a young second housemaid who learned entirely too much when she innocently went to dust the music room — and what did she find? His wife nodded knowingly as Mr. Mc-

Dougal waggled his eyebrows.

"I was just a young one then," he said. "But I well remember the hysterics she had in the kitchen. Such an uproar! The cook finally had to give her a good shot of the cooking brandy, since the butler-that-was, old Grimthorple, was rather tight with the key to the spirits cabinet. Ah, well."

"I don't rightly think that this earl should be compared to his father," said his wife comfortably. She ran the laundry, linens, and weaving section of the castle operations, and what she didn't know about castle occupants wasn't worth knowing. "These two are sweet on each other and newly married. And the countess is no slip of a girl. Even if one does see them kissing now and again, she is always respectful and courteous to me."

"And Ira," she told her husband for the third time, "you could have knocked me over with a feather when she came to me and said, 'Mrs. McDougal, I have found a few slight indescrepancies in the housekeeping records, and I wondered if you might help me understand them?' Ira, you could have knocked me over with a feather. That Mrs. McLean — some housekeeper she is! — has been filching linens from my very cupboards practically as long as she's been here, and no one has taken a bit of notice. You can tell our lady has been brought up the right way."

Mr. McDougal acknowledged that he too

liked the young countess: Who would not, given her kindly, sweet manner? But he ventured to say that he shouldn't like *his* daughter to be seen kissing her husband in back of every statue in the gardens, and hadn't Mrs. McDougal told him herself that the countess's French maid said she was spending most of her time sewing buttons back on her mistress's clothing?

"She's French," Mrs. McDougal replied, assessing the evidence of a Frenchwoman at a very low rate indeed. "But even if Marie were telling the truth, what's the matter with a few buttons lost between a man and his wife, eh, Ira?"

Her husband chuckled appropriately and talk passed to other things.

Meanwhile the master of the castle kissed his wife behind statues, scattered small pearl buttons around the matrimonial bedchambers, and played with his child in the castle garden. And when the time came for the family to travel back to England, the three large coaches stayed together, if only because Pippa switched frequently between her mama and papa's coach and that of her own dear nanny. So the coaches wound toward London as slowly as the servants' coach had found its way up, and Charlotte buried memories of tearful nights by romping half the night with her husband in the same inns.

No one who saw the young countess on the way back to England, rather than on the way to Scotland, could have said she looked distant or snobbish. Due to Pippa's frequent presence in the coach, Charlotte often looked rumpled; but if the truth be told, even when Pippa was not in their coach, her husband took over the job of rumpling her himself.

The day after the first coach, drawn by four prancing steeds, drew up before Sheffield House in Albemarle Square, Sophie York swept past the butler with an airy "Charlotte expects me."

"So," Sophie demanded impudently. "Tell me *all!* How is married life?"

Charlotte blushed.

"That good?" Sophie asked, laughing.

"What has happened to you in the last two months?" Charlotte asked.

Sophie twinkled at her, just to show that she noticed Charlotte's evasion, and then she wound into a long tale of Braddon Chatwin's pursuit (having missed his chance with the one reigning beauty, Charlotte, he had adroitly turned to the other, Sophie). Charlotte alternately laughed and choked. In fact, she found herself wondering whether she had missed most of Sophie's jokes before she got married. Would she have understood Sophie's joke about the newlywed Lady Cucklesham, who married for money and then wore her maidenhead on her finger in the likeness of a large diamond?

"Were I minded to be the wife of a fool," Sophie said a little moodily, "I couldn't do better than Braddon. He would never bother to question what I was about: He's eternally good-natured and discreet. If there's one thing I can't stand, it's ungentlemanly behavior." She gave a little shudder.

Charlotte looked at her friend sympathetically. Everyone knew that the Marquis of Brandenburg could not resist a Frenchwoman, particularly when he drank overmuch.

"Don't do it, Sophie," she urged, a little surprised at her own fervency.

"Why ever not?"

"Because . . . it is wonderful being married to a man who isn't a fool."

"They are *all* fools," Sophie said rather shortly. Then she smiled wryly at Charlotte. "I don't mean to take away from your married bliss. But in my experience — granted, only gained by observation, but none the worse for that — in my experience, even the best men take to foolish behavior like a duck to water."

"Still," Charlotte persisted. "You could find a fool whom you like more than you like Braddon."

"That's just it. I *do* like him. He reminds me of the little brother I used to wish I had. I spent hours sitting in the nursery, which was just above my parents' bedroom. And I could hear my parents yelling at each other; my mother used to care a good deal more about my father's inability to resist a lovely Frenchwoman than she does at this point. I would wish and wish that I had a little brother: someone uncomplicated and loving. And Braddon is like that, Charlotte. He's very uncomplicated. I know he's loving — I overheard Sir Bredbeck say that Braddon has more mistresses depending on him than a lawyer has cases. Although, to do him justice, he keeps his mistresses out of the ballroom."

Charlotte involuntarily giggled, even as she winced at the sad image Sophie offered of her childhood.

"But, Sophie, you can't have children with someone who is like a little brother!"

"I want to marry someone who will be — a pleasant acquaintance. That strikes me as the best kind of *ton* marriage." Sophie said. Then she brightened. "Have you heard how well your protégée, Chloe van Stork, is doing? I vow, that girl is in a fair way to claiming some of my suitors! Not that I mind. She could even have Braddon but the gossips suggest she is waiting for Will Holland."

Charlotte thought back to her wedding ball. "Chloe liked him very much," she said.

"Well, she doesn't show any signs of grief, although he's still in the country. She has four or five constant beaux — they accompany her everywhere, hanging from her every word. I hear that they are betting in the clubs that she will take Lord Winkle."

"I'm glad," Charlotte said decisively. "She's a lovely girl and she deserves to be admired."

As Sophie chattered on about the particular snub that Lady Skiffing dealt Camilla Prebworth, the wife of Captain Prebworth, Charlotte's mind wandered to Alex. She knew exactly where he was: He had been pulled into his study by his long-suffering secretary, Robert Lowe, to deal with the correspondence that had built up over the last months.

Just then her husband appeared at the door, and Charlotte's face unknowingly lit up.

"Alex!" she cried, springing up from her chair.

Alex winked at Sophie, whom he had come to like a great deal over the two insufferably long months of his engagement, took his wife in his arms and slowly, deliberately, backed out of the door of the salon.

Sophie's clear laughter echoed after them as Alex stood in the marble hallway of Sheffield House, passionately kissing his bride until her knees trembled and she clutched the front of his coat.

"Alex, we have to go back into the salon," she whispered. "I can't just leave Sophie alone like this. It's too impolite."

"Swear that you'll meet me in one hour, in our chambers."

"I shall not."

"Swear that you will or I won't let you return." Alex traced a fiery path down Charlotte's throat to the rapidly beating pulse at its base. He licked it, and she almost moaned out loud.

"Alex!"

"Swear!"

"No. I have an appointment to visit Monsieur Carême in two hours."

"I'll get you there," Alex promised hoarsely. "I'll drive you in the phaeton." He showed every sign of going even lower in his outrageous kissing.

"I swear," Charlotte finally gasped.

But her husband wasn't listening. Having ascertained that there were no footmen stationed in the hallway at the moment, Alex was craftily trying to maneuver his wife against the wall. The moment he had her back to the wall he crushed his body against hers, thrusting his knee between her legs and grinning down at her wickedly. His hands swept down her back and cupped her buttocks, pulling her up against his erection. Charlotte's bottom was so curved and delicious that Alex could have wept.

The next second his wife pushed him away indignantly, although Alex noted with satisfaction that her hands were trembling and her cheeks were deeply rosy.

"Alex!" Charlotte snapped.

She whisked into the salon where she had left Sophie. Sophie was peacefully eating lemon wafers and drinking tea. She laughed out loud when she saw Charlotte. Charlotte's hair looked as if she had been in a high breeze; even the vagaries of Monsieur Pamplemousse's fashionable haircut couldn't explain the countess's current look.

Alex didn't seem to have followed her, so Sophie felt free to comment on the situation. In fact, Alex was staring at the Oriental birds that adorned the wallpaper in the hallway and waiting for his rigid arousal to subside. These knitted pantaloons really were inadequate, he thought glumly. At least for the kind of raging lust he felt for his wife. A tiny grin crept over his face.

"Does he kiss well?" Sophie asked. "You know I deserve an answer, given that you simply deserted me."

Alex inched a little closer to the open door. Surely it wasn't eavesdropping when the subject was as important as this one.

Charlotte gasped and then laughed. "Yes, he does," she replied. "He only has to kiss me and I —" she broke off, shrugging her shoulders.

"You what?" Sophie asked. Sophie knew a great many sophisticated jokes about erotic matters, but she didn't, in fact, see much point in carnal relations.

"Well, I just melt, that's all."

"It sounds like such an uncomfortable encounter," Sophie said. "Mind you, I'm not quite sure I understand exactly what happens — but please don't feel you have to tell me, Charlotte. While I feel certain that my mother will never get around to explaining the facts, at some point I'm going to accept one of these dunces who are courting me, and I'm sure he'll explain the whole awkward business."

Charlotte turned even pinker, if that was possible. "Well, it is awkward, but it's rather magnificent too."

Sophie looked at her curiously. "My mother told me that marital relations are a matter of extreme discomfort, and must be endured in return for one's place in society."

"That's not . . . it's not like that with Alex."

"Just my luck," Sophie said gloomily. "You take the one man in London who has any idea how to make the business comfortable, and I'm left with old Braddon. I'm sure he would explain it to me by reference to his stables. Sometimes I think he considers me to be prime bloodstock, just like his best mares."

"It's more than comfortable," Charlotte burst out. She was dying to tell someone, and she couldn't discuss it with her mama. "It's actually rather — glorious. Sometimes it's the only thing I can think about, all day," she confided.

Sophie was staring at her, blue eyes wide. "Maybe I *shouldn't* marry Braddon," she finally said. "I am quite sure that I would never think about him all day, no matter how he kissed. Does your husband kiss better than Will Holland does — or did?"

Charlotte blushed again. Sophie thought they were talking about *kissing*, and she had been talking about . . . She probably shouldn't discuss anything like this with an unmarried woman. Sophie seemed so sophisticated, but she obviously wasn't.

"What do you mean 'did?' " Charlotte replied, adroitly changing the subject. "Isn't Will kissing anymore?"

Out in the hallway Alex leaned his head back against the wall. There was no way he could ever join them in the salon. Hearing Charlotte's confession that she thought about sex during the day had made him harder than a rock. He groaned and set off toward his study. He might as well go through the rest of his correspondence. Given that he wasn't going to be able to do anything intelligent until Charlotte met him an hour hence, the least he could do was make Robert happy.

Another month passed. The London season was drawing to a close. Charlotte's and Alex's lives had fallen into a comfortable pattern. Charlotte painted in the morning. She embarked on a portrait of one of the kitchen maids, a large, bony girl named Mall who'd grown up near the Welsh border. At first the countess and the kitchen girl regarded each other circumspectly; Mall's certainty that her mistress was stark-raving mad didn't make sittings any more comfortable. But Charlotte persisted. Ever since she had seen Mall's face when she restocked the fireplace one morning she had wanted to paint her. After a while they became friends, and Charlotte learned all about Mall's seven brothers and sisters, and even some gossip about the staff. The butler, Staple, for instance — he sounded like a veritable tyrant. And if she understood Mall's marked Welsh brogue correctly, he wasn't behaving as he ought to around the younger female staff, either. That very night Charlotte dismissed

Staple, who seemed inclined to argue about it. But Charlotte was not the daughter of the Duchess of Calverstill for nothing. She drew herself up and gave him a duchess look, a stiff-necked, extremely unpleasant look. And Staple found himself walking right out of the room, willy-nilly.

Charlotte wrote a note to Mr. McDougal in Dunston Castle. Would he and Mrs. McDougal like to move to London? Since there was no housekeeper at the moment in Sheffield House, they would both be more than welcome. Charlotte named a salary well in excess of Staple's.

While she was painting, Alex worked in his study. In the first few weeks after they returned to London he used to wander into her studio and read a book on the days when she didn't actually have Mall sitting with her, but after a while Charlotte banished him. Not only could she not concentrate properly with him in the room, but he consistently put down his book and sprang on her.

"Like a tiger with its prey," Charlotte complained.

"It's not my fault," Alex said, grabbing his prey. "You have wanton eyes. You look at me over your easel and I know that you are silently begging me to caress you."

"If you do it only for me, you can leave off," Charlotte said pettishly. "I was thinking of my work, not of you."

"You can't fool me. You had *such* a melting

look around your mouth. . . ."

"Why don't you go fence with Lucien? You can play your games with him!"

"Because," her husband growled, "I like private play, at private houses. *This* house." And with that he bore her off to the old settee in the corner, and there was another morning lost. So she banned him from the studio, and he took to fencing with Lucien every morning.

"I have to do *something!*" Alex would complain. But Charlotte knew he loved the rough maleness of the fencing studios, the sharp give and take of insults that accompanied fencing matches. He always came back to the house glowing — and ready to lure her upstairs.

In the afternoon Charlotte played with Pippa, and in the evenings she and Alex went to the usual round of balls. Even if Charlotte occasionally affected a fashionable air of weary sophistication, she enjoyed balls as she never had before. There was nothing as delicious as meeting your own husband unexpectedly in a hallway, and having him whisper a promise in your ear that made you rosy-pink for the next hour. Or having your husband pull you so close during a waltz that people whispered — but we are married, Alex would reassure her. Or he would smile at her devilishly and say, "Let's do something for the benefit of my reputation," and kiss her right there, on the dance floor.

By the time Charlotte had been married four months, she was certain of two things. One was that she wasn't pregnant yet, and she would have to inform her husband of this signal fact (thereby curbing their joyful and button-liberating nightly activities), and the second was that she was falling, or had fallen, deeply, irrevocably in love with her husband. Her heart danced to see him; she was diminished when he wasn't in the room. Whenever they made love, the words almost burst out of her mouth, but she stopped them. What had he said when he asked her to marry him? Love was built from trust. And she wasn't sure he trusted her yet. Her mind wove into tangled, tiresome explanations of why she shouldn't tell him. But the truth was, she was a little afraid. He said so bluntly that he didn't love her, before. Charlotte felt shy, and vulnerable, and . . . well, as if she would rather not be the first to say "I love you." What if Alex thought she was trying to bribe him, to make him forget that she didn't tell him about her lack of virginity?

So she kept silent, and when she felt most like saying "I love you," she covered his face with passionate kisses instead, or offered to rub his back until he went to sleep. And then when she was quite sure he was fast asleep she would whisper "I love you" into his thick curls or against the rock-hard surface of his chest. The tension would drain out of her until the next time she caught sight of him laughing and found herself fighting the impulse again.

That night Alex found himself up against the ladylike training that Charlotte was, generally speaking, ready to toss to the side. But not to-night. In fact, she had secretly thought she was pregnant, since she hadn't had her flux during their entire married life, but it started that morning. And Charlotte was determined to follow her mama's outlines regarding just this contingency.

"No!" she said, looking at Alex in fascinated horror.

"Why not?" her husband said in his sweetest tones, kissing her neck. "Six more days?" Alex asked against her lips. "Six more days, Charlotte? I can't make it; I can't live through it."

Charlotte didn't dare answer. Her whole traitorous body was urging her to give in but she wouldn't, she wouldn't.

"I will not," she finally said. "I'm really serious, Alex. Perhaps I'd better sleep in the other room tonight."

"Oh, no," Alex said hastily, giving up. He had no real hope, but he certainly didn't intend to forgo Charlotte's sweet, curvaceous self lying next to him in the bed. Later he managed to reduce his wife to a flushed, longing beauty without even getting her long white nightgown above her knees, but still she was adamant.

"Six more nights," she said firmly. "Seven days is what my mama said, and I'm sure she's right about this. Perhaps I *should* go sleep in the other room."

Alex rolled over on top of Charlotte hastily, just in case she was really thinking about getting out of bed. He rubbed her nose gently with his, exactly as they both often did with Pippa. "I love being married to you, do you know?" His dark eyes stared down into hers as if they looked to the bottom of her soul. That's almost like saying "I love you," Charlotte thought.

The next morning Alex was sulky as a bear at breakfast, and then suddenly made a wry grimace at Charlotte.

"Is it just me?"

"I feel as if someone dumped itching powder on my head," his wife replied, smiling.

"Well, at least I'm not alone." Alex returned to the newspaper and then strode off to his study. Later that morning he uttered a muffled curse and dropped the piece of paper he was holding. Robert looked at him sympathetically. Then he moved forward and handed his master a heavy, embossed envelope marked *Department of Foreign Affairs* across the top.

"There's this one too," he said.

Alex read the message and let out a loud, heartfelt "Damnation!" Any other time he would be delighted with the invitation contained in these pages — invitation? Command, more like, he thought, his eyes skittering over the elegantly scripted letter from Lord Breksby, the Secretary for Foreign Affairs. He couldn't leave Charlotte now, he thought, his blood heating at the very thought of her. But he couldn't bring her; it was far too dangerous. He crumpled the heavy parchment in his hand and threw it violently into the corner.

"Send around a message telling that fellow that I will wait on him at four o'clock this afternoon," he barked at Robert. "And tell Lucien I will be at his house at five." Then Alex strode out of the study.

Alex tracked Charlotte down in her studio. She was frowning over the portrait of the third kitchen maid. Sophie was sitting with her and regaling her with Braddon's latest marriage proposal, attempted while they were both riding in Hyde Park.

"Was there something unpleasant in your correspondence?" Charlotte rang the bell for tea. She wasn't sure whether her husband looked so glowering because of last night, or due to another reason.

"I don't want tea," Alex said impatiently. "Tell the maid to bring me some brandy."

Charlotte came back to the divan, her eyes puzzled. Alex rarely drank in the afternoon. But he clearly didn't want to discuss the problem. Sophie, with her ever-present sensitivity to the moodiness of the male sex, was already gathering up her wrap and talking lightly of seeing them tonight at Lady Combe's ball.

Charlotte and Alex arrived at Lady Combe's ball late that evening. Even for a couple who had shocked and delighted the *ton* by their shamelessly affectionate behavior, their conduct at Lady Combe's ball was outrageous. For example, the countess was waltzing with the Honorable Sylvester Bredbeck when her husband simply barged onto the dance floor and swung her into his arms, without even a word of warning. All he did was grin at Sylvester — who took it very well, everyone thought — and announce that he had to hold his wife now. *Hold his wife* indeed! That wasn't something married people said about each other, as Lady Skiffing punctiliously pointed out.

And then the way they danced! Needless to say, there was no light visible between their bodies. Intriguingly, Lady Prestlefield swore that later that evening she saw the two of them having a squabble on a balcony. The Earl of Sheffield and Downes had his face buried in his wife's hair, but she looked fit to be tied, Lady Prestlefield recounted with relish.

She was more than fit to be tied. Charlotte was enraged and terrified by turns. Alex was setting off on one of the most foolish, quixotic journeys she had ever heard of. Who cared if he had perfect Italian and could pass as an Italian? No one in their right mind would venture to spy on the French, given the fragile truce holding between Napoleon and the English government. As for Lucien! She always liked her husband's friend before; in fact, ever since she realized at the picnic that Lucien had lost both wife and child in France, she had felt tenderly affectionate toward him. But now! If he *dared* to present himself to her, she would say something horrible to him.

"And don't tell me this is just female scruples, Alex!" she flashed at her husband later that night. "No one with the slightest consideration for your well-being would ask you to do such a thing. Go to France! Pretend to be Italian! Look for some girl who has likely, poor thing, been discovered and guillotined, and then try to get you both out of the country. Let alone traveling with a well-known French count — it will get you guillotined in a minute!" Charlotte rigidly controlled her tears.

"Lucien won't be with me," Alex explained patiently. "He'll be waiting in a boat off the shore of France. It would be too dangerous for him to enter the country. But Charlotte, there's more than a chance that we can rescue Lucien and Daphne's little sister. How can I deny that request? It's a simple thing, after all. Italians are free to travel throughout France. I simply enter the country as a prosperous merchant, travel a short way over the border, pick up this girl in the milliner's shop, and there we are. You mustn't worry too much, love. Paris is full of Englishmen at the moment: Remember, we signed a peace agreement with Napoleon."

"No, Alex, no," Charlotte said chokingly, winding her arms around his neck. "It's too dangerous. You can't leave me and Pippa. You can't! I'll die without you."

"Listen, darling." Alex drew back and looked down into Charlotte's clear eyes. "I was born a gentleman. That was extremely lucky; I should have greatly disliked to have been born a chimney sweep, for example. But that same *honor* to which I was born means that I cannot refuse Lucien's request simply because of fear. Even given that I hate the thought of leaving you and Pippa. Nor can I turn down Lord Breksby's gently worded command to pick up a package, whatever it is, in Paris. They need someone they can trust. They can trust me, because I was bred to a position that made me trustworthy."

Charlotte wanted to shake him. What a silly, stupid reason to risk one's life. Yet she could see from Alex's beloved face that he believed every silly word. Frustrated tears rose to her eyes.

"Lucien's youngest sister is only thirteen years old," Alex said. "I can't leave her there, Charlotte. It was a terribly dangerous act for this milliner to have taken her in. Apparently he told everyone that she was his niece, but there's a good deal of money offered for aristocrats, no matter how young."

Charlotte buried her head in his chest, her shoulders shaking with sobs. "Why can't someone else go?" she finally wailed, the ageless cry of wives and mothers watching beloved ones go fight in foreign wars.

"Because I look so very un-English," Alex said wryly. "And thanks to Maria I also speak idiomatic Italian. Darling, I will be perfectly safe, I promise you. I will be back in England before you even finish your portrait of that rawboned kitchen maid."

"Then why so soon?" Charlotte pulled away, walking to the window and staring out at the dark gardens. She felt utterly disconsolate.

Alex came up behind her and pulled the thick curtains shut. "There's no time to be lost." Charlotte knew what he meant. The thirteen-year-old . . . He wrapped his arms around her from the back, and Charlotte leaned against him. Her hands absently twisted a length of the rich velvet curtain.

"I don't see why Lord Breksby needs *you* to go to Paris. Surely Paris is the most dangerous place of all!"

"Actually not, darling," Alex said, his deep voice unruffled. "Italians go in and out of Paris all the time, and it isn't as if I am being asked to bring back a person from Paris. I am going to pick up a small package. It should take a matter of hours, and my carriage can be searched on the way out without any risk. The French government is allowing business transactions to continue, you know."

"Well, I still don't see why Lucien can't simply hire someone," she retorted. "You just said yourself that rescuing people is dangerous."

"If you were trapped in France, darling, I would ask my closest friend. If Patrick were not in England, I would ask Lucien. I would never just hire someone I didn't know. Lucien lost both his brothers to the guillotine, so he *has* to ask me. But even so, he didn't ask me face-to-face. He left me a way out by asking me on paper. But it wouldn't be right, Charlotte. I couldn't live with myself afterward. What if we heard in a month or two that the girl had been imprisoned? Until now Lucien didn't even know she had survived at all."

There was a little silence. Then Charlotte resignedly turned about and reached out her hand to ring for Maria. It was time for bed. Alex had to leave at five in the morning, and that was a mere three hours away.

She looked up at her husband. He was looking at her with an imploring hunger that made her heart turn over. Well, so what? She had broken every other rule that governed a lady's marital relations. Odd that while she blithely broke the most sacred rules regulating the conduct of a lady, Alex was risking his life to keep to the rules of being a gentleman, Charlotte thought wryly. But her flux seemed to be unusually light anyway, so there would be nothing embarrassing about it.

And she wanted to, she realized. She wanted to as much as he did.

"Will you act as my maid, my lord?" she asked, dropping her hand from the bell cord.

Alex took her delicate face in his large hands, kissing her sweet mouth. "I don't deserve you," he said. "I don't deserve you, Charlotte."

Charlotte's arms slipped slowly from his shoulders, down his back and rested on his buttocks. Alex's body went absolutely rigid. His wife was slowly learning to be bold, but she was only just learning how much her touch inflamed him. Charlotte splayed her fingers and pulled her husband's large, powerful body against hers.

"Just in case you don't come back," she whispered achingly, "I am going to memorize your body tonight."

His hands shaking with a potent combination of lust and tenderness, Alex turned Charlotte around and started unbuttoning her gown. Pearls, yanked from their moorings, hurdled across the floor with the sound of scampering mouse feet. As Alex unbuttoned, he kissed, and as he kissed, he moved lower and lower until he was on his knees. He turned his wife around again and simply pulled her gown forward and down until it draped low on her creamy stomach. Then Alex wrapped his arms around Charlotte, resting his face against her soft skin.

"I thought you were pregnant," he said. "When I get back, I am going to make love to you every night and every afternoon until your waist grows so large that I can't get my arms all the way around you."

Charlotte chuckled. "That won't ever happen," she said. "My mama told me that people didn't realize she was pregnant at all until practically the last month. We're so much taller than the average woman."

She stared down at her husband's curls. Did he want an heir, or their child? "Do you . . . would you like to have a child, even if it were another girl?" she finally asked, tentatively.

Alex rocked back on his heels, his hands stroking Charlotte's slim sides. "I would love to have a little girl who looked just like you," he said, so sincerely that Charlotte knew he meant it. He looked up and caught her eye. "I want to be there for the birth, you know." Charlotte's eyes widened.

"You couldn't *possibly*," she gasped.

"You watch," Alex said, grinning. "I saw a baby born in Italy, when I was traveling around the countryside and a woman simply gave birth right in the *taverna*. It was wonderful. Even dragoon guards couldn't keep me out of the room if you were having a baby!"

Charlotte didn't know what to say to that. She swallowed. If her mama ever found out, she would faint on the spot.

Alex ran his hands over Charlotte's flat stomach. Then he felt a surge of strong, masculine annoyance. By God, he was starting to get maudlin! He had to watch it, or he *would* start thinking he was in love with Charlotte. And he had made up his mind that he simply wouldn't allow any woman to have that much power over him, ever again. Not even his own Charlotte. *No* woman, he reminded himself. Expertly he began giving Charlotte little licking, nipping bites, working upward toward her breasts.

Charlotte giggled. With a mock growl, her husband lunged at one of her breasts, taking the nipple in his mouth and rolling his teeth over it. Charlotte's giggle died in her throat, replaced by a ragged moan. Alex scooped up his wife and laid her on the bed.

The next morning at five o'clock, Charlotte and a very cross Pippa waved good-bye to Alex from the steps of Sheffield House. Pippa hadn't wanted to wake up, but Charlotte was determined that she say good-bye properly. Not like the last time, when Pippa simply woke up to find that her papa was gone. And if — Charlotte only let herself think this in the far recesses of her mind — if Alex did not come back, at least Charlotte could describe how he kissed and kissed Pippa's face, later, when Pippa was old enough to understand.

The next day Charlotte told everyone the story that Alex had prepared — that he had to go to Italy suddenly, to attend to some business. Only Sophie and her parents knew the truth.

"I told you," was Sophie's response. "Every man plays the fool at some time or other. Why didn't Lucien simply hire one of the Bow Street Runners? I thought they were so good at dangerous business."

For a second Charlotte's heart leaped. But no, it was too late. By now Lucien and Alex would be at Southampton, boarding a ship bound for Italy. Lucien was traveling as Alex's personal servant: These days there was nothing surprising about having a French manservant.

"No," she said. "I doubt Bow Street Runners speak Italian. Alex made it all sound so simple."

"Nothing is that simple," Sophie said flatly. "Particularly not when it comes to the French."

Charlotte tightened her grip around Pippa, who was peacefully sleeping in her lap. She hadn't let her out of her sight all day. Then she sighed and looked up at Sophie.

"When this little bundle wakes up, would you like to go shopping? I can't possibly face my studio today. Besides, I need to buy some larger clothes."

"Larger clothes?" Sophie asked. "Why on earth?" Then her eyes widened. "You're having a baby!" She jumped up and gave Charlotte an impulsive hug. "When?"

"I'm not sure," Charlotte said with a small smile. "You see, I thought my monthly had started and that I wasn't pregnant, but then it stopped. And my mama told me this morning that a little blood was quite common. So I could be as far as three months along, I suppose." She looked down at her slim waist a little dubiously. "I feel just the same."

Sophie smiled at her gaily. "Well, why shouldn't you? Did you tell Alex?"

"No, because I didn't know. I didn't understand what was happening, and so he thinks I am definitely *not* pregnant, and here I am, three months pregnant. When he gets back, I'll probably look like a cow."

"A very beloved cow," Sophie said with an affectionate grin. "Alex will be ecstatic. One evening he and I were sitting next to each other — was it a musicale? I'm not sure where you were — and he told me that he wanted a large family, four or five children."

"Really?" Charlotte asked, fascinated.

"Oh, yes," Sophie said. "He's besotted. Only besotted men want children."

Charlotte blushed and just stopped herself from asking if Sophie really thought Alex was besotted. She had to keep a little bit of dignity. Pippa stretched and yawned; Sophie rang the bell.

"Do you want to take Pippa with us?" she asked.

"Yes."

Sophie gave her friend an understanding smile. Pippa looked so much like Alex.

"You'd better change your dress first," Sophie observed. "There's a big wet spot where Pippa was sleeping."

Chapter 17

That night Charlotte circled the bed that she and Alex usually shared, staring at the slightly crumpled, fine linen sheets. The night seemed to stretch endlessly before her; night after night alone. Six weeks, Alex had said. Or two months at the most. Two months! Charlotte wanted to scream at the unfairness of it. By the time he got back she would look like a pumpkin, and he wouldn't want to make love to her. One tear slid coldly down her nose. But Charlotte stopped herself. She couldn't spend the next two months weeping. She would have to organize such a busy life that she fell into bed exhausted every night, so tired that she couldn't dwell on her memories.

Finally Charlotte crept under the cool sheets. She was wearing one of her long white nightgowns, the kind that Alex hated. Thinking about nightgowns made her remember Alex's impatient hands running up her body, pulling her nightclothes out of the way with a muffled oath. Charlotte smiled a little. Bed with Alex had become the focus of her days. He could be frowning at the morning papers, totally absorbed in the report of activities in the House of

Lords, and she would suddenly remember the dusky intensity that overtook his eyes as he watched her undress at night. Or Alex would come back from fencing, his hair ruffled, body glowing with exercise, and Charlotte would remember how his chest heaved, after . . . He used to roll over with a moan of simulated exhaustion and growl that he would never recover. Charlotte bit back more tears. Two months wasn't very long. She would finish the portrait of Mall.

The portrait was causing her some trouble. She had chosen Mall because of the angularity of her face, but she was having a good deal of difficulty capturing Mall's rough, lively person. One day her face looked like a cartoon of a Welsh country girl, all nose and chin. The next day, Charlotte would work hard on bringing back Mall's contrary girlishness and shrewdness, and then the portrait would take on the air of a little girl trapped in a grown-up face. Thinking about the painting made Charlotte feel much calmer. After all, there's more to life than Alex and this bed, Charlotte told herself with a twinge of amusement. Someday they would be old and gray, and they would be tired of making love.

Suddenly there was a squabbling noise at her door and Charlotte sat up.

"Who's there?" she called.

"Oh, my lady, I am so sorry," came an anguished voice from the door.

Charlotte lit the candle by her bed. The door opened and she dimly saw Pippa's nanny, swathed in a large robe, clutching a kicking, squealing Pippa.

"She ran out of the room before I realized she was awake," Katy continued. "I'm so sorry she awakened you, my lady." Pippa let out a furious wail.

"Pippa," Charlotte said. "What on earth are you doing awake in the middle of the night?" And then, "It's all right, Katy. Let her go."

Pippa trotted over to the bed, her little bare feet patting on the wood floor.

"Papa?" she asked, her voice quavering. "Where's Papa?"

"Oh, sweetheart," Charlotte said, her heart turning over. "Papa had to go away for a while, but he will come back."

Pippa gave her a look of total disbelief and sat right down on the floor. She began to cry, not the angry sobs of an almost two year old, but the heartbroken sobs of a baby deserted again.

Damn! Charlotte thought furiously. How can he leave her? She hopped out of bed, shivering as her bare feet came down on the drafty floor. Katy was standing quietly in the door.

"She's been asking all evening, my lady," Katy said, in response to her unspoken question. "I've told her that her father is coming back, but she doesn't believe me."

Charlotte knelt down and pulled Pippa onto her knees.

"He *is* coming back, poppet," she whispered into Pippa's soft curls. "You remember when we went to Scotland together, and Papa was there waiting for us?" Charlotte stood up, still cuddling Pippa, and turned back to the bed.

"Katy, I will keep Pippa here tonight," she said with sudden determination. Katy curtsied and closed the door silently.

Charlotte climbed back into the bed, tucking a sobbing Pippa up against her left side.

"Pippa," she whispered. "Shall I tell you a story?" Pippa didn't say anything. But Charlotte remembered loving the stories her nanny told her when she was young. So she started a story about a mama hen and her three naughty little baby chicks. After a bit Pippa stopped crying and turned her face up toward Charlotte's. Then, when Charlotte was chirping the *peep peep* of the three naughty chicks as they left their house to look for trouble, she felt Pippa's body relax and her head grew heavy against Charlotte's arm.

Charlotte lay for a moment in the warm darkness. Suddenly the bed didn't seem so large and unfriendly anymore. Pippa was curled on one side of her, and in her womb Alex's baby was growing larger every moment. Charlotte smiled. Soon she would have two little chicks.

The next morning Charlotte started all over on Mall's portrait, to the kitchen maid's mingled distress and pleasure. Mall loved sitting in the mistress's airy studio; she vastly appreciated the time to rest her feet. But she was eager to see a picture of herself too. Even staring into the cracked mirror upstairs hadn't told her why the mistress wanted to paint her. Mall was hoping that she would be transformed into a great beauty, on canvas at least.

By two weeks later, Charlotte had made more progress on the portrait than ever before. She had also dragged Sophie to two balls, two musicales, and the opera.

"I abhor musicales," Sophie complained, waving her fan gently. "We are not dressed to our best advantage. I don't appreciate myself in chaste white muslin. Just look about you: Every woman looks like a little white ghost. We appear sheeplike, and that inspires men to become dull admirers of themselves and make their court to nothing but their cravats. Look at that fop who calls himself my cousin." She waved at the Honorable François de Valcon, her mama's nephew, with an enchanting smile. Then she turned back to Charlotte. "He is more concerned at the disordering of his cravat than I would be at having my skirt fly above my ankles."

"That is because you admire your own ankles as much as François likes his skill at tying cravats," Charlotte whispered back.

Sophie laughed. "Musicales are particularly boring because we just sit about and listen to singing. I like to dance. There's always the chance I'll be able to admire my ankles, or at the least, I can provide the occasion for someone else to admire 'em. Look at this room. There's not a man here who isn't a skirter, paying his lazy addresses to *us*, but actually conducting business only with his mistresses."

"You shouldn't use that kind of slang, Sophie!" Charlotte protested. But as she glanced around the room, she had to agree with Sophie. Musicales were for the bored and the foppish; Mrs. Felvitson's Russian singers were unintelligible and monotonous. The room was full of young matrons like herself, accepting the languid compliments of fairly uninterested fops.

"And all these old women: They are hoping for a scandal to erupt," Sophie continued disgustedly. "We should leave, Charlotte. They're such dowdies, just longing to kick up some dust. If a libertine walked in the door and happened to look at a woman, they would build some sort of a tale out of it."

"Let's go then," Charlotte replied, standing up. But as she stood, her eyes caught sight of a tall man just bowing his welcome to Mrs. Felvitson.

"Alex!" she cried. She took one step, but the combination of shock and the fact she had just jumped to her feet blurred her eyes. Without a word, and for the first time in her life, Charlotte fainted clear away. Luckily Sophie had just risen to her feet, and when Charlotte suddenly swayed, she automatically reached out her arms. A minute later she found herself sitting on the floor, Charlotte's head and shoulders in her lap, completely bewildered. Then Sophie looked up, and at the same moment Charlotte opened her eyes.

The man smiling down at the two beautiful women saw a puzzled expression on their faces that he had seen a thousand times before. Patrick squatted down on his ankles, patting his new sister-in-law's hand.

"How do you feel?"

"Are you Alex?" Charlotte whispered. Sophie didn't say anything. To her mind, this man — obviously Alex's twin — only looked like the earl from a distance.

But Charlotte was still half in a swoon, her mind foggy. She reached out and touched Patrick's cheek wonderingly. "You aren't a ghost, are you?"

Patrick's eyebrow shot up. Was his brother's wife touched in the upper works? Sophie shot him an admonishing look.

"Will you please help the countess off the floor?" she said, with something less than full social politeness. "This is your sister-in-law, as I'm sure you have realized."

Surprised, Patrick looked at the little termagant who was clutching his brother's wife. Then he smiled back at Charlotte, dismissing Sophie from his mind.

"I am your brother-in-law, you know," he said winsomely. "Not Alex at all."

"I apologize," Charlotte said more firmly. "I can't imagine what came over me. But I would like to get up now." She was uneasily aware that there was a cluster of people hovering around them. She quickly sat up, and then put her hand to her head. Lord, her head was swimming!

In a second Patrick scooped her off the ground and stood up with Charlotte in his arms. She struggled, feeling with real distress the sharp eyes of all the gossips standing around them.

"This isn't proper," she whispered. "Put me down, please."

Patrick strode over to the nearest divan and deposited her with aplomb. Then he stepped back and gave a flourishing bow. "I am Patrick Foakes, my lady, and very pleased to make your acquaintance," he said. "I just stepped off the ship this morning. When I came by to see Alex I was told of your existence, and of the fact that you were at this lovely musicale." He smiled at Mrs. Felvitson's sharp little face, hovering at his elbow.

"Oh, dear," Charlotte said lamely. "Alex did send you a letter telling you of our wedding, in the diplomatic pouch."

"Must have been already traveling when it arrived," Patrick said. "Would you like me to accompany you to the house? There seem to be a plaguey amount of people watching us here."

"Yes." Charlotte stood up, composed again. She made a graceful apology to Mrs. Felvitson for interrupting the music (even those Russians had been craning at her lying on the ground!) and left the room on Patrick's arm, Sophie trailing after them.

They left behind them a far more excited crowd than had originally graced Mrs. Felvitson's soirée.

"There's nothing to it," Sir Benjamin Tribble said in an extremely unconvincing manner.

"No, indeed!" Sylvester Bredbeck agreed, his sharp eyes scanning Sir Benjamin's melon-colored jacket in an unpleasant fashion. "The countess was surprised to unexpectedly meet a man who looked exactly like her husband, that's all!"

Everyone had to acknowledge the value of this statement, and the whole subject may have fallen into silence, except for two factors. One was Lady Prestlefield's excellent memory, and the second was Lady Cucklesham's acute irritability.

"I dare swear you are right, Sylvester," Lady Prestlefield said in her customary brisk manner. "Except that those two dear children do know each other. Alex — that is, the earl — told me himself that the countess, such a lovely girl she is, met his brother years ago, before he went off to the East. He said it to me flat out. In fact, he said that when he, Alex, met Charlotte at *my* ball, she first mistook him for his younger brother."

"You are *too* severe, Sarah," Lady Cucklesham cooed. She preferred to maintain a sweet tone at all times. "Why, if one were to believe that they knew each other already, some inconsiderate soul might think the worst of that tender gesture she gave him, brushing his cheek with her fingers as she did."

"Nonsense," Sylvester said stoutly. "That's a pack of nonsense, Sarah, and you ought not to repeat it. Charlotte had never met Patrick

434

Foakes before in her life."

"Yes, yes, you are right, Lord Bredbeck," Lady Cucklesham said. "Now, Sarah, darling, you must *not* repeat a word about the fact that Charlotte was so well acquainted with the earl's younger brother before he went abroad, because I dare swear the truth of the matter is that they merely met once or danced . . . or something of that sort."

Sylvester Bredbeck cast Lady Cucklesham a glance of acute dislike. He always thought she was a puffed-up turnip, and now that she had finagled her way into a marriage with a man forty years older than herself, it certainly hadn't done her temper any good.

Sylvester bowed rigidly and left the musicale. It wouldn't make any difference if he were to defend Charlotte any further; better to let it blow over, he thought.

But London society was rather thin since the season was drawing to a close. There wasn't much to talk about. The matches that would happen this season had already been made, the documents signed, the couples happily or unhappily embarked on forty years of matrimony. Some two weeks ago there had been an elopement, but it was *very* unsatisfactorily concluded, to everyone's mind — the young bride banished to the country and the groom sent off to the continent.

So by the next evening every member of the *ton* who had enough self-respect to keep abreast

435

of current gossip knew that the Countess of Sheffield and Downes, who had only been alone for a few weeks, had greeted her husband's brother in the most tender and affecting manner, actually fainting from happiness at the sight of him. And although no one could actually remember seeing them dance together during Charlotte's first season, quite a mythology sprang up overnight about what must have been a brief but passionate romance before Patrick was ordered off to the Orient.

"Only the most unkind," Lady Skiffing observed, "would think that Charlotte had married the elder in place of the younger. If only on a practical level, no girl would marry a second son when the first was asking for her hand."

Her little circle considered this a very fair observation. "You have so much good nature, my dear," Lady Prestlefield said comfortably.

"Yes, indeed," chimed in Sir Benjamin Tribble. "Why, those who don't have your forbearance, Lady Skiffing, might be persuaded to wonder about dear Alex's previous marital problems. . . ."

"That's just an example of the ill nature some people exhibit," Lady Skiffing exclaimed. "It is such a consolation to me to think that none of *us* would repeat anything so indelicate about the earl!"

The little circle thought with satisfaction of the kindly news they had spread far and wide. In fact, Sir Tribble had gained quite a bit of fame this week due to having been actually present when the lovers met again. Tribble had a way with words, and his account of the countess's white, imploring face and the way she pressed her trembling fingers to Patrick's face was taken to be a most affecting account.

So, no matter how many times her mama protested that there was no truth to the report, and her friend Sophie York ("a bit wild herself," those same unkind people might say) stoutly insisted that Charlotte had merely mistaken Patrick for her husband, by the end of the week all of London understood that Patrick had broken Charlotte's heart by going off to the Orient without marrying her, and that she had only married Alex as second choice.

Charlotte didn't know what to do. She was, quite simply, bewildered by the storm of scandal that had broken over her head without warning.

"I wouldn't worry about it too much," her mama said consolingly. She had come to say good-bye. The season was over, and rather than retire to the country the duke and duchess were taking a long-promised trip to America to visit their eldest daughter, Winifred, who had married a wealthy American.

"I hate to leave you at such a delicate time," Adelaide said, "but the fact is, darling, that one simply cannot get through one's life these days without at least one major scandal erupting out of nowhere. When I think of the things that were said about your father, for example, when we were young! Someone told me, quite seriously, that Marcel was on the verge of leaving me and running off to France with a young opera singer. And when I finally got up the courage to mention it to your father, he had no idea who this woman was! All he could say was 'France? France? Deuced uncomfortable country!'

"The part that really bothers me is leaving you while you are *enceinte*," Adelaide said. "Pregnancy is such a tiresome business. Still, the baby is a perfect excuse for you to stay in the house, dearest, and rest. For goodness sake, don't give anyone fodder for gossip. I'm afraid you will just have to wait and become acquainted with Lord Foakes after your husband returns."

Charlotte listened silently as this flurry of advice descended on her. "But Mama, Lord Foakes sent me a note saying he would wait on me this afternoon at four o'clock. I can't send him a note telling him nay. It would be so impolite."

Adelaide had the perfect solution. "Simply tell him to send away his carriage, darling. His servants can take the horses around the park and no one will be the wiser. But you mustn't spend any time with him in public. That would be fatal."

Charlotte looked at her mama's serious expression and promised to avoid Patrick at all costs.

"Now we will just pray that some poor foolish soul decides to elope with her footman," her mama said bracingly. "Because this kind of story — especially when there is nothing to keep the fire burning — always disappears within a matter of weeks. Why, in a year or so you can dance twice with Patrick and no one will even notice." Then she hesitated. "Darling, *was* Patrick the man in the garden?"

"Oh, Mama, of course not!" Charlotte was disgusted. *No one* believed her, not her mother or her husband. "It was Alex, as I told you."

Adelaide was without measure relieved. She had manfully hidden her worry from Charlotte, believing that anxiety was bad for pregnancy. But it made her feel ill to see just how close this whole scandal came to the truth. That was the worst of it. She was glad to be leaving for America because she was not the best of liars and she was always afraid that people could guess when she told half-truths.

Finally Charlotte dutifully kissed her mama good-bye. Adelaide departed with a muddled lecture about pregnancy, birth, midwives, doctors and wet nurses. Charlotte listened numbly. She still couldn't believe she was pregnant. There had been no sign, unless one included her fainting spell. She began to think that fainting must be a sign of pregnancy, because every time she rose too quickly she felt as if the room were spinning. But she didn't want to see a doctor yet. Charlotte shuddered. She was perfectly healthy; she must simply remember to stay seated or risk making a fool of herself.

So that afternoon Charlotte smiled engagingly at her husband's brother and waved him to a chair without getting up.

"You see," she confided, "I, or rather Alex and I, are having a baby, and it seems to make me rather light-headed."

Patrick's eyes cleared. He was relieved to hear that his brother hadn't married a vaporish woman whose sensibilities were so fragile that she fainted constantly. Although he wouldn't have blamed him, Patrick thought. Lord, but Alex had found a dark beauty.

"Alex will be pleased." Patrick grinned. "He always wanted a large family. I used to twit him about it because it didn't seem to fit with his . . ." Patrick trailed off. He had forgotten that one didn't make jokes about one's brother's propensity for wild starts in front of his new bride. Let alone acknowledge that Alex once thought family life was pretty flat.

But Charlotte only heard confirmation of the fact that Alex wanted children. "Yes, it is splendid, isn't it? He doesn't know yet."

"I won't tell him. What the devil is he doing over in Italy?" Patrick asked.

Charlotte swallowed. Alex said not to tell anyone, but surely he didn't mean his own brother?

But Patrick continued without pause. "I know: winding up the affairs of that virago he married," he said. He changed the subject politely, and they talked of his travels for a few minutes, but the atmosphere was strained.

Finally Patrick took the bull by the horns. "I

440

suppose you know about the stories that are circulating about us."

"Oh, no!" Charlotte cried, looking up suddenly. "I forgot to ask you to send away your horses!"

"Do you really think that's necessary?" Patrick said, his brow darting up in a gesture of aristocratic disbelief that was *so* like Alex that Charlotte couldn't help smiling.

"My mother thought it would be a good idea."

"In that case I'll send them off directly."

Charlotte rang the doorbell but no butler appeared, only a rather flustered looking upper housemaid.

"Don't you have a butler?" Patrick enquired.

"I dismissed him, and the new one hasn't arrived from Scotland yet. Molly, will you ask a footman to attend us, please?"

"Yes, my lady." Molly dropped a curtsy. Then she hesitated.

"Molly?"

"Oh, my lady, there's such an awful man outside! He says he's from *The Tatler*, and we can't get rid of him."

"My goodness," Charlotte said, startled. "Who exactly has tried to evict the man?"

"Well, there's three footmen have been out to see him, but no one can stop him from lurking about the house and sneaking up to the windows."

Patrick rose threateningly to his feet. "I'll —"

"No, you certainly won't!" Charlotte snapped.

"You can't be seen here at all. I suppose your coach is waiting for you in front?"

"I don't know," Patrick replied. "I had a fresh team this afternoon, so Derby may have taken them for a spin."

"Molly, send a footman out to intercept Lord Foakes's carriage and send it off to Hyde Park."

"No, no," said Patrick, his deep voice amused. "He can tell Derby to go home and I'll take a hackney later."

Molly curtsied and left the room. There was a moment of silence. Then Patrick laughed ruefully.

"Do you know, I have never had an affair with a married woman? I begin to see that it must be remarkably uncomfortable."

Charlotte chuckled. Now that she saw Patrick more clearly, she couldn't believe she ever thought he was Alex. They were entirely different. Patrick looked as if he was always about to burst out laughing or say something whimsical. Whereas Alex . . . Charlotte thought longingly of Alex and the way he would grimace when she teased him for wearing his "brooding look."

"London is dashed dull after India, anyway," Patrick said frankly. "I thought I might go into Leicestershire for the hunt. I shall be off in the morning, and that ought to kill the gossip." He looked disgusted. "All this devilish propriety! I never could abide it. Although I must say I have never got up to as freakish an exploit as Alex did in Italy, and he always seems the sober one. Annulling his marriage!" Patrick had caught up on all the family gossip the night before, and he was feeling rather refreshed at the thought of his somber twin getting himself into such a bumble-bath.

Charlotte blushed faintly. She felt a bit diffident about the subject of Alex's first wife.

"Anyway, how the deuce am I to get out of here?" Patrick demanded. "I'm very pleased to have met you, but unless I'm to spend the night I need to find a back door, or some such."

Charlotte had been thinking this over. "The problem is that you're so very tall," she said, dismissing her idea of disguising her brother-in-law in a maid's dress. She had read a novel in which that worked, but somehow it didn't seem very likely in reality.

"I'll just wait until the cove outside lopes off."

"The cove outside lopes — off?" Charlotte repeated in a bewildered tone.

Patrick gave her an irrepressible grin. "I'll attend your ladyship until that gentleman who is creeping about your house gives up and goes to find his dinner."

"Oh. Is that Indian slang?"

"No! It's flash talk, from the streets behind your house," Patrick said with asperity. He had forgotten how sheltered English women were. The well-bred ones, at least.

"Oh," Charlotte repeated. There was a knock and Molly entered again. Charlotte looked up

443

thankfully. Patrick made her feel muddleheaded and tired. It must be the baby, she thought.

"This arrived for you, my lady." Molly held out a somewhat worn envelope. "I thought, under the circumstances, that you would like to see it directly."

"Thank you, Molly," Charlotte said, taking the envelope. She knew instantly it was a letter from Alex. It was quite brief.

Dearest Charlotte, it read. *I dislike writing letters, so this will be quite short. I'm afraid we have run into more problems than we anticipated. While Lucien's business is completed, I have yet to acquire the merchandise I told you of, as it was not available in Paris. It will take a while to arrange the transfer, but then I shall be coming home.*

At the bottom, written in a less formal, sprawling hand, Alex had written *Beloved*. And then, *Alex*. Charlotte stared at the letter in disbelief. This was *it*? An obscurely phrased note about merchandise from Paris? He must have been afraid that the letter would be intercepted, she thought. Well — but "beloved"? That must mean her. She felt a warm glow creeping over her. This was even better than Alex saying that he loved being married to her. "Beloved" is close to "I love you," she thought. Then she realized the room had been silent for several long moments. She looked up and blushed.

444

"Do forgive me, Lord Foakes. It is a letter from your brother. He reports that he won't be able to return from Italy as early as he planned. In fact," she frowned, "he doesn't exactly say *when* he thinks to return!"

"Kicking up a lark!" Alex's brother said knowledgeably. Then he caught Charlotte's eye and almost blushed himself. "No, no," he said. "I didn't mean that. I'm sure Alex will be on the first boat back to England."

Charlotte's heart felt very light. "You think he's gone on the mop?" she asked cheerfully. "Or piked the bean?"

"One 'pikes on the bean,' " Patrick corrected, a large grin splitting his face. He had suddenly discovered that his new sister-in-law was not only lovely, but enchanting as well. "And, no, my elder brother has definitely *not* run off. Alex was always the more responsible of the two of us. But where in the world did a well brought-up young lady learn those terms?"

"From our third housemaid, whose name is Mall," Charlotte replied.

"Mall . . . Mall is a good friend of yours?"

"Oh, yes. We have spent quite a lot of time together. Mall is from the Welsh border." Charlotte smiled at her perplexed brother-in-law. Served him right for treating her as if she were a silly nincompoop.

"Well," Patrick said finally, when it became clear that she was not going to explain any further, "why don't I look out the servants' en-

445

trance, and if I don't see anyone I'll lope off and if I'm lucky no one will smoke me!"

Charlotte laughed. "I shall have to ask Mall for an appropriate retort to that proposal." She got up cautiously and held out her hand. Her eyes danced; Patrick was surprised to feel a twinge of jealousy of Alex. What on earth for? *He* didn't intend to get married, even to a lovely girl like this one.

"Here's my famble," he said jokingly, taking Charlotte's delicate hand in his. He stooped and kissed her cheek. "I am very glad you have joined the family," Patrick said in an entirely different tone. "Alex deserves the best, and I think he might have found it."

Charlotte smiled into Patrick's dark eyes, eyes so alike Alex's and yet so different. It was odd that she could find one face soul-shatteringly beautiful, and the other — practically identical to Alex's — just a nice, handsome face.

"Thank you," she said sincerely. "I hope when all this fuss has died down we can come to know each other better."

"As do I, my lady." Patrick bowed formally, and left the room. When he didn't return in five minutes, Charlotte assumed he had found the coast clear. It was time to think about moving the household to the country. She had been waiting for Alex, hoping not to have to supervise such a large, complicated endeavor by herself, especially without a butler. But what could she do? Clearly Alex didn't have any idea when he would be returning to England. And now that winter was drawing in, coal smoke was starting to darken the streets. She remembered the article she had discussed with Alex long ago, about the black little lungs of autopsied babies, and shuddered. They would wait one more month for Alex to return, and then she and Pippa must leave London.

Meanwhile Mr. Peter Taffata, better known as Taffy Tatler (one of *The Tatler*'s best rattlers, as they were called) waited patiently outside Sheffield House. He knew that the Earl of Sheffield and Downes had a younger brother named Patrick, and he knew that this Patrick was inside the house, doubtless being entertained by the young countess. Taffy had no personal animosity against either of these two people. As a matter of fact, he had a good deal of sympathy for the countess. It was a crime that her parents had married her off to an impotent man. Still, her shenanigans with her husband's brother looked as if they might warm up to a really good story, perhaps even a whole page to himself.

He'd been puzzling over one question for the last hour or so, rather like a bullterrier with a cow bone. That's why I'm so good, Taffy thought absently, because I keep at a problem when I find one. And the problem here was: Why hasn't a fancy butler come out of the house and told me off soundly? Usually Taffy had to deal with butlers who were more puffed up than their masters, their noses so far in the air they couldn't smell their own toes. But this house didn't seem to have a butler. In Taffy's experience, that meant that the butler had either scampered — or got himself fired. And Taffy liked the latter idea better. Because, he thought, who ever left the employ of an earl? The three footmen who had tried, very inefficiently, to get him to move his stumps had looked well-fed enough, and they were dressed in spry uniforms.

So it was just a question of catching one of the kitchen maids and getting her to cough up the name of the ex-butler, and then he, Taffy, could get a real story.

Taffy looked at the unwelcoming eyes of Sheffield House. He had a strong sense that the footmen had tattled on him, and that Lord Foakes had snuck out the back of the house. Of course, he could report that Foakes never left, but stayed the night. . . . He chewed this over for a while, but finally dismissed it. Too risky. What if Foakes had gone off to his club? Bound to have: In six years of chasing gossip Taffy had noticed that gentlemen headed back to their clubs like flies to a horse.

He needed to find that ex-butler. Taffy headed around the back of Sheffield House with renewed energy. One hour later he was possessed of a trembling, weeping kitchen maid who kept protesting how she shouldn't 'av, even as she hotly clutched ten shillings in her hand. And from the kitchen maid had come a name, Staple, *and* his favorite pub, The Raven.

Taffy knew The Raven well; it was a rather less than reputable place, on a dingy street called Ram Alley. Not the kind of place your better butlers would frequent, that was for certain, sure, Taffy thought. Why most of these butlers were stuffier than their masters; you never caught them taking a pint of th'best in the local, with a baker on one side and a wagoner on the other. No sir, butlers gathered in flash pubs and traded discreet gossip amongst themselves. He felt a glimmer of hope about Staple. This was likely to be a man influenced by a bit o'th'ready, in Taffy's opinion. Fired by the mistress herself, the kitchen maid had said, delight stiffening her tone. Fired for not behaving like a gent, it sounded like.

Better and better, Taffy thought. Butlers what as thought themselves one step under God himself were likely to get their noses out of joint when they were told they weren't acting like gentlemen. Taffy cast one more look at Sheffield House. Lord Foakes must be gone by now. Taffy set off for The Raven.

Chapter 18

Two weeks later Taffy achieved what he felt sure was the apex of his career. He unfurled his morning *Tatler* and looked at it lovingly. He had the whole gossip section to himself, just as they had promised him. He checked his own name first. There it was: Mr. Peter Taffata. He sighed in satisfaction. Last time they had spelled his last name with one *F* and it gave him indigestion for days. "Butler Tells All," he read. "Honeymoon Crisis; Wedding Trip Canceled, the Countess's Tears." Lovely. Really Lovely. And then his favorite headline: "All's Well That Ends Well: the Countess and the Twin." Taffy really liked the literary touch — using the title of a Shakespeare play. He thought it gave the article a touch of class that *The Tatler* didn't usually get. His thoughts wandered to a dream of writing for the *Times*.

Charlotte took one look at the paper that Molly silently brought to the breakfast table, and almost gagged. Her wedding night was down in black and white where everyone could see it. A wave of humiliation flooded over her. She couldn't even read the whole page; she pushed back her chair and ran upstairs, tears prickling her eyes.

At the top of the landing, Charlotte stopped. Where was she going? She turned into her room, picturing the eager faces of ladies reading the gossip column and shuddered. I have to leave immediately, she thought frantically. What if someone calls around to sympathize? Or to ask questions? Charlotte clenched her teeth together, hard, and ordered herself fiercely not to cry. She had to leave *now*, within the hour.

The only refuge was outside London. She would go to Alex's country estate. If only Alex were here! Alex would find their ex-butler Staple and put him in jail. Despite herself, tears filled Charlotte's eyes. She didn't want to arrive at Downes Manor by herself, a countess without a husband.

She fought to control her raging emotions until finally the look in her eyes turned from anguished mortification to determination. Taking a deep breath, Charlotte battered back the hysterical wish to throw herself onto her bed and cry. Instead she rang the bell, summoned Marie, and calmly told her that the entire household must be ready to leave in one hour.

She had last seen Pippa two hours ago, when Pippa toddled into her room for their early morning hot chocolate. They had snuggled together in the bed, Charlotte tickling Pippa's round tummy. Charlotte walked quickly down the hallway to the nursery, and told Katy their change in plans. Pippa was sitting on the ground, clanking spoons together in a business-like way. She looked up, sensing a new tone in Charlotte's face.

"Mamaaa!" Pippa said gaily.

"Of course, my lady," Katy replied. Katy never seemed to be ruffled by anything, not even when Pippa had upended a chamber pot on the kitchen cat.

Charlotte smiled at Pippa and then knelt down beside her as Pippa held out her arms. Somehow with Pippa's tight grip around her neck, the scandal didn't seem so insurmountable. Who cared what the *ton* thought of her? After this scandal, Alex would probably banish her to Scotland anyway . . . but she would have Pippa. And her baby. Charlotte's new, gently rounded tummy was evidence that Alex's child was nestled under her heart.

In her rush Charlotte completely forgot that Chloe van Stork had been asked for tea that afternoon. But her oversight was just as well. Because Mr. van Stork read Taffy's entire article, thoroughly, and then laid down his paper and announced that Chloe was not going to Sheffield House for tea, not now and not ever. His daughter's protests left him unmoved. He wasn't going to risk Chloe's engagement to Baron Holland — and that's just what might happen if she were associated with someone like the Countess of Sheffield and Downes.

"Not that I blame *her,* you understand," Mr.

van Stork explained ponderously. "Though why all the tears on her wedding night? I can only assume that her parents explained nothing to her!"

"Explained *what?*" Chloe cried in frustration.

Mr. van Stork looked at her in exasperation. "Lord Foakes is not wholly a man," he said and then closed his mouth firmly. Chloe knew that was all he was going to say on the matter. She turned to her mother, who was slowly digesting the article.

"It is the fault of her parents," Mrs. van Stork exclaimed. "All this fuss is clearly the result of the girl not being informed. I never understood their decision, never," she said. "Why marry your daughter when there will be no grandson?"

"The settlement," Mr. van Stork replied. "You send her a note, miss," he said to Chloe. "You'll have to cry off; you can use any excuse you want."

"Poor girl," Mrs. van Stork said with a sigh. "It's not the only excuse she'll get in the next few days."

Chloe was tremendously relieved when the footman returned with her note still in hand, saying that Sheffield House was closed up and only a skeleton staff left in residence. Perhaps Charlotte didn't even know about this terrible article. Chloe had finally managed to finagle the paper from her mama, who felt that she shouldn't read those kind of details. But Katryn van Stork had reminded herself that Chloe was a grown-up now, engaged to be married, and it might not be bad to read about wedding nights.

After all, if Baron Holland kept his word, Chloe herself would be married by next year. So Chloe read, horrified.

Yet to her mind the article didn't make much sense. Her beloved Charlotte had had an argument with her new husband; that was clear. Someone had thrown a jar of cream against the wall. The family had abruptly changed their plans, not gone to Italy, and Alex had made Charlotte ride in the servants' carriage.

"Why?" she asked her mama. But Mrs. van Stork didn't know.

"I can only suppose that the poor girl was not told," Mrs. van Stork said heavily, "that the earl cannot have any children."

"But they are so happy together!" Chloe objected. "You have not seen them together since they were married, Mama. She loves him."

"I assume the countess came to terms with her husband's disability — as is appropriate," her mother said. "But her behavior now is most improper. She should not be associating herself with the earl's brother. The author of this article says that she entertained Lord Foakes in her house. If she were a true lady, she would not welcome a man into the house when her husband is not in the country. And it doesn't matter if the man is her brother-in-law," Mrs. van Stork said, in answer to Chloe's unspoken challenge. "She is in a most delicate position, given her husband's incapability. Her behavior must be above reproach."

"It's not fair," Chloe protested. "I'm sure Charlotte has done nothing untoward with her husband's brother. She is not that sort of person!"

Mrs. van Stork looked at her. "You will have nothing to do with Lady Sheffield from now on, Chloe. Your reputation is most fragile. When you marry the baron, everyone will be watching to see whether your "city' birth comes out, and you show yourself to be less than a gentlewoman. Lady Sheffield may well be innocent, but she is ruined now. If you are not careful, the same injustice could happen to you."

Chloe nodded. But silently she decided that after she married Will she would not repudiate Charlotte. Her mother was wrong. Chloe had made plenty of friends among the aristocratic girls she went to school with, and Charlotte was different from most of them. You could read her heart in her eyes, Chloe thought, with an unfamiliar touch of poetry. The sight of Charlotte and Alex's first waltz together as a newly married couple had emblazoned itself on her mind. Charlotte loved Alex. She would never, never betray him, even if she did discover that they could have no children. Of that Chloe was sure.

Mercifully, Charlotte herself found so many aspects of her husband's country estate needing attention that she had little time to think about wedding nights, brothers-in-law, or ruined reputations. Alex's father had spent almost no time at his county seat, Downes Manor: The curtains were moth-eaten and in some rooms wallpaper was actually peeling from the walls. Charlotte hired an army of local women and had all sixty-five rooms cleaned from top to bottom. She spent hours with Percy Rowland, a representative of one of London's best fabric houses. True, Percy eyed the notorious countess curiously on his first visit to the estate, but after the first few minutes Charlotte's meticulous eye for color absorbed all his attention.

With Percy's help, she refinished three sitting rooms, the grand dining room, and the ladies' parlor. Items of furniture were hauled off to be re-covered, only to return a few weeks later swathed in dull gold or plummy crimson. Charlotte's stomach grew large and her back twinged protestingly every time she rose from a chair; she turned her attention to the nursery. The nursery became a charming fairy castle, its walls covered with fanciful murals — but Charlotte was starting to view the stairs up to that nursery with a distinct lack of enthusiasm. She had a water closet installed on the first floor of the house and began thinking about the moldering, dark master bedchamber. And by the time Alex's bedchamber had been transformed into an elegant, airy set of chambers, papered in a Florentine design, Charlotte was heartily tired of both Percy and pregnancy.

The weather grew warmer, and she and Pippa spent the afternoons wandering about the grounds of Downes Manor. Charlotte was slowly introducing new ideas about gardening to the ancient, clutch-mouthed gardener who ran the outdoor staff. After much coaxing he put up an airy lattice frame south of the house and began to train roses to grow over it. Charlotte hung the inside with light pink cotton and she, Pippa, and Katy would escape the afternoon sun by sitting in rosy shade. After a while she asked the footmen to bring them tea there, and one day the three of them even stayed through a brief shower. Pippa shrieked and shrieked with delight as water pummeled the light roof, making a sound like hundreds of grenadiers beating drums.

Charlotte was trying to paint a landscape for the first time: the gentle slope of the hill down from the summer house to the river at the base of the garden. But it wasn't terribly satisfying. She missed the struggle and frustration of drawing faces, trying to catch a kernel of emotion that was present one minute and lost the next.

The portrait of Mall was finished. In the end, Charlotte set her in a little courtyard, outside. Somehow what finally came through in the picture was not the young, strong, funny Mall that she wanted to catch, but the bone-weary, exhausted Mall at the end of a hard day. The Mall who had polished too much silver and carried too much hot water. Charlotte showed it to her tentatively, afraid that she would think it ugly. But Mall burst into tears. She stood in front of the picture, choked with sobs.

"But, Mall . . ." Charlotte wasn't sure what to say.

"It's *her*," Mall gulped. "It's me mum."

Charlotte looked back at the portrait. She looked through Mall's eyes — and there was a tired, rather fierce, angular Welshwoman staring back at her. Mall had stopped sobbing and was just staring at the picture.

"She died after me brother John was born. It was just too many: eight children, just too many. I couldn't do anything. She never even got to see John. . . ."

"Take it. Take it home to John."

"Oh my lady, I couldn't!"

"Yes, you can. I am giving it to you. And I am going to send you to Wales, Mall. Did I tell you that I own a house there? Well, I'd like you to go with Keating and see what shape my house is in," Charlotte said steadily. There was an acid tightness at the back of her throat. She knew what it was: just a little fear. Women died in childbirth all the time. That didn't mean she would.

"Me?" Mall stared at her with wide eyes.

"Yes."

"But I'm just the third housemaid, my lady."

"Well, now you're going to learn to be a house-keeper, Mall. And I want you to stop off at your father's house and spend a good week with your family before you begin your new position."

Charlotte dispatched Keating and Mall to Wales with directions to open the house and to make extensive lists of those things needed to refurbish it. The roses crept over the top of the lattice house. Pippa learned to say whole sentences, made up of three words. She developed a passionate love for the kitchen cat, who rapidly became adroit at recognizing her small footsteps and disappearing.

Still there was no news from Alex. Charlotte allowed herself to think about him only in small snatches — first thing in the morning or last thing at night. She shied away from imagining his rage when he saw *The Tatler* and found out that the horrible Staple had not only detailed the ugly shambles that was their wedding night, but had invented quite a few things himself, such as the fact that one of the maids supposedly heard her crying out "Alack! I shall have no children!" Charlotte still shuddered every time she thought of *The Tatler.*

When Sophie arrived for a visit, she was impudently cheerful about the scandal. She didn't tell Charlotte that her mother had forbidden her to visit and that Sophie had wrangled with her for a full week until Eloise finally gave her permission. In fact, the marchioness had relented only when Sophie threatened to create a scandal the next season that would cast Charlotte's little problems into the shade. Even so Sophie had had to be fairly graphic about exactly what she would be caught doing before her mother finally quailed and allowed her to visit Charlotte.

"Alack!" Sophie said blithely, when she and Charlotte were sitting in the newly furbished

Green Room after dinner. "Alack! I shall have no children! I fear me that Braddon has given up the chase."

Charlotte glared at her. "Don't be funning about this, Sophie! Alex is going to be furious when he returns. *If* he returns."

Sophie rolled her eyes. "The most besotted man in all of London — and you're afraid he won't return? What do you think he's doing?"

"I don't know," Charlotte admitted. "He said he would be gone for two months, and he has been gone well over twice that. And he has only sent one letter. Here I am, eight months pregnant" — she gestured faintly toward her growing stomach — "and he doesn't even know we're having a child yet. Oh, Sophie," Charlotte said wrenchingly, "do you think he went into France and didn't come back out?"

"No. Because in that case the Foreign Office would inform you. Have you tried writing to the rascal who sent him off on this excursion?" Sophie shared Charlotte's sense that the whole idea of picking up a "package" in Paris was ridiculous.

"Yes. Lord Breksby sent a note about two weeks ago saying that I should not worry, and the project was taking longer than planned. His tone was not — entirely nice. The worst of it was that I had the distinct impression that he felt the mess here was so awful that Alex was *making* the project take longer than it need have."

"I doubt that," Sophie replied. "For one thing,

how would Alex know about it?"

"I don't know, I don't know. But I keep thinking that even though they didn't tell me exactly where he is, probably those men in the Foreign Office know his location. And what would stop one of them from sending over a copy of that terrible *Tatler* article?"

There was a moment of silence. "That would be difficult," Sophie agreed. "Do you know where Alex's brother has gone?"

"No. He said he was going hunting in Leicestershire," Charlotte said. "But what good could he do even if he were here? I don't want to *see* him again! *The Tatler* made it sound as if he may have stayed in our house all night — when he was only there an hour at the most! Oh, dear . . ." Tears fell down her face.

Charlotte had spent so much time keeping up a serene front that it was a great relief to see Sophie. For example, she was acutely aware that none of the neighbors had called as would be normal. They must think that I am a scarlet woman, she thought miserably. She instinctively placed her hands on her growing tummy.

Sophie interposed. "You're probably right; Lord Foakes would just make things worse." She decided to change the subject. "I must say, you don't show the baby very much," Sophie said. "Are you sure that you are eight months along?"

"I saw a doctor, and he seemed to think so. My mother said her pregnancies didn't show much until the very end."

Thank God, Sophie thought, *Maman* has no idea about Charlotte's pregnancy. That would be the straw that broke the camel's back. Sophie could just imagine the scandal that Charlotte's rounded belly was going to provoke.

"Perhaps you should write a letter informing Alex of the pregnancy, and send it to him care of the Foreign Office," Sophie suggested.

"I thought of that," Charlotte answered. "But what if Alex isn't planning to come back at all? He told me once that he was on the point of leaving his first wife for good when she proposed the annulment. He was going to join the army, or something of that nature. I'm afraid that someone told him how shocking I am, and he has simply decided to stay in Italy."

She was sobbing hard now, her face buried in a sofa cushion. Sophie moved over and stroked Charlotte's shaking shoulders. She wasn't sure what to say.

"I'm afraid that he doesn't love me enough, Sophie. He doesn't trust me, and now he never will," Charlotte said chokingly. "And I love him so much! I don't think that I can live without him."

"Hush," Sophie said, "hush. You don't have to live without him. I think you are exaggerating the importance of Alex's absence. I expect he is sitting in an Italian *taverna* at this very moment, having the time of his life, and hasn't heard a thing about the *Tatler* article."

"But how can he have such a good time?"

Charlotte sobbed. "I miss him so much; I dream about him every night. It *hurts!*"

"Men are different," Sophie retorted. "You can see that easily enough, Charlotte. Women may love one man, but men simply love the person they see before them. That old chestnut, absence makes the heart grow fonder, doesn't work for men. They are like children with toys: They move onto the next shiny object if you take the old one out of their hands."

Charlotte pulled herself upright. "You're so bitter, Sophie," she said. "Why are you so bitter?"

"My father," Sophie replied succinctly.

"Oh," Charlotte said unhappily. Everything in her resisted the idea that Alex, her dear beloved Alex, was like Sophie's father, the Marquis of Brandenburg. But if Alex wasn't akin to the marquis, where was he? Four, no five, months had passed, and while she counted each day off as if it were a year, Alex was apparently frolicking about Italy, perhaps not even thinking about the wife he had left at home.

When Charlotte tried to imagine how he was feeling about her, all she could think of was his black rage in Bournemouth, when he thought she'd betrayed him. She pushed the terrifying image from her mind. He promised, he *promised* to trust her. She simply had to hope that he would keep that promise. But her mind circled endlessly, moving unhappily from the facts of Alex's first marriage, which made him so apt not to trust her, to their blissfully happy time to-gether. Surely that would count with him, more than any silly article published in his absence!

"He said he loved being married to me," she told Sophie, her voice shaky. "And he said he wanted to have children. I'm sure he'll be happy when . . ." Her voice trailed off.

In Sophie's warm hug she read disbelief; in the recesses of her heart the same disbelief hovered. If Alex loved her, truly loved her, he would have found a way to come home by now. She drew a deep breath and hoisted herself from the couch.

"Prospective mothers need to sleep." Sophie held out her hand, her blue eyes loving, coaxing, sympathetic.

Charlotte smiled, a little, peaked smile. "Do you think . . . could you stay with me for another month, Sophie?"

"Well," Sophie said teasingly, tucking her arm through Charlotte's elbow and drawing her to-ward the door, "it will be a great sacrifice, of course. Braddon undoubtedly plans to propose at least three or four times during the coming month, and woe is me if he turns his attentions to another. My mother, for one would be furious —" she chattered on. But when they were climbing the stairs, Sophie said casually that it would be a sound test of Braddon's affections if he didn't see her for at least two months. And Charlotte's heart lifted, warmth creeping into the empty space left by her tears.

Chapter 19

In fact, Alex knew nothing of the *Tatler* article. At the very moment when Charlotte was sobbing over his absence, he was involved in an animated argument over the relative merits of a certain year of *vin santo*, a strong Italian wine. Yet even as he agreed with the owner of a little bar that this particular *vin santo* was very strong but not too strong, and disagreed with him over the merits of adding a touch of pepper, he was thinking of Charlotte. When Signor Tonarelli finally stopped talking and bustled into the room behind his counter to fetch the famous "package," Alex found himself thinking not about the extended chase which this package had led him over the last five months, but of his wife's lovely, slim legs. He fancied they were particularly beautiful above the knees. When she lay on her side, he would run his hand slowly, slowly up the perfect slow curve, over the little bump of her hip, his thumb falling inside and teasing the delicate hollow that lay just over her hip bone.

Alex stared absently at the wooden shelves that lined the back of Bar Luce, the only restaurant, so to speak, for miles. He had found his way up to this little Italian village only after months of enquiry. Slowly he had traveled through the countryside and finally up the mountain, tracing the path of a weary old Frenchman. Where the man had been going before he died in this little village, Alex had no idea. Signor Tonarelli claimed to have never seen him before.

Mario Tonarelli came back out of his inner room, clutching a small, grungy bundle.

"Grazie! Grazie mille," Alex said enthusiastically.

"Prego," Signor Tonarelli responded. He was delighted to have been of service to this rich and powerful stranger. The man was from Rome, Signor Tonarelli had decided, given his accent. But he was much friendlier than the average Roman — a nasty, suspicious lot, as all mountain folk knew. What on earth the Roman was doing in his small *osteria*, picking up a bundle of old clothes, he didn't know. Tonarelli knew they were just old clothes, because of course he and his wife had taken a careful look when the old Frenchman died, practically on their front door. He said — the Frenchman did — that someone would be along to pick up the package, and he was right. But neither Mario nor his wife, Luce, could figure out why on earth anyone would ever want to recover the old Frenchman's clothes.

They buried him in the cemetery at the back of the little village, but Mario hung on to the package. Sure enough, along came a Roman only six months later, asking for it.

Mario's eyes lit up. The Roman seemed to be counting out a little pile of gold lire. Who cares why he wanted those musty old rags?

"Grazie!" Tonarelli said, with true gratitude in his voice. He stood for a second in the door of his *osteria,* watching the Roman return to his carriage. He was a good-looking man, the Roman. Tall, with an arrogant, powerful walk that Mario much admired. He himself had grown rotund from eating too much of Luce's mushroom pasta; but even so, he had never walked as this man naturally did. Like a wolf, Mario thought. His hand closed firmly on the pile of coins.

"Luce," he bellowed, as Alex's carriage began its long, winding way down the mountain. Mario's sudden shout frightened the chickens who were pecking about the piazza, the square in the center of the village that was ringed by three stone houses, his bar, and the church.

"Is he gone?" His wife appeared breathlessly around the side of a building. She had been doing their washing in the stone bath behind the fountain, and her dress was splashed with water.

In answer Mario simply held out his hand, showing the coins.

"Grazie a Dio!" Luce said simply. Mario smiled and walked over to her, a little of the stranger's arrogant lope in his stride. "I shall take some flowers to the grave today, to the old man," Luce added.

Mario nodded. He deserved flowers, that Frenchman. He had made them rich by dying on their doorstep. Now they could not only buy a cow, but perhaps even spend some money to buy another mule. Their mule, Lia, was sixteen years old, and she staggered as she climbed up the mountain every couple of weeks, dragging a cart full of things to sell in the bar.

In the carriage Alex looked broodingly at the package he held. He hated the cursed thing by now. He had arrived in Paris only to find the house that he was looking for had been torched by the police a few weeks before. Rather than show any undue interest, he had been forced to leave Paris immediately and hire a dingy French spy to go back and find out what had happened and where the inhabitants had gone. That took a blasted two months, over two months.

And all Alex himself could do was go through the motions of being an Italian merchant interested in exporting French wines. He was careful, however, not to enter France again until the day he casually crossed the border, drove his horse straight to a certain milliner's house, and left three minutes later with a very frightened French girl, Lucien's sister Brigitte. The recovery of Brigitte was as smooth as cream. They weren't even stopped at the border into Italy, just waved through by a couple of bored soldiers.

Hearing the story of how the mob came to Lucien's house, how his wife and son died, and how Brigitte escaped capture only by hiding in a pile of laundry made Alex itch to go home. Of course, Pippa and Charlotte were happy and healthy in England. Yet something about Lucien's still white face and the way he clutched his little sister to his chest made Alex feel precariously mortal.

He found himself thinking about Charlotte all the time: not even imagining sex as much as Charlotte's laughing face in the morning when Pippa clambered into the bed and spilled chocolate on the sheets. The way she would bite her lower lip as she concentrated on painting. The fierce manner with which she would counter his arguments when they disagreed over decisions made in Parliament. The consummate pride he felt as he gave a speech in the House of Lords that was not exactly as it would have been had he not discussed it with his wife the night before. Discussed it, ha! Battled over it was more accurate.

I love her, Alex realized one morning. Blast it, I'm *in* love with her. After that it was as if the icy wall that he had built around his heart during the marriage to Maria simply tumbled to the ground. Alex feverishly longed to hold Charlotte in his arms, to kiss her all over until she was crying out with desire and need, and then whisper "I love you" in her ear. She'll cry, he thought, picturing her huge dark eyes filling with loving tears. She would see that he forgave her for everything before their marriage, that he really trusted her. He even forgave her for not being a virgin when they married. He was prepared to forget that she had slept with his brother before him. Alex was so impatient to board the boat back to England that he could hardly sit still.

He toured vineyards in Italy and established what would later prove to be a lucrative chain of vineyards prepared to import wine into England from Italy, rather than into Italy from France, as he pretended. The activity served his cover, so to speak. But even as he conducted the leisurely conversations that precede every Italian business transaction, Alex was aflame, burning to return to England.

Yet as he lay in his stiflingly hot bedroom, arms crossed behind his head, Alex sometimes felt disgusted at his own eagerness. Hadn't he already played the fool, thinking that a woman would be honest? He felt a deep, brutal shame, remembering the shambles of his marriage to Maria, her promises to be faithful to his bed. Shades of his old cynical self haunted the edges of his soul, cautioning that even Charlotte was no virgin when he married her. Maybe she was just another Maria, out for what sex and money she could take. The gaping, raw anger he felt when he walked in on Maria with the footman still echoed at the back of his mind.

But for the most part Alex nourished his dream of a grateful, loving Charlotte. Charlotte was no Maria. She loved him. Alex thought about how her body fitted to his like a glove during the night. If he drew away she would sigh and move restlessly until she snuggled up against him. How had she slept without him? It had been almost five months; she must be used to sleeping alone, he thought rather sadly.

All those weeks of waiting had culminated in a bundle of old clothing. Alex stared, stupefied, at the bundle he had just opened. His carriage jolted uncertainly over the stony track down the mountain, taking him to the sea. One part of his mind rejoiced at being finally on his way. But another part felt a mounting rage.

How in the hell could that unmitigated fool Breksby send him all the way to Italy to serve as a secondhand clothing merchant? He picked up the pieces of clothing distastefully. They were shabby, black, the clothes of a poor Parisian merchant. There was a pair of old trousers, ripped in the upper thigh, a coarse shirt that was probably white at some point in its distant past, a heavy, unwieldy jacket. Distastefully he felt through the pockets of the jacket and trousers, but there were no letters, no money, nothing. But then Alex's eyes narrowed. The fat innkeeper had said that the old Frenchman had told him someone would pick up the clothing. There *must* be something valuable here.

In a few minutes, he had it. Or them, rather. They had been folded many times, worked into tiny squares and placed inside the lower seam of the jacket. They were letters, and Alex had no idea how in the world they ended up sewn into a shabby black jacket. Because they were love letters, in French, and by the end of the second sheet Alex had a very good idea who had written them. They were letters from Napoleon to Josephine. And they were written *before* the couple were married. As a matter of fact, they were clearly written while Josephine was still married to General de Beauharnais.

Alex whistled a bit, reading the third letter. Then he grinned. He had heard that Josephine was beautiful . . . but beauty didn't seem to be her only desirable attribute. By the time he had finished reading the letters, Alex's face was somber. He could make a good guess about what the English government intended to do with these letters. The French still had many aristocrats locked up in their dungeons, and he held the ransom for at least a few of those unfortunate people in his hands. Alex folded the letters carefully, putting them in his breast pocket.

Suddenly the five months he had been stuck in Italy seemed inconsequential. He had a beloved, beautiful wife waiting for him in England. Lucien's wife and his young son would never return. The letters had appeared too late to save them. But it might ransom a different family out of Bonaparte's prisons. Alex shouted up at his driver with new purpose. These letters needed to be back in England, even more than he himself needed to be there.

Five months after he had left England, Alex stood on board ship, smiling into a cold, dank wind blowing off the English coastline. There is nothing as bone-shakingly chilly as a rainy coastal breeze, and yet there is nothing that smells so heartwarmingly English either, he thought. Slowly the rain-stained cluster of pubs that marked the London wharf came into view as their boat meandered up the Thames. Lighted windows winked and disappeared through the sheets of rain that were dashing to the shore. Lucien appeared at his side, tightly bundled against the storm.

Alex cast an affectionate arm around his shoulders. "We made it!" he shouted against the strained creaking of the small ship as it jarringly came into port. Instantly stevedores began trotting up and down the gangplank, carrying boxes of wine out to the dock.

"Gently!" Alex shouted, his voice booming over the noise of slanting, falling rain. One of the seamen looked up, startled, but the stevedores paid no attention, nimbly finding their way over the piles of cargo, winches, ropes, and garbage that festooned the dock.

"They pay you no mind," Lucien chuckled. "They know their work."

"I'm not worried they will drop a box," Alex said. "But if they shake the port, it will have to settle for two years . . . and I could use a drink at this moment."

Lucien turned and gathered his sister, Brigitte, into his arms. "Didn't I tell you to wait for me in the cabin?" he scolded. Alex could just see glowing, bright strands of hair peeking out from beneath Brigitte's hood. He had become very fond of Lucien's courageous little sister over the past few weeks on board the ship. She was finally losing her white strained look and beginning to take on the normal air of a mischievous thirteen-year-old.

"I wanted to see England," she said in her marked French accent. "It is my new home, no?"

Alex put his arm lightly around her shoulder and they stood together, the three of them, watching the last of the cargo being taken off the ship. Alex knew to the bottom of his soul that he would never be more proud of anything he did in his life than he was of his trip into France. The fact that this effervescent, lovely girl was alive was due in part to him; from what Brigitte had told them, the milliner was being asked more and more questions about his supposed "niece." It was only a matter of time before Brigitte would have been brought into the police for questioning.

Alex gestured toward the shore. "Your new home lies before you. Shall we disembark?"

"Daphne will be waiting for us," Lucien said to his sister.

"Do you think Daphne stayed in London after the season ended?" Alex asked curiously. "Won't she have retired to the country?"

"Oh, no," Lucien said with calm, absolute certainty. "She would never leave London under the circumstances."

Alex's heart gave an odd lurch. He had never even considered the possibility that Charlotte

474

might still be in Sheffield House. But what if she was? What if she too waited for him, not wanting to miss a moment of time with him?

On shore, he saw Lucien and Brigitte off into a carriage and then hailed a hansom cab himself. Even as they rounded the corner into Albemarle Square he saw that the house was closed, the shutters down, and the knocker off the door. Charlotte must have taken Pippa to the country. Well, what else could she do? She had no idea when he would return. He had only been able to send his wife one cryptic note during the five months. Still, he supposed Lord Breksby had been in touch with her. First thing tomorrow he would deliver the Napoleon letters to Breksby and by the day after that he could be crushing his wife into the bed. Alex smiled to himself wickedly.

If there seemed to be an air of strain among the few servants left in Sheffield House, Alex didn't notice. Keating, his man, had accompanied Charlotte out to the country, and it would never occur to Alex to give a thought to the odd way the two remaining footmen eyed him. He didn't bother going to his club. Instead he had a long bath and fell into bed, grateful to be on solid ground again. There was really no point in going to White's, Alex thought drowsily. All his friends would be out of London. Parliament was closed; the season was finished; even the law courts weren't in session. Only civil servants like Breksby would remain in London's sooty streets.

But in fact Lord Breksby had also gone to the country. "He has retired to his estate," Alex was informed. And so it was that one of Lord Breksby's underlings, one Ewart Hastings, had the pleasure of informing the Earl of Sheffield and Downes what a shocking scandal his wife had created in the last five months. The newest tale was that she was pregnant, presumably with his own brother's child. Alex listened to Hastings's tale with an absolutely unmoving face. Inside Hastings shivered and thought he'd never seen a more devilish look, but he didn't stop talking. The allure of telling such an arrogant member of the Quality that his wife had been acting like a tramp was just too strong. As a junior in civil service, Hastings had put up with endless condescension; he relished every minute of this set-down. So he told it all: Charlotte's faint when she first encountered Patrick; the *Tatler* article; the fact that Charlotte entertained Patrick in Sheffield House; her subsequent pregnancy.

"About four or five months along," Hastings said cheerfully, adding, "I'm very sad to say, your lordship." It had suddenly occurred to him that he himself was in a precarious position. A nerve was pulsing in Alex's jaw, and his eyes were glowing with rage. Hastings's mouth shut, and then opened only to say, weakly, "I'm sure there's no basis in fact for this report, my lord." Alex just looked at him. Then he reached across Hastings's oak desk and ruthlessly grabbed his carefully arranged cravat, jerking him to within

476

an inch of Alex's furious glare.

"I should hate to hear that you ever repeated any of this foul, slanderous information," Alex told him through clenched teeth.

"I will not," Hastings managed to squeak. He could feel sweat pouring down his back. Alex disdainfully pushed him back. Hastings took in a shaky breath. Alex turned on his heel and left without a word.

The minute the door shut, Hastings sat down plumply in his chair. He was trembling like an autumn leaf in a high breeze, he realized. Insane — that's what Alexander Foakes was. A lunatic. He, Hastings, had only told Foakes what any man on the street could tell him. Just what did Foakes intend to do? Threaten half the population of London?

Hastings carefully cracked the knuckles on his left hand. It calmed him, and his heart began to slow down. Really, what a madman, he thought with a touch of conceit. He started on the knuckles of his right hand. Finally a little smirk touched Hastings's mouth. His high and mighty lordship could abuse as many civil servants as he wished; it wouldn't change the fact that his new wife was a trollop who was sleeping with his own brother. Hastings's smile widened. He leaned back in his chair and began to hum a little tune.

Hastings disliked his own wife — a penny-pinching, quarrelsome woman, he thought — but he could say without the slightest hesitation that she would never sleep with anyone but him.

Indeed, she hated the whole performance, as she'd often told him. But if a man's wife is not his own, well, that man is poorer than the poorest chimney sweep. That's a fact, Hastings thought. And if that fact made the high and mighty earl a bit touchy, Hastings could understand and sympathize.

Alex stalked out to his carriage, absolutely calm. He gave the coachman the address for his solicitor, and sat back in the carriage. Thankfully, he felt nothing. A reasonable voice in his head reminded him that such a scandal was only to be expected, and he agreed. Still, he felt as if someone had poured cold steel through his veins. He didn't even feel bitter, he thought, a little surprised. He must have known, all along. If anything . . . he felt a little pain that Patrick would do this to him. Patrick was his other arm, his boyhood companion, his twin. How could he betray him? Yet even this, the grossest of the betrayals facing Alex, didn't really bother him.

On the other hand, Mr. Jennings of Jennings and Condell found himself bothered indeed. Normally nothing flustered Jennings. No matter what disaster — forged wills, foolish lawsuits, illegal duels — was recounted to him, Jennings maintained a tranquil front. In fact, to his mind the law had the remedy for anything. But surveying the huge, dispassionate earl standing before him, Jennings felt an unfamiliar tremor of panic. If only his father were still alive; his father was so good at handling irate peers and irascible earls. He could talk them out of their bluster and fury in about twenty minutes, blending his soothing voice with large draughts of the very best port. But every instinct cautioned against offering this particular earl a glass of port. He looked murderous, in Jennings's opinion.

Jennings bowed very low. "My lord," he said calmly, "won't you enter my study?" Once Foakes was settled in his comfortable, book-lined study, Jennings took out a folder. Inside was a copy of the *Tatler* article in question. Jennings sat down in a large leather armchair opposite Alex. He crossed his legs and made a tent out of his delicate fingers.

"I called on your lady the morning after this article appeared," he said, watching Alex scowl as he read the details of his wedding night in *The Tatler*. "However, I just missed her. Her entourage left for the country that morning. I cannot say I disagree with her decision," he said in his thin, rather acid fashion. "It would have been remarkably unpleasant had she remained in London. The article, naturally, caused a good deal of excitement."

He paused. Alex sat back, absolutely composed, tapping his fingers on the arm of his chair. Since he said nothing, Jennings continued.

"I took the liberty of hiring an investigator after the article appeared." He drew another sheet of paper out of the folder on his knee. "I have found that instigating a suit for slander can be remarkably efficacious in quelling a scandal brew of this type. However, detailed information is needed before such a course can be contemplated." This was Jennings's way of saying that there wasn't any point in suing for slander if the *Tatler*'s charges were factually true. "This sheet specifies the activities of your brother, Lord Foakes, during the week in which he was in London. You will see that he made no effort to contact your wife until he arrived at your house and was informed of your marriage. To my mind, this casts a good deal of doubt on the supposition that the romance was of long standing."

He paused again. Alex didn't say a word, but his teeth involuntarily ground together. Of long standing! Damn right it was, given that it included the taking of Charlotte's virginity.

Jennings continued. "Your brother accompanied the countess back to Sheffield House from Mrs. Felvitson's musicale, but he left immediately. He then returned two days later at four o'clock, by appointment. He exited the house at approximately five thirty, by the back entrance. He left by the servants' entrance because he was aware of the presence of a reporter in the front. Lord Foakes spent the rest of the evening in White's, where he lost over two hundred pounds at play. The next morning he rose early and left for Leicestershire in company with Braddon Chatwin, the Earl of Slaslow." Alex looked up. Barring himself, Braddon had been Patrick's closest friend in school.

"Hunting?"

"That would be my surmise. After that point, of course," Jennings added primly, "I saw no reason to continue investigating the activities of your wife and Lord Foakes. Consequently I can cast no light on the reports of her pregnancy." He regarded his tented fingers. "Of course, if the child is born in the near future, there would be no reason for anxiety." Jennings took a deep breath. What he had to say next was not pleasant. "There is nothing that can be done, legally speaking, about the rumors circulating about your wife. Her future reputation hinges on two things: the birth date of this child, and your attitude."

Jennings looked up, meeting Alex's steady eyes. "I am sure I need not tell you how quickly your actions will prove or disprove these rumors in the eyes of the world, my lord."

Alex nodded. Then he tapped the newspaper on his knee. "And this?"

Mr. Jennings slipped another piece of paper out of his folder. "*The Tatler* was served papers for slander six days after the report was published. They were, of course, expecting this response on our part and had thought to shield their report by labeling your wife 'the Countess' and your brother 'the Twin.' However, my brief noted that there is in fact only one countess, your wife, who stands in any familial relation to a male twin and therefore they infringed upon the law, which is quite strict with regard to personal slander. After consulting with his solicitors, who naturally concurred with my brief, Mr. Hopkins, the editor, approached me with a quite handsome proposition. They published a full retraction." Jennings handed Alex another sheet of paper.

"However, this retraction has no real effect, given that the season was over," Jennings pointed out. "I put this to Mr. Hopkins with some force. I also ventured to name a sum in pounds that I was confident the court would assign to us, should this lawsuit continue. Mr. Hopkins therefore has agreed to publish a further article about 'the Countess' and 'the Twin,' in the spring when the season begins again. This article will carry no reference to the lawsuit, and will appear to be simply a further piece of news. However, it will retract all the innuendo that was suggested by the earlier article. The article will be read and approved by yourself and your ladyship before publication. I judged, under these circumstances, that it was better to overlook the report of your wedding night." Jennings tactfully refrained from mentioning that according to his investigations the article was dead right about that night.

"All this will depend," Jennings said heavily, "on the birth date of your child, unfortunately." Silence fell in the room. Jennings stared assiduously at the glowing colors of the Oriental rug that adorned his study.

Finally Alex spoke. "Prepare a bill for divorce," he said abruptly. Jennings nodded. Delicacy forbade him from mentioning that the already prepared document reposed in the same folder poised on his knee. Alex rose. "I will contact you about whether you should proceed with the divorce."

Jennings bowed, and Alex left the study. He needed to think about all this in peace and quiet. Clearly nothing had happened in London between his wife and Patrick. The fact that Charlotte had fainted when she saw Patrick brought the first twinge of pain that he had felt so far. Of course, she must love him. Women never forgot the man who took their virginity. A deep ache moved through Alex's heart and was ruthlessly banished.

The babe was obviously the key. If it was his child, Charlotte would now be unwieldy, large, on the verge of giving birth. But it was unlikely, he thought, remembering that he had left in the midst of Charlotte's monthly bleeding. She wasn't pregnant when he left, so whose baby did she carry at this moment? He was perfectly conscious that Jennings had talked of "the child"; there was no doubt that Charlotte was carrying someone's baby, then. It must be Patrick's.

Abruptly Alex realized that he had mindlessly walked down the street, away from Jennings's office in the Inns of Court. He cast a look over his shoulder. His groom was following him down the street, walking the horses. The horses were fresh; he might as well head out to Downes Manor. He had horses housed on the Oxford

Road, and he could ride alongside the carriage. The last thing he needed after weeks in a ship was to be confined in a small, swaying carriage for two days. Alex raised his hand, summoning the groom and carriage, and barked a few commands. One of the footmen hopped nimbly off the back and disappeared down the street. He would gather Alex's clothes and send them after him to Downes Manor.

I forgot to mention the presents, Alex thought, staring absently after the footman. He had lovingly chosen presents for Charlotte and Pippa over the last months, picking up a piece of glowing blue silk here, a carved wooden toy there. Somehow they had mounted into stacks, evidence of the irresistible presence of his wife and child in his mind over the last five months. Just as well, Alex thought matter-of-factly. He had made enough of an ass of himself, even allowing himself to *think* about Charlotte while he was away. She clearly didn't give him another thought after he boarded the ship. He felt a twinge of regret at the idea of Pippa's presents. Still, he could use them to make her feel better when they returned to London without Charlotte.

Alex stared coldly ahead as he sat in the carriage, easily adapting to the swaying movement as the horses trotted onto the high road leading to Oxfordshire. As the imperturbable Jennings had said, it all depended on the birth date of the child. He would know as soon as he entered the room where Charlotte was. If Charlotte was not very large with child, he saw no reason to discuss any of this unpleasant business with her. Why bandy words? Alex's heart hardened into cold steel at the image of his wife pleading with him, perhaps even promising — again — that she was trustworthy.

The silence that settled in the carriage was ominously empty, devoid of kindness or warmth. Alex had an acid taste in his mouth and a cruel pain flickering behind his eyes; he felt as if some important part of himself had been discarded somewhere on the road, back in the dusty column that rose behind the galloping hooves of his horses. He kept thinking: *Stop!* Put it back the way it was . . . someone, please, put it back the way it was before I went to the Foreign Office, before I went to Italy, before I left Charlotte's side.

But no one offered to do that small service for him, and so Alexander Foakes drew further and further ahead of that other Alex, back in the dust: the pre-Hastings Alex, the pre-Italy Alex, the Alex who loved and was loved.

Chapter 20

By the time that Alex's horse was galloping down the straight row of oak trees that lined the road to Downes Manor, he had rebuilt, step by step, the icy wall which memories of Charlotte had toppled in Italy. The last two nights he lay awake, great slashing blows of humiliation shaking his body. Finally he had got to the point where his lips twisted in a wry smile. By God, Patrick always said I had terrible taste in women, he thought.

The whole scandal seemed horribly appropriate, looking back over his thirty-plus years. He had fallen in love for the first time to a prostitute-in-training, in a garden. And then he had tried to recreate that experience in marriage. Finding a trollop among gently bred women didn't seem to be so difficult. The problem was that his garden girl had gone on to her chosen career, and the woman he married. . . .

Well, Charlotte's record spoke for itself. Alex's chest felt very tight. He was determined not to lose his temper, as he had in the inn at Bournemouth. What was the point of shouting at someone who was simply acting in the only way she knew?

Alex caught himself up. He had to keep Maria and Charlotte separate in his mind. After all, Patrick was the first man Charlotte loved. She gave him her virginity. That was not the same as Maria, sleeping with any man with two legs and equipment to match. If he walked into the room and found Charlotte on the point of giving birth he would know it was his child. If she wasn't, well then the child was his brother's and, a bitter voice in his head remarked, that baby will probably be your heir. He was done with wives and women, after this. He was giving up the idiotic dream of finding someone as wild and tender as the garden girl. He'd find a woman when he needed one, and leave the titles and land to Patrick's heir — even if that heir was Charlotte's child.

Alex had no idea just how much he was counting on finding a large, bulky Charlotte waiting for him at Downes Manor until he was directed to the new summer house, behind the manor. And there she was. He stood for quite a while, an eternity, it seemed. Charlotte was sitting on the floor of the breezy terrazzo.

Pippa was sitting across from her, and they were playing with dolls. Charlotte's doll was talking, and now Pippa's doll seemed to be clumsily dancing on the floor . . . but it was Charlotte's waist that commanded Alex's eyes. She was clearly pregnant. Her beautiful figure had bloomed around the waist; her breasts, softly caught up in a white muslin day dress, looked lush and generous, blooming from her low-cut gown. And she was glowing, lovely, more beautiful than he remembered. Soft curls fell down her neck, and from his angle long, inky eyelashes brushed her cheeks. She was so lovely that he felt a twist of agony around his heart, as if someone had twisted a key in his chest.

Just then Pippa's nanny looked up and saw her master standing just outside the summer house. One glimpse of the earl's hard, hard eyes and Katy nearly panicked, something she never did. Instead she acted instinctively to protect Pippa from whatever unpleasantness was about to happen.

"My lady, Pippa and I will be in the schoolroom." Katy stooped and picked up Pippa, totally ignoring the angry wail that accompanied her rapid decision. Pippa hated to be abruptly swooped into the air. Her small doll fell from her hand and her wail turned to a howl.

Charlotte pushed dark curls out of her eyes and looked up, absolutely confused. Katy was already walking briskly toward the main house, Pippa's voice growing smaller and smaller as Katy walked. Then Charlotte knew. She turned her head to the left, and there he was, staring down at her.

Her heart leaped with joy to see him. "Alex!" she cried, her face lighting up. He didn't move. Charlotte smoothly rose from her place on the ground, adjusting her white high-waisted gown.

The French styles suited pregnant women terribly well; there was nothing like a waistline under the breasts to diminish one's girth, Charlotte thought self-consciously. Alex was staring at her middle.

Charlotte's eyes danced. Well, of course, he didn't know she was pregnant. "We're having a baby," she said happily. He still didn't move or speak. Charlotte was beginning to feel uncomfortable. She took a few tentative steps toward him and stopped.

"*We're* having a baby?" Alex finally said, his voice rasping. His eyebrow flew up, in the way she loved, except that now he was looking at her with utter disdain. "Shouldn't you say, *I* am having a baby?" His voice settled to its normal deep tones; he was practically purring. "Or let's see, I think I like this phrasing: The Countess and the Twin are having a baby. Congratulations, everyone!"

Charlotte's heart dropped to the bottom of her stomach. She literally couldn't find any words. She had pictured Alex's rage over their butler's depiction of the wedding night. Of course, she knew that he would be furious about the scurrilous innuendo about his brother and her. But she had never thought he would actually believe the article. Because he promised to trust her . . . She didn't say a word, just stared at him, eyes wide.

As for Alex — all his planned calmness and control flew out the window. His wife was so beautiful, gazing at him in bewilderment, as if she had no idea what he was talking about! And yet she was so clearly only a few months pregnant. Black, filthy rage slashed his heart.

"You're a whore," he said, almost casually. "It seems I have a remarkable affinity for women of that stamp." His laugh was like nothing Charlotte had heard before. "Yes, indeed," Alex said savagely. "You might say I specialize in whores. But this — this was something special! Why are you looking so surprised? Did you think I would forget that you had your flux when I left?"

He strolled toward her, his large, lithe body as controlled as a pacing tiger. Charlotte opened her mouth, but he took her chin in his strong hand, holding it brutally tight. "I don't think so, darling. I don't want to hear any pleas, this time. The calendar is so deadly factual, isn't it? I don't think even you can talk your way out of this one.

"I have figured out the rest of our married life. If Patrick wants you, he can have you. I've instructed my solicitor to make up a bill of divorce. If Patrick doesn't — and I don't see why he should, given that he's already had the goods — you can go and live in Scotland. If the baby is born in the near future, he or she will come with me to London. I'm not having my children, *either* of my children if there are two, brought up by a tart."

Charlotte instinctively wrapped her arms around her stomach. He was mad, absolutely mad. She pulled her chin away from his hand. Alex looked at her, a muscle jumping in his jaw.

His eyes were as black as pitch. Charlotte shook her head a little, to clear it. Could this really be happening? Was this the man she had waited for and dreamed so passionately about?

"You promised," she half whispered. "You promised." Her face was drawn with pain, but she stood firm, pulling her slender shoulders back to look at his face with dignity. She would not allow herself to curl into a hedgehog and scream aloud.

Alex's lip curled. "*You* promised. You promised to love and obey. *With my body I thee worship*," he sneered. "I think they had better take that line out of the marriage service, don't you? It just doesn't suit the times."

Charlotte stared at him numbly. He was so handsome, even with stark rage written on his face. Part of her longed to throw herself against Alex's chest, to beg him to listen, to hug him and kiss him. He was in pain: She could see it in his shadowed eyes and the fierce hunch of his shoulders. But she would not . . . could not beg him. What she had to do now was protect her child. And Pippa. Pippa couldn't be pulled from her side after losing her mother. Pippa wouldn't be able to bear losing another mama. The thought gave steel to Charlotte's backbone. She thrust the utter despair in her heart to the side.

"You mustn't take Pippa away," she said. "She has suffered too much already."

"It will be better for her," Alex retorted. He turned away from Charlotte and stared across the great, soft green slope leading toward the house. Then he turned back and looked at his wife. "How can I leave her with a woman who is sleeping with my brother, Charlotte? Will you answer that? Even when I thought you had been false to me before marriage, I didn't really believe you would keep up that behavior after we married. More fool I."

"I didn't —" Charlotte stopped. This was a reiteration of their wedding night. He didn't believe her then, and he would never believe her now. He was simply too influenced by his first marriage. She felt such a leaden pain in her chest that she almost fell over. There was no point in talking. But one thing she had to say.

"You promised to trust me," she said, looking straight into his eyes. "You *promised.*" Then she turned and walked away, and no voice called her back.

Charlotte kept her back very straight, all the way into the house. But she climbed the stairs slowly, one hand on the small of her back. She felt like an old, a very old woman. The baby seemed to be pulling her forward. She finally reached the second floor and, turning left, walked straight into Sophie's bedchamber.

Sophie gasped and sat up. She had been drowsing in the warm afternoon sun, puzzling over a book of love sonnets written in Portuguese — Sophie, to her mother's great annoyance, showed an acute and unladylike passion for reading literature in its original language.

"What's the matter?" she asked sharply. Charlotte was standing in the doorway, swaying slightly, her face dead white.

"The baby's coming!" Sophie swung her feet over the edge of the bed, alarm shaking her to the bottom of her fingers. It was too early; the baby wasn't due for three weeks.

"No." Charlotte shook her head slowly from side to side. "No, no, no. He's back." She paused and collected herself again, her body visibly trembling.

"Who's — oh," Sophie said. She had wondered over the last month whether she should warn Charlotte of Alex's possible reaction. But then she kept thinking that anxiety wasn't good for pregnancy, and perhaps Alex wasn't as rash and stupid as the majority of men she had met in her life. But obviously he was just the same as the others.

"He doesn't think the baby is his," Sophie said flatly.

Charlotte's eyes flew to hers. "You knew!"

"I thought it was likely. Men are such unmitigated idiots."

"He wants to take the unborn babies away . . . my baby and Pippa. He *is* going to take them away." Charlotte was clutching her stomach, very close to hysteria. Sophie cast a worried eye on her. Hysteria probably wasn't any better for unborn babies than anxiety.

Sophie moved over and stood in front of Charlotte, her eyes commanding her friend's attention. "Don't get overwrought, Charlotte. It's not good for the baby. We have to *think*." Sophie pushed Charlotte into a sitting position on her bed.

"Where is he now?"

"I don't know . . . I left him in the summer house." Sophie felt a perk of approval at that news. At least Charlotte had left him, rather than the other way around.

"Are you absolutely sure about what he plans to do, Charlotte? Perhaps he just spoke in the heat of anger."

"He said he couldn't have his children brought up by a whore, and if the baby was born in the near future he would take it with him to London." Charlotte's voice was deadly calm. "He also said that he had already told his solicitor to draw up a bill for divorce." When she looked at Sophie her face was frozen, tearless eyes looking from a dead white face. "I can't let him do it, Sophie. Do you think he can?"

"The law is on his side." Sophie was thinking fast. What they really needed around here was Patrick, the big gallump who had encountered them at the musicale and started all this mess. If anyone could convince Alex that Charlotte was innocent, it was Patrick. But where was he? Perhaps Alex knew.

Sophie looked back at Charlotte. She looked fractionally more like herself. "I'm leaving," Charlotte said. Her eyes met Sophie's. "I'm leaving and I'm taking Pippa with me. I love her;

I love her as if she were my own child." You thought she was your own child, a voice screamed in her mind. Charlotte steadily ignored it. She couldn't afford to listen. "I can't leave her here with a madman," she said. "We'll go to Wales. I doubt that Alex would remember that I have a house there."

"Don't be stupid!" Sophie snapped. "He's your husband — everything belongs to him now."

"No, it doesn't. My father negotiated a peculiar dowry based on the rumors surrounding Alex's first marriage. He believed Alex, but he demanded that I retain my own property. And Alex . . . Alex didn't care." She pushed away the memory of a laughing Alex, insisting that he didn't give a snap of his fingers for her money. That was Alex before their wedding, when he thought she was a virgin. What a tangled mess this is, she thought in a moment of dispassionate logic.

"So the house in Wales is my property. I shall go there until the baby is born, and then I am going to travel to America."

Sophie thought about this. Charlotte was clearly hysterical, even given her collected tone. She couldn't take Alex's children and move to America; they would find her and throw her in jail. On the other hand, Sophie judged that Alex probably needed a cooling-down period. Not too long, because he had to be there for Charlotte's delivery or he might never believe that the child was his.

"All right," Sophie said with sudden resolution. "How are we going to get out of the house without Alex knowing?"

"Oh, Sophie. You are a sweetheart, but you can't come with me. You'd be ruined."

"Don't be a fool. I won't be ruined."

"Yes, you will," Charlotte insisted passionately. "You won't be able to get married if you run off with me — my God, you probably shouldn't even be visiting me now!"

Sophie looked at Charlotte wryly. Clearly this was the first time such a thought crossed Charlotte's mind. She was such an innocent!

"Sweetheart, don't you realize that it's all about money? I am my father's heir. Nothing could ruin me except being found absolutely naked in someone's bedroom."

"I don't believe you, Sophie. Look what ruined me: a faint and a touch on Patrick's cheek."

"You're married," Sophie explained. "Once you are married, it's all different. A married woman can sleep with as many men as she wants, as long as she is absolutely discreet. Because common adultery is not really interesting. You may make the gossip columns but you won't be ruined. But a wrong move in an interesting direction — say, showing affection for your husband's brother, and compounding that with getting pregnant in his absence, *and* not showing how close you are to giving birth — well, that can ruin a woman. But even that kind of ruination can be salvaged, because you are so very rich,

Charlotte, and so is Alex."

Charlotte digested all this in silence. "It doesn't matter," she finally said flatly. "Because Alex thinks I did sleep with his brother. I suppose if I stayed here and the baby was born tomorrow, he would believe that the child was his. But he would still take the child away. He thought I was a . . . a trollop before."

"Why?" Sophie asked.

Charlotte hesitated. She had never told Sophie the reason why she and Alex had had such a tempestuous wedding night.

"I slept with him before we got married," Charlotte said. "I slept with him at a ball." She couldn't bring herself to say it was at the Hookers' Ball, so-called. "And he doesn't remember it, and thinks I slept with his brother. So to him all of this gossip just confirmed that I really love his brother. Oh, God, how could I have been so stupid!" Because now Charlotte realized that of course Alex would have believed the article. Of course he wouldn't think the child was his.

Sophie was looking at Charlotte with fascination. She sat down next to her. "You slept with him . . . at a ball!"

Charlotte nodded.

"And he doesn't *remember?* Lord, how many women has he deflowered at a ball?"

Charlotte shook her head helplessly. "We never discussed the place. He jumped to the conclusion, on our wedding night, that I had slept with Patrick. And then he refused to talk about it again. He promised . . . he promised," Charlotte's voice caught on a sob, but she steadied herself. "He promised to trust me."

Sophie gave her a sympathetic squeeze. She had virtually no belief in male promises, but it didn't seem the right moment to point that out. Charlotte was extraordinarily beautiful when she was her ordinary self, but pregnant . . . she was exquisite. It was very hard to believe that a man had allowed sex with Charlotte to slip his mind.

"I still can't believe that he doesn't remember sleeping with you — especially given that you were a virgin."

Charlotte shrugged. "He says he never met me before."

"Who do we need to bring with us?" Sophie said practically.

"Katy, Marie, and your maid," Charlotte replied. "Keating and Mall are already in Wales, thank goodness."

"The problem is that we need to get Alex out of the way. Let me take care of it," Sophie said with sudden vigor. She left Charlotte to find Katy and instruct her to pack Pippa's things. Sophie walked down the stairs, straining to hear Alex's deep voice. The house was silent. Her feet resounded on the marble floor of the entranceway as she hesitated a minute. Then she headed for the library. She entered and closed the door, leaning back against it.

Alex was drinking a glass of brandy, his third that day. He looked up without interest.

"If you have come to plead her case, you might as well forget it," he said curtly.

"Where is your brother?"

Alex measured Sophie's length with his heavy lidded eyes. "I feel sure that my lovely wife can answer that question better than I can," he sneered.

"You need to find your brother," Sophie repeated. "Where is he?"

"In Leicestershire, they say. Hunting."

"Can you find him?"

"Why bother? I'm sure he'll show up here sooner or later. He can't have had all he wants of Charlotte's body, even if she is pregnant." He threw back the glass of brandy and poured himself another.

"Can you find him?"

"I suppose," Alex said with deadly irony. "But why bother?"

"Because you are an idiot and there's always the chance that your brother can bring you to your senses," Sophie said, speaking with just as much irony as he had used. "On the other hand, he *is* your brother; maybe he won't be able to remember who he slept with in the past five years or so."

Alex flashed her a look of acute dislike. "Hellion," he said unemotionally.

"I may be a hellion," Sophie bit back, "but I wouldn't ruin my family when there was no evidence to justify it. Surely your conscience won't allow you to throw away your wife like a used cravat before you even *speak* to her supposed seducer?"

"Seducer? I would say that she was almost certainly the seducer," Alex growled.

"You're splitting hairs, my lord," Sophie replied. "Are you afraid to talk to your brother? What will you do when he tells you that he only met your wife twice, for extremely brief periods of time?"

Alex stared at her, a small pulse beating in the corner of his mouth.

Sophie stared back, her eyes steady. "Will you simply condemn your own twin brother, out of hand, as you have condemned your wife? Without asking for an explanation?"

Alex felt as if a band was tightening around his forehead. "Just what would you have me do?" he asked harshly. "I left my wife when she had her monthly bleeding, and I return to find her pregnant. Exactly what explanation could she offer?"

Sophie ignored this statement. She was none too clear about the progress of pregnancy, and certainly not enough to quibble over medical facts.

"She says you promised to trust her."

The words dropped into the charged silence between them like small leaden weights. Alex kicked the log burning in the fireplace. Maybe he should seek out Patrick. What the hell was he to do tonight, anyway? Banish his wife to Scotland in the dark?

"Can you find him and return before three weeks?"

"Yes," Alex said absently, not even thinking about Sophie's odd question. Braddon Chatwin lived two days' ride from Downes Manor. "All right," he said finally, straightening up with a last vicious kick at the burning log. "Tell my wife" — bitingly — "that she should be ready to travel to Scotland a week from now."

Sophie nodded and slipped back out of the door of the study. She didn't trust herself to speak again, she was so angry. Ten minutes later the front door slammed and Alex shouted for his horse.

Sophie and Charlotte looked at each other over the piles of clothes littering Charlotte's bed. Three maids were bustling about, helping Marie pack. Charlotte fingered a little pile of soft white baby garments.

"He didn't . . . show any signs of relenting?" she whispered.

Sophie shook her head. Charlotte took a gulping breath of air. Sophie said firmly, "After we get to *Scotland,* Charlotte, you can buy more things for the baby."

Charlotte looked at her, startled. Sophie nodded toward the four women in the room and drew Charlotte toward the door. "Come on, darling. Let's go play with Pippa. We can leave first thing in the morning."

"No!" Charlotte protested in the hallway. "I want to leave tonight!"

"It's not good for the baby. You need to rest." Sophie's voice admitted no arguments. "If we tell everyone that our destination is Scotland, it will throw Alex off the trail for a week or so."

Charlotte nodded. It was true that every bone in her body ached to lie down, especially now that she knew Alex was out of the house.

"I'll send a tray to your room," Sophie said consolingly. "We can leave first thing in the morning."

That night Charlotte fell into a sleep so deep that she hardly stirred on the pillows. Toward morning a dream flowered, a seductively tender memory. She was back in Scotland with Alex, in the days when they were so happy. They had gone for a picnic on the banks of Grouse Lake. Katy had taken Pippa back to the house for a nap, and Alex's eyes were glowing as the carriage bore their child away.

"The coach won't return for at least fifteen minutes." Alex's deep voice was seductive, suggestive. He slipped off one of Charlotte's peach-colored slippers and ran his fingers over the delicate arch of her foot. "It's not enough time for . . . a five-course meal," Alex murmured. He bent his head and white teeth bit her toes gently.

He plucked a white daisy from the tender green grass by her feet and rubbed it on her thigh, just above the top of her stockings.

Waves of erotic heat washed up Charlotte's legs. Alex began to move up her body with small wolfish bites, laughing at her gasping remonstrances. In her sleep Charlotte's face eased into a blissful smile.

But then the dream suddenly changed. She was standing on the wharf that led out into the lake, and a fog had come up. Tendrils of snaky white were twining about her feet, drifting off the water. Fogs came up so quickly in Scotland; one minute the sun was shining and the next minute the world was ghastly, faintly shiny with dew. She looked about, calling for her husband. Then to her horror she heard a floundering, splashing noise and a little voice calling,

"Mama! Mamaaa!"

Charlotte woke up, her heart beating so fast that she felt as if she were ill. The baby in her womb had woken up too and was dancing a brisk tattoo. She breathed in gasps, trying to calm down. She was in her own bed, and Pippa was fast asleep in the nursery. Pippa was not drowning in a black Scottish lake, calling for her mama.

Finally Charlotte's heart slowed and she leaned back. Something in me has changed, she realized, soothing the small, sharp bumps that were her baby's kicking feet. Pippa . . . I have to protect my children, Charlotte thought fiercely. To hell with Alex's kisses and his passion. It was empty; without trust; based on lust. He had *used* her, like a meal spread out before him, and then he dumped her as casually as he might reject venison if he felt like eating veal.

And he didn't care about the babies anyway. He waltzed off to France without a second thought about Pippa. Charlotte spread her hands on her tummy, caressing the round bump that she thought was perhaps a head, or maybe a bottom. "I promise," she whispered into the hushed night. "I promise I will love you, and trust you, and never, never let you drown in a lake." Her eyes filled with tears despite herself. It would be so lovely if there were two of them, if Alex and she could love each other *and* the babies. But there wasn't any way that could happen. And so for yet another night the Countess of Sheffield and Downes cried herself to sleep.

Chapter 21

Alex found his brother only after four hard days of riding. He reached Braddon Chatwin's country house in two days but found to his intense irritation that the "young master" had left a few days earlier. Alex slapped his gloves against his leg, staring with unconscious, arrogant rage at the wilting butler before him.

"What do you mean, man, you're not sure where they went? Either you know or you don't. If you don't, say so clearly."

"What I meant," Treble said humbly, "was that his lordship expressed the intention to travel to Bath — and of course your brother, my lord, was accompanying him. But the party may well have stopped at Singleton Manor, that would be the Earl of Slaslow's estate in Kent."

"The *party*," Alex barked, "what is this, a summer parade? Are there women traveling with them?"

Treble cast his eyes on the marble floor at his feet, looking vainly for support. He looked up only to say, "I used the word loosely, my lord. The group consisted of the Earl of Slaslow and your brother. And —" he half mumbled, "there is also an acquaintance of Lord Foakes's, a young female, my lord."

It was Alex's turn to lapse into silence. "Female" could only mean one thing: Patrick was transporting a ladybird with him from hunting lodge to hunting lodge. Nothing new there. Except that it meant that Patrick had left a pregnant Charlotte alone in order to disport himself with a mistress. Treble shook with terror, seeing how the earl's face seemed, impossibly, to grow even darker and more menacing.

"Did this — *female* — arrive with my brother?"

"Yes, my lord." And when Alex stared at him, his eyes boring into his skull, Treble added uncomfortably, "The young woman arrived shortly after your brother and the master came from London; that is, I believe that the assignation was made in London and the young, uh, lady simply took a few days to pack. She is traveling with a good deal of clothing," Treble said with feeling. It had taken his staff almost five hours to unload the trunks from the roof of the carriage; it was worse than receiving a duchess, in his opinion. The girl didn't travel with her own sheets the way nobility did, but she had brought forty-eight hats, each in its own hatbox!

Alex turned his back with a curt thanks and walked back down the marble steps. Before him the sky was streaked a bitter orange color, layers of clouds stained by the setting sun. Alex stared at it blindly. He was beginning to have a very curious sense of uneasiness. Would Patrick have tired of Charlotte's body so soon? He himself had *had* her, Alex thought savagely, for some three months and he knew with a deep inner certainty that he would have happily taken her body to bed with him for the next three — hell, the next thirty — years.

Perhaps Charlotte had cut off the affair. Perhaps Charlotte did love him, and she only succumbed to Patrick because she had lost her virginity to him. Alex scoffed at himself. What was he thinking? She slept with his brother for old times' sake? Out of nostalgia?

The brutal fact was that Charlotte was bleeding when he left and when he returned she was pregnant. And nothing mattered but those two facts. He ignored the plaintive voice of Treble calling after him, asking whether he wished to spend the night at Selfridge Manor. The last thing he wanted to do was sleep anywhere his brother had been. Alex strode over to his waiting horse and swung up in one swift, muscled lunge. He nodded at the mounted manservant who was leading Alex's stallion, Bucephalus.

"I'm going to the Fox and Keys, Harry," he said curtly. "You'd best walk Bucephalus. It's been a long day."

Two days later, Alex galloped into the drive of Singleton Manor, one of Braddon Chatwin's country houses, around nine in the evening. His eyes keenly swept the front of the sprawling stone manor and he felt a glow of satisfaction.

He'd finally caught them. The pale gray stone of the manor house was darkened by glowing candlelight shining from many of the house's windows; Braddon had to be in residence.

Alex threw Bucephalus's reins to the bowing footman. He paused for a second next to the portly butler as he held open the eight-foot-high door.

"Where is he?" Alex snapped.

"It is an honor to see you again, my lord," Braddon's butler Vorset said gently. He was too old to be bullied by young sparks like this one, he thought to himself. "The master and Lord Foakes can be found in the library."

Alex paused for a moment, his stern face cracking into a reluctant smile. "I'm glad you're still on your feet, Vorset." Vorset had never snapped at the ill-behaved twins when they visited Braddon during school holidays, years ago. To tell the truth, Alex and Patrick had led Braddon into some of his worst scrapes, which Vorset knew but never revealed to Braddon's parents.

Vorset nodded slightly, his eyes kind. Like the rest of England, he knew something of Alexander Foakes's marital problems. "The library is off to the right, my lord," he murmured, leading the way.

Alex followed the old butler down the well-known, wide passageway to the library. Lord, he hadn't been in this house for some ten years. After his mother died he and Patrick had been farmed out to whomever was available for holidays. They used to tear about Braddon's house as if they were wild pigs released indoors by accident.

Vorset opened the library doors without announcing him, a tribute to his closeness with the family. As Vorset disappeared back down the corridor, Alex paused in the doorway. There was a huge fire burning in the marble fireplace, taking the spring chill off the air. The draft going up the chimney was making the candelabra flicker. Still, the scene before him was clear enough. Braddon Chatwin was moodily reading what looked to be a stud report. And nestled in a settee before the fire was Alex's brother. For a moment Alex forgot his rage and just let his heart feel glad to see Patrick again. His twin was like his arm, he realized suddenly. No matter how much he hated him, he would be devastated if anything happened to him. Patrick looked thinner, his skin tanned dark brown by the Indian sun. He was whispering into the ear of a lovely redhead, who was giggling softly at whatever nonsense Patrick was murmuring.

Alex cleared his throat deliberately. Braddon looked about; no one else even looked up. Braddon's clear blue eyes met Alex's for a brief moment and then he said,

"Patrick, my buck, there's someone here to see you."

Patrick didn't move, his black curls bent over the mass of red hair seated next to him.

"Patrick!" Braddon insisted.

Finally Patrick looked up. But something about Alex's coiled aggression as he leaned casually in the doorway made him pause. The twins could always read each other without speaking; Patrick knew from the other side of the room that Alex was filled with a cold, cold rage, greater than anything Patrick remembered.

Patrick walked slowly over to Alex and stopped in front of him. His arching eyebrows flew up as he asked his twin a silent question.

Alex's black eyes raked Patrick's face. For a moment the library was absolutely still, and no noise broke the air but the hiss and crackle of green logs burning in the fireplace.

"Hell," Alex said quietly. "You didn't do it, did you?"

Patrick stayed where he was. "I didn't sleep with your wife, if that's what you mean."

Alex's face was a tight, cold mask. When he didn't respond, Patrick dropped an arm around his brother's shoulder and turned him around. Alex turned automatically, as if he were sleepwalking. The two men walked out of the library without looking backward.

"Lud!" Miss Arabella Calhoun breathed. (She was the red-haired enchantress who had been sharing Patrick's sofa.) "He's a mean-looking one, isn't he?"

When Braddon didn't answer she stretched a dainty foot out before her and carefully inspected it on all sides. She quite liked these slippers. They were French, of course, and pale blue, embroidered with small white doves.

Braddon drifted over and rested his arms on the back of the sofa.

"What do you think, Braddon?" Miss Arabella asked dreamily. She used the earl's first name because she believed in maintaining terms of the greatest intimacy with all male friends of her current *amour*. And the minute Patrick walked out of the library with his brother she realized that in fact her particular *amour* might be a thing of the past. Patrick appeared to have family problems. Arabella shuddered. She hated family problems: so dreary, so tiresome, so unromantic.

"Think of what?"

"Think of my shoes!"

Braddon stared at them. This is why he never got anywhere with women. What could a person say about shoes?

"They're very . . . they're very small."

Arabella shot him an annoyed look. This one was a lout, that was for sure. But he was looking at her so anxiously that she relented.

"Well, Braddon," she said, patting the cushion next to her. "Since Patrick took himself off without even bothering to say a word, why don't you join me?"

And it was a good thing she extended that invitation. Because around an hour later, when Vorset appeared to offer drinks and refreshments, he announced that the Earl of Sheffield and Downes and his brother had both galloped off without mentioning when they might return.

"Well, I like that!" Arabella said, her eyes filling with easy tears. She turned to Braddon, who was sitting very close beside her. "Isn't that the rudest thing you ever heard? I didn't have to accompany that bounder all the way out into the country. Men line up by the theater door every night just to ask me to dinner!"

"I know," Braddon said, taking Arabella's hand. "I was one of them." He stared soulfully into Miss Arabella's eyes, and she felt herself perk up a bit.

After all, as she confided to her maid later that night, one man is much like another, aren't they? And while Patrick was more handsome, Braddon was much more amenable. Shoes — hats — everything was so expensive these days!

As a silvery slip of a moon swung into the sky above the dark forest lining the road, Patrick reached out and jerked on his brother's reins. Alex's horse was lathered with sweat and panting heavily, his sides blowing in and out painfully as they drew to a halt.

"We must stop now, Alex."

Alex shot him a ferocious glance. Patrick calmly ignored it, leading his horse off on a road to the right whose crooked sign read *Buffington, One Mile.*

"There's a decent inn in Buffington," Patrick shouted back over his shoulder.

Then he stopped and wheeled his horse about, sensing that his brother wasn't following him down the Buffington road.

"For goodness sake, man! She's not going anywhere; Charlotte is pregnant. She'll be there waiting for you, and a few hours won't matter."

Alex's face was an immobile, dark shadowed mask. Patrick walked his desperately exhausted horse back the few steps to the cleft in the road. Alex looked at him.

"She's going to leave me, Patrick," he finally said, hoarsely. "I promised I would trust her, and I failed her. I have to get to the house and follow her. I have to find her."

Patrick sighed. He hadn't been able to get any sense out of his twin since Alex grasped the fact that his brother not only had no part in his wife's pregnancy, he hardly knew the woman.

"Charlotte is not going anywhere! She's *pregnant*. Pregnant women don't travel." Patrick vested his voice with a deep layer of authority, dismissing his memory of pregnant women trundling happily up and down the roads of India. "Think of Mother. Don't you remember when she was pregnant? She went to bed for months."

It was an unhappy thought, one that drained the last bit of color from Alex's face.

"My God," Alex whispered. "What if she's like Mother, what if she dies, Patrick?"

"Charlotte is a sensible woman, Alex. She wouldn't endanger the life of her child. She will be sitting in Downes Manor waiting for you when you get back. I'm not saying that she won't take your head off. But she won't risk the child's life to run away."

Alex blinked. That was the first argument he'd heard which made sense. Maybe he was wrong in his deep conviction that Charlotte was, even now, riding away from him on some road. That he would never see her again. She wouldn't endanger the babe, that was true.

Patrick sensed his victory and grabbed Alex's bridle again, forcing his horse to walk off toward Buffington.

"We'll be up at dawn. Even if she did decide to travel to Scotland — and mind you, I think the chance is exceedingly slim — she necessarily will go very slowly. We won't have any trouble catching up with her."

Alex didn't respond, just nodded. They plodded their way into the Queen's Ankle, Buffington's best inn, ate squirrel stew (the only food available), and fell into the two beds that graced the innkeeper's sole spare room.

"Lord," Patrick said crossly. "When do you suppose that fat ass downstairs last had the straw turned in this damned mattress?"

Alex didn't bother to respond. He was staring up at the uneven planks above him, wondering where his life went wrong. What led him to suspect Charlotte of adultery? His mind kept replaying the scene in the little summer house, as if to torture himself. Charlotte would rise, a tremendous sweetness trembling in her eyes and mouth, and then . . . he would reject her. When he finally spoke, his voice was harsh and grating.

"If she's gone, I don't know what I'll do, Patrick."

Patrick rolled his eyes in the darkness, thanking his lucky stars for never having been touched by the tender emotion called love.

"She's not going *anywhere*, Alex. For God's sake." They fell silent.

Given Alex's punishing speed, it only took two and a half days to return to Downes Manor. The minute they entered the drive Patrick's heart sank. Alex was right. The house had an odd, eerie stillness.

Alex dropped Bucephalus's reins right there, in the drive, and charged through the front door. It wasn't locked and a startled footman leaped out of the library as the door slammed open.

"My lord!"

"Where's my wife?" Alex bellowed.

The footman's eyes were glued to the floor. "I couldn't say, my lord . . . that is, I have no idea," he stammered.

Patrick strolled forward, opening a door and looking into a salon to the left. Behind him Alex reduced the footman to quivering jelly. The footman appeared to be suggesting that the countess had proceeded to Scotland. Patrick turned around, asking mildly,

"Where's your butler, Alex?"

"The butler! Where's the butler?" Alex added a string of expletives.

"You don't have one in this house, my lord,"

the footman said with some dignity. "My lady had interviewed several candidates and I believe she was about to appoint a butler, but you returned. . . ." His voice trailed off.

Patrick noticed with interest that although the man was clearly unnerved by Alex's shouting, he showed no signs of being cowed. In fact, when he raised his eyes to Alex's face, surely he looked — could he be contemptuous?

Patrick intervened again. "Did the countess take her maid with her?"

The footman shifted his eyes to the floor once again. "Yes."

"Was anyone else traveling in the party?" When the footman hesitated, Patrick added, "Your loyalty to your mistress is —"

But his sentence was broken off by Alex.

"Of course! Sophie York was here. They must have gone to her mother."

"I doubt it."

"Why the hell not?" Alex turned his burning eyes on Patrick.

"Because the Marchioness of Brandenburg would never admit your wife into her house," Patrick said. "Charlotte has been branded a whore the length and breadth of England. I am very surprised to hear that Sophie York was allowed to visit at all."

"Was Charlotte that scorned?"

"I would be surprised if anyone would speak to her at all," Patrick said gently. "I'm sorry, Alex. There was nothing I could do; I stayed as far away as I could. If I had even been seen in her vicinity, it could only further ruin her reputation."

"But Sophie York was here when I returned."

"She looked like the loyal type," Patrick said. He remembered very well the clear, fierce eyes of the girl who had caught Alex's wife when she fainted at the musicale. Sophie looked at him with such condemnation that her eyes actually haunted him for a few days, until he shook off the memory by chasing and winning Arabella Calhoun, the much-admired singer at the Theater Royal.

Damnation, Patrick thought with a start. I left Arabella back at Braddon's house. It was the first time she had crossed his mind since Alex appeared in the doorway of the library. Then he dismissed her with a mental shrug. Bella would always land on her feet.

"Oh, God," Alex said. His words dropped into the silence filling the hall.

Cecil, the footman in question, nervously cast his eyes at the floor. It sounded as if the earl was sorry for all the problems he caused; it sounded as if the madness was over. Cecil thought nervously of Marie's whispered analysis. She had said that the earl was the only one who could stop the scandal and allow her mistress to return to society. So should he, Cecil, reveal his mistress's whereabouts?

Patrick shot a sharp glance at the footman. That man knew where Charlotte had gone, that was certain. But Patrick judged that if he pushed him the servant might become obstinate out of pure loyalty.

"Time for dinner," he said to the footman. "Is there a chef in the house?"

Cecil nodded. "Oh, yes, my lord, the countess hired a chef immediately. He's been here for months. His name is Rossi. He's Italian. The countess —" He looked at his master. "The countess felt that the earl might appreciate Italian food after his sojourn in Italy."

"Oh, God," Alex repeated.

"You're starting to sound like a bronze gong," Patrick said cheerfully. He pushed open the door to the yellow salon.

"Bring us some drinks, will you? What is your name?"

"Cecil, sir."

"Well, Cecil, you're the butler-in-charge. I'd like some whiskey, and so would my brother."

As the doors swung to behind the brothers, Cecil swallowed nervously. Had he done the right thing, keeping it secret that he knew where the countess had gone? No one else in the household knew. They all thought she had set off for Scotland. But of course Marie had told him the truth, that the party was heading for Wales.

Then Cecil trotted off, shelving the problem for the moment. Rossi might be Italian, rather than French, but he was just as temperamental as the French chef in London. He'd need to be warned as soon as possible that he was required to produce a proper seven-course dinner.

In the yellow salon Alex slumped on a couch, staring straight ahead. Patrick wandered around the room, picking up small objects and looking at them absentmindedly.

"This room looks different," he said.

Alex didn't look up. "I need to find out when she left," he said dully. "Do you think she went to Scotland?"

Patrick didn't bother to answer. He had the full intention of screwing the whole truth out of that footman — but not until after dinner. If he knew Alex, his brother would insist on riding off for parts unknown before dinner. Patrick was sick of galloping down dangerous roads at night, vulnerable to highwaymen and God knows what else. Maybe he wouldn't approach the footman until tomorrow morning.

"Were you responsible for refurbishing the house, or was Charlotte?" he asked, with an air of mild curiosity.

"I haven't entered the house since before father died."

"Your wife has an eye for color."

"She's a painter."

"Hmmm," Patrick responded.

"She's a real painter," Alex barked. "She paints portraits, and they're brilliant. She said she might paint me. . . ." He lapsed into silence again.

Patrick was examining a painting on the wall, with some interest.

"Not that," Alex said irritably. "That's a Rossetti. I feel as if someone threw a black sack over my head and was slowly choking me."

Patrick came back to the couch and sat down in the opposite corner from his brother, stretching out his long, muscular legs. He threw his head back and looked up at the ceiling. Charlotte had had its peeling, faint decoration restored; the ceiling bristled with lazy-looking noblemen and their ladies, picnicking by an elaborately winding stream.

"Why *did* you do it, Alex? I only met Charlotte twice, but I would have judged her effortlessly honest and true as steel. More, she loved you," he said ruthlessly. "I felt sorry for her, suffering through an obscene scandal that broke out over nothing: but I never thought that you would subscribe to it."

"When I left for Italy she told me she had her monthly," Alex replied. "I found she wasn't a virgin on our wedding night, but she told me that she had lost her virginity to me. I knew that wasn't true, so I decided she must have lost her virginity to you. Then when I returned, I heard about her fainting when you appeared, and there she was, pregnant."

"You're a fool," Patrick said, not unkindly. "Have you remembered when you slept with her?"

"You've met Charlotte, Patrick. Do you think you could forget taking her virginity?"

"You should give it serious thought. She's not a liar."

"Well, what about you?"

"As it happens, virgins have been few and far between in my life. I tend to give 'em a wide berth. I deflowered one woman, and she was an Indian maiden on the banks of the Ganges River. It's a nice memory, but irrelevant."

"We're even. I too slept with one virgin, but she had red hair, and it took place at the Hookers' Ball."

Patrick thought about the implication that his sister-in-law had attended the Hookers' Ball. He opened his mouth — but then he closed it again. He was tired and hungry and didn't feel like wrangling over details with Alex. Once they tracked his wife down they could sort out the particulars.

There was a discreet knock and the door swung open. Cecil stood there, blinking nervously. He held a silver platter in one hand but said nothing.

"How on earth did you get the name Cecil?" Patrick asked with a touch of malice. "Did your mother have delusions of grandeur?"

Cecil shook his head from side to side. "She admired the nobility," he said briefly. He advanced into the room and bowed before Alex. "A message has arrived for you, my lord."

Alex snatched the white envelope off the silver salver, almost tearing it in half in his eagerness to open the letter.

"My God," he said. "It's from her, Sophie York. They're in Wales. She says" — and his voice strengthened with indignation — "that if I would like to attend the birth of my child I should make haste."

"You deserve it." Patrick eyed the footman, who was looking distinctly relieved. "Off with you," he said curtly. "You had a lucky escape."

Cecil bowed his way out of the room, agreeing with younger Foakes with all his heart.

Patrick was feeling distinctly sour. He could see dinner disappearing from before his eyes. Sure enough, Alex had already bounded out of the room and started howling for his horse. Patrick dragged himself out of the comfortable couch, throwing a last look at the happy ladies frolicking about on the ceiling. Taking Alex's punishing speed into account, it would take them two days to get to Wales. Two more days before he could have a decent meal. In the hall he pulled on his greatcoat and strolled out the door slowly, just to annoy his brother who was already mounted on a nervous steed. With a sigh Patrick leaped on top of a fresh horse, loosed the rein, and pounded after his brother down the dark, tree-lined drive.

Chapter 22

Charlotte's voice rose to a shriek. "No! No! No!" She hunched over, protecting her huge belly. "He's only here to take my baby! Make him leave —" Her voice broke off as she stumbled against the bedpost, swallowed into a great slashing wave of pain. The room was silent except for Charlotte's harsh pants.

Alex stared at his wife in horror. Had he been blind? She was wearing a light shift, drenched with perspiration. The swollen outline of her belly was clearly visible. She was bigger than the woman he saw give birth in Italy, he thought with a pulse of alarm. The baby must be enormous.

A hand grasped his arm. "My lord, you must leave this room," said a courteous voice at his ear. Alex swung about wildly. A doctor was standing before him, looking at him gravely but with an unmistakable air of command.

"You're very young," Alex said.

"You must leave this room now," Dr. Seedland said. "Your wife's birth is proceeding well, for a first baby. But she cannot lose strength arguing with you. The child is large."

"Please . . . please make him go away!"

Alex looked back at Charlotte. She had been clinging to the bedpost, but she pulled herself up. Her hair was roughly pulled back from her face; her eyes were enormous and black. Oh, my God, she's in pain, Alex thought. He felt such a wave of tenderness that he instinctively started toward her. But the doctor's arm tightened on his like a vise.

"Out," he said. "You must not remain here."

"Go away," Charlotte said pleadingly. Her pupils were so dilated that her eyes looked like black pools. "Please, please, go away." She broke down and started weeping.

"My lady." The doctor turned around, frustrated. "You must not waste strength like this!"

Sophie wrapped her arms around Charlotte's shaking shoulders and met Alex's eyes with a silent order. Slowly he backed out the door, even as he heard Sophie's soothing words.

"It's all right, darling. I won't let him take your baby. I'm here."

And, as the door swung to, he heard a wailing scream. Charlotte had been hit by another contraction.

Alex stood outside the door, struck to the core with the enormity of his own idiocy. His wife — *his wife!* — was delivering his child, and she had looked at him with utter terror. His heart wrenched with grief and self-loathing. It would be better if he just went out and shot himself.

But at that moment Patrick's strong arms circled around him in a rough, unaccustomed hug.

They stood for a moment, two large, powerful men. In the twilight of the corridor they looked uncannily identical. The silence was broken by a shuddering scream, and another, and another, arching above the murmur of voices in Charlotte's bedroom.

The doctor's voice rose above the rest. "My lady, you *must* stop screaming and conserve your strength. Lower your voice!"

Alex struggled in Patrick's arms. "My God, he's yelling at her. I'll kill him!" he said through clenched teeth.

Patrick gripped his hands on Alex's shoulders. "Have you seen a woman give birth before?"

"It was different," Alex said fiercely. "She just lay down and there was the baby . . . blood, but then she had a glass of wine, and the baby started sucking."

"Probably the fifth or sixth baby," Patrick said. "You know that women die in childbirth, Alex. Think of mother. It happens all the time, and most frequently with the first baby. Charlotte has to conserve her strength. The doctor is right. I saw a woman die, in India. She simply didn't have the strength after a while."

Alex pushed out of his brother's embrace and leaned against the corridor, shuddering all over. There was silence in the bedroom. Then the horrible cries erupted again. Patrick gave him a little shake.

"I'm going to take your daughter into the village and leave her with the vicar's wife," he said.

"Charlotte can be heard all over the house." He strode away.

Alex leaned against the wall without replying. By two hours later he was praying, fiercely, promising anything and everything he owned. Charlotte had stopped screaming, but he didn't know whether that was bad or good. It didn't sound good. The contractions were still coming, but all he heard were whimpers and harsh, groaning breathing.

He couldn't even think, caught in the grip of an agonized grief so large that he felt black water closing over his head. Charlotte was his heart and his soul. She was being tortured in the next room and he couldn't even hold her in his arms because he had made her too afraid of him.

The hours crept by. Patrick brought him a slice of meat and a glass of wine, which lay untouched on a tray. He brought a couple of chairs and sat down next to Alex, a silent, comforting presence. Alex couldn't bring himself to sit down. He stayed propped against the wall.

Then Sophie's voice came through the heavy oak door, sounding desperate.

"Charlotte! Charlotte! You must not give up! Wake up, wake up!"

There was an agitated murmur of voices. Alex straightened. The doctor could go to hell. He was going in there. He opened the door. The little cluster of people didn't even look up. Charlotte was on the bed now. She was naked, her belly swelling from her slender body. A pulse of

526

pure terror struck Alex's heart. He could just glimpse her face and it had the look of death. She's going to die, he thought. She's going to die. My lovely, lovely Charlotte is going to die.

He walked over to the bed. "Get out," Alex said fiercely. The doctor didn't look up; he was waving smelling salts under Charlotte's nose, but she didn't even tremble at the fierce acid smell. Alex grasped his arm and flung him back.

"Get out!" he bellowed. The little flock of women fell back from the bed in alarm.

The doctor finally looked at him, his eyes exhausted but steady. "My lord, the child is still alive. I can try to rescue the child." The words fell into the silent room like heavy drops of water.

Alex stared at him in disbelief. Then he hissed through his teeth. "Get out."

Dr. Seedland gave him a look of compassion. "I will be outside. I can give you ten minutes," he said. "After that point it will be too late to save the child either." He put his hand on Charlotte's forehead for a moment, looking down at his patient. Then he ushered the three serving women out of the room.

Only Sophie stayed exactly where she was, next to Charlotte's head.

Alex looked down at Sophie's fierce, unforgiving face. "I have to tell her," he said, his voice breaking. "I have to tell her."

"She can't hear anymore," Sophie said flatly.

"Please, Sophie," Alex said. "Please." She

looked at him and in the deep blue depths of her eyes he met a contempt that he had never encountered from another human being. It pierced his heart like an arrow.

"Please."

Sophie bowed her head. She leaned down and put a kiss on both of Charlotte's closed eyelids. They were dark violet, the veins swollen from her labor. Charlotte's breath was very faint and far away; she hardly stirred as a contraction rippled her stomach.

"Good-bye," Sophie whispered. "Good-bye, sweetheart, good-bye." Strong arms pulled her away. Patrick pushed her over against the door. Then he came back and hauled his brother around.

"You must wake her up, Alex. Wake her up and help her push. She has to push the baby out, or they will both die." Alex looked into his brother's face. Patrick's eyes burned into his, giving him strength.

Patrick turned and gathered up Sophie, who stood motionless by the door where he had deposited her. He opened the door and they walked into the empty corridor. Seedland has probably gone to find a chamber pot, Patrick thought. He looked down at the fierce little person beside him. She was shaking with deep, wrenching sobs, so strong that they could not escape her chest. She struggled to breathe. Patrick gathered her into his arms and carried her into the bedchamber across the hall. He sat in an armchair, reflexively stroking her hair.

"I killed her," Sophie said, gulping for air. "I killed her and I loved her. Oh God . . ."

Patrick was startled out of his fearful attempt to hear across the hallway and into the master bedroom. *"What?"*

"I killed her. If I hadn't sent the message, she would be fine. I thought, I thought that he should know, so he couldn't suspect her of changing the baby's birth date. I thought that if he was here for the birth, he would realize how stupid it was to suspect her."

"You were right to do it," Patrick assured her. He had no clear idea what Sophie was talking about, but he kept stroking her silky curls.

"No, no, I wasn't," Sophie choked. "Because everything was going well before *he* came. They were about to send me out of the room, and even though it was painful, she was brave . . . but when he appeared, and she thought he was going to take the baby when it was born, it just stopped. It stopped working. I told her, I kept telling her, that I wouldn't let him take the baby, but she didn't believe me." Sobs took over her voice again.

Patrick cursed softly, under his breath. When he spoke, his voice was as ragged as hers. "It's not Alex's fault," he said. "And it's not your fault. Births don't always work, especially with the first baby. The baby, or the mother, can die."

"Or both," Sophie said drearily.

"Or both," Patrick said. He rested his cheek

against the head of the woman whose name he hardly knew. "But it's not your fault. Alex realized what an ass he'd been, and he was on his way back. He loves her, you know. He was a fool, but he loves her. So he should be there. When I saw this happen before, in India . . ." he trailed off.

Sophie raised her head and looked at him, her blue eyes drenched in tears. "Did she suffer? I mean, at the end?"

"No. No, they called the husband, and he went in the room and was with her."

Sophie dropped back against his chest, exhausted.

"How long has it been?" she whispered.

"About three minutes." They both listened, but there was no sound from the hallway, not even the doctor's returning footsteps.

In the master bedchamber Alex sat down on the bed beside Charlotte. She was very far away, in some private space of her own where there was no pain. He could see it in the frail whiteness of her face and her hushed breathing. He took her hands in his. As always, her delicate hands were dwarfed by his huge fingers. He had a sudden flashing memory of her fingers deftly holding a thin brush as she turned about to laugh at him, flicking a spot of red onto the front of his white shirt. He had growled in mock anger and swooped down on her, carrying her to the divan. He was such a fool! Why didn't he know that a man and woman don't make love like that, heart and soul infused into each other, unless there is true emotion between them? He had confused Maria's cold, loathsome couplings with their joyful passion.

A great numbing coldness invaded Alex's limbs. He had killed Charlotte. It was his fault. Unlike Patrick, he needed no explanations for what had happened. He had frightened his wife so much that she thought he would wrench the baby from her arms. So she gave up. Alex's heart lurched in his chest. He hadn't felt this agony since he was eleven and his mother died in childbirth. His mother would hate him if she knew what he had done to his own wife.

Something burning, hot, fell on his wrist. Alex realized it was his own tears. He hadn't cried since his mother . . . He couldn't lose her. He couldn't lose Charlotte.

"Charlotte!" His voice emerged desperately from his strangled chest. "Charlotte, come back." There was no response from the white figure on the bed, only a faint twisting as her body shook from another contraction.

"No!" Alex howled in agony, "No, God, no!" He bent over, putting his lips to Charlotte's ear, holding her hands as tightly as he could.

"I love you, Charlotte, I love you. Oh, God, please hear me. Please, please, don't go, don't go without hearing me. I found out how much I loved you in Italy. I was afraid . . . I was afraid that you didn't love me, or that you were like

Maria. Oh, God, Charlotte, please wake up!"

But there was nothing. Tears fell down Alex's face and he leaned forward, pressing his face against Charlotte's warm cheek. The silky warmth bolstered him, strengthened him. She wasn't dead yet!

He took a deep breath. Bring her back, Patrick had said. Bring her back and help her push. He put his hands on her swollen tummy and the faint flicker of life he felt sent fire through his veins. Their child was there as well, fighting for life.

Alex bent over again, putting his hands on Charlotte's cheeks. His voice was low and insistent this time. "Charlotte, you must wake up. You must come back. The baby will die if you don't come back, Charlotte. Our baby will die." He paused and looked down at her. Had her eyelids flickered? Alex put his mouth so close to her face that his breath warmed her skin. He kissed her, breathing warmth into her, pouring his strength into her. "Charlotte," he said again. "You must wake up or our baby will die. Don't let our baby die, Charlotte!"

Charlotte heard him, but only as if his voice were a long way off, in a dream. It was Alex, she knew that. And he wasn't shouting at her; he was pleading, almost begging. And then she understood what he was saying and with the last bit of her energy she opened her eyes. Almost instantly a contraction gripped her and she moaned, eyes closing, willing herself to fall back into the sweet, blessed darkness without pain. Long eyelashes drifted down over her white cheeks.

But Alex's voice wouldn't let her. "Don't, Charlotte, don't! Our baby will die." His voice was rasping with agony, but it was fiercely commanding as well. Charlotte opened her eyes again.

"Oh, God, Charlotte," Alex said. He cradled her face in his hands. "I love you, do you know that?"

And Charlotte, looking at him with pain-drenched eyes, saw agony and tenderness and unbearable guilt in his eyes, and nodded, once. She smiled a little and turned her face against his hand, sliding back into the warm nest he had pulled her from.

Alex roughly pulled her into a half-sitting position. Charlotte groaned, but she was looking at him again.

"Our baby," he was saying, "our baby, Charlotte!"

Slowly it came back to her. Her baby; where was her baby? Right on cue, another bone-shaking contraction crept up her abdomen. She opened her mouth to scream, but no sound came out. Alex was gently caressing her shoulders. The pain passed and she opened her eyes.

He was looking at her, his eyes wild and desperate. Charlotte blinked. "Charlotte, on the next contraction, we're going to push the baby out, do you understand?" Alex's voice was so commanding that she answered.

"I tried." Her voice was a wisp of sound.

"This time we're going to push together. You were alone before; now I'm going to push with you. Feel how strong I am, Charlotte?" She nodded. He was gripping her hand as if he would never let go.

The door opened and Dr. Seedland slipped through, alone. His eyes went instantly to the bed.

"All right, Doctor," Alex said without turning his head. "On the next contraction Charlotte and I are going to push the baby *out*. Because we want our baby to live, Charlotte. And if it doesn't come out, the baby will die." He kept his eyes fastened on hers, as if he could hypnotize her into strength.

Charlotte took a deep breath. She was fully back now; back in her pain-wracked, exhausted body. Somehow logic had come back as well. She had to get the baby out. Yet logic, in fact, had deserted her, because as she explained later, Alex said *he* was going to push the baby out, and she agreed. She was too tired; it would be good if he could take over now.

So when the contraction started, instead of trying to control the pain Charlotte just relaxed into it and when Alex's hands tightened and his voice beat at her head, saying "Push, push!" she thought about the baby dying, and that Alex was pushing, and she wrenched her whole soul down to her stomach. And pushed.

"I see the head," Dr. Seedland said unemotionally. He looked at Alex with a gleam of approval. "We need one more like that, my lord."

Alex turned back to Charlotte. She was lying back, hair plastered to her scalp with sweat. She looked as if she'd been in a good fight and had come out on the losing side. She was the most beautiful thing he'd ever seen. He bent down and kissed her mouth. Charlotte didn't stir. He bit her lip sharply. Her eyes flew open.

There he was again, bothering her. She frowned at him.

"We need to do it one more time, Charlotte. Come on, the contraction is coming. We can get the baby out this time, Charlotte!" And then, in answer to her unspoken plea, "Just one more time, Charlotte." And he hoped it was true.

So as the pain wrenched its way up her legs and into her chest Charlotte clutched her husband's hands and pushed, one last time.

There was a shout from the end of the bed. "I've got him!" Dr. Seedland said hoarsely. And a second later there was a fierce, thin wail.

In the room across the hall, Sophie and Patrick had given up. They were curled up in the huge armchair like a pair of hibernating animals, taking pure animal comfort from each other's nearness. For a while they listened carefully, but when Alex shouted "No, no!" Sophie slumped back against Patrick. She was too tired even to cry anymore. Patrick was stricken with grief for his twin. In the back of his mind, he knew that Alex would never get over this, never. He loved

Charlotte; he had failed her; she had died. Mentally, Patrick sat in the chair gathering his strength to fight for his twin's life.

But then a baby's tiny wail pierced their silent thoughts. Patrick literally leaped from the chair and Sophie was launched into the air and flew down to the ground: *whack!* She fell on her left shoulder.

Sophie screamed with pain, and Patrick instantly scooped her up into his arms. They poised there, absolutely silent, until another spiraling wail hit the air. An uneasy thought occurred to Patrick. Had the doctor "rescued" the baby? Or did Alex succeed in waking up Charlotte? He had told his twin to wake her up, but he had almost no hope that it was possible. Patrick set Sophie on her feet and opened the door into the hallway.

The door to the bedroom was open. Sophie's heart quailed; the bed was absolutely soaked in blood. But then . . . there was Alex, striding toward them, a huge grin splitting his face. And in his arms was a tiny, tiny little scrap of humanity.

"See?" Alex held back the flap of the white blanket so they could see a red face and small mouth, opening and shutting.

"He's hungry," Sophie said, fascinated. "Or, she's hungry?"

"She," Alex said. He looked about. Charlotte's carefully chosen wet nurse had gone off to the kitchens long ago, and was at that moment drowning her sorrows in a tankard of ale. Mall, who had stood by Charlotte's bed for hours, was weeping, head down on the kitchen table.

Alex looked down at his daughter's small mouth and walked back to the bed. Charlotte was propped up against the bed board, still ashen white, but without the faraway, lost look she had before. She seemed to be asleep. The doctor had pulled a sheet up around her after the delivery. Alex pulled it down to Charlotte's waist and carefully settled his little daughter against her breast.

Charlotte opened her eyes, startled, as a tiny flailing fist hit her.

"Ohhhh," she breathed. The baby opened its black eyes and stared at her; then she turned her head restlessly and opened her little mouth again. Instinctively Charlotte brought her up to her breast and the baby closed her small lips around her nipple.

Charlotte's eyes met Alex's and her free hand clasped his. Alex cupped his large hand around his daughter's tiny head.

"She's beautiful," Alex said. "Look! She's sucking."

Suddenly the midwife, the wet nurse, and Mall erupted back into the room.

"I'll take the little babe," the wet nurse said importantly. She had been living at the manor for two days, waiting for the baby to come.

"No!" Charlotte said, as the wet nurse reached down to take the baby. "Alex!"

Alex felt a swell of pride. Charlotte had looked

to him to save her baby; she obviously didn't still think of him as a kidnapper. He grinned at the wet nurse.

"The countess has decided to nurse the child herself," he explained cheerfully.

"My lady!" The wet nurse was aghast. Ladies *never, never* nursed their children. She bent down next to the bed. "My lady, your breasts . . . they will never be the same."

Charlotte looked at her uncomprehendingly. She felt as if she were half-asleep, and sounds only reached her through a thick cotton blanket. She looked away from the woman and down at the baby's tiny bald head. It was so fragile. Charlotte caressed the baby's head tentatively, running her fingers delicately over her rosy shell-like ears. When the woman kept saying something to her, she looked up at Alex in silent appeal. Alex took the wet nurse by the arm and led her out of the room, passing her over to the housekeeper with a muttered remark about compensation. Slowly the room emptied.

To his surprise, Alex realized that he knew Charlotte's housekeeper. The woman in front of him, who was obviously the housekeeper given her ring of keys, was the young girl Charlotte had been painting in London. Although she didn't seem so young now. At her direction he went back to the bed and bent down.

"Darling, I'm going to carry you into another room now." Charlotte smiled exhaustedly, a flicker of a smile. Alex's strong arms came under her and she gratefully laid her head against his shoulder. In her arms nestled their little baby, still suckling irregularly, although her eyes weren't open anymore.

Alex laid his wife and child tenderly in the room Mall pointed out. When Charlotte's maid appeared with a bowl of water, he waved her away and washed Charlotte's body himself. She hardly seemed to notice as the warm sponge glided over her body. The baby was asleep now, its cheek tucked against Charlotte's breast.

Finally Alex snuffed out most of the candles and climbed on the bed too. He couldn't bear to be parted from them. In a gesture that broke his heart, Charlotte handed him their daughter, adjusting the babe's little head against his arm. Then she snuggled against his side and fell instantly into a deep sleep. Alex lay awake a long time, staring blindly at the opposite wall.

An hour or so later Pippa trundled into the room in her nightclothes, shrieking with delight to see her papa. Charlotte didn't even stir. Alex showed Pippa the new baby, but she showed almost no interest. Instead she said, "Mama!" and crawled over Charlotte's body so that she could nestle on her other side. She butted her head up against Charlotte's shoulder, clutched a bit of Charlotte's nightgown, and closed her eyes, absolutely blissful.

Alex nodded to Pippa's nanny, who left. Then he leaned back against the headboard, sick with self-loathing. How could he have thought to separate this family? If Charlotte is generous enough to give me a place in the family again, he vowed with all the silent strength of his soul, I will guard it with my life and never, never be the one to pull it to pieces.

Alex lay unmoving in the huge bed until dawn began to creep through the curtains, rearranging the puzzle pieces of life: the garden girl and how she led him to marry Maria, and Maria's wild sexual gyrations, and how they had nothing to do with Charlotte. And perhaps, most important, his own destructive rage at Maria, which he unfairly directed at Charlotte.

As his new little daughter sighed and stirred and opened her black eyes, peering about in a dazed, half-blind sort of way, Alex remembered the anguish in Maria's eyes as she'd begged him to be kind to Pippa, and to love her. Whatever Maria had been, she was a good mother, Alex thought. Healing remembrance flooded his soul: He, after all, was alive. He didn't have to say good-bye to Pippa, or to Charlotte, or to this little scrap of humanity in his arms. Alex shuddered inwardly. But he smiled too. The burning, corrosive rage was gone. When he thought of Maria now, he knew he would remember the dying mother, tears streaming down her face, telling him in a broken voice that she hadn't allowed Pippa into the room for three weeks so that their daughter wouldn't catch scarlet fever.

Alex's new child opened her delicate red mouth and cried the desolate, high wail of a hungry newborn. Charlotte's eyes snapped open and she sat up, bewildered. Then she held out her arms, smiling as Alex gently arranged their daughter's round head against Charlotte's breast. And when Alex's eyes met the forgiving eyes of his wife over the head of a noisily sucking infant, there was no man in all of England who could claim to be happier than he.

Chapter 23

For the first few weeks, as Charlotte's body mended, she pored over her baby, learning every little bump and curve, the enchanting dip of her eyebrows, the sturdiness of her body, the wildness of her hungry eyes, the bliss of the little grunts she made while eating. When she thought about Alex at all, it was with gratitude: He got up in the dark and went to the door in answer to Katy's soft knock, bringing Sarah for a feeding. He played with Pippa in the afternoons. Alex and Charlotte curled together like spoons at night, at least the part of the night during which she wasn't nursing Sarah. And after the first few weeks, Sarah only roused once a night for a feeding. Charlotte would wake up, wondering where Sarah was, and find a warm, masculine arm curled around her stomach, or a muscled leg carelessly thrown across her own. It made her heart glow.

Sarah was a very even-tempered baby, easy to care for and undemanding. Charlotte soon began to feel like herself again. One morning when Sarah was around two months old, Charlotte was woken by the faint jiggle as her husband swung his legs out of bed.

Marie had been in the room early in the morning and had drawn the curtains. Morning sun puddled on the carpet and lit up the glinting silver in Alex's hair. He was standing stark naked by the window, staring down at the gardens. Charlotte sleepily allowed her eyes to drift up his long, muscular legs and the line of his back, all the way to his towering shoulders. Alex's hair had grown longer during the past two months; curls touched the back of his neck.

"Alex," Charlotte said, before she thought.

Alex turned around at the soft sound of her voice as if he'd heard a gunshot. Charlotte was propped up on her elbow, her velvety black hair cascading over her shoulders. She was wearing a fine lawn nightgown with wide shoulders, suitable for nursing, and the neck had slipped down leaving a creamy shoulder bare. Alex's body responded immediately.

Charlotte was staring at him in fascination, not saying a word. A faint pink flush rose up her neck.

Alex walked over to the bed, consciously making himself stroll as if the center of his body wasn't jutting into the middle distance.

"Charlotte?" he asked.

Charlotte didn't say anything. She was trembling and she couldn't seem to stop staring at him. Alex's eyes were black, so black that she couldn't see the pupils at all, and one of his eyebrows was arched. He sat on the bed when she didn't answer.

Slowly his hand reached out and stroked her

neck, his fingers trailing down to the ivory mounds peeking out from the lace surrounding her night rail. Slowly, slowly, almost holding his breath in hopes of not startling her, Alex bent over and put his lips gently on her rosy mouth.

Instinctively Charlotte opened her lips and Alex's tongue swiftly invaded. Charlotte's arms wrapped around Alex's neck and he lowered himself onto her. Charlotte gasped. His weight was so delicious. She'd thought she would never feel it again, the way his hardness settled onto her soft curves, making her feel tingling and tight at the same time.

Alex's hand swept down Charlotte's body and pulled up her gown with one swift wrench. He wasn't going to give her a chance to remember that she hated him. They had never discussed everything that happened before Sarah was born, but Alex knew that in the depth of Charlotte's soul she must hate him. She was letting him stay with her while the baby was so small . . . but inside his wife must hate him for almost killing her and Sarah, for mistrusting her and leaving her.

But that realization hadn't stopped him from loving Charlotte — and wanting her. Sarah was his daughter; he knew that with every fiber of his being. But even if she hadn't been, even given Charlotte's lack of virginity, he didn't care. What he wanted was this warm, laughing, exquisite person to be next to him his whole life.

Alex's hand found her and Charlotte moaned, her body bucking against his palm. Alex's mind clouded. She was ready for him.

"Charlotte?" he whispered. "Are you sure it's all right? It's only been a few months since Sarah was born."

Charlotte opened her eyes and looked into Alex's eyes. Hers were unfocused, glowing, until they saw the concern in Alex's eyes. His face was strained with the effort of holding himself back.

In response she opened her mouth and ran her tongue along the line of his lips, a delicious, teasing gesture that made a silent pronouncement. With a groan Alex took her mouth and in the same breath he thrust into her, a jagged moan leaping from his throat.

When he didn't move again Charlotte nudged her hips up against his. Her heart was racing. Her entire being was focused on the incredible sensations radiating from her hips. The racing heat in her belly demanded that he respond, that he adopt the fierce cadence she remembered in her dreams. Why wasn't he moving?

Alex stared down at his wife as Charlotte's long eyelashes fluttered. Her eyes stared bewilderedly into his.

"I can't do it," he said brokenly. "Charlotte, please . . ."

Charlotte stared at her husband in absolute perplexity. What on earth was he asking for? She bucked her hips gently against his, closing her eyes a minute, coaxing him to leap into movement. But Alex remained still, so she opened her eyes again.

He was looking down at her silently, eyes strained and vulnerable.

"Alex?" she asked hesitatingly. "What is it? Doesn't it . . . don't you want to?"

"Oh, God." Alex groaned. "Can't you feel me? Don't I *want* to!" He pulled back and thrust into her again, just to show her how much he wanted to be where he was. Irresistibly he did it again. But just as a broken moan drifted from Charlotte's lips, he stopped again.

"Alex?" To her horror, Charlotte saw that his eyes were bright with tears. "Alex!"

Abruptly Alex withdrew, pulling away and swinging his legs over the side of the bed — as if he were leaving, Charlotte thought with alarm. She reached out and touched his elbow.

"Alex?"

Sitting on the edge of the bed, Alex dropped his head into his hands.

"Alex, what's the matter?" Charlotte hastily pulled her nightgown past her hips again. Then she sat next to her husband.

He lifted his head to look at her, eyes bright with self-condemnation. "I almost took your life and Sarah's, Charlotte. I can't make love to you as if that didn't happen. I shouldn't *be* here with you; you should have tossed me out the door long ago. God knows, Charlotte, I deserve it."

Charlotte bit back a smile. Lord, but she had married a man of extremes. When Alex first pulled away, she felt a pulse of alarm, thinking he was going to erupt in a fury. Although, now that she knew with utter certainty how much he loved her, even a jealous rage couldn't really disturb her happiness.

"Do you love me?"

Alex leaned forward and just touched her lips with his. "You know that I do," he said hoarsely.

"Do you think I love you?"

A wry smile lit Alex's eyes. "In my more optimistic moments."

"Don't you see, Alex?" Charlotte reached out and cupped his face in her two hands, her grasp both sensual and confiding. "Don't you see how lucky we are? You loved me so much that you were able to save my life — you pulled me back from the edge of death. And I loved you enough that I followed your voice back, even though I had given up."

Charlotte leaned forward and caressed Alex's mouth with her lips, sweetly, with all the truth that lay in her eyes. Then she whispered: "To have and to hold, in sickness and in health, till death do us part."

Silently Alex pulled his wife into his arms, burying his face in her sweet-smelling curls. The silky roughness against his cheek soothed the tightness in his throat, the burning in his eyes.

"I don't deserve your love, Charlotte. I'm a jealous idiot," he said. "I couldn't stand the idea of anyone else touching you — and the thought made me irrational. I'm sorry. I'm so sorry I was cruel." Tortured guilt strained Alex's voice.

Charlotte rubbed her cheek against Alex's

shoulder comfortingly. "You *are* an idiot, Alex," she said. "Why would I ever want any other man to touch me when we make love the way we do?"

But still Alex held back. "You don't know how stupid I was, Charlotte. I kept praising myself because I was going to forgive you, but you have to forgive me. If . . . if I promise not to go insane again, will you ever trust me?"

"I trust you," Charlotte said simply. "In all ways: in bed and out of bed."

"I couldn't ever sleep with another woman," Alex answered, speaking to the question of beds.

"Well," Charlotte said with a lopsided, teasing smile, kissing the honey dark skin of Alex's shoulder, "can you imagine sleeping with *me?*" She trailed small, heated kisses along the ridge of Alex's collarbone and up his neck to his beating pulse. Then she stopped, throwing back her head and looking straight into her husband's coal-black eyes.

"I love you, Alexander Foakes. I love you so much that I will undoubtedly forgive you again and again and again, for anything you do."

Alex's eyes burned down into hers. "You couldn't love me as much as I love you."

The words hung in the air between them. Now Charlotte's eyes were dewy. Alex lowered his head, passionately kissing her eyes, her cheeks, the whirl of her ears. As each tear slowly slid down her creamy skin he kissed it off. Finally they fell back onto the bed together.

Charlotte's hands clutched Alex's shoulders as

he sunk into her warm depths.

"We're together," Alex said.

"Together." In Charlotte's voice was a promise.

"With my body," Alex said hoarsely, looking straight into Charlotte's eyes. "With my body I thee worship." In his voice there was a promise — a promise, a vow, a benediction.

Postscript

Alex rode through the warm autumn twilight with Lucien Boch and Will Holland, all three men silently enjoying being outdoors at the very moment when the sun began to wink under the edge of the heavy woods surrounding Baron Holland's country estate. Their horses pranced, sensing that they were finally heading home after a long day.

"This is a lovely spot you have, Will."

Will smiled and then checked his horse as they approached the gatehouse. "Excuse me a minute, won't you? My gatekeeper's wife has been ill and I'd like to enquire about her." Will jumped off his horse and disappeared into the thatched cottage.

Lucien pulled his horse up and turned to face Alex. "You have never let me thank you properly," he said, his voice lilting slightly with a French intonation.

"There's nothing to thank me for," Alex replied.

"Yes, there is," Lucien insisted. "I know, of

course, of the scandal that your wife had to suffer in our absence. Had I not asked you, you never would have left her, especially at such a delicate time. If only you had told me she was pregnant!"

"We didn't know," Alex said lightly. "Besides — it has resolved itself. Charlotte put up with a little gossip, but it's all settled down now; no one would *dare* to suggest that Sarah was not my child." She was his to every curve of her face and twitch of her baby eyebrows.

"Yes, but I am very regretful that —"

"Lucien. It was nothing."

Will emerged from the gatehouse and swung back up on his mount, ending their conversation. Alex nudged his horse to a gallop, eager to return to the house. He had been gone for hours, looking over the grounds and being shown Will's new mills. He missed the children . . . and Charlotte.

Lucien caught up with Alex again. "I understand it is your birthday," he said slyly. "I believe there is a surprise in store for you."

Alex shot him a sideways glance. "The devil you say."

Lucien gave him a secret smile. "So I believe."

But there was nothing surprising about the fact that Pippa dashed toward him across the velvet lawn before Will's manse. Well, perhaps it was an exaggeration to say that Pippa dashed — she trotted toward him, shouting "Papa! Papa!" in a piping voice. Alex jumped off his horse and swung his daughter up on his shoulder where she whispered blackberry-flavored secrets in his ear about the kittens in the barn and the berries that grew in the kitchen gardens.

And there was nothing surprising about the fact that his wife's eyes met his with such a stir of love and desire that Alex found himself barely under control, and right there in the drawing room had to stroll over and examine Chloe Holland's china cabinet — as if he were a teenager again! His wife's gurgle of laughter was nothing new either, even if it did make him long to toss her over his shoulder and head for the bedroom.

Dinner passed without incident. Chloe presided over the meal with an engaging lack of formality — she had taken to her role as Baroness Holland with effortless ease. The party talked of the possibility of a Napoleonic invasion and of the unsavory death of Bishop Burnham (in the arms of a woman with a dubious reputation). No one mentioned Alex's birthday at all. Alex almost felt piqued. But then . . . perhaps Charlotte was planning a special treat for him in their bedroom. His wife, tied in a large bow. He rather liked the sound of that. The ladies rose and retired to the drawing room; Alex, Will, and Lucien settled in the library with tumblers of scotch.

The door to the library swung open to reveal Will's butler. He was French and professed to speak no English.

"My lord," said the butler. Alex looked up

enquiringly. The butler held a white card in his gloved hand. He bowed magnificently and handed it to Alex.

Alex glanced over at Lucien and saw his secret smile break out again.

"My birthday?"

"Quite so," his friend replied.

Alex broke the seal and read the note rapidly. Then he crooked an eyebrow at Lucien.

"I am instructed to proceed upstairs and dress appropriately."

"Then by all means, Alex, do not let us keep you." Will jumped up, a conspiratorial grin covering his face.

"Does everyone know what my wife is planning?" Looking at his two friends, their eyes lit with mischievous laughter, Alex knew the answer to his question. He ran quickly up the marble stairs, his mind racing to elaborate pictures of what "appropriate" dress might be. What would Charlotte be wearing, for example?

But the master bedroom held no one but Keating — no dressed, or deliciously undressed, wife.

Keating had laid out formal dress on the bed. Alex's protest died on his lips. Obviously this was a surprise that Charlotte had elaborately planned. It would be churlish of him to refuse to comply. Still, he knit his brow when Keating swirled his old green domino around his shoulders.

"Am I going to a masquerade? In this godforsaken part of the country?"

"I couldn't say, my lord. I am merely following the countess's orders." Keating didn't mention that Charlotte had asked him to take Alex's green domino out of the attic some two months ago, and that the birthday excursion had been in the planning stages somewhat longer than that.

Finally Keating ushered his perplexed master out of the bedroom. Will's butler was waiting in the hall, a devilish French smile on his face, Alex thought rather crossly. The butler majestically led the way to a carriage outside.

Finally, Alex thought, quickening his pace. He climbed inside, brushing off the footman's extended arm.

But the carriage was empty, and before he could register the fact, the door was flung shut behind him and the horses picked up.

"For Christ's sake," Alex said blankly, to himself.

They didn't go far: perhaps twenty minutes. Alex helped himself to a basket placed on the backseat, clearly for his pleasure. But even a glass of excellent champagne didn't soothe his feelings. Where was his wife? What was the delight of drinking champagne alone? His eyes grew dark as he imagined her sitting opposite him in the carriage. Then he smiled wolfishly. He'd have his revenge for this lonely birthday party! She'd have to be in the carriage on the way home, after all. . . .

So by the time the carriage jolted to a close, Alex's mood was restored. In fact, he was feeling quite cheerful, having finished near to the whole bottle of champagne.

He tossed open the carriage door and jumped out, only to find himself face-to-face with Keating. A quick glance showed him that they had stopped in the manicured driveway to a country house.

"Keating!"

"My lord," his valet said quietly. He had apparently just climbed down from the driver's seat; his cheeks and nose were bright red with cold.

"Good God, man, what are you doing here? And where are we?" Alex demanded.

Keating hesitated. In his hands he held a black piece of cloth.

"My lord, I must ask you to turn around," he replied.

Alex glanced at the cloth and then at his embarrassed valet's face. Charlotte was going a long way with this masquerade. He shrugged and turned around, allowing his valet to fit the black cloth snugly over his eyes.

Keating guided him back into the carriage and it jolted off, up the drive, unless Alex missed his bet. He was starting to sour on the whole business again. If his wife wanted him blindfolded — or tied up, for that matter — why didn't she just do it herself? Why all this rigmarole involving the servants?

The carriage stopped and Keating put a hand under his elbow. Alex shrugged it off and stepped out of the carriage. Oddly enough, it sounded as if they had arrived at a party. He could hear the shrill laughter of women and the chords of a small orchestra.

"My lord," Keating said softly. And this time Alex suffered him to take his elbow and steer him up some ten steps and into what seemed to be a crowded hall. The party-goers were intrigued by a blindfolded man, Alex heard that. But he also heard some very surprising accents. This wasn't a party solely attended by the gentry.

Alex was about to wrench off the blindfold and demand an explanation when Keating stopped him, saying,

"Beware, my lord. You are at the top of a flight of stairs."

Then he felt the tie of the blindfold ease and the cloth fell away.

Alex stood at the top of a flight of marble stairs, looking down into a very crowded ballroom. He scanned the room in surprise. The ballroom was hot, and the heat was exacerbated by the aggressive smell of tallow dips and overheated dancers. Long forgotten memories stirred, telling Alex that he'd been in this room before.

On the dance floor ruffled skirts competed for space with soiled-looking Greek robes. A few women sported small masks, but lavish makeup seemed to be a more common disguise. Alex frowned. Where on earth was he? The French windows were hung with shabby maroon velvet. . . .

Of course! This was Stuart Hall — and — and this must be the Hookers' Ball. The Saturday Hookers' Ball. It was a Saturday, Alex thought numbly.

His eyes rose, and stopped. There she was. Next to a statue of Narcissus was a slender woman dressed in a black domino, powdered hair piled high. With a sense of leaden inevitability Alex skirted the exuberant revelers on the steps and walked down into the ballroom. He walked through the crowds of dancing party-goers, his green domino brushing against the powdered shoulders and garish frills of ladies of the night. But he didn't look either to the left or the right. He didn't want to break eye contact with his wife.

For her part, Charlotte felt as if she had been waiting her whole life for this moment. There was her beloved, beloved footman at the top of the stairs, in his green domino with his silver-shot hair. But he looked for *her* this time. And when Alex's eyes met hers, a message of such tender passion passed between them that she shivered and had to hang on to Narcissus's cool stone arm in order to catch her balance.

Then her shiver turned into a grin. Alex was striding through the ballroom as if the hookers, servants, merchants, and the rest didn't exist. No one, watching his combination of unconscious arrogance and effortless grace, could reasonably think him a footman. Even in a cloak some ten years old he was clothed in the nameless confidence of high blood matched by high intelligence. Finally, after an eternity, he stood before her.

Her hair was powdered. Her skin was so white that her hair *had* to be red. She was wearing a black domino, and sheltering herself in the shadow of a statue. She was herself . . . she was his garden girl . . . she was Charlotte.

Without missing a beat, Alex wrapped his wife in his green domino and kissed her so possessively, so lovingly, and so passionately that Charlotte's knees gave way and she had to cling to him for balance. She slid her hands inside his formal black coat, hands drifting over the faintly rough texture of his fine lawn shirt, over the muscled expanse of his back.

Alex looked down at her from underneath his black eyelashes. "I should kill you for this trick," he said, his voice hoarse with emotion. "Or I should kill myself for being such an utter, unmitigated idiot."

Charlotte grinned up at him impudently, still leaning against his chest.

"Happy birthday, love."

"Vixen," Alex growled, bending his head again.

When a patron of the ever-popular Hookers' Ball swept through the throng of revelers holding a woman in his arms and headed up the stairs, hardly anyone in the assembly spared him a second glance. And the fact that the man in the green domino pulled his *amour* into his lap the minute they were settled in the carriage, without exchanging a word, would have been considered unsurprising as well. It wasn't until much later that night — nearly morning, actually — that the Earl and Countess of Sheffield and Downes had the time and breath to discuss the earl's birthday present.

"You see," Alex said, pulling Charlotte's head against his shoulder so that he could punctuate his words with kisses dropped into silky curls, "I put together the fact that you looked like Maria, but I didn't want to think too much about it. The clanger was that I never thought of the fact that I married Maria *because* she looked like the girl in the garden, and that meant that you looked like her too, and . . . that meant you were the girl in the garden." He gave a wry, self-condemnatory grimace. "I'm an idiot, darling. You've married an idiot."

Charlotte brought Alex's hand to her lips, kissing his palm. Her mouth curved against his hand in an irrepressible grin. "Luckily, I've always been fond of fools," she said, her teasing reply half muffled by his warm skin.

"I am an idiot, a dolt," Alex continued indomitably. "There were so many times I should have known. Do you remember when I asked you to marry me in your mother's Chinese salon, and afterward I touched you?"

A rosy glow suffused Charlotte's face, but she nodded.

"You said thank you, afterward." Alex's voice was full of tormented self-hatred. "And I thought — fool that I am — how surprising it was that for a moment you reminded me of my garden girl, but I didn't think any further. Because, you see, the garden girl thanked me too, and you were the only two women who were ever so courteous . . . I deserve to be whipped," he said savagely. "I caused you so much misery —"

Charlotte broke off his speech by the simple expedient of clamping her hand over his mouth.

"Don't!" she cried. "Don't you see . . . Don't you know how happy you make me? The only thing that matters is that it was *you* . . . it was *you* all the time. And now you know, and what does it matter that you didn't remember immediately? You still wanted *me*, don't you see?" she whispered achingly. "If you had come back and you had remembered taking my virginity, I never would have been able to trust that you wanted me for myself. I would always wonder whether it was your gentlemanly sense of honor. Do you know what I remember most clearly from the time we spent in the Chinese salon?"

Alex shook his head, mesmerized by her glowing eyes.

"You said . . . you said that you didn't want to continue kissing me because you would ruin me, and you didn't want to do that. And all I could think of was thank God you didn't remember that you had ruined me before, because it meant you wanted me now. Not just to make up for a moment's indiscretion in a garden, but for my-self."

Alex pulled her into his arms, burying his head in her neck. "You're too good for me," he said. "I don't deserve you." There was a moment's silence between them.

"But it wouldn't have been like that if I had been less of a bumble-head and able to put things together," Alex said more calmly. "In many ways the course of my whole life has been dictated by that garden girl: you. Do you know that I dreamed about you for weeks afterward? You were crying and I was trying to comfort you, or you were lying in my arms, and I was kissing you. Either way the dreams were a torment. I forced Patrick to go back to that Hookers' Ball with me the next week, but I couldn't find you. I went to five *ton* balls in the next two weeks, but I couldn't find you there either. And then I went to Rome, and I thought I found someone who looked like you . . . and so I married her, but she wasn't you either. And finally when I met the daughter of a certain duke in London, even though I had no idea she was my garden girl, I wanted nothing but her. I planned to marry you about two minutes after meeting you at the ball, you know."

He smiled down at his wife's dazed expression. "I'm afraid, my love, that you must be my fate."

Charlotte clung to him, relishing the feeling that came from being in his arms. And now there were no shadows between them.

"I missed you," she whispered. "I missed you so much."

"I missed you too. I missed you even when I was the most furious. Do you know, I always knew that we would be together again? Even as I raged about the house saying hideously stupid things, I knew that no matter what you'd done I had to have you back, because you are part of my heart. Losing you would be losing myself."

Alex's wife smiled up at him, her clear eyes shining with love. "You couldn't lose me, darling. Next time you storm out of the house I'll follow you wherever you go."

"But don't ever leave me, Charlotte. I couldn't bear it."

"I won't."

"And I will cherish you," Alex whispered. "Until we are old and gray: past that time, for all time."

Charlotte made no answer to Alex's promise, for the promises they exchanged then were silent ones, given in sweetness, taken in sweetness, remembered forever.

A Note about Potency and the Pleasures of Scandal

In 1612, the unhappy marriage of Robert Devereux, the third Earl of Essex, erupted into a prolonged and contentious scandal. His countess, Frances, declared to all and sundry that Essex was impotent and that their marriage had never been consummated. One of London's notable gossips reported that "there was a divorce to be sued this term twixt the Earl of Essex and his lady, and he was content (whether true or feigned) to confess insufficiency in himself." But when it came to the actual trial Essex refused to acknowledge impotence — except in matters of his wife. A group of gentlemen were invited to witness his manly potential and agreed to its general working order; a group of ladies in turn inspected a heavily veiled Frances and pronounced her a virgin. After months of acrimony King James ordered the marriage dissolved on grounds of nullity. The Lord Chamberlain himself reported (with some glee) that "it was truth that the earl had no ink in his pen." But many London gossips firmly maintained that Frances had petitioned for divorce solely because she was in love with a dashing, handsome young lord, the Earl of Somerset, whom she married shortly after the annulment of her first marriage.

Alex is only roughly modeled on the Earl of Essex — my Earl of Sheffield and Downes is not and never was impotent — but the pleasures and dangers of scandal as depicted in *Potent Pleasures* are fully historical. The third Earl of Essex was plagued by charges of impotency throughout the remainder of his life. When his second marriage produced no children, the whispers grew louder. On the other hand, Frances was never free from scandal either. When she was accused of murder some years later, most of England linked the charge to her dubious claims of virginity.

Yet scandal and love are sometimes true bedfellows. Frances and her second husband, the Earl of Somerset, lived together until her death in 1632. Their marriage — consecrated in the midst of intense speculation — was celebrated by the poet John Donne in one of the most beautiful of English love poems:

Now, as in Tullia's tomb one lamp burnt clear
Unchanged for fifteen hundred year,
May these love-lamps we here enshrine,
In warmth, light, lasting, equal the divine.
Fire ever doth aspire,
And makes all like itself, turns all to fire,
But ends in ashes; which these cannot do,
For none of these is fuel, but fire too.

This is joy's bonfire, then, where love's strong arts
Make of so noble individual parts
One fire of four inflaming eyes,
   and of two loving hearts.

The employees of Thorndike Press hope you have enjoyed this Large Print book. All our Large Print titles are designed for easy reading, and all our books are made to last. Other Thorndike Press Large Print books are available at your library, through selected bookstores, or directly from us.

For information about titles, please call:

(800) 257-5157

To share your comments, please write:

Publisher
Thorndike Press
P.O. Box 159
Thorndike, Maine 04986